Also by Mark Henshaw

Cold Shot

Red Cell

THE FALL OF
MOSCOW
STATION

A Novel

MARK HENSHAW

TOUCHSTONE

NEW YORK   LONDON   TORONTO   SYDNEY   NEW DELHI

Touchstone
An Imprint of Simon & Schuster, Inc.
1230 Avenue of the Americas
New York, NY 10020

First Touchstone hardcover edition February 2016

For information about special discounts for bulk purchases, please contact Simon & Schuster Special Sales at 1-866-506-1949 or business@simonandschuster.com.

The Simon & Schuster Speakers Bureau can bring authors to your live event. For more information or to book an event contact the Simon & Schuster Speakers Bureau at 1-866-248-3049 or visit our website at www.simonspeakers.com.

Manufactured in the United States of America

1   3   5   7   9   10   8   6   4   2

Library of Congress Cataloging-in-Publication Data

Henshaw, Mark, 1970-
The fall of Moscow station : a novel / Mark Henshaw.
      pages ; cm
         I. Title.
   PS3608.E586F35 2016
      813'.6—dc23
      2015027887

ISBN: 978-1-5011-0031-4
ISBN: 978-1-5011-0032-1 (ebook)

To those foreign agents betrayed by traitors
like Aldrich Ames and Robert Hanssen,
men and women with dreams of liberty cut short;
and to those who tried to save them

THE FALL OF
MOSCOW
STATION

PROLOGUE

U.S. Embassy

Santiago de León de Caracas

Bolivarian Republic of Venezuela

"Operator." Alden Maines gripped the phone tight, his eyes closed, his teeth grinding hard together. This line was reserved for one purpose only and he had only one case officer on the street tonight. There were twenty people standing around him, all silent, watching him. They'd come the moment the phone had called for their deputy chief's attention.

"GRANITE . . . site MANGO." It was Kyra, he was sure, but her voice was slurred.

"GRANITE, report your status," the deputy chief of station ordered. There was no reply. He repeated the order and heard nothing but silence, the line still open. Maines cursed under his breath and cut the connection to stop the locals from tracing the call to either end.

"Abrams! Raguskus!" he called out. Two members of the circle jerked hearing their names. "Get down to the garage and fire up the van. Search and rescue—"

"Don't move, any of you!"

Maines looked over at the man who had countermanded his order, fury drawn on his face. Sam Rigdon, chief of Caracas Station, came into the room, wrestling his way through the line of bodies surrounding his deputy. "Was that Stryker? If she's in trouble, she can sit and wait it out. She probably screwed up the op and led the SEBIN right to Carreño. I'm not going to throw any more bodies at Chávez's people. She can get herself home. You keep your butt in that chair."

"No."

"Excuse me?" Rigdon replied, surprised.

"I said no," Maines told him again. He turned back to Raguskus and Abrams. "Go get the van ready," he ordered again.

"If anyone moves, I'll send 'em back to Langley—" Rigdon started to threaten.

"Then you'll send us all back!" Maines yelled. "You know that Stryker didn't lead anyone to Carreño! He used you to lead her to them! Everyone here but you knew that Carreño's a double, but you didn't want to believe it. But you were worried enough that we might be right that you decided not to go find out for yourself, so you fed Kyra to the lions instead. You're a coward, Sam. You've run this station into the ground, you've put everyone here at risk, and now the most junior officer we've got might be bleeding out in a safe house because you didn't have the stones to go out and man up to your own dumb mistakes. So we're done taking orders from you. You want us to follow you? Then get behind the wheel of the van and help us get Stryker home. Otherwise get out of the way."

"This is insubordination!" Rigdon yelled.

"I prefer the word 'mutiny,'" Maines told him. "But yeah, 'insubordination' works for me."

"You leave this room and I'll be on the phone with the director of national intelligence before you—"

Maines's fist drove itself deep into Rigdon's stomach, bending the station chief over and driving the air out of his lungs in a hard, gasping wheeze. The deputy pulled his fist back and pulled it upward, slamming into his superior's nose. Maines's knuckles made an audible crack as the bones fractured against Rigdon's skull. The station chief's head snapped up, the blood already flowing from both nostrils as he fell onto his back, the carpet doing little to cushion his hard landing.

"I'll dial the number for you," Maines told him, shaking his hand. "Feel free to tell him I did that, and let him know that if he tells me to stand down and abandon Stryker to the SEBIN, he'll be telling Congress why. And if you get in our way again before we bring Kyra out of the safe house, you'll end up in the infirmary before she does, you got me?"

Rigdon couldn't answer for the blood rolling down his face. "Anyone else on his side?" Maines asked.

"Screw 'im," someone from the back said. "We ought to trade him to Carreño for Kyra." Murmurs of assent and open curses erupted from the group.

"Thought not," Maines said. "Raguskus, call the infirmary and have some of the people standing by. Sounds like she's hurt. I don't know how bad, but she was unresponsive. Then get a trauma kit down to the van," Maines ordered. "Kain, you line us up some transportation out of the country. If she's seriously wounded, we won't be able to get her out on a commercial flight, so you'll have to get creative."

"I'll figure something out, boss," the woman said. She pushed her way past the two men behind her and ran for her desk.

"Good," Maines said. "Winegar, get a group together and start monitoring the local police bands and any of the SEBIN frequencies that NSA has cracked open. If they're getting anywhere near MANGO, I want to know about it . . . and we might need some help avoiding their people on the way in and back out again."

"Will do," a tall, older man replied. "Raguskus, Pitkin, you're with me." The group of four marched out of the room.

"Good . . . and if he"—Maines pointed at the bleeding senior officer on the floor—"if he tries to get up, someone feel free to drag him out to the street and out him to the first policeman you can find.

They probably already know who he works for, just let 'em know that we don't want him anymore."

"Long as you don't care what shape he's in when they get him!" somebody called out.

"Doesn't matter to me. If we're getting charged with mutiny, let's make it a story they'll tell at the Farm for the next hundred years," Maines ordered. "We roll out of here in ten."

He was on foot now. The SEBIN cordon was enormous, at least twelve blocks square, which meant there were holes everywhere. The deputy station chief had worked his way inside easily enough, but Raguskus and Abrams were still probing for some way to get through in the van. The rain had picked up in the last hour, the drizzle turning into a drenching gush from the dark gray heavens and cutting visibility down to a half block in any direction.

The safe house was on the fourth floor of a high-rise apartment complex ahead. It was inside the SEBIN search radius from what Winegar had been able to discern from the radio calls, but Maines wondered if the Venezuelans were either patient or organized enough to search every domicile in the area. He doubted it. The real question was whether Kyra Stryker was in stable condition and could survive in place long enough for the security services to give up the search.

He looked at his watch. It had been an hour since Kyra's emergency call. *This could all be moot*, Maines told himself.

A police car roared by him, siren screaming out, the tires spraying him with a heavy wall of water. He ignored the discomfort. Maines was soaked through already.

He turned north up the alleyway off the Avenida Urdaneta. The service entrance was ahead on his left, a few dozen feet. He pulled his spare key, unlocked the entry, and slipped inside. The rain resumed pounding on the metal door, like the angry fists of the locals trying to batter their way into the building.

Maines shook the water out of his hair, took a few steps ahead, and stopped, looking down. Spatters of blood made a dotted line across the dirty tile floor to the hallway. He cursed. The rain had erased whatever blood trail Kyra had left on her way to the building, but any idiot could follow the line inside.

He ran out into the hall, walking along the red trail himself, praying it didn't lead to the safe-house door. The lighting was dim, and the blood was hard to see on the grubby floor. That was cause for hope. He stepped around it, tracing the line to the stairs, then up and ending at the fourth floor. There was no question in his mind now.

Maines ran down the hallway, still looking down until the blood stopped in front of one of the apartments. The number matched the one in his memory and the station chief cursed again. He pulled his key, unlocked the door, and let himself inside.

"Stryker?" he called out. There was no answer. The lights were on and the red line led into the bedroom. Maines pushed the door open.

Stryker was on the bed, not moving. He ran over, saw her eyes were closed. "Stryker!" he repeated. She didn't answer.

Her leather jacket was on the floor alongside one of her shirt-sleeves, crumpled in a bloody red heap. A crude bandage was wrapped around her upper right arm. He checked the rest of her limp form for wounds and found none, then exhaled the deep breath he hadn't realized that he was holding. *Flesh wound*, he thought. She won't bleed out. He searched around, found the empty QuikClot package and morphine syringe in the bathroom. *Good girl*, he thought. Kyra had packed her own wound with the coagulant, then dosed herself to kill the pain. She'd probably ingested too much morphine, but she would survive that if it hadn't killed her by now. Her breathing was still regular, her pulse thready and fast, but not enough to scare him.

Could move her, he thought, *if Rags and Pitkin can get the van here*. The blood trail in the hall was still a problem . . . *or an opportunity*, he thought.

He dug through the trauma kit in the bathroom and extracted a ziplock bag and a pair of the latex gloves inside. He donned the gloves, then retrieved Stryker's blood-soaked sleeve from the floor and stuffed it into the plastic bag.

Maines ran back out into the hall, then down the stairs to the first floor. He pulled open the bag, pulled out the shirt, and began to squeeze the cloth gently onto the floor, extending the woman's blood trail away from the stairs. *Hate to do this to some poor sap, but better them than us,* he thought. He dripped the blood down the hallway another thirty feet, then curved the line to a random apartment door. The bloody sleeve went back into the bag along with the latex gloves. Maines stuffed the gory package into his coat pocket and sprinted back to the service entrance. A janitor's closet was nearby, locked, and he kicked the door in. A mop and bucket were sitting inside. He lifted the bucket into the utility sink, filled it a quarter up with water, and hauled it and the mop back to the stairs. It took him less than ten minutes to run the wet implement across the forty stairs to the fourth floor, erasing the bloody line that led to the door. Another thirty seconds cleaned up the tile leading to the safe house, and then he was inside again, the evidence of Kyra's run wiped away. The Venezuelans would still be able to find the trail on the stairwell using luminal and a UV light, but he prayed they wouldn't be so thorough once they found the second trail he'd created.

Maines touched his earpiece. "This is MALLET," he called out, the broadcast encrypted by the radio clipped onto his belt behind his waist. "I've located GRANITE, condition stable. Site MANGO is not secure, repeat, not secure. What's your status?"

"Still looking for a hole," Raguskus called back. "Bad guys are everywhere. We're parked five hundred meters from your position, engine cold, lights out at the moment."

"Hold your position," Maines ordered. "Will advise . . . wait." The sirens, which had been rising and fading since he'd dismounted from the van, had gotten close now. He moved to the window, split the blinds a hair, and looked down.

At least five cars, some unmarked, had stopped on the street. Men in tactical uniforms were spreading out along the sidewalk, some senior officer directing his subordinates down the side streets. "Hostiles at my position," he reported. "They'll be coming in the building."

"Any possibility of evac?" Pitkin asked.

"Negative," Maines replied. He looked back at Kyra. The woman was still unconscious on the bed. "I'd have to carry GRANITE out . . . no good cover for action on that one."

"Roger that," Pitkin answered.

Maines moved to the apartment door, leaned against it, listening for voices or footsteps. They were four stories up, and he doubted he would hear anything, but the stairwell was close.

Two minutes passed and he heard a yell, then other cries . . . heavy footsteps somewhere below, he couldn't tell how many, but he would've guessed a dozen men if he'd had to lay money on a number. Then yells again, cries of surprise, someone protesting in guttural Spanish. The SEBIN search team had found the blood trail and followed it to its obvious end. They'd found nothing, assumed the family living in whichever apartment Maines had set up had treated their wounded prey and helped her escape to some other site. They would spend a long night in an interrogation room. Maines truly hoped that the SEBIN would accept their story and let them go, but if not, it was not his problem.

"This is MALLET," he called out. "Hostiles have been diverted. Wait fifteen, then start her up and see if you can't find a hole. I think the cordon will start to break up."

"Roger that," Raguskus called back.

Maines parted the blinds again and watched the SEBIN lead a struggling couple out of the building into the street. The man and wife had no raincoats and they were soaked to the skin in seconds. Their hands were bound in front with zip ties. They protested their innocence and no one cared. The security team forced them into a waiting van, then boarded their own cars, and pulled out. The area was clear within ten minutes except for the onlookers and gawkers, still awed and amused by the spectacle.

"MALLET, this is PIGGYBACK, we have a hole," Pitkin called out. "Will be at the way point in two minutes."

"Roger that," Maines replied. He let the blinds fall closed, moved to the bed, and checked Kyra's pulse. The girl was still down, but her pulse was steadier now. He grabbed her leather jacket and lifted her in his arms, her head cradled against his shoulder.

He moved slowly, careful to avoid the doorframes, handrails, and walls as he maneuvered his unconscious charge through the apartment, the hallway, and down the stairs. Maines didn't bother to look around corners or down bends on the stairwell. If there were still SEBIN in his path, he would not be able to outrun them with Kyra in his arms. He encountered no one. The blood trail on the bottom floor was smeared now from the bootprints of a dozen soldiers who hadn't been interested in collecting evidence for a prosecution.

Maines reached the door to the service entrance and managed to open it. The rain outside hadn't slackened in the least. The van sat five feet beyond the door, engine idling. The double side door slid open and he lifted Kyra in, Raguskus reaching out to pull the unconscious woman inside. He didn't bother to close the building door behind him and Pitkin had the van in motion before Maines could slide the van door closed.

"What've we got?" Rags asked, opening the trauma kit.

"One gunshot wound to the right triceps. Looks like she packed the wound, tied it off, and dosed herself with morphine without checking the syringe. Lost a significant amount of blood, but I don't know how much," Maines replied. Abrams nodded, checked Kyra's handiwork, and set to work fixing her shoddy bandage. "Any word on an exfil plan?"

"I talked to Kain five minutes ago. She's got a private cargo flight lined up out of Colombia. We'll have to drive her across the border, but I know a few back roads across that aren't patrolled by the locals. Chávez uses them to ship supplies to the FARC, so we'll have to watch out for guerrillas, but we can manage them. We'll meet up with one of our pilots at a small airstrip outside of Cúcuta. Flight runs to Panama, then to Florida, then to Dulles. It'll take her a couple of days to get home and some of the puddle jumpers will be running pretty low to the ground and the Atlantic, so I hope she doesn't get airsick."

"From the looks of her, I don't think that's going to be a problem," Rags said. "It's a nasty wound, boss. She lost a chunk of muscle most of the way down to the bone. We'll have to keep her on morphine the whole way there. She'll need surgery when she gets back, and physical therapy after. I don't think she's going to remember much about the next few days. But she'll make it."

Maines nodded. "Good to hear. Question is what to do about that idiot back at the station."

"Nothing we can do," Pitkin replied, disgusted. "Director of national intelligence put him in there, nobody below him can pull Rigdon out. But I'd bet after this, none of us are going to be down here very long. Stryker just proved that our best asset is a double agent for Chávez. We're probably all burned now. We might as well not bother coming back once we cross the border."

"Roger that." Maines looked down at Kyra's face one last time, then leaned back against the van's metal bulkhead and closed his eyes, the tension starting to drain from his own body. *Seventh Floor idiots at Langley*, he raged to himself. *No, not just there. At Liberty Crossing and the White House too. Making a political donor a station chief. They don't care about who they put in front of the guns. They just want to run their little wars and push their little armies around. We're all just cannon fodder . . . loyalty only running in one direction. Didn't used to be like that, and no way to fix it. No way at all.*

Maines opened his eyes and listened to the rain pounding on the thin metal walls of the van and the broken asphalt under the tires. "SEBIN know all of us now, thanks to Rigdon. Might as well not bother coming back once we cross the border," he repeated, his voice quiet.

Fools. They're all a bunch of fools up there.

There were more borders in the world than the ones on the maps.

CHAPTER ONE

Vogelsang Soviet Military Base (Abandoned)
65 kilometers north of Berlin, Germany

General Stepan Illarionovich Strelnikov kept a steady pace as he walked through the abandoned streets, though not fast enough to satisfy his impatience. He could not walk faster, not anymore. The cushions between several of his vertebrae were eroding, so the doctor had said, and walking any serious distance was agony. He had taken the painkillers before setting out this morning, but they weren't up to the task. He ignored the pain as much as his discipline allowed, which was very little.

The road was familiar. That wall of trees to his right hadn't been there in his youth, and now, though pleasant on the eyes, it blocked his view of the old buildings he knew were sitting beyond. No matter. Strelnikov hardly was paying attention to the scenery. Vogelsang brought back memories thick as the flies swarmed these woods during the summers. He had been stationed here in his youth, when the first Soviet nuclear base outside of the *Rodina* had sheltered fifteen thousand soldiers and their families. It had been a lively place, an entire Russian town cultivated inside East Germany, where the signs all had Cyrillic letters and children had always been running between the buildings, some to the cinema, others to the school or the playground.

Now Vogelsang was a desolate waste, empty and crumbling, with trees growing up through the floors of some of the buildings. Grass erupted in straight lines through the concrete seams of the open spaces, and the buildings were all turning a uniform gray as their paint eroded. There was hardly an intact window anywhere, though most still had metal bars covering the openings. Doors were missing or hanging open. The wind made an ugly sound as it passed through the structures, the cracks in their facades creating a symphony of whistles and moans that combined in random tunes. The Germans wanted to level this reminder of the days when they had been in bondage to his country, but it seemed like nature was determined to do it first.

Why meet here? he wondered. The old general's knees had quivered when he'd recovered the meeting instructions that his CIA handler had left at the dead-drop site in Moscow. He'd had to read them twice, but there had been no mistake. Was it all coincidence, or did the CIA know his history? If that, what purpose could they find in calling him here? That was a question they were going to answer before he would answer any of theirs.

He stopped to orient himself, trying to remember which decrepit building was which, and his old mind wandered. His memory of the place became as real as the world around him and for a minute the pain in his back was gone. Strelnikov recognized the old theater across the intersection, where he had met his wife. He'd courted Taisia here and they'd dreamed of building a dacha a few miles north to retire in the German woods—

Foolish old soldier, he cursed himself. "No time for that," he muttered. Maybe after the meeting.

He found the building after another half hour's walk. The base commandant's office had been a high-class facility in its prime. Now it was a shell, but good enough for a clandestine meeting, he supposed. He trudged up the small flight of concrete steps onto the landing, pulled open the door, and stepped inside.

The loop came down over his head. Strelnikov thought it was a garrote, and he was sure a metal wire was about to crush his windpipe and choke off his air. But the attacker pulled it short and Strelnikov felt a fat cotton rope force itself between his teeth, to stop him from biting down.

In that instant, Strelnikov knew that the man behind would not kill him, not in the next few minutes anyway.

One hand pushed his head forward and down while others seized his arms and pulled them high over his head, spreading them like a chicken's wings flapping in the air. The pain surged in his shoulders, narrowing his vision into a black tunnel, and for a moment he was sure the men would keep pulling until the rotator cuffs tore, but finally they stopped before he passed out. More hands stripped his coat and shirt from his body. The Russian general offered no protest.

There are no suicide pills hidden in my clothes, young comrades.

When he was stripped to the waist, Strelnikov's arms finally were allowed to fall free. The men behind him pulled a hood over his head and suddenly he was blind.

His pants were pulled down to his ankles and Strelnikov was pushed down to sit on a stool. His shoes were pulled from his feet. More unseen hands covered with latex gloves searched his body, leaving nothing untouched. His captors forced him to stand, then bend over.

You will find nothing in there either, he assured them in his thoughts, but Strelnikov didn't bother saying the words. He had no plan to end his life on his own terms, but his promises would carry no weight with these men and he held his silence. Strelnikov had known the cavity check would be coming, but it was painful all the same. Suicide pills were small and the men were thorough, if not gentle. The rope in his mouth was a convenient outlet for that particular pain, and Strelnikov bit down hard until the clinical search was finished.

He was pulled by his arms, pushed around corners, and marched in circles until he could not longer orient himself by memory. They dragged him forward and up a staircase, then into some room, and he heard a door close behind. He was made to dress in what he knew to be a blue jogging suit. His modesty restored, his assailants removed the hood. The men wore no masks and Strelnikov knew soldiers when he saw them. The hair, the bearing, the efficient manner told him that these men were Special Forces.

They checked his mouth with a penlight and a dental pick for false fillings or other implants. Strelnikov offered no resistance. These men had specialized tools for wrenching open the jaws of anyone who stupidly thought they could keep their mouths shut as far as the rope allowed. Finding nothing, they finally removed the cord, cleaned up their kit, and evacuated the barren room. Strelnikov watched them go, waiting for the door to close before turning to the interrogator he knew was still inside.

"Good evening, Stepan Illarionovich." General-Major Arkady Lavrov, director of the Main Intelligence Directorate of the General Staff of the Armed Forces of the Russian Federation (GRU), sat in a cheap wooden chair by the corner of the door.

Strelnikov said nothing for several seconds, his mind pondering the surprise, and then he spoke. "Good evening, Arkady Vladimirovich." He made his way to the lone wooden stool in the room. It looked like it was original to the building and he hoped it wouldn't crumble under his weight.

"It looks so very different, does it not, the old base?" Lavrov asked.

Strelnikov exhaled long and slow. "It's hard to say. Time is cruel to memories," he said, making no effort to hide the sarcasm. What he'd said was true in so many ways. To admit that this country was a better place now than when the Soviet empire had controlled its eastern end would have been to admit that he had spent his life in the service of a mistake.

Lavrov waited for the other man to say something else, then finally spoke when the silence grew too painful. "It has changed, very much. A testament to our failures." He pressed his lips together. "We were in Berlin that night. Do you remember, on the embassy roof? We watched the people dancing on the Wall."

"I do," Strelnikov said. "That was an unhappy night."

"Yes, it was. I question, sometimes, how we did not foresee what happened that evening," Lavrov admitted.

"We did not see it," Strelnikov advised him, "because we lacked the great virtue that would have let us predict it."

"And that would be?"

"Honesty. The Kremlin would not hear of failure, so we would not let ourselves consider the possibility."

Lavrov let out a quiet laugh after a moment. "Yes, you are right, but not all of us were so blind."

Strelnikov sighed. He'd pushed away his memories on the walk here and he was in no mood to let his old friend indulge in them now. "You were the one who left the instructions at the dead drop in Moscow for me to come here. I must congratulate you on your penetration of the CIA. I was told that my case files and reports were being held in a very secure compartment."

"They are," Lavrov agreed. "And our new asset is impressive. It is regrettable that he cannot be allowed to remain in place, but your betrayal has forced me to exfiltrate him. He doesn't know it yet, but he will very soon."

"How long have you known?" Strelnikov asked.

"Not long," Lavrov admitted. "Your knowledge of my operations left us little choice but to act quickly. But you are my old friend, Stepan, and I had to be convinced beyond any doubt that you truly were guilty. There was no question once you left for Berlin. Your fellow GRU officers dismantled your dacha. I'm told they found the smartphone and software the Americans gave you to use, among other toys. It doesn't matter where you've hidden whatever money they have paid you, you will not see it."

"There was no money," Strelnikov told him. "I asked for none. I did not do this for money."

"I had hoped not." Lavrov looked to his comrade, a painful sadness twisting his face. "More than forty years we have been friends. So, please, tell me why you turned to treason," Lavrov demanded.

"Do you truly want an answer?"

"Of course. It will not change what comes after, but I prefer knowledge to ignorance." His desire to know was genuine, Strelnikov knew. Lavrov needed no confession to condemn him at a tribunal. An answer to the question could not hurt him more and perhaps might do some good.

"My grandfather was a Jew, Arkady. I never talked about him, of course. There were so many Jew-haters among the chekists. Still today too, though not so many. You are not one of them, I know, but still you and your foundation threaten my grandfather's people . . . my people."

"Ah," Lavrov said. "The assistance I gave to the Iranians."

"Yes," Strelnikov said. "You should not have sold them nuclear technology. And now the new device you want to sell them—"

"We must help our allies," Lavrov said, as though that simple fact alone was justification enough.

"Our allies are butchers, Arkady."

"And we are not?"

"We have been, but we could be better men. We can restore the *Rodina Mat* in other ways than this."

Lavrov sighed, feigning a loss of energy. "I will have your clothes returned after they are inspected. I will give you that dignity. But you already *were* a better man, Stepan Illarionovich. I know you were."

"It was not my head but my heart that made my choices, Arkady," Strelnikov said, defiance in his voice. "As it always has."

"In honorable men, *true* men, the head and the heart speak with the same voice," Lavrov told him. "I regret that you forgot that. Remember it now and you might find some peace." The senior Russian official stood to leave.

"Arkady . . . a question for you," Strelnikov pleaded.

"Yes?"

"Why this place? Why bring me back here?"

Lavrov smiled, rueful. "Death and resurrection, old friend. This is the place for it." He turned away from Strelnikov and walked outside.

Aqid (Colonel) Issam Ghazal of the Syrian Army had learned, of necessity, to be a patient man. With no familial connections to advance his career, his promotions had come through careful maneuvers and waiting for those more ambitious and less careful than himself to make mistakes that could not be dismissed. Such steps created enemies and each rise in the ranks forced him to be ever more deliberate. Greater heights put him under more scrutiny, and ever-smaller mistakes could be his undoing. Still, his self-control was rigid now and he enjoyed the thought that his enemies were going slowly mad waiting for him to make mistakes that never came.

But patience did not mean he could not be mindful of the time. Ghazal checked his watch, a Suunto Core digital that he'd picked up in a highbrow Berlin shop the day before. He wished he could afford one of those finer Swiss watches, one of the TAG Heuers that he'd seen under the glass, but those would stay beyond his means until he could secure a promotion to flag rank.

The Russian general, Lavrov, had been inside the decrepit mansion for a half hour before emerging. "Colonel Ghazal," he said. "It is my great pleasure to meet you again."

"General Lavrov," Ghazal replied, bowing slightly.

"If you will walk with me, I will escort you to the test site," Lavrov requested.

"You don't want to drive?" Ghazal asked.

Lavrov shook his head. "I would like my car to be in working order after the weapons test." He extended an arm and Ghazal began to trudge across the cold ground with the Russian, their boots crunching in the hardening mud.

"That was a spectacle that your men put on a few minutes ago," Ghazal noted. "Who was the man they detained?"

"Regrettably, an old friend," Lavrov said. "But one who could not find it in himself to remain loyal."

"Ah," Ghazal said, his manner sympathetic, "that is always regrettable. The foundation of any friendship is always loyalty."

"Indeed," Lavrov replied. "And to violate it is the unpardonable sin. Trust cannot be recovered once lost. Doubt always remains after treason, no matter what a man says or does thereafter."

"Yes," Ghazal agreed. "I presume that you wanted me to see that so I could reassure my superiors that your operation is secure."

"Correct," Lavrov admitted. "The debacle our Iranian friends suffered last year caused many of my clients to question our ability to be discreet. I wanted to show you that we can manage the problem."

"I do not think that was ever in doubt," Ghazal said. "But they do not want it managed, only prevented. At our level, one breach is too much." The Syrian ran a hand through his dark beard. "If that man taken in the house truly was your friend and a loyal officer for decades, then anyone else could be vulnerable. If the Americans could persuade him, who could they not reach? No, I do not think my superiors will be convinced that your operation is secure."

"The Americans did not persuade him," Lavrov countered. "He had a weakness that led him to falter. A relative of his was Jewish, so my dealings with the Iranians and now with you worried him."

"Zionists and their friends are everywhere. How many more like him might be part of your organization? We can never know." Ghazal sighed. "I am under orders not to pay you nor take possession of the material until my superiors are convinced that you have reestablished your security," he said. "My leaders do not want trouble with the

Americans like the Iranians suffered last year, much less with the rest of NATO or, Allah forbid, the Israelis."

Lavrov frowned. "What are their terms?"

"They are not asking for changes to the contract," Ghazal admitted. "They simply do not want it executed until they are sure there will be no unexpected publicity."

"That will happen very, very soon," Lavrov said. "The man who identified Stepan as a traitor can identify any others in my organization who are disloyal."

"That is reassuring," Ghazal replied. "And you will be pleased to hear that I have convinced them to pay you interest for the time spent cleaning out your own house."

"A small investment now that will save you from greater problems in the future," Lavrov advised. "But for now, come, I have something to show you."

The Großer Müggelsee Lake
Treptow-Köpenick District
Berlin, Federal Republic of Germany

The gray clouds made the day look as though it was already dying despite the morning hour when Sigmar Mueller stepped out of the Mercedes Vito onto the wet grass. The vegetation had grown wild and thick along the lakeshore here, and the recent storms had fueled its growth as much as the Müggelsee water. Some underpaid labor had not mowed along the roadside and the green shoots rose to a height that reached up past his boots and darkened his pants where they touched his legs. He closed the car door, trapping some of the wet plants inside the cabin, and Mueller muttered something indiscreet about the work habits of immigrants hired to keep the grass down.

The marshy ground pulled at his feet as the grass gave way to cattails that gently hit his thighs until he reached the paved trail, but the damage was done. The old man, tall, graying hair, and smooth faced, ignored the feeling of his trousers growing more damp and cold with each stride. It hardly qualified as an annoyance. The senior investigator for the Bundeskriminalamt, the Federal Criminal Investigation Office, had been called to study corpses in locations far more hostile and personally uncomfortable than this one. The worst had been the dead prostitutes that some patrons of the street had stuffed into sewer holes. Those pictures in his mind stood out in his memory, which was impressive given the many competing images. Mueller hoped that dementia might help him forget them all someday after he had given up the job.

The Müggelsee had been an attraction for him since he'd been a child, a lake so large that one could always find some quiet solace on a weekend near a tree line. He brought his family here often during the gentler seasons, the October fall and the April spring before the air turned either frigid or humid, and he prayed that what he would soon see here would not put him off this place. But he supposed the lake's size and secluded shores that made it such a draw for him would eventually call for less benign reasons to the organized criminal groups that operated out of Berlin, sixteen kilometers to the northwest.

The highway encircled the lake, no more than a few dozen meters from the shore at the farthest point, but trees hid the water from the road in places and early September rains had left the ground a humid bog on the southeastern side. Mueller muttered to himself, then chuckled, amused by his own absurdity of wanting to ask murderers to accommodate him and his fellows by depositing their victims in convenient spots. They would earn an extra measure of his gratitude if they would also concede to pick less onerous seasons to do their work. He had missed enough Advents and Christmas days with his family and feared he would have too few left to make up the difference.

He cleared a slight rise, the far side of a low swale where the water had pooled an inch deep, creating a tiny marsh that sank under his feet until the dirty water covered the toes of his boots. He pushed himself up the embankment, then pulled himself forward by grasping an exposed root, scrambled up, and saw that he had arrived.

The body rested under a blue plastic sheet held down by rocks to keep the cold breeze from carrying it away. Two uniformed officers from the local *Polizeibehörde* stood over the departed and Mueller realized that he didn't know which town was closest to this point of the lake. No matter, he supposed. The locals had called for the federal police, he had arrived, and their duties here would be done by the day's end. Other officers had roped out a perimeter larger than he needed for the purpose of his visit, and civilians were blessedly absent except for two—a young man, bearded with short brown hair, and a woman, petite with a pixie cut, both sitting in a covered police Gator that someone had managed to drive through the thick woods.

One of the local police, this one a woman dressed in civilian clothes and an overcoat, saw him coming and moved to meet him. "Herr Mueller?" she asked.

"*Ja,*" he replied.

"I am Johanna Adler. It is a pleasure," the younger woman replied. She was a head shorter than Mueller, blond, probably half his age and overweight, which he observed from her rounded cheeks, but not so much that young men would find her unattractive.

"The pleasure is mine," Mueller replied in their native tongue. "Though not so much to be here."

"I must agree with you," Adler replied, her voice quiet, unnerved.

"Your first murder scene?"

"*Nein,*" Adler said. "My second, and at this lake, if you can believe it."

"And who was the first victim?"

"A young British man, a photographer and hiker, pulled from the lake last month." Her cheeks were flushed red, whether from embarrassment or the cool air Mueller didn't know. "I used to love the Müggelsee. Now I am starting to dread seeing it."

"I hope you will be able to spend happier days here," Mueller said. "How was the victim found?"

"By the two witnesses, there," Adler said, pointing to the young couple sitting in the Gator. Closer to him, they looked to be barely more than teenagers to Mueller's eye, but he was old enough that most everyone looked like children to him now. The woman was distraught enough that she probably had been incoherent an hour before. The man was holding her and saying nothing except to answer an officer's questions with as few words as possible. Adler pulled out a notebook and read her own handwriting off the pages. "Thomas Gauck and Angela Weidmann. He brought her here this morning at sunrise to propose marriage. He says that he had spent a week wandering the lakeshore to find the best spot and finally settled on this one yesterday afternoon. He hadn't counted on the rain, but decided not to postpone. They arrived on foot at six forty-five this morning. When the sun finally rose, they saw the victim in the shallows. The body was facedown in the silt, with no shirt or shoes. Mr. Gauck insists that he would have seen it yesterday afternoon had it been there, but the state of decomposition seems advanced, so it is unlikely that someone merely left the body here overnight. That spurred me to call your office. Our local office is not equipped to identify a victim so . . . unrecognizable."

Mueller walked over to the blue shroud on the ground and saw Adler avert her gaze as he lifted a corner. "Not so bad," he said. "The dirt from the water makes him look worse than he really is." It was true, but Adler had not been entirely wrong. The deceased was bloated enough that identification would be problematic. Obviously male, a little under two meters, and moderately overweight, though his swollen tissues made his true weight difficult to estimate. Mueller scanned the muddy ground around the corpse and saw no sign of disturbance. Adler looked ill to him, trying to control her rebellious stomach, but questions had to be asked. "And there were no other tracks on the ground?"

"None that we could find other than those left by Herr Gauck and Fräulein Weidmann."

"The ground is too soft for anyone to come and go and leave it unmarked," Mueller observed. "It seems likely that the body floated here."

"*Ja,*" Adler replied. "The Spree River inlet is a half kilometer from here, close enough to create a slight current that could have pushed the body from there to this point overnight."

Mueller nodded. "I cannot say there was violence involved in this, but if so, it is possible that it could have been deposited here in the lake a few days ago, improperly tied and weighted, and worked its way to the surface. Decomposition creates gases in the tissues that make the corpse buoyant. They can be quite difficult to keep submerged."

He'd recited the science as pure facts, not thinking about the woman standing to his left. He heard her make an unpleasant sound and he turned, seeing Adler's face pale at the thoughts his words had drawn in her mind. *Poor girl,* Mueller thought. *Such a thing to see before the holiday.* He regretted that she would have to suffer through for a few minutes more. Procedures had to be observed. "Did you examine the body for distinguishing marks?"

"Only the areas we could see without moving it," she said, her voice tenuous. "Obviously, the rigor has passed, but we did not want to disturb the site until you had a chance to inspect the area. He has a military tattoo of some kind on his left shoulder, but I'm not an expert on such marks. We did find something unusual when we checked his pants. If you'll check the interior label—?"

Mueller donned a pair of latex gloves, then followed the young woman's suggestion, turning the waistband of the wet blue jogging suit over. Adler saw the older man's eyes widen when he saw the marking. He let the pants go, extracted a pair of glasses from his overcoat, put them on, and repeated the inspection.

Mueller let the pants go and pulled the suit top away from the corpse's shoulder until he could see the tattoo. He stared at it for several seconds, committing it to memory, then stood, removing the glasses and the thin gloves. All sense of charm had vanished, replaced by a more serious demeanor in the time it had taken him to come to his feet. "I will talk to the witnesses and call in a forensic unit. We will take responsibility for the remains and the site, but I doubt there will be any evidence to collect here beyond the body itself. If you would share your interview notes and any suspected evidence, I would be most grateful. And could I trouble you to please summon the Bundesamt für Verfassungsshutz? The Federal Office for the Protection of the Constitution might have some domestic intelligence that could be useful. Interpol may also become involved."

Adler's brow furrowed deep. Mueller saw her confusion. "You recognize Cyrillic letters when you see them, yes?" he asked.

"Of course, Herr Mueller."

He nodded. "I am familiar with military tattoos. The one on the victim's shoulder is not uncommon among soldiers of the Russian Main Intelligence Directorate. You might know them as the GRU, the old masters of the Spetsnaz Special Forces. That and his suit label together suggest this gentleman was a Russian intelligence officer at some point in his life. If he was still a military officer at the time of his death, then this is almost certainly a murder. No Spetsnaz soldier, past or present, would drown in the water unless he suffered a cardiac arrest or some other medical issue. The gray in his hair and his weight, even accounting for the bloating, suggest that he's likely an officer, possibly a senior one. Enlisted soldiers of the Russian military are typically conscripts, and tend to be younger and more trim. So we face the possibility that a ranking Russian Special Forces officer died on our soil, possibly from misadventure or natural causes, but murder seems more likely to me. Unless we can rule that out, we must consider this as a potential national security matter, possibly involving espionage or organized criminal activity. So you are freed of responsibility for this matter."

Adler exhaled. "I cannot say that I am sorry for that, Herr Mueller," Adler said. "My men and I will be most grateful not to have to work this case."

"I would say that you're most welcome, Fräulein, but I'm not pleased to catch such a case myself." He was past the age where he sought the big cases that promised recognition and advancement.

"I understand," Adler said. "I will fetch my case notes for you and place the call."

"*Danke.*" Adler trudged away toward the officer interviewing the witnesses and Mueller knelt down again and pulled back the plastic sheet. *Thus ends my holiday, I think*, he told himself. Perhaps next year.

Flughafen Berlin-Tegel Airport

Tegel, Borough of Reinickendorf

Berlin, Germany

The Boeing 777 carrying Alden Maines arrived late, which chafed him but created no real inconvenience. Nothing short of incarceration would truly upset his schedule. That was a real possibility, though a small one and not enough to cause him any anxiety as he made his way through customs. If the Germans had known to detain him, they would have sent men onto the plane before allowing anyone off. His logic proved right and the customs officer hardly looked at his face as she processed his passport and waved him into the Federal Republic of Germany without a welcome.

A driver was waiting for him, holding a card with the cover name the Russians had assigned him. The car was more average than Maines thought he deserved, but he supposed that anything expensive would've drawn attention. The driver gave him a sealed envelope before leaving him at a boutique hotel near the St. Clement-Kirche Chapel and the Hebbel Theater. He opened the letter in the privacy of his room, and the cryptic instructions inside ordered him to dine at a local eatery before calling a contact number. The operator at the other end of that call sent him another mile northwest on foot to a pub in Tiergarten, giving him time to walk a surveillance detection route and buy the current copy of the *Economist*. He held the magazine in his left hand at the intersection of Stulerstrasse and Cornelius at 2:45 local time to signal another driver, who was punctual.

Maines would've preferred some time to shake off the jet lag before the meeting, but he knew that he wouldn't have slept. The world was going his way. The Russians had sampled the product he was offering and liked it enough to pay him a nice sum and ask him to come here. They would want to control him, of course, but he was the one selling the secrets, so the advantage was his. The Russians would follow his lead or they would lose his services. It was his neck on the block, wasn't it?

The driver made the final turn and Maines was surprised at the destination. He'd expected a safe house.

The Russian Embassy in Berlin was a great stone slab of Stalinist design, hollowed out in the center and surrounded by a low rock parapet and wrought-iron gates. The white walls and trees in the courtyard at the building's front tried to persuade onlookers that the embassy wasn't some granite pustule erupting out of Berlin's underside, but the pilasters and parapets above advertised the building's cold, austere spirit. The enormous complex violated German laws governing the height of buildings along the Unter den Linden highway, but East Germany had been in no position during construction to ask its Soviet masters to obey regulations.

The car passed through gates manned by Russian guards and pulled into an underground garage. The driver gestured for Maines to follow and the two worked their way through back hallways and little-used stairwells. He supposed that his sponsors didn't want the staff to see an American expatriate walking the corridors, but the small office where the sentry finally delivered him was disappointing. After he'd made peace with being at the embassy, he'd assumed that the meeting would take place in one of the finely furnished conference rooms on the building's top floor. Maines had owned a larger office at the U.S. Embassy in Caracas, and the chairs in this one hardly qualified as comfortable, much less ornate. The light was harsh, the walls concrete, and the pipes in the ceiling exposed. It was hardly a place to fete a man who could provide the information he held.

They made him wait another hour, the driver standing at the door to make sure he didn't wander, and his temper was at a full rolling boil when his patron finally approached.

"*Spasibo.*" Arkady Lavrov ignored the American in favor of the sentry. "*Pozhaluysta zakroyte dver.*" The escort nodded and closed the door as he'd been asked after Lavrov stepped inside. The Russian GRU director went to his seat on the other side of the small desk, then leaned back and studied the American sitting across from him. "Mr. Maines, it is a shame that you are here. Do you love your country?"

Maines's brow furrowed and he stared at the Russian. "I . . . of course I do." *What idiocy was this?*

"That is unfortunate."

Maines drew his head back. "General, I'm here to help my country." He'd told himself that enough to believe it. "Relations between us have suffered because my president is a moron. Our two nations will benefit from having someone like me who can explain to you what my leaders are thinking—"

"You have no access to President Rostow," Lavrov observed.

"I've been with the CIA for twenty years. I know how the White House and the Agency operate."

"No doubt. But I question whether you understand what this will cost you."

Maines's features twisted in confusion. "What are you talking about?"

"I'm concerned about your soul, Mr. Maines." Lavrov leaned forward, clasped his hands, and rested his arms on the desk. "I truly wish you were a mercenary, just giving up your country for money. It would make the new arrangement that I will propose easier on you. I have seen more than a few men commit that treason, some for money, others for revenge or ego, a few for reasons of conscience. The ones who do it out of principle, like yourself, almost go mad from the shame and the homesickness, once they are discovered and have to live in exile. Even the ones who do it for less honorable reasons and are beyond feeling guilt simply never know another day without fear, another peaceful night. They wonder whether this won't be the day that the knock comes at their door. The money or the vengeance or the excitement never can cure that. So I fear for you, Mr. Maines. If you truly are doing this for principle, then I wish that you had been faithful to your country."

"I fingered a traitor to *your* country," Maines protested. The anger was starting to rise in his chest now. He'd run this meeting through his mind over and over, and no imaginary version of it had ever followed this course. "I helped you neutralize a serious threat to your operations to prove my sincerity—"

"Yes, you did," Lavrov said. "I almost wish you hadn't. General Strelnikov had been my very good friend for a long time. It hurt me deeply to know that he had been unfaithful to us. You are correct that he was jeopardizing our work, but it saddened me all the same. He thought he was helping a country that he loved. It's just unfortunate that he loved two countries and imagined that he could divide his loyalties. I know how he would have suffered for that through the years had you not told us what he had done."

"'Would have suffered'?" Maines asked.

"He was executed."

"Huh," Maines grunted in surprise. He should've expected that, wasn't sure why he hadn't, but it didn't rankle him much. Men had been sacrificed before to prevent hostilities between nations, and the leaders who'd sacrificed them were hailed for it later. The masses sometimes needed a few years to realize the wisdom of the choice, but the historians were usually kind.

"He cannot hurt the *Rodina* anymore, for which I am glad, and now his conscience will not torture him, for which I am also glad. But you will come to regret what you have done, I think," Lavrov said.

Maines fought the urge to roll his eyes at the man's stupidity. The entire conversation had left him off balance. The casual way that Lavrov had denied him control of the discussion, deflecting every attempt to seize the initiative from the outset, was maddening. *Get on with the business*, he thought, but did not say. He pushed ahead. "General, if you don't want my information, I'm sure there are others in your government who would appreciate what I have to offer," he said. "But I don't know why you would be stubborn about security or money. You already paid me fifty thousand dollars."

"That will not be necessary," Lavrov told him. "You are here and your information will be useful. So I am prepared to hear what you have to tell me. As for money, you will receive none."

Maines frowned, confused. "What are you talking about?"

"After your flight to Berlin had left America's airspace, I had one of our people in Washington inform your FBI that you were defecting to the Russian Federation."

"You . . . what? I don't—"

"Like Cortés in Mexico, I burned your ship after you landed in the New World, as it were." Lavrov reached into his coat pocket, pulled out a sheet, and slid it across to the American. "You will not be going home, Mr. Maines."

Maines looked at the sheet and started to rock back in surprise before he caught himself. He stared at the paper, a copy of an Interpol Blue Notice with his photograph . . . the one from his Agency badge, in fact.

Maines, Alden

**WANTED BY THE JUDICIAL AUTHORITIES OF THE
UNITED STATES OF AMERICA FOR PROSECUTION**

IDENTITY PARTICULARS

Present family name: **Maines**
Forename: **Alden**
Sex: **Male**
Date of birth: **10/09/1980 (39 years old)**
Place of birth: **Los Angeles, California,
                     United States of America**
Language(s) spoken: **English, Russian, Spanish**
Nationality: **American (USA)**

PHYSICAL DESCRIPTION

Height: **1.8 meter**
Weight: **77 Kg**
Colour of hair: **Brown**
Colour of eyes: **Green**

CHARGES Published as provided by requesting
entity

Charges: **Treason, corruption**

IF YOU HAVE ANY INFORMATION PLEASE CONTACT

Your national or local police
General Secretariat of INTERPOL

INTERPOL

Lavrov smiled. "You will tell me what I need to know, and once that is done, I will take you to Moscow and see to it that you get a permit for work and residency. I will also help you secure an apartment. That should be enough for you to start building a life."

Maines's face twisted in disbelief at the words. "What I know is worth millions of dollars, tens of millions, and I'm only asking for a fraction of that."

"Mr. Maines, please." Lavrov shook his head in pity. "I am surprised that someone who has lived in the United States so long should have such a poor understanding of capitalism." He paused, then leaned back in his chair and thought for a moment. Each empty second stretched out in the air. Finally he spoke. "Intelligence secrets are strange things. We collect them at great cost, and they are valuable not because they tell us what to do, but because they tell us what not to do. They prevent mistakes of judgment and save us the costs of wrong guesses. And yet, once such a secret is revealed, it loses all its power. The enemy realizes that we know his secret and changes his behavior. He shuts off the means by which we stole his secrets. We lose the power of the secret itself and some of our ability to gather more through the same means. So the cost of collecting our enemy's secrets goes up."

Lavrov leaned forward again, his features hardening. "One does not pay a mole to reveal his country's secrets. One pays a mole for his access, which is much more valuable. Time destroys the value of any information he gives up, no matter how important. Secrets are just another perishable commodity and a mole is the broker. We pay a broker not for his product, but for his ability to provide that product." Lavrov leaned back, gathered his thoughts again, then smiled. "Now you have no access and you are a wanted man. So you need my protection and the only currency you have to barter for it is the information you have in your head. And without the ability to acquire more, what you have devalues as we speak. Your value to me diminishes by the hour. So, cooperate now and we will grant you residency with no extradition. From time to time, we will use you to embarrass your government and highlight its hypocrisy, and you will smile and cooperate with our networks and newspapers to do it."

Maines ground his teeth together, his face flushing red. "I'll take my information to someone else."

"A poor threat," Lavrov advised. "If you will not share your information with us, then your only value to me will lie entirely in the goodwill I will earn from the Germans and the Americans when I walk you out the front door where the German federal police will be waiting."

Maines's head was throbbing now. His desire to murder Lavrov right here, smash his brains out against the table, almost overcame his own desire for self-preservation. The driver was still outside the door, and he was probably Spetsnaz, more than a match for a mildly obese CIA officer just past his prime. But this was all beyond his control . . . not how this meeting was supposed to have gone. He couldn't even walk out of the embassy now. "So why not just toss me in a cell?"

"You're not a prisoner," Lavrov told him. "You are just not in a position of leverage."

"So that guard outside the door is just a free concierge service you offer all of your clients?" Maines asked. He suspected the sarcasm would be lost on the Russian.

"Not at all," Lavrov said. "He will make sure you do not roam the embassy. You were a CIA officer, and there is always the possibility that you are not a true defector. We don't want you to steal any more of our secrets than you already have." The Russian pushed away from the table and smiled. "I do enjoy honesty. Do you not, Mr. Maines? We get so few opportunities to indulge in it. It is a rare delicacy for men of our occupation."

"I don't think you want me to indulge in honesty much right now," Maines warned him.

"So long as you are truthful when you give us the names, the rest I will forgive," Lavrov replied. "But it is not in your interest for any negotiation to drag on. Time is no friend of yours now. I suggest you make your decision within the next day or so."

Lavrov stepped outside into the hall and closed the door behind him. Maines heard his footsteps shuffle away from the small room and was left to listen to the buzz of the harsh lights and his own thoughts.

CHAPTER TWO

Office of the Deputy Director of National Intelligence
Liberty Crossing Complex
McLean, Virginia

Kathy Cooke's new office was quite austere. Six months into her new appointment, the former CIA director had enjoyed little time to arrange it to her liking. Papers sat in manila folders organized in neat stacks on the desk, edges aligned as with a ruler. Personal trophies that meant nothing to anyone but the owner occupied the shelves that other people would have used for books, including several ceremonial weapons that were probably illegal to have in a federal building. There were no diplomas or performance awards hanging on the walls, and the pictures were all of family, with none of the usual vanity photos of the occupant shaking hands with this president or that foreign leader. Humility was a rare trait among senior government officials, but Cooke had learned early on that a healthy dose of meekness tended to save her a lot of trouble later on.

She'd always kept her office at CIA mostly impersonal for the duration of her five-year tenure, in no small part because she'd never expected to hold the job very long. Leaders at that level of government service tended to have short terms in office, usually lasting only until some new president was elected. That she had survived under two surprised her more than anyone else, and Rostow had made it no secret that he'd wanted her out. She hadn't really wanted to retire from the job, but the president was no respecter of the Agency and Cooke had resisted his maneuvering more to protect the people at Langley than out of any personal ambition. Had Rostow been a better man, she would have been happy to retire. She wasn't yet fifty, her professional options would have been legion, and she and Jon could finally have gotten on with the personal life they'd kept on hold for too long.

Jon, she thought. Cooke hadn't seen the chief of CIA's Red Cell for almost a month now. Langley was just a few miles up the road to the northeast, but her promotion had put more distance between them than the geography. Her schedule was hardly conducive to having any kind of personal life.

Cooke had no idea how her boss had convinced the chief executive to promote her. She hadn't wanted the job, had even thought about rejecting it when the DNI had called. But she served at the pleasure of the president, even when the man was a hostile, arrogant cuss. The Senate had confirmed her fairly quickly, and the only votes not cast in her favor had been abstentions.

She'd decided to give it three years. Three years would satisfy her sense of duty, she thought, and then she would walk away. But there were still issues to resolve before that happened. The most distressing was the one she could do the least about at the moment.

Cooke stared down at the copy of *Der Spiegel*. CIA had attached a printed translation of the lead article on the German daily's front page.

The German Federal Criminal Investigation Office reported today that its officers recovered a drowning victim from the Großer Müggelsee Lake southeast of Berlin. Forensic investigators have identified the victim as retired lieutenant general Stepan Illarionovich Strelnikov, director of Russia's Foundation for Advanced Research . . .

The secure phone rang, interrupting her reading. She knew who was calling and what the subject of conversation would be. She'd told her secretary to block every other call from anyone who ranked lower than herself, which was almost everyone in the intelligence community now. She picked up the handset. "How's Berlin?" she asked without preamble.

"Depressing." Clark Barron's voice was deep, the resonance masked by the digital encryption, but the man's somber tone came across the line perfectly clear. The CIA director of the National Clandestine Service was an unhappy man at the moment. "I've got a cable coming your way with the details, but I wanted to give you an informal report first," he said. "The Bundesnachrichtendienst let me see the body and their forensic evidence. It's Strelnikov, no question. Coroner says he drowned." The Bundesnachrichtendienst was Germany's foreign intelligence service.

"He *drowned*?" Cooke asked, incredulous. "How does a former Spetsnaz officer drown?" The question was entirely rhetorical.

Barron answered it anyway. "By having someone hold his head under," he offered. "I think Maines gave him up, but this isn't the way the Russians do business. They keep suspects stuck in the homeland while they build airtight cases, and then they nail them. They don't send them abroad to execute them, and they sure don't move this fast. Doesn't make any sense to me."

"Yeah," Cooke acknowledged. She stared out his window, then shut her eyes tight, wishing the reality away. One of the CIA's most important assets was dead. The only question now was how the Russians had found him out, and the most likely answer promised more disasters to come.

Cooke shunted her emotions aside and set herself to the business. "Clark, I'm going to send Jon and Kyra out to you. They're good at pulling things like this apart."

"Yeah, they are," Barron confirmed. "How fast can you get them out here?"

"I'll have them on a plane to Berlin by tonight."

Cooke couldn't see the NCS director nod his head on the other side of the Atlantic. "I'll pick them up. One question . . . do they have a blank check to follow this thing into Moscow?"

"If that's where the trail leads. Your discretion," Cooke said. "One more thing, Clark?"

"Yeah, boss?"

"If you get a chance to bring Maines home, you don't need to be gentle with him on my account."

"Understood," Barron replied. "He'll come home breathing and mentally undamaged. He'll have to consider anything else a bonus."

"Roger that," Cooke said. "Good hunting." She didn't wait for her subordinate to hang up the phone before doing it herself. She swiveled her chair around to face her computer and checked the in-box. Barron's promised cable hadn't arrived yet. The DNI was waiting for his own briefing and she wasn't going to deliver it until she had the official report in hand. She was tempted to call over to CIA's operations center to ask about it, but decided to wait. No doubt Barron had marked up the electronic report with all of the code words and crypts that would send it screaming through the system to his in-box as fast as the system would allow. It would be on her screen within the hour, barring inattention of incompetence of the ops center staff, and, if not, the thrashing they would receive wouldn't be dished out over the phone.

Cooke exhaled in frustration, checked her watch, and the waiting started again.

Flughafen Berlin-Tegel Airport
Tegel, Borough of Reinickendorf
Berlin, Germany

The morning fog covered the German fields in gray smoke, hiding the fields until the plane was nearly on the ground. Kyra Stryker couldn't see the sun or sky once the aircraft was on the tarmac, which was slick from a storm that had passed through during the night. Silver puddles were scattered across the blacktop, spraying in all directions as planes and support trucks drove through them.

She had not expected to visit Germany during her career, certainly not during her first ten years anyway. European assignments were so often reserved for senior officers who had served their time in less desirable posts and had the personal connections on Langley's Seventh Floor to lock up the positions they wanted. Getting the truly prized assignments required both a track record and inside help. Kyra knew she could and would be good at it, but three years' working in the Red Cell had left her wondering whether she wanted to try.

Kyra exhaled hard. The man next to her looked at her sideways. "Nervous?" Jonathan Burke, the chief of the Red Cell didn't turn his head to confirm the guess. Jon wore his usual khakis and an oxford shirt, no tie or jacket. He kept both on a hanger behind his office door but she'd never seen him wear them. *Only God and the White House get a coat and tie*, he'd once said, and she'd never seen the middle-aged man break that rule for anyone else. Few noticed. He avoided people as much as they allowed.

"About the mission? No," Kyra said after a moment's thought, surprising herself. "After you've been shot at, not much else gets the blood pressure up. It's hard to care about what people think after someone's made a serious effort to kill you. But it does get really hard to put up with stupidity."

"And now you see why people consider me prickly," Jon said.

"They're not wrong," she teased.

Both customs and the luggage handlers lived up to the myth of German efficiency, and the analysts were in the city within the hour. Berlin fascinated Kyra as it passed by in the window. She'd seen so many cities that had sacrificed their character for modern amenities, but Berlin had retained a look of old history. There were few true skyscrapers jutting above the stone buildings and rounded domes that looked centuries old. It was impressive, she thought, given how much of skyline had been bombed into wreckage by the Allies during the Second World War and how much had been rebuilt while the city served as the front line of the Cold War. These Germans had survived hell itself for decades and Berlin was now the testament to their endurance.

The hotel was a decent choice, and Kyra had breakfast brought up to her room. She rarely slept on planes and the pilot stubbornly had plowed through a series of Atlantic storms, robbing her of what little rest she might have enjoyed. Jon was always telling her not to substitute caffeine for sleep, but time was a zero-sum game in counterintelligence, always working for the hunter or the prey, but never both. Kyra didn't want to give Alden Maines or the Russians more time. German coffee and energy drinks would solve the jet-lag problem for one day at the cost of shaky hands, but she would manage it.

The U.S. Embassy was close, eight blocks away on foot. The Marine guards ran their IDs and let them pass. Like them, Clark Barron was a visitor with no office in the building of his own. It took some time to find the man and an unused classified space where they could talk.

The conference room was government standard except for the high-backed leather chairs that surrounded the table. The windows gave a view to the north and a small curio case of foreign gifts sat in one of the opposite corners. Relief maps of every continent but their own hung on the walls.

"Good to see you both again. It's been a while since Pioneer and the Farm," the NCS director said.

"Better times than this," Jon agreed. "What can we do for you?"

"To keep it short and blunt, we've got a case that makes no sense. And it'll probably be the most tightly compartmented case you'll ever get read into at the Agency."

Barron set a copy of *Der Spiegel* on the table with a printed translation of one article attached. "Three days ago, the German Federal Criminal Investigation Office pulled a body out of the Großer Müggelsee Lake southeast of Berlin. Forensic investigators identified him as retired lieutenant general Stepan Illarionovich Strelnikov, director of the Russian Foundation for Advanced Research, their version of DOD's Advanced Research Projects Agency. The *Moscow Times* ran his obituary today. The Russian government says he drowned while going for a swim."

Jon pulled the article across the table, turned it around, and scanned the translated page. "It's not every day that a retired Russian flag officer drowns, is it?"

"Not one who's the Russian equivalent of a Navy SEAL." Barron handed the analysts a folder. The first page was Strelnikov's biography, with a stapled photograph of a man dressed in a Russian general's uniform, portly, with pronounced jowls, dark eyes, and the dour expression that seemed to be a Russian birthright.

Biographical and Leadership Report NC1232
Leadership Division/Office of Assessment

STRELNIKOV, Stepan Illarionovich
Professional Biography
- DoB: 19 Nov 1960
- PoB: Volgograd, Volgograd Oblast, Russia
- 1982: Graduate, Moscow State Technical University imeni Bauman
- 1984: Graduate, KGB Higher Communications School, Kharkov
- 1984: Company Commander, 72nd Independent Radio-Electronic Combat Regiment, Bagram, Afghanistan
- 1985: Deputy Chief of Staff, 413th Special Radio-

Electronic Combat Battalion, Group of Soviet Forces
Germany, Karl Marx Stadt

- 1986: Executive Officer, 4th Special Warfare Brigade
  (SPETSNAZ), Kabul, Afghanistan
- 1989–1990: Professional status unknown; stationed at
  Soviet Embassy, Berlin, Germany
- 1990 (Dec)–1991 (Feb): Defense Attache's office, Baghdad
- 1991–1994: Professional status unknown (Serbia?)
- 1995: Graduate: Military Academy of the General Staff
  (was: Voroshilov Military Academy)
- 1996: Commander, 11th Radio-Electronic Combat Regiment (Grozhny)
- 1996–1998: Professional status unknown
- 1998–2000: Liaison officer attached to Serbian Army
- 2000–2002: Commander, 7th Independent Undersea
  Warfare and Special Reconnaissance Regiment, St. Petersburg (SPETSNAZ)
- 2002–2003: Liaison officer (Defense Attache's office),
  Baghdad
- 2004–2005: Commanding officer, Voronezh Higher Communications Academy
- 2006–2007: Commanding Officer, Second Directorate
  (USA & Canada) Main Military Administration (GRU)
- 2008–2012: Senior Military Attache, Caracas, Venezuela;
  retires from active military service with the GRU, Federal
  Security Service of the Russian Federation
- 2013: Listed as Vice President for Communications
  Security, "Zelyonsoft" [zelyeniy is Russian for "gold"], St.
  Petersburg. Strelnikov is introduced at UN conference on
  global Internet governance as Zelensoft Vice President for
  Strategic Investment; Strelnikov tells UK/SIS officer at
  conference he is "retired military."

- 2014–2016: Strelnikov leaves Zelensoft, is named Special Advisor to President Putin for Information Security
- 4 January 2017: Strelnikov named Director, Foundation for Advanced Research.

"He was a new asset, barely a year on the books, and a volunteer," Barron told them. "We had high hopes for him, until someone gave him up."

"A mole?" Jon asked.

"A defector," Barron corrected him. "Kyra, I'm sorry about this one." The next page showed a photograph of a middle-aged man, midforties, thin, with black hair lightening at the temples. He had bright eyes, green, with a Roman nose and a day's stubble. The man wore a suit and stood before an American flag. Burke recognized it as the kind of photo that senior leaders were privileged to take when they reached sufficient rank. Not every Agency officer got to take one during his career.

"Alden Maines," Kyra said before Barron could name him.

"You know him?" Jon asked.

"He was deputy chief of station in Caracas when I was there," she said, her voice flat. "He got me out of the country after I was shot." She took the file out of Jon's hands, dropped it on the table, and leaned over it, hands in her hair.

"After our station down there was torn to shreds, he couldn't work South America anymore," Barron added. "He put together the operation to get Kyra out on the fly, and I thought that was worth a reward. I also wanted to see what he could really do, so I brought him back to headquarters and made him deputy chief of Russia House. But I'm told he didn't like the desk. Then the current chief of Russia House retired and Maines applied for the job, but I was having second thoughts about him by then. Maines had been showing contempt for leadership since he got back from Venezuela . . . started abusing the people under him too. I interviewed him and he displayed a nasty mix of narcissism and sadism. So I chose the other candidate. I was going to move Maines to some other assignment, where we could sideline him and he couldn't put ops or people at risk."

"I guess Alden didn't like that decision," Kyra observed. "He was never like that in Caracas. I always thought he was one of the good ones."

"It doesn't look that way," Barron agreed. "The FBI was tailing a Russian diplomat who was on their list of suspected intel officers. They followed him out to the Banshee Reeks Nature Preserve in Loudoun County, twenty miles west of Dulles Airport, and figured that he was using it as a dead-drop site. They put the area under surveillance. A week later, he loaded the drop. The special agents on the scene were smart enough to let him go, then crack open the package and take pictures. Then they holed up and watched to see who came for it. Maines showed up. Pictures are in the folder."

Kyra turned Maines's photograph over and found several more underneath, one of a stack of bills, another showing an out-of-focus letter with a transcription clipped onto the back.

> *Dear friend: welcome!*
>
> *Acknowledging your letter, we express our sincere joy on the occasion of your contact with us last week. Your information was very helpful and we firmly guarantee you for a necessary financial help. You will find in a package 50.000 dollars. Now it is up to you to give a secure explanation of it.*
>
> *As to communication plan, we want to share one soonest with you. We have designed a secure and reliable one we will share with you at GLENDA as we have arranged for you in our previous contact. We await your reply and we shall be ready to retrieve your package from BROOKE since 20:00 to 21:00 hours on the 12th of September after we would read you signal (a vertical mark of white adhesive tape of 6–8 cm length) on the gazebo closest to Battlefield Parkway at the*

Route 15. We shall fill our package in and make up our signal (a horizontal mark of white adhesive tape). After you will clear the drop don't forget to remove our tape that will mean for us—exchange is over.

Please, let us know during the September meeting at GLENDA of your opinion on the proposed place (DD "Amy"). For our part we are very interested to get from you any information about possible actions which may threaten us.

Thank you. Good luck to you.

Sincerely,

Your friends

"That stack of hundreds in the package works out to be something like fifty thousand dollars . . . probably *bona fides* money," Barron said. "Maines had to give the Russians something juicy to prove that he was a serious turncoat. Most Russian assets get a pittance, if they get anything at all. The last ones they paid that kind of money to were Robert Hannsen and Aldrich Ames."

"I assume that giving up Strelnikov would've been worth fifty thousand?" Jon asked.

"Ten times that much, easy," Barron replied. "Maines gave him up cheap. Anyway, FBI Director Menard put a surveillance detail on him and got a warrant for cell-phone and Internet taps. Five days ago, Maines made like he was going to work. Surveillance lost him, he never showed up at headquarters, and he never came home."

"A deputy chief of Russia House defecting to the Russians could shut us down in Moscow," Kyra observed.

"He knows about all of our tech ops and key assets," Barron agreed. "If he's talking to the Kremlin, there's probably not an intel officer in the city from any of the English-speaking countries who's safe, much less our assets. I've suspended all human operations there as of this time yesterday and the chief of station is preparing to exfiltrate our key assets, but it'll take a few weeks to get the resources in place."

Jon turned the file on the table, looked at Maines's biography, then turned it back. "Sounds like a straightforward greed-and-revenge defector," he said, the boredom in his voice clear.

"It was until three days ago," Barron agreed. "First, Strelnikov turns up dead just a few days after Maines fingers him. That's not how the Russians operate. They're methodical. They build airtight cases so they can rip our operations open in a public trial. They watched Oleg Penkovsky for months before they grabbed him and he was giving up nuclear secrets."

Barron leaned across the table and offered the analysts another photograph. Kyra took the picture . . . Maines standing in a customs line at an airport. "Second, two days ago, the Russian ambassador walked into Main State and gave that up. We've identified the airport where that was taken as Berlin Schönefeld. The ambassador told SecState that Maines was defecting."

Kyra's eyes grew wide "He's here?" she asked, incredulous.

"Looks that way," Barron said. "What we can't figure is why the Russians burned him. Maines could've been an incredibly valuable asset to the Russians. There was no good reason to burn him that we can see, and now he won't be worth anything to them in a few months. I would say they were dumb, but I have the feeling someone is getting played and I don't want it to be us."

"It's not us," Jon said, his voice flat. "It's Maines."

"I want to believe that more than you know," Barron said. "What're you thinking?"

"Maines wasn't planning on defecting. Look at the letter . . . this sentence here," Jon ordered, pointing to the second paragraph.

> *As to communication plan, we have designed a secure and reliable one we will share with you at GLENDA very soon as we have arranged for you in our previous contact.*

"You don't establish a covert communications system for an asset unless you're expecting him to keep working for you," Kyra observed.

"That's not even the interesting part," Jon said. "The money is."

"How so?" Barron asked.

"Given how tight the Russians are with a ruble, not just any-one could authorize a fifty-G payout," Jon offered. "Add onto that Strelnikov's former military rank and his position as the head of the Russia's DARPA, and it's obvious that not just anyone could order his execution."

The NCS director frowned but his expression betrayed his agree-ment. "Makes sense," Barron replied. "Still doesn't tell me why they burned Maines."

"There's only one reason that makes sense, don't you think?" Jon asked, looking at Kyra.

The woman stared down at the photograph of Maines in the air-port. "Running an asset is slow business," she started, thinking as she talked. The puzzle unraveled in her head in an instant. "Impatience will get your people killed, but the Russians are being impatient, which means they're worried or scared. They're in damage-control mode, trying to protect something or someone very important. So whoever took out Strelnikov has leaks he needs plugged, he wants it done fast, and Maines knows where the leaks are. So Strelnikov's killer tricks Maines into leaving the U.S. and then burns his bridge back. Now Maines has to depend on him for protection, and the cost of that pro-tection will be a complete download of everything he knows."

"You're saying that the Russians are blackmailing their own asset?" Barron asked, incredulous. "That doesn't make sense if he's already playing for their team."

"It does if you consider that Maines is a new asset . . . so new that the Russians don't really know him or what his motivations are," Kyra explained. "Some traitors still have morals or principles, and won't give up everything they know. But that's not acceptable if this Russian really is desperate to plug some leaks and doesn't think he has much time to do it. So he needs leverage to force Maines to give up everything right now."

Kyra realized that she'd been staring into the distance, unfocused on the men in the room as she'd thought through the story. She looked down. Jon was smiling, Barron was horrified. "Sir," she said, "if that's right, you may not have a few weeks to exfiltrate any of those assets. The Russians could start dropping them anytime. They might kill them as fast as Maines identifies them, the same as Strelnikov."

Barron muttered a curse. "If that's true . . . we have no way to figure out who's at the top of the hit list."

"No, there is a way," Jon disagreed. Barron looked up, hopeful. "Figure out who ordered Strelnikov's execution and what he's trying to protect. Do that and you can identify which remaining assets are his biggest threats. But . . ." He trailed off.

"Yes?"

Jon hesitated, then looked to Kyra. *He doesn't know how to say it gently,* she realized. Kyra tumbled the thought about in her mind for a few moments before deciding that there were no gentle words for it. "We can start with Strelnikov's file. That might give us an idea of where to start. But after that . . . dead assets might be the only other clues we'll get to answer the question."

"That's not acceptable," Barron said, his voice turning cold.

"The only other option is to talk to Maines," Jon said. "If the Russians have pulled a bait and switch on him, he might not be happy about his current situation."

"And how, exactly, would we get in the same room with him?" Barron asked.

"If Maines really is in town, he's either at the Russian Embassy or a safe house," Kyra said, thinking aloud. "If it's a safe house, someone at the embassy will know where. So we go to the embassy."

"Good luck even getting the Russians to admit they have anyone in our business at the embassy," Jon mused.

"They can do a lot worse than say no," Barron warned. "If the Russians really are desperate to use Maines's information to plug some leaks, there's no telling how they might react when you show up asking for him."

"I don't think," Jon said, his mind engaged now. "They were the ones who told us where he was. They had to expect that we'd come asking about him. They might even be planning on it."

"And it might offer some clues besides dead bodies that will help us figure this out," Kyra added. "So let's go knock on the door."

Kyra sat in the empty conference room, focused on Maines's file to distract herself. She'd read it twice already, and had found it surreal to read about the operation he'd led to save her from the Venezuelan SEBIN. Moving on, she saw that Barron's clinical words about narcissism and sadism had softened his description of the true problem. She'd only known Maines a few months before she'd been pulled from the country, had liked him well enough. He'd been a decisive leader, amiable, with a concern for his subordinates that she'd thought genuine at the time. The papers on the table had shaken that conclusion.

On the first reading, the file seemed nothing more than the record of a solid career, with no obvious signs of personal or professional distress. Her second review revealed that the high marks and bureaucratic language used to avoid legal issues were hiding a flawed man. There were no reprimands or disciplinary actions in the records, but performance covered a multitude of sins. Case officers considered sin itself a tool for plying their trade, and if the practitioners indulged on occasion, that was the price of business so long as they didn't cross certain lines. But pride and wrath were capital vices too, and Alden Maines's arrogance and temper both had bloated until he couldn't accept that his decisions could be faulty or see any better way to deal with his failures than making his staff into targets.

The file had been thin, which Kyra hoped was the result of some nervous counterintelligence manager's fear that giving away too much would jeopardize the investigation. There were less noble reasons why such files often were thin. Information was the life's blood of intelligence, but it was also the black-market currency of bureaucrats and only reluctantly did they give it away for free if they thought it had some value they could trade for favors or some other advantage. But there was enough in the papers to ensure she would lose sleep tonight trying to dissect the puzzle Maines had left behind. One line in the Russians' dead-drop letter stood out in her mind.

This is why we suggest you use some money in this package to meet us in GLENDA very soon as we asked in our previous contact.

Kyra had parsed the words so many times that she'd lost count, but the implication never changed, like a quiet voice in her mind. *They're in a hurry*, she thought. The Russians knew that they had a rich source to tap and they wanted to start mining him immediately. Maines imagined that it was so they could talk face-to-face, issue him taskings, and settle on a communications plan in hours that would take them weeks or months to work out through dead drops alone. But if Jon's theory was right, the Russians were more impatient than that. Maines could've been a long-running source, like a deep mine in a mountain, full of endless veins that could produce valuable ores for years. Now the Russians were prepared to strip-mine that resource in a single stroke, looking for only a few tidbits of Maines's information that they considered more valuable than his long-term potential.

What operation is so important that it's worth burning an asset like him? Kyra wondered. Any of the answers she could imagine scared her more than she wanted to admit even to herself.

She finally heard Jon enter. "Barron approved your plan," the man said.

Kyra stared at her mentor, taking in his face. "You're worried about it."

He nodded and his eyes stared off at some point in the distance as he always did when he was talking and thinking at the same time. "The Russians are vicious. We've tangled with the Chinese and the Iranians and the Venezuelans and came out with everything attached, but the Russians play on their own level. Anyone who isn't scared of the Russian intel machine is either stupid or ignorant."

"They're not perfect," Kyra said. "You're the historian. You know our people outplayed them plenty of times during the Cold War."

"'Quantity has a quality all its own,'" Jon quipped.

Kyra frowned. "What are you saying?"

"That was something Stalin said when a critic pointed out that his enormous army was mostly untrained conscripts. When the other guy has enough people on his side, he can afford mistakes. It's the one who's outmanned that has to be perfect, and even that might not be enough. If the enemy is big enough, sometimes he only has to hit you once and the fight's over. The only question is whether you're humble enough to stay on the mat. Can't fight when you're dead."

Kyra felt an ache in her arm, under the scar that a Venezuelan bullet had left behind years before. "Jon, we have to help."

He glared at her. "Leading with your heart is a fine way to get yourself killed."

Kyra smiled. She'd seen him surrender to the inevitable before. "God hates a coward," she said.

"Your plan is only marginally insane," Barron said. To be fair, the analysts had only worked on it for an hour before approaching him, but he supposed that time was working for traitors today. The proposal Kyra had offered him had taken less than two minutes to explain.

"I'm open to a better one," Kyra told him.

"I called Langley. No one there has anything either. Honestly, I don't mind a little insanity when it's called for. The Russians practically sent us an invitation to come talk, but they've got some agenda and I've got no idea what it is," Barron admitted.

"I could talk to the ambassador . . . see if he'd be willing to send one of these State Department boys in to talk," Kyra suggested.

"I thought about that," Barron told her. "But they don't know the right questions to ask, and Maines is our problem anyway. Plan approved. When are you going?"

"First thing in the morning, as soon as we can get a disguise in place," she replied. "Maines will know who I am, but there's no sense in giving the Russians an easy picture of my real face."

"Agreed," Barron replied. "How's Jon doing?" The tone of his voice suggested he wasn't asking about her partner's professional performance.

"The same," she admitted. "He's been this way ever since Marissa was killed last year. He's never been the happiest man I ever met, but I'm pretty sure he's clinically depressed. I tried to get him to see one of the Agency psychologists, get him on something that'll help him climb out of the dark, but he won't go."

"I guess I'd be feeling down if one of my old flames died in front of me like that," Barron said. "Doesn't help that Kathy left either. She's the one person who could really help him, but the DNI is keeping her busy. Do you know if they've talked?"

"I don't think so, not for a few months anyway," Kyra said.

"Do you think he's a danger—"

"No," Kyra answered, too readily. "He's usually pretty morose anyway. I'm sure he'll come through it eventually."

"Keep an eye on him," Barron ordered. "If it looks like he's becoming nonfunctional, let me know and we'll bring him home. The

Russians are too good at the game for us to keep anyone in the field who can't keep themselves together."

"I will, sir."

"Good hunting."

"Thank you, sir," Kyra said. She sat back, closed her eyes, and wondered whether Barron should ever have let her friend come to Berlin.

CHAPTER THREE

The Embassy of the Russian Federation
Berlin, Germany

The etched metal plate by the gated entrance displayed an imperial eagle with two heads, both crowned, holding a scepter and orb, under the words *Botschaft der Russischen Föderation*. Kyra spoke no German, but the words were plain enough.

The devil's den, she thought. *Are you in there, Maines?*

She had waited in the rain two hours to get this far in the queue. Every few minutes the line shuffled forward a few feet, and most of the supplicants kept silent. The couple in front of her had said enough to identify themselves as Russians, the family behind her, German. She heard no English. The natives walked past the granite complex without a glance, leaving only the tourists to stare at the building, a mix of trepidation and amazement on their faces. *Probably the way the Russians like it*, Kyra thought.

Her disguise was more superficial than she would have liked, but time hadn't allowed for better. Given a few days' notice, the Agency's Directorate of Science and Technology could have turned her into an overweight old man missing a limb. As it was, she was still a woman, though her hair was now raven black and longer, her chest larger, and her face rounder courtesy of glasses and small wads inside her cheeks. The acne was her true masterpiece given the lack of time and supplies, and the ill-fitting jacket and skirt were an insult to fashion. Her false ID was a larger worry. It was good enough to pass cursory inspection, but nothing more. There had been no time to manufacture anything better. If the Russian desk officers manning the visa line were as bored as the U.S. State Department officers at their own embassy seemed to be with the same job, the plastic card might pass muster.

The true challenge would lie in convincing the Russians to let her into the same room with Maines. Strelnikov's file had given her a possible way around that problem, but she would have to find a Russian bureaucrat who wasn't completely obtuse.

The guards waved her and a few others through the entrance. Kyra walked through the ornate metal doors and wiped her feet on the mat before stepping onto the gray stone floor and taking in the room. The room was more modern than she'd imagined. Her Russian hosts clearly had renovated the space in the recent past. Only the Roman columns standing in the corners hinted at the original architecture. The walls were off-white, with pictures of current Russian officials and the Kremlin breaking up the monochrome. The room was also quiet, with a few Russian staffers speaking German with accents so fierce that even Kyra could tell they were mangling the language.

The line snaked along inside the building for another hour before she finally reached the visa desk. The consulate officer was a young woman with short, dark hair cut in a bob and unfashionable glasses covering green eyes. *"Aufenthaltserlaubnis bitte?"* she asked. Her German accent was rough, even to Kyra's unfamiliar ear.

"English?" Kyra asked.

The Russian girl looked up, nonplussed. "English?" she asked. Kyra nodded.

The girl frowned, stood, and walked into another room, leaving Kyra at the desk. Another ten-minute wait gave her time to admire the friezes bordering the ceiling until a Russian man, neatly dressed in a dark suit and equally black tie approached her. "I am told you need assistance in English?" he said. The accent was still strong Russian, no hint of an accent from the UK or any other friendly country.

"I've come from the U.S. Embassy. I'm here to speak to Alden Maines," Kyra told him.

"That is not a Russian name."

"No, it's an American name. Mr. Maines has, shall we say, applied to become a resident of the Russian Federation and is living here at the moment."

The man stared at Kyra in surprise. "I am sorry, I do not know of any such person here," he said.

"Two days ago, a Russian consulate officer visited FBI headquarters in Washington, D.C., to tell my government that Mr. Maines was defecting. As proof, he provided a photograph of Mr. Maines taken at the Schönefeld Airport. So he either came here, or someone here knows where he's staying in Berlin."

The embassy officer smirked. "I cannot help you. Clearly, your information must be incorrect."

"Clearly," Kyra said. "I will need to speak with one of your intelligence officers."

"I believe you have been misinformed," the man said after taking a moment to collect his thoughts. "Unlike many other countries, intelligence officers do not work in our embassies."

Kyra smiled faintly at the brazen lie. "Of course not," she said, her condescending tone lost on the man. She pulled an index card and a pen from her coat pocket, scribbled a word and four Cyrillic letters on it, and offered it to the man. "Show this to whoever is handling Mr. Maines upstairs. He'll know what it means. I'll wait here."

The consulate officer took the card and stared at it. His face turned sour as he read it, and he turned and left without a word. Kyra smiled at the confused young Russian girl, then walked to an empty chair along the wall and took a seat.

"General Lavrov?" The guards had held the consulate officer in the hallway for a half hour. The doors finally opened and Lavrov and several other men the diplomat didn't know were emptying into the hallway.

"Yes?"

"My apologies for disturbing you sir," the consulate officer said, walking alongside the senior official, trying to match his pace. "A young American woman came to the visa desk a short time ago and asked to meet with an 'Alden Maines.' When I told her that I did not know of any such man, she asked to see an intelligence officer. I advised her that that would not be possible, and she gave me this. I took it to one of the GRU officers in residence and he told me that I should show it to you, that you would know what it meant." He held out the index card.

Lavrov stopped, took the card, and read the lettering.

Strelnikov
А Б Ю Я

"Where is the this woman now?" Lavrov asked.

"She said that she would wait by the visa desk for your answer."

Lavrov exhaled, folded the card in half, and placed it in his shirt pocket. "Escort her upstairs."

"Where shall I bring her?"

"The roof."

Kyra hardly needed her talent for reading body language to see the mixture of stunned embarrassment and anger spread across the consular officer's face as he crossed the room, but she was in no mood to indulge in schadenfreude. A surge of anxiety rose in her chest faster than she could suppress, and her heart began to pound, the adrenaline adding to the tremors that the Red Bull had left in her hands.

"If you will please accompany me?" the Russian said, his language more courteous than his manner. She doubted he knew how to change his voice when speaking English to show irritation.

Kyra stood and followed the man. An embassy guard joined them at the door and walked behind them. She wondered how many CIA officers had ever seen the inside of this building, and this level in particular. It had to be a small club.

The officer and the guard led her to a utility stairwell, which they climbed for several stories until it reached a gray metal door. The officer pushed it open and motioned Kyra through. She stepped onto the roof, the guard followed, and the consulate officer closed the door behind them.

Kyra scanned the open space and saw the British Embassy to the west, the U.S. Embassy just beyond, and the Brandenburg Gate farther west and north. The Russian building on which she stood was larger than both allied embassies together, she realized. *I guess you can do that when you own the city around it for fifty years*, she thought.

A man stood on the far edge of the roof, looking down at the Unter den Linden traffic below. *Maines?* No, the man was too old. She began to trudge across the roof, stepping around the larger rain puddles, hands deep in her coat pockets to hide the tremors. *Time to play*, she told herself.

Arkady Lavrov heard the footsteps and turned to see a young woman making her way across the wet stone. "And you are?" he said. His English was rusty but his accent was still light.

"My name isn't important," Kyra told him. "I'm with the U.S. Embassy—"

"I think not, but that is not important at this moment," Lavrov replied. "Why are you here?"

"I think my request to your people was clear."

"It was," Lavrov said. "Quite forward of you to come here and make such a demand."

"You're the ones who told us he was defecting and sent a photo to prove it. You had to know that we'd figure out which airport he was in," Kyra replied.

"Of course," Lavrov mused. That had never been in doubt. That the Americans would be so brazen as to walk into the embassy and demand to see their most recent Judas was the real surprise. But the FSB general was a soldier and appreciated the willingness to take the initiative. "Still, walking in and asking to see a potential defector is hardly the customary way of handling such affairs." He held up the card Kyra had passed to the embassy functionary. "Nor is admitting that you know the dead-drop signals we had assigned to the asset."

"Diplomatic protocols in matters such as these can be tedious, and tedium costs time. I know that yours is valuable, and it would benefit both our countries to resolve this matter quickly," Kyra advised.

Lavrov turned his head and stared at the woman, as though the American had lit some spark of interest in him. "If Mr. Maines has requested asylum in my country, then it is a matter for the Foreign Ministry, not for an intelligence service," he said. There was a playful tone in his voice, as though he was enjoying some new game.

"That would depend on why Mr. Maines requested asylum and what he's offering for it," Kyra replied. She clenched her hands and ordered her heart to slow down. It disobeyed.

"Any man who would draw such a bold response from your organization would surely have much to offer us. So the question naturally must turn to the counteroffer your friends would be willing to make."

"Oh, I think that's premature," Kyra disagreed. "Obviously, we couldn't determine that until we confirm his location and what . . . assets he may have already used to establish his value." *You show me yours and I'll show you ours.*

"I understand that desire, truly, but you realize that I must consider any future opportunities we may have to attract talented individuals from your organization in the future. It would become difficult if prospective converts knew we were open to returning them to their home countries for a price."

Kyra nodded. "Of course," she said. "Forgive me, sir, but you appear to be an older gentleman. Did you spend any time here in Berlin before the Wall came down?"

"I did," Lavrov said. Did this American know who he was, know his biography? If so, this game would be far more interesting than he had thought. "I was here the very night that the Wall fell; on this roof, in fact. We could see the Wall there, to the west of the Gate." Lavrov pointed toward the Brandenburg Gate, waving a gloved hand to the northwest. "The plaza was full, people were on the Wall itself. To shoot them would have started a massacre. I saw that much, but I could not understand why the guards would not pull them down at least." He dropped his hand. "That was the night the Warsaw Pact fell, you know. The historians say that came later, but it was that night. The Wall coming down was a shot to the belly . . . a painful death, and a lingering one."

"I'm sure it was a memorable night for you," Kyra said, speaking directly for a moment. She'd been a toddler when it had happened. "So you knew about the East German practice of having the Stasi arrest political prisoners and ransom them back to the West as a way to generate hard currency?"

Lavrov shrugged. "I heard that such things happened. Why do you mention it?" He'd helped arrange a few such kidnappings-for-ransom in his youth. Did this woman know? If so, how? Had the CIA uncovered something in the old East German archives?

"Only to point out that ransom payments aren't unheard of in our business." She wondered if this man would give up Maines for money. Not likely, but stranger things had happened between intelligence agencies.

The Russian didn't bite the hook. "But if Mr. Maines has applied for asylum, then he is no hostage," Lavrov noted. "Quite the opposite would be true."

"I doubt that," Kyra said. "Your country told mine that Mr. Maines was defecting. That act made Maines a fugitive from justice in the United States. You invited him here, then closed his door back. Now he can't set foot on the street here without risking arrest and extradition, leaving him no real leverage for any bargain. So you don't have to pay him one ruble to make him talk, do you? You can extort him for everything he knows just by threatening to run him out the front door and calling the German police ten minutes before you do. So I think if Maines is here, he's very much your hostage."

Kyra studied the man, hoping that the Russian's body language would scream his thoughts and emotions to her, but his control was practiced and very precise. She could only divine small glimpses, but for the moment, his pleasure was obvious.

"*Zamechatel'nyy!*" he muttered. "I truly wish you would tell me your name, young miss."

"I must disappoint you," Kyra said. The Russian might find out anyway. She'd seen at least three security cameras here on the roof and doubtless they'd passed a few dozen on the way here. They would have her picture and her disguise was not total.

"But you intrigue me so very much, *devushka*," Lavrov said. "I will consider what you have to say. But for the moment, I suggest you enjoy the view from our rooftop. The view of the Gate is quite nice."

Kyra stared at Lavrov, tried to read his face, and finally gave up, unable to tell what he was hiding behind his smile. That had almost never happened to her. "Most kind of you."

Lavrov bowed slightly. "Until our next meeting." He turned on his heel and walked toward the rooftop door.

Strelnikov's file was spread out on the table, the man's photograph pinned to the wall.

Jon had been staring at the papers since Kyra had left for the Russian Embassy. Research was his preferred remedy for anxiety and his younger partner was a bottomless source of it. He'd wondered sometimes if she wasn't an adrenaline junkie, an addict whose preferred fix was risk. She'd almost succumbed to alcoholism two years back and he suspected that her addictive personality was always seeking another outlet. But there was nothing he could do for it at this moment. She was inside the Russian building and he could hardly go charging in after her.

Kyra had been right that the file was thin, but the reports officer who had assembled it had been organized and thorough. The Russian's grandfather had been Jewish, Lithuanian by birth, and a farmer until the Nazis had invaded from the west. *No requests for money, personally wealthy, so he didn't commit treason out of greed. Retired at flag rank and made the head of the Foundation for Advanced Research a year ago . . . so you're not like Maines, not angry because some superior didn't give you your due*, Jon thought. *Ideological defector? Soft spot for Israel?* He checked the date of the first report. *Ten days after Kyra found Iran's nuke in Venezuela*, he realized.

Ideological defectors want to make a difference, to protect something they love or cripple something they hate, he reasoned. A Russian GRU general, even a retired one, would have had access to a huge amount of material, but another pass through Strelnikov's reports showed that the Russian had given up nothing that wasn't directly related to the Foundation. *You wanted to protect Israel, but you didn't want to hurt Mother Russia?* Jon reasoned. *So assume he's ideological. No way for Strelnikov to make a difference in Iran's nuke program unless the Foundation is involved in the program.* Even so, the general's tranche of reports revealed nothing about the Foundation's actual research projects. The man had restricted himself to revealing its organization, budget, manpower, areas of interest, but nothing that would have allowed CIA to cripple a specific program. Perhaps the good general's conscience had been putting up a fight.

Jon hunted for Strelnikov's biography, laid on top of the pile, and started to read again.

The Russian had been well traveled. *Afghanistan in the eighties, Berlin when the Wall came down, Serbia in the late nineties, Baghdad during the war, Venezuela in the late aughts when Chávez was cutting deals with Ahmadinejad and the Iranians . . . all of the hot spots.*

The connection to the Iranian program was apparent. Kyra had uncovered Iran's illegal nuclear device in Venezuela the year before, and Strelnikov had been in that country when the foundation for that ugly partnership had been laid. *Maybe he brokered it?*

Something else was pulling at his thoughts. *What am I not seeing?*

Jon stared at the biography for another hour before he saw it. *Idiot,* he cursed himself. It had been there, on the page in plain sight.

The Embassy of the Russian Federation

Kyra stood in the drizzle for another fifteen minutes before the door opened again. She heard the rusting hinges squeak in the rain and looked at the new visitor.

Alden Maines trudged across the rooftop toward her, frustration obvious in his features. He thought about stopping, looked backward over his shoulder, saw the black-suited Russian officer guarding the stairwell, dark glasses on his face despite the overcast sky, and decided to keep up his walk.

Kyra's heart rate picked up again, for a different reason now. The anxiety was gone, and she felt anger flood into her chest to replace it.

Maines slowed for a second when he saw the woman. He frowned, then continued on. "Who're you?"

"I think you know," Kyra told him.

The man's head turned in surprise at the sound of her voice and his eyes flitted in several directions as his memory tried to match the sound with a person. The answer finally came through and Maines's shoulders slumped.

"Long way from Caracas. I guess Barron sent you? How is the old man?"

"Ready for a family reunion at your earliest convenience."

"Yeah, good luck with that," Maines said. "What do you want, Kyra?"

"You'd have to be very, very stupid not to know the answer to that question."

"You really had the stones to march into the Russian Embassy so you could ask me to come back with you?" he asked

"I thought I would make things simple for you," Kyra advised. "Come with me and I'll tell the Bureau you cooperated. You might get a shot at parole after a couple of decades in prison."

"Your turn to not be stupid."

She'd thought she was ready for his hostility, but the delta between the man she remembered from three years before and the dark figure here was wide enough to unnerve her, if just a little. Kyra hid the emotion behind a casual shrug. "I just wanted to confirm that you were here. How you end up back in the States in chains and a jumpsuit isn't really my problem."

"The Russians aren't going to hand me over," Maines said. Kyra had expected a smirk or a smile, but the man's expression was cold. "I'll be good PR for them if nothing else once we get to Moscow."

"And you come cheap, don't you? I just had a discussion with one of their intel officers," Kyra told him. "They refused to pay you, didn't they? You came here looking for a fat paycheck, but the Russians said they'd burned you and now they want you to give them the family jewels just to stay out of jail. In fact, I think that the reason they decided to let me see you was to prove that they really had burned you, to crank up the pressure in case you were thinking they'd lied."

Maines laughed, rueful. "You really don't know why I did this, do you?"

"I really don't *care* why. There's a difference," she told the man. "You can explain your reasons to Barron and the Bureau. I'm sure they'll be amused."

Maines grunted. "You should care." He wished he had a cigarette or something to hold in his shaking hands. "I did this because of you, in a way." He laughed, pure contempt and derision. "After we all got reassigned from Caracas and Barron sent me over to Russia House, I thought it was a good place to land. I actually kind of liked it, until last year. One of our people got pulled out for a few days to join a task force. It turns out that two *analysts* got trapped in Venezuela when the revolution started. Did you know about that?"

Kyra dearly wished, for a single instant, that she could tell him exactly what she knew about it. "I heard something about it" was the answer she gave him.

"Can't wait for that one to get declassified in twenty-five years. Anyway, Kathy Cooke tasked a group with trying to help those analysts figure out how to infiltrate a military base. It was the most insane thing I'd ever heard. Instead of pulling them out and sending in a real team, the CIA director let an analyst execute the op. And then a day later, the president decided to just blow the base up and dropped a Massive Ordnance Penetrator on the place and almost blew those analysts up along with it. How those two got out alive, I'll never know, but it got me thinking. We're just one bad leader away from getting killed, and the Agency is full of 'em. One Seventh Floor moron or one selfish politician makes one bad decision, and we're all cannon fodder. You know that. That idiot of a station chief almost got you killed. You wouldn't have made it if I hadn't pulled you out of that safe house in Caracas. So when Barron decided not to make me the chief of Russia House, I just decided that I'm going to get mine before somebody like him gets me or somebody on my team shot."

"So you're going to sell out our assets—"

"I haven't told them anything," Maines said. "Don't really plan to either."

"You gave up Strelnikov."

"Wasn't counting him. I didn't know they'd execute him. Just thought he'd wind up in a gulag."

Nice confession, Kyra thought. She burned the words into her memory so she'd be able to repeat them for a judge. "So you just don't count the ones who the Russians execute? And you tried so hard to convince me you weren't a moron. They drowned him, by the way, in case they didn't share that tidbit. Took him out to the Müggelsee Lake, held him under, and didn't bother to pull him out when they were done."

Maines shrugged, though not dismissive. *Fatalistic? Or just a psychopath?* Kyra wondered. *Thinks it wasn't his fault? Or really doesn't care?*

He interrupted her thoughts. "If I was giving up assets, they would've shut the Agency down in Moscow by now."

"Again, not my problem," Kyra replied. "I'm going to leave now. I'm going to walk back to our embassy over there, and I'm going to confirm for FBI that you're here. After that, the Germans will be obligated to arrest and extradite you if you set foot outside. Sooner or later, the Russians will give you up."

"That's not going to happen."

"You have a lot of faith in your new friends," Kyra told him.

"No, I have a lot of faith that you're going to help get me home."

"I'd be happy to," Kyra advised. She didn't try to keep the contempt out of her voice. "You shut your mouth until tomorrow. I'll call

Barron and have him ask the president to promise to commute your sentence to, say, twenty years in prison. You come home, do your time, and you don't die in prison." She had no authority to make a deal, but decided it was worth trying.

Maines smirked. "Kyra, you be a good girl and go tell Barron my terms for a deal. He convinces the president to give me a pardon and fifty million in the bank, and I won't give the Russians another name or tell them about a single operation. I don't get that and I'll tell them everything I know."

"How about I throw you off this roof instead?" Kyra proposed.

"I don't think my friends would let you."

"I guess you would need your friends," Kyra spit back. "You're a coward."

Enraged, Maines lunged forward, hands out, reaching for Kyra's neck. He'd saved this ungrateful woman's life and she—

Kyra pivoted on her feet and hips, turning sideways, and she swept her right arm across her body in an arc, guiding his arms to the side. She brought her arm over his, holding them down for the second she needed to bring up her left to hold his away. Kyra's right came back up, fingers turned in, and she clawed his face hard enough to draw blood. The man screeched, his hands coming up to protect his face from another assault. Kyra pivoted again, facing Maines head-on, and she grabbed his shirt, and pulled hard. Her forehead smashed into his nose. His head snapped back, stunned, the blood starting to flow from his nose. She pulled again, Maines stumbled forward, off balance, and she drove her knee into his groin hard enough to lift him onto his toes. The traitor fell back, then dropped onto his knees, the blood rushing out of his face.

The Russian guard by the door moved to run toward them, but saw Kyra make no further move toward her victim and stopped.

Maines cursed . . . and then the real pain hit him, erupting out of his pelvis like a fire burning through his nerves and stealing his breath. He curled up on the ground in a twitching heap, groaning and gasping for air.

Kyra stepped back, far enough that he couldn't grasp or kick her. "I'd tell the Bureau to add assault to your indictment, but it's already a long list." She squatted down so he could see her face. "I'll tell Barron about your offer, but you're not going to get your deal. And even if you do get to Moscow, CIA defectors have a bad habit of falling down long staircases after they're not useful to their Russian friends anymore. So I wouldn't plan on a peaceful retirement, back home or in Moscow."

"Uh-uh," Maines grunted. "Full . . . full pardon . . . and fifty . . . million." He sucked in some air, then pushed himself up onto his hands and knees. Kyra didn't move, ready to defend herself again. "I get that," he wheezed, "I keep my mouth shut. I don't . . . and I tell the Russians everything . . . take my chances."

"If you want the president or anyone else to take your offer seriously, you need to give something up first."

"What's that?"

"The name of your handler," Kyra told him.

"I don't think . . . he'd like that," Maines said, his chest rising and falling rapidly. The pain between his legs was fading enough to manage. He pushed himself back onto one knee. "If Barron gets me the deal, you stand out front of the embassy tomorrow at noon . . . wear a red jacket. If you're there, I come out. If you're not, I take care of myself." He was catching his breath now, but his legs were still too shaky for him to stand.

"Either way, I'll be seeing you pretty soon." Kyra turned around and walked toward the door.

"I should've left you in that safe house," Maines said, his voice still weak from the abuse she'd dealt to his crotch. "I see you again and I'll kill you."

Kyra made an obscene gesture without looking back.

Kyra turned to the last page of the photo album and stared at the surveillance photos, giving each a few seconds of her attention. It was wasted time. None of the men in the color pictures was a match for the one in her memory. She closed the book and set it on the stack of four others she'd already reviewed. "He's not here," she said. *Who are you, old man?* She leaned back, stared at the ceiling, and dissected her own thoughts.

"That's all of the mug books that we've got on the Russians stationed here," Barron replied.

"Then it must be someone who's not stationed here," Jon advised. "The books don't include pictures of short-term visitors."

There's your faulty assumption, Kyra realized. Maines's handler had convinced him to come to Berlin, but that didn't mean his handler was stationed in Berlin itself. "The Russians might have sold it to Maines as an out-of-country meeting," she said. "Assume the Russians considered him a high-value asset," Kyra started. "His case file would be compartmented. Not everyone would know about him. The man I talked to on the roof was older, a graybeard. He had to be a senior officer. Maybe somebody who came from Moscow just to meet with Maines?" The Russian Embassy to Berlin was enormous, large enough to shelter a thousand intelligence officers. *So the man from the roof either was new enough to Berlin that the Germans and CIA officers here had no photograph of him yet or he had never been recognized as an intelligence officer at all*, she decided. *A short-term visitor senior enough to be read into Maines's compartment . . . at least senior enough to be running him.* But which intel service? The Russians had eleven, not so many as her own country, but enough to complicate the problem.

"Maybe," Barron agreed. "But if he's an intel officer, he would have to be from one of the Russian services that runs foreign assets abroad," he said, following her silent line of thinking. "That eliminates most of them."

"The two largest that qualify would be the SVR and the GRU," Kyra added. The Sluzhba Vneshney Razvedki was Russia's Foreign Intelligence Service and the one that seemed the most likely. But there was still the GRU, the Glavnoye Razvedyvatel'noye Upravleniye, the Main Intelligence Directorate of the Russian military. Far larger than the SVR and, she'd heard, more ruthless, if that was possible. She suspected it was. The GRU controlled the Spetsnaz, for the most part. Kyra dearly hoped that she would never have to tangle with one of the Kremlin's Special Forces soldiers. There were few men in the world trained so well in the dark arts of covert military operations. She had been in a few fights during her short career and come out of them well enough. The Agency had trained her in self-defense and she'd studied Krav Maga and some other disciplines on her own time and dime, but she had no illusions how long she would fare in a fight with one of Russia's most elite soldiers.

"Strelnikov was GRU," Barron said. "He was Spetsnaz, once upon a time, and the GRU controlled a lot of the Spetsnaz units back in the old days."

Kyra picked up Maines's file and looked through the papers twice, but nothing caught her attention. She looked at the dead-drop letter again.

The answer finally broke through her subconscious mind. "Do we know who left Maines's dead drop in the woods at Banshee Reeks? It's not in the file."

"Yes, a GRU officer, Russian military intelligence," Barron replied. "The Bureau's going to pick him up the next time he leaves their embassy grounds. He's probably got diplomatic immunity, so State's going to declare him persona non grata and send him home. I don't remember his name . . . those Russian names all sound alike to me. But I can look it up."

"Actually, it wasn't his name I needed, just the intel service."

Jon nodded. "Bring up the files on the GRU leadership," he suggested. "There are probably hundreds on the list, but might as well start at the top and work down."

Kyra complied, and after a few minutes of searching, she opened the first file . . .

. . . and fell back in her chair, eyes wide. "That's him." Kyra paused and stared at the photograph again, to be certain there was no mistake or trick of the light.

"Unbelievable," Barron muttered. "Arkady Lavrov. Chairman of the GRU."

Office of the Deputy Director of the National Intelligence

"What's the word?" Cooke asked.

"Maines's here," Kyra said. The audio quality of STU secure phones had improved in recent years, but the static and noise mixing with Kyra's voice showed that the Agency's speakerphones had not. "I met with him."

"What did you find out?"

"The Russians definitely are trying to screw him over," Kyra replied. "I think that's why they let me see him, to ratchet up the pressure on him. But he admitted burning Strelnikov, but claimed that he hasn't given up anything since, and he's offering us a deal. He says that he'll walk out of the embassy and come home if he gets a full pardon from POTUS and fifty million in the bank. We don't deliver and he'll burn every operation we have in Moscow to the ground."

"Amazing," Cooke muttered. "He thinks he can burn an asset, then blackmail us and walk away?"

"Might be worth it." Cooke recognized Barron's voice. "If they bleed him for what he knows and we get shut down in Moscow, it'll take us a decade and a lot more than fifty million to get things started back up."

"True, but it's not our call," Cooke said. "And it's extortion. We pay this and it won't be the last time. Every narcissistic slacker with a security clearance will think he can run a protection racket on us. Make us pay up to keep our assets safe. We can't do business like that. So I'll be stunned if the president approves it, but we have to give him the option."

"Kathy, if I may?" It was Jonathan's voice now.

"What is it, Jon?"

"I've been studying General Strelnikov's file. I think there's a bigger problem than just Maines burning our Moscow operations to the ground."

"As if that wasn't enough. What's your theory?" Cooke asked.

Jon's explanation took ten minutes. Cooke said nothing in response for almost another minute. "Jon, stay by the phone. I want you to explain that to the president. Then everyone hold tight until I get back from the White House."

"Yes, sir," Barron said. He pressed a button to disconnect the call from his end.

U.S. Embassy
Berlin, Germany

Kyra grinned at her partner. "You going to brief POTUS," she said.

"At least I don't have to put on a tie," Jon replied, deadpan.

She nudged him gently. "You'll kill it. Now, if you gentlemen will excuse me, I have to go shopping."

"For *what*?" Barron asked, incredulous.

"A jacket," she said. "Something in red today, I think."

It took Barron a few seconds to absorb the implications. "You won't need it. The president isn't going to go for the deal," he said, as though explaining it to a child.

"Maines doesn't know that," she said.

The Embassy of the Russian Federation
Berlin, Germany

Kyra had expected that the president wouldn't approve a pardon for Maines, and he had neither surprised nor disappointed her. Jon wasn't happy about President Rostow's obstinance, but her partner was a logical man and the refusal wouldn't bother him for long. Jon was simply doing what he did, deconstructing a problem into the simplest parts to find the most efficient solution. Jon was very nearly a misanthrope and people were just variables to him at such times. If the best solution to a problem allowed one person to profit or suffer unfairly, that was just the price to be paid. He simply wanted the puzzles solved, and when his variables failed to make the decisions that would resolve matters, Jon would curse their stupidity and then look for an alternate pathway. It was a rare thing for him to care about such things on a personal level.

But Jon had never been a case officer, had never felt protective of an asset. Kyra had been responsible for a man's life. She had run through the streets of a hostile city, trying to fulfill the Agency's debt of honor and save a person from execution. The case officer unchanged by that didn't deserve the job. A man who was willing to see them executed for his own gain deserved the electric chair, Kyra thought, so just bruising Maines's ego and his manhood hadn't even come close to sating her sense of justice. Hunting traitors was never a business of cold calculation. There was always a layer of passion and hatred underneath it all.

Leading with your heart is a fine way to get killed? she thought.

You're wrong, Jon. It's the only real edge we ever have in this business. Training and tools could always be countered, but the will to act, to keep pushing on against the enemy . . . that was harder to match.

So it was ironic, she thought, that she was pushing against the enemy by standing still. Kyra leaned against one of the trees that lined the wide median between the opposing lanes of the Unter Den Linden, ignoring the tourists and locals walking behind her. Cars rolled past, almost within arm's reach, but she never moved or looked away from the embassy. The wind picked up, imparting a chill to the air.

Kyra zipped up the red jacket.

There were German Bundeskriminalamt officers hiding in tourists' clothing at both ends of the block, ready to seal off both ends of the street and take Maines into custody after he walked out the front door. The president of the United States had refused to offer a pardon to Alden Maines, but Maines didn't know that. With that realization in hand, Kyra had thought she might be able to shut down Maines's threat before nightfall. All he had to do was believe that his deal was within reach.

You asked for me, Maines, she thought. *Get out here.*

Alden Maines stared at the embassy sidewalk from the conference room window, failing to repress a smile. *The president signed off, and I get to go home*, he thought. Maines had sold out his country, made $50 million in the process, and the president himself had agreed to forgive it all. The world was dancing on his strings.

"It is a good view," he heard Lavrov say. Maines turned and saw the Russian general come up behind him. "Not so nice as it was before the Wall came down, but it still has much to recommend it."

"I wouldn't know," Maines said. He had nothing left to say to the man.

Lavrov smiled, a small one. "She is quite a pretty girl, isn't she?"

"Who?"

"The young lady in the red coat down on the street," Lavrov said. "The one I allowed you to meet yesterday."

"Not my type," Maines said. "I don't like the pudgy ones." *I've got my pardon now, you moron*, he thought. *You don't want to pay, you get nothing.*

"Oh, surely you recognize a disguise when you see one," Lavrov protested. "Hers was a very good one, but I suspect that she is much prettier without it. She would make a most agreeable companion for an evening out, and good entertainment after if she were persuaded. But I doubt she would entertain any such notions with you. I'm told that she left you clutching yourself on the roof."

Maines gritted his teeth but refused to look at the Russian. Of course Lavrov knew about his humiliation. Another reason to spit in Stryker's face when he walked out the front door of this building in a few minutes. *You won't be so full of yourself then, General.*

"A woman of intelligence, beauty, and spirit," Lavrov said, approving. "I would like to know her name."

"She didn't tell me." It was technically true.

"Perhaps, but I think you know who she is," Lavrov suggested. He held out a large manila envelope.

Maines opened it and pulled out the contents, three photographs, medium resolution, clearly stills taken from security-camera footage. The first was an image from the roof, Stryker arguing with him yesterday, then driving her knee into his crotch. The time stamp confirmed what Maines's own memory told him.

The second picture was grainy, poor resolution with odd lighting. Even so, the detail was enough for the American to see that it was Stryker again, no disguise, dressed casual. She was handing something, likely her passport, to an airport customs officer. *China*, he thought, from the Mandarin lettering on a wall sign, *Beijing*, he supposed.

"This picture was taken in Beijing two years ago. Our facial recognition software says that there is a very high probability that it is the same woman despite the differences," Lavrov said, confirming the guess. "Our Chinese friends sent it to us after the incident in the Taiwan Strait with the U.S. Navy, asking for help identifying the woman. Some days after this was taken, she helped a Chinese intelligence officer escape surveillance, likely as part of an operation to bring the man to the United States. She assaulted one Chinese officer during the escape, and another on the street some days earlier. That one spent a significant amount of time in a hospital after she beat him with a steel bar."

Maines stared at the woman's picture. *You landed on your feet after Caracas better than I did,* he realized, and he felt a hatred for the woman welling up inside him. She'd moved on to lead a key operation while he had sat rotting at headquarters, even after he had saved her. *Should've been me.*

"The man she helped escape had shared information on a research program that the People's Liberation Army had been running for seventeen years with my assistance," Lavrov continued. "A few days later, your country's navy destroyed a unique stealth plane that was the focus of that project. The radar telemetry collected during the battle shows that your navy had established a system to detect the plane."

Maines stared at the picture again. "Sorry," he lied. "Still don't recognize her."

Lavrov tapped the third photograph. It showed Stryker at another customs desk, this one in some Latin American country, judging by the Spanish signage. The picture was higher quality. Stryker was blond again, no glasses, athletic build, not a short, overweight brunette with bad eyesight like yesterday—

—then he recognized the place. *Caracas.*

"Our Venezuelan friends shared this with us last year. The

woman infiltrated a munitions factory near Puerto Cabello and was instrumental in stealing the nuclear device that the Iranians were building there with the help of their hosts. She assaulted the Venezuelan national intelligence director inside the base and later in an airport hangar. She crushed his nose and shattered his cheekbones with a rifle butt, and she detached one of his retinas. He identified her some days later from the airport security footage after his eyes could begin to focus again. Apparently, she had been in his country before and was wounded in a counterintelligence operation he had led. She seemed to take it quite personally."

Maines gaped at the photograph and cursed silently in amazement. *Kyra broke into that military base last year?* He'd been wrong. It hadn't been an analyst who Cooke had tapped for that operation. He'd just assumed that Kyra had joined the Red Cell later. *You went back to Caracas.* He might have been impressed had his anger not been crushing every other feeling in his head.

Still, Lavrov had insulted him and Maines was in no mood to give the man free information, or even show that he was unhappy. "Yeah, I bet. Still can't help you," he repeated.

"She is a concern. You see, the Chinese and the Iranians were both clients of an ongoing project that I oversee. This woman appeared and both efforts were disrupted within a few days. I do not believe that is a coincidence." Lavrov pointed to yesterday's photograph. "And now she is here."

Maines shrugged and dropped the picture on the desk.

Lavrov studied Maines, ran his eyes over the American's face, looking for some signal of deceit. There was no reason to bluff and Maines let the Russian watch him. "You are lying to me, Mr. Maines," Lavrov finally announced. "One woman has disrupted two critical GRU operations that we were running in concert with important allies, and now she is here in Berlin while you and I are here while I am advancing a third. I think that your Agency knows about my operations, and I believe you know her name. You wish to say that is not the case?"

"Yeah, that's what I'm saying," Maines protested. "Look, if the Agency is on to you, they figured it out some other way because I never heard a whisper about your big operation, whatever it is."

Lavrov nodded slowly, took the pictures back, and replaced them in the folder. "It will be a shame to disappoint such a woman."

Maines frowned. "What do you mean?"

"She's wearing a red jacket. I believe that was the signal she was to give you if your country accepted the proposal made to her," Lavrov said, as though a child should have understood his meaning.

Maines understood it perfectly well, and his eyes widened. Lavrov saw it. "Of course, we heard everything. Surely you knew that?" the Russian asked, his question entirely rhetorical. Whether Maines had thought of the possibility or not was moot now. "I would like to hear the story about how you saved her from a safe house in Caracas, but at this moment I have an operation that is waiting for your information to proceed. So please don't lie to me again about whether you know her name."

"You want to know what I know? The president of the United States just agreed to pay me fifty million dollars not to tell you jack, including her name," Maines said, pointing toward the street at Kyra. "So if you want me to talk, that's the bid to beat."

Lavrov frowned. "Such obstinance. But I will counter the offer. I will give you my bid . . . eight hundred rubles."

"Eight hundred rubles?" He did the math in his head. *Twelve dollars?*

Lavrov raised a hand and motioned with two fingers. Three younger men, all muscular, entered the room, one carrying a small bag. Two of them took Maines by the arms and forced him to the table, ignoring his curses and protests. The American struggled, but he was in no shape to hold his own against either of the men, much less both together. They forced his arms out, putting his hands palm down on the brown oak.

Lavrov pulled out the chair on the other side of the table and sat down, looking Maines in the eyes. "Yes, eight hundred rubles . . . the price in Moscow for a good Russian-made hammer." Lavrov nodded to the man carrying the bag. The younger Russian opened the satchel and pulled out a small club mallet.

"No! You can't—" Maines started. Without hesitation, the Russian swung the small metal sledge and slammed it down on Maines's outstretched hand.

Maines screamed as the hammer shattered his metacarpal bones into fragments. On reflex, he tried to rip his crippled hand away from the two men holding him down, but they had expected him to fight and kept him pinned. The hammer slammed down again, this time just behind where the first blow had landed, and the *crunch* of grinding carpals in his wrist was heard for a brief second before Maines's howl of agony drowned it out.

"She will not be disappointed when you don't come out to meet her . . . more angry, I think," Lavrov told him. "So she will go back to her embassy and report to her superiors that you refused the deal, which I suspect will not be extended a second time. They will believe that you never intended to accept any deal, and perhaps will think that you were only buying time to let us act on your information. You were clever to try to build a bridge home after I burned your ships back. But now I am burning your bridge too." He nodded to the Russian holding the tool and the man swung it down without hesitation.

Five more strikes with the hammer made sure there were no more unbroken bones in Maines's right hand. The two assistants at his sides let him go and Maines hardly moved. He tried to lift his arm and moaned in pain as the agony of bits of bone grinding into his muscles and skin sent new spasms of agony cutting through his brain. He whimpered, trying not to cry, only just succeeding, and he squeezed his right arm at the wrist as though he could bottle the pain up in his hand and keep it from passing through the nerves up into his mind.

Lavrov stared at the pathetic sight. "Now, Mr. Maines, you have lied to me, but I must confess that I also lied to you. You must forgive me for that. My time is not unlimited, as I suggested, and your grace period is gone. You have information that I need and you will give it to me now. There is morphine in the infirmary waiting for you, but you don't know where that is, do you? These men will be happy to show you the way after I am satisfied. But for every minute you make me wait to begin from this moment, you will get the hammer. We will save your spine for last if you are still intransigent, but I think you will not let matters go so far."

Lavrov took a small notebook out of his jacket pocket, then a Montblanc pen. He opened the notebook and laid it on the table, then uncapped the pen and laid it on the first blank page. He looked at his watch and marked the time. "Now, Mr. Maines, shall we talk? First, I want the name of the young woman outside on the street. Second, I want the names of all of the CIA officers currently stationed in Moscow. And third, I want you to tell me everything you know about this CIA unit you call the Red Cell."

Kyra's own watch confirmed that she'd waited an hour and a half on the bench, more than fifteen minutes after Maines's deadline. *He's not coming*, she concluded. Why not? *Did he know there really was no deal?* That was unlikely, she thought. There were only five people who even knew about the traitor's proposal, including the president and Maines himself, and she refused to believe that either Jon or Barron was a turncoats himself. *The Russians found a way to tap our secure phones?* That thought was almost more upsetting than the first, and the notion seemed just as unlikely.

Maybe he's dead. That would be more good fortune than she

could expect, and she couldn't assume the possibility anyway, given the price to her country if she was wrong.

Was he trying to buy time for the GRU to move on our assets? A deception operation would explain why the old Russian had been so willing to let her see Maines the day before. And if Maines had cooperated with it, then the man's treason had gone beyond simply giving up names to the enemy.

Kyra started walking west and pulled an encrypted cell phone from her pocket and dialed a preprogrammed number. The call took thirty seconds to connect and encrypt.

"Barron."

"It's me," Kyra announced. "He didn't show."

"That wasn't unexpected, but good try," Barron said. "I doubt his new friends would let him walk out the front door even if he wanted to."

"Probably not," Kyra agreed. "I'm headed back to the embassy. You should thank our friends here for being ready to help. I'm sorry they came out for nothing."

"They'll understand." The call disconnected, Kyra replaced the phone in her coat and started the short walk to the west.

U.S. Embassy
Berlin, Germany

Barron cradled the phone. "Well, that's that, I guess. Maines didn't come out."

"Nothing is ever so easy," Jon mused.

"No, but sometimes the universe smiles." Barron hunched over the table, his weight on his fists, his head down, thinking. He looked up at the analyst. "I guess the question now is what Lavrov is doing? You said we might be able to save some assets if we figured that out, but I don't know where to even start with that."

"I think the starting point is obvious," Jon told the NCS director.

Barron furrowed his brow. "You and I have very different definitions of 'obvious.'"

"Strelnikov was killed three days ago, and Maines showed up the day after," Jon observed. "They could have taken off for Moscow anytime after that. So why is Lavrov still *here*?"

"You think he came to Berlin for another reason?"

"All of his obvious reasons for being here are finished," Jon noted. "Maybe Lavrov lured both Strelnikov and Maines to Berlin because he was already going to be here."

"Good thought, but where do we start with that?"

"You're a case officer," Jon said. "And you were the station chief in Moscow once upon a time. So why did you ever travel outside of Russia?"

"Right now I came here to meet with the Germans to confirm Strelnikov's death," Barron replied. "But that's a weird case. Usually I traveled foreign to meet an asset someplace the Russians wouldn't be watching."

"So let's assume that Strelnikov was here to meet someone. Any candidates?" Jon asked.

Barron pondered the question. "When I first met with the Bundeskriminalamt about Strelnikov, we talked suspects. They did say that a Syrian army officer managed to evade surveillance on a drive north of the city. That would've been a day or so before they found Strelnikov's body floating in the lake, and the day after Lavrov came to town. But they found the Syrian coming back into Berlin along the same road later in the day."

"How long was he gone?"

"Less than four hours," Barron said.

"All right, let's assume Lavrov was meeting with the Syrian somewhere up north," Jon said. "Assuming they talked for at least an hour, that would mean their meeting site would be within a ninety-minute drive of Berlin."

"That's still a big search area."

"Yes, it is," Jon conceded. "I don't suppose the Germans were following Lavrov."

"The chairman of the GRU? Yeah, they'd follow him anywhere and everywhere. But a guy like that could find a way out of the Russian Embassy without being seen if he really wanted to."

Jon nodded. "The only other angle we can work is Strelnikov's murder itself. The Germans didn't find any forensic evidence that could identify where he was killed?"

"They didn't mention anything," Barron replied. "Between the rain that week and the body being in the lake for a few days, anything useful probably got washed away, but I'll check with them again."

"Ask about anything unusual, no matter how minor," Jon suggested.

"Will do."

Barron took three hours to respond. "The Germans have nothing," he told Jon, the man's voice slightly broken up by interference on the cellular network. "It was a straight-up drowning. Toxicology was clean and no signs of defensive wounds or bruises on him. Assuming he really didn't drown going for a swim, whoever took him out was a professional."

Jon frowned. "There must be something to grab on to."

"Afraid not," Barron said. "The only unusual thing about Strelnikov's death was that his was the second body they'd pulled out of the Müggelsee in a month."

"Do tell," Jon said, interest in his voice.

"Late August, the local police pulled a guy out of the water on the other side of the lake, British kid. I've got the name . . . hang on . . ." Jon heard the rustling pages of a notebook over the receiver. "Graham Longstreet."

Jon scribbled the name on an index card and handed it to Kyra. She read the name, leaned over a laptop, and began typing. "Okay. That's it?"

"Yeah, that's it," Barron said. "On my way back."

The call ended and Jon hung up. "You think the Russians took out this British kid too?" Kyra asked.

Jon shrugged. "Could be a coincidence," he admitted. "Got anything?"

"The obituary," Kyra said. She pulled up the web page detailing the young man's demise and scanned the report. "It says he drowned, names the usual surviving family, loved hiking and environmental causes."

"He loved hiking," Jon said, his voice quiet. "Did he have a web page? A blog? Facebook or Instagram accounts?"

Kyra clicked the computer's mouse a few times. "Yeah, a web page . . . looks like he was one of those guys who likes exploring abandoned sites. He's got pictures here from the Six Flags park in New Orleans, the one that got wiped out by Hurricane Katrina a decade ago. Here's some from Pripyat, Ukraine. That was a whole city that got abandoned after Chernobyl in '86. I would've run from that one, too. There's a bunch of others here . . . Willard Asylum in New York, Canfranc Rail Station in Spain, Château Miranda in Belgium." Kyra scrolled through the online album, disbelieving. "I guess everyone needs a hobby, but this is morbid. These places look like sets for horror movies."

Jon leaned in over her shoulder. "Any abandoned sites like that in Germany on his list?"

Kyra scanned through the entire list. "None that he visited." She looked up at her mentor. "Maybe he was here to correct that little problem."

Jon smiled at her. "Search it."

Kyra turned back to the keyboard and began typing.

ABANDONED SITES GERMANY

The search results appeared and Kyra scrolled through the list. "Amazing how many places just get left to rot," she said, awe in her voice. "Half of these sites were built by the Russians during the Cold War and then abandoned after the Wall fell in '89."

"Any within an hour's drive north of Berlin?" Jon asked.

Kyra needed five minutes to find the answer. "Vogelsang Soviet Military Base. It's enormous. They housed fifteen thousand men and their families there, and somehow the Agency and every other Western intel agency missed it for years. Looks like the kind of place where an abandoned-site junkie would have on his bucket list."

"And every other sane person on the planet would want to avoid," Jon said. "A hundred dollars says that Lavrov was assigned to Vogelsang at some point when he was younger."

"I'm not a GS-14 like you, so I don't get paid enough to gamble," Kyra replied. "So Longstreet goes to Vogelsang a month ago, stumbles across Lavrov or his people, and they kill him to protect whatever they're doing. They dump the body in the Müggelsee, which is a good two hours away, so nobody comes looking for him around the base," she offered. "Then, a month later, Strelnikov gets lured out there, and they follow the same procedure."

"Not a bad theory," Jon agreed. "It's pretty thin on the evidence."

"We know how to fix that, don't we?" Kyra asked.

The Oval Office
The White House
Washington, D.C.

Daniel Rostow had been in this office less than three years, but his youth already was paying the price for his ambition. The end of his first term was still little more than a year out and the man's brown hair already was streaked through with white. The dark circles under the eyes disappeared only when a makeup artist covered them up before he went before cameras or Congress, and his frame had thinned since his inauguration despite the personal chef and Navy stewards at his disposal. Barron had heard rumors that the doctors were worried about his weight loss and confirmations that Rostow hadn't seen the inside of the White House gym in over a year. The presidency offered no true downtime, no matter how often the occupant went to Camp David or the putting green or the movie theater in the White House. Aides came and went with tidbits and papers to be signed with no regard for personal time, phone calls had to be taken when they came. Rostow's schedule was parsed in five-minute increments, with thirty-second meetings scheduled for the times he would be walking from one room to another.

Kathryn Cooke wondered if the man wasn't suffering post-traumatic stress disorder. She had known many subordinates who endured that. The White House had been sending her case officers into war zones at a rapid clip for more than a decade now, and more than a few had been forced to fire weapons in anger. But any severe, prolonged stress could lead a man down that same road and there was no question that the commander in chief's job included a daily serving of that. If Rostow had joined that particular club, Cooke was sure the man's stress evaporated only when he could finally escape into the oblivion of sleep, and then only on the few nights it wouldn't follow him into his dreams. Her own time struggling to justify to herself the condition her orders had imposed on her people had left Cooke with her own theory as to why so many presidents had affairs. The world thought such dalliances were about power and indulgence. Cooke was sure they were seeking new forms of stress relief.

She wondered whether the paper in Rostow's hand would send the man off in search of some.

IMMEDIATE DIRECTOR
MOSCOW 76490

1. FURTHER TO REF. RED CELL OFFICER STRYKER ADMITTED TO RUSSIAN EMBASSY BERLIN 1115 HOURS MORNING OF 26 SEPTEMBER. EMBASSY STAFF INITIALLY DENIED THAT CIA DEFECTOR MAINES WAS PRESENT BUT RELENTED AFTER STRYKER PRESENTED CONTRARY EVIDENCE.

2. STRYKER WAS ESCORTED TO EMBASSY ROOF AND INTERVIEWED FOR TEN MINUTES BY SENIOR RUSSIAN OFFICIAL LATER IDENTIFIED AS DIRECTOR GRU ARKADY LAVROV. LAVROV WAS EVASIVE ABOUT ANY ROLE PLAYED IN MAINES' DEFECTION AND INTIMATED THAT MAINES HAD REQUESTED ASYLUM. STRYKER CAREFULLY SUGGESTED THAT LAVROV ENTERTAIN A DEAL FOR MAINES' EXTRADITION, BUT HE REFUSED.

3. MAINES WAS ESCORTED TO EMBASSY ROOF AFTER LAVROV'S DEPARTURE, WHERE STRYKER INTERVIEWED HIM FOR TEN MINUTES. MAINES ADMITTED IDENTIFYING RUSSIAN GENERAL STEPAN STRELNIKOV (RET) AS A CIA ASSET TO PROVE BONA FIDES BUT CLAIMED HE HAD NOT BELIEVED THE RUSSIANS WOULD EXECUTE HIM.

4. MAINES ADMITTED THAT HIS RUSSIAN HANDLERS WERE NOT PAYING HIM COMMENSURATE WITH HIS EXPECTATIONS. STRYKER SUGGESTED THAT MAINES CONSIDER RETURNING TO CONUS IN RETURN FOR COMMUTATION OF PRISON SENTENCE. MAINES REFUSED AND MADE A COUNTEROFFER, PROMISING TO NAME NO FURTHER ASSETS

IN RETURN FOR A FULL PARDON FROM POTUS FOR ALL OFFENSES COMMITTED AND FIFTY MILLION US DOLLARS. MAINES SET A DEADLINE OF TWENTY-THREE HOURS LOCAL TIME FOR STRYKER TO ARRANGE THE DEAL AND TOLD STRYKER TO STAND IN FRONT OF RUSSIAN EMBASSY BERLIN WEARING A RED JACKET TO SIGNAL THE DEAL WAS ACCEPTED. IF DEAL IS NOT ACCEPTED, MAINES PROMISED TO REVEAL NAMES OF ALL RUSSIAN ASSETS IN A BID TO GAIN AS MUCH GOODWILL WITH HIS RUSSIAN HANDLERS AS POSSIBLE.

5. STRYKER EXPRESSED HER DISPLEASURE AT MAINES' ACTIONS BUT PROMISED TO INFORM USG OF MAINES' PROPOSAL.

6. REGARDS. END OF MESSAGE.

Rostow stared at the cable report in his hand and read it twice before looking up. "Having trouble keeping the house in order?"

Cooke ignored the dig. "Defectors are an occupational hazard, but a rare one."

"Rare?" Rostow asked, disbelieving. "Last I heard, the intelligence community's had a few dozen moles since '47."

"Moles, yes," Cooke replied. "Defectors, not so many. There's a difference."

"Not much," Rostow scolded. "After Snowden practically burned Fort Meade to the ground, I would've thought that you people would've locked Langley down tight. But no, you've got not just a mole, but a *defector*, and somebody in your shop or Langley or the Bureau will leak it to the *Post*. Half the country will think I can't protect national security, and the other half will hail Maines as a hero and call me an unethical tyrant who likes killing children with drones. And that's assuming Maines doesn't leak it himself. It used to be that defectors had the decency to at least slink off and spend their golden years hiding out in a slum somewhere. Now they literally wrap themselves in a flag and get on the cover of *Wired*. So now my entire domestic agenda running into the election season is going to get blown out of the papers because one of your people ran off and will start spewing classified information to the press any day now." He tossed the Maines cable across the Resolute desk toward her.

I suppose you want leaking classified information to remain your prerogative, Cooke thought.

"You know," Rostow continued, "the last time the director of national intelligence was in this room, he threatened to resign if I didn't promote you. I agreed on the one condition that you never set foot in my office again."

"I wouldn't know about any of that, Mr. President," Cooke said, certain that a refusal to be baited would do more to upset the man than any retort she could conjure up.

"He didn't tell you?"

"It wouldn't have made a difference if he had," Cooke said. "I'd still be here. I volunteered to come."

The president frowned. "Why?"

"Alden Maines was one of mine when I was CIA director," Cooke replied. "I promoted him. I put him in the position where he had access to the information he's giving to the Russians. So I want to deal with the problem. The DNI shouldn't have to take the political heat for this."

"You want me to take Maines's deal," Rostow said.

"I can't recommend a decision one way or another," Cooke reminded him. "I can only explain what we think are the opportunities and implications of decisions."

"Not much difference," Rostow groused.

"Sir, if I may?" The words erupting out of the speakerphone on the Resolute desk were polite, making them a mismatch for the tone of the voice.

"What was your name again?" Rostow frowned.

"Jonathan Burke, sir."

"Mr. Burke is the chief of CIA's Red Cell," Cooke said in Jon's defense. "He's also one of the two officers who recovered the Iranian nuclear warhead last year."

Rostow froze. "You were in Venezuela?"

U.S. Embassy
Berlin, Germany

"I was," Jon confirmed, trying to keep his voice as neutral as he could manage. *And you almost got me killed.* He would've known better than to say it even without Kyra's coaching. "Sir, I believe that this isn't just about preserving our operations in Moscow. There's a larger problem here."

"Which is?" Rostow asked. The condescension had drained from his voice.

"I've been looking at Strelnikov's biography. You have a copy in your file." He heard some rustling of paper and he suspected that Cooke had had to help the president find the right page. "Note that Strelnikov was a liaison officer to the Serb Army in '99."

"I see it," Rostow said. His irritation was entirely lost on Jon.

"That was the year the Serbs shot down one of our F-117 Nighthawks," Jon explained. "We know some of the wreckage was sold to the Chinese, but the Serbs were in Russia's pocket. We've got pictures of Serb military escorts walking Russian generals around the crash site. The Serbs wouldn't have sold so much as a screw to the PLA without Russian approval. Then, three years ago, the PLA sent an experimental stealth plane against the USS *Abraham Lincoln* during the Battle of the Taiwan Strait."

"The 'Assassin's Mace,'" Cooke said, her voice quieter. The deputy DNI must have been sitting across the desk from the president, putting her farther away from the speakerphone's mic.

"The stealth technology wasn't the only interesting bit," Jon said. "After the Navy shot the plane down, U.S. and Taiwanese engineers reconstructed the wreckage they were able to pull out of a crater on Penghu Island. The engines were similar to the design found in the Russian T-50, which is a fifth-generation fighter. The PLA has struggled with sophisticated engine design. They couldn't have developed that engine without help."

"Any evidence that they bought 'em?" Rostow asked.

"The engines were too badly damaged to confirm whether the Chinese built them, but there was no question that the design was a major advance for them," Jon confirmed. "Now look at the bio, five lines further down."

"*Senior Military Attaché, Caracas, Venezuela,*" Rostow read off the page, more curious than annoyed now. "The back half of the last decade."

"That was the same period when Hugo Chávez was forging partnerships with Mahmoud Ahmadinejad and the Iranians, and with the Russians. Chávez bought four billion dollars in Russian weapons during that period . . . fighter planes, naval vessels, small arms, you name it. Chávez was Russia's biggest weapons customer in 2011. And last year, we recover an illegal warhead that Tehran and Caracas built together on Venezuelan soil. The engineers at Los Alamos National Labs tore it apart and found that it was a two-stage fusion-boosted design . . . much more sophisticated than any of the plans peddled by A. Q. Khan, the North Koreans, or any of the other candidates likely to sell blueprints to the mullahs. The Iranians only figured out how to enrich uranium to weapons-grade a decade ago. They couldn't have developed that kind of warhead on their own."

Rostow cocked his head. "Two cases of technology transfer."

"Both of which depended on prior events at which Strelnikov was present," Jon noted.

"So Strelnikov was an arms dealer—" Rostow began.

"Not just an arms dealer," Jonathan cut in. "A strategic military *technology* dealer. My theory is that he was selling research and materials that hostile countries need to build next-generation weapons that they couldn't build on their own for another decade or longer."

The Oval Office

Rostow sat back in his Gunlocke chair, crossed his arms, and looked down at the paper. "Even if that's right, he couldn't have done it on his own, or at least without a lot of people looking the other way."

"I would agree," Jon said. "It's one thing to sell some guns and old tanks. Plenty of Russian officers did that after the Soviet Union fell apart. Moscow didn't even know what it had in the warehouses. But stealth tech and nuclear weapons designs? That stuff goes missing or shows up in some other country and very important people start getting unhappy and asking questions. And they sure don't put the thief in charge of their Foundation for Advanced Research unless they're happy with his track record and want to expand his efforts."

"Then Strelnikov got to the Foundation, saw what they were working on, and it scared him enough to come to us," Cooke added. "But Maines burned him before he could give up the really good stuff."

"Mr. President," Jon continued. "Selling guns . . . that's just about money. Selling technology is about balance of power. When Vladimir Putin set up the Foundation back in 2012, he said its purpose was to get Russian weapon R and D back on par with ours. But if the part of its raison d'être is getting other Russian military allies on par with us, then we have a more serious problem . . . and General Strelnikov's death leaves Maines as our best source of information on General Lavrov's current operations. Anything Maines knows about Lavrov's dealings could be critical."

Rostow looked at the phone, replied nothing, then looked away. He pushed himself back from the desk, crossed his hands in his lap. "And you're sure about this connection with Arkady Lavrov?" he asked.

"We have a high level of confidence in that assessment," Cooke concurred. "The woman who met with Lavrov on the roof of the Russian Embassy was Jon's partner, Kyra Stryker. She was the other officer who recovered the Iranian warhead last year, by the way." That bit of news heightened Rostow's discomfort. She wished that Jon and Kyra could have seen it. "NSA says that Lavrov signed Strelnikov's travel orders to Berlin. Then Lavrov flew to Berlin the day before Strelnikov left, requesting emergency counterterrorism meetings with the German Federal Intelligence Service . . . some crap story about Chechen rebels trying to smuggle arms through Berlin. Given Lavrov's connections, he probably could have faked that if he needed cover for the trip."

Rostow nodded, almost unconsciously. Cooke studied the commander in chief's face, trying to divine some clue as to his thoughts. *He's actually taking CIA seriously.* It was a rare thing.

But Rostow's face hardly moved and Barron could do nothing but listen to the white noise coming from the phone speaker as Jon held his peace four thousand miles away. Rostow stared down at his desk for a full five minutes, saying nothing.

The president finally looked up. "No."

"Sir?" Cooke asked.

"No deal. No pardon, no money, no nothing," Rostow said. "Maines can enjoy life in Moscow until the Russians off him or he can come home and take his chances."

Jon was smart enough not to protest over the phone. Cooke took her time assembling her thoughts and finding the most politic way to tell Rostow what she thought of the young president's decision.

"Mr. President, Jon was correct when he said we can tell you about the implications of decisions, and it's my duty to tell you now the implications of the one you've just made. Sir, if we don't make this deal with Maines, people will start dying in short order, ours and theirs. The FSB or the GRU will begin arresting Russians working for us, one after another, and they will be executed, without exception. We will be forced to try to exfiltrate as many as we can, but we will fail to save most of them. We won't have the time, the people, or the resources, so we will be forced to improvise. But we will be operating on Russian soil and the Russians have, without question, the most efficient, skilled, and ruthless counterintelligence operation in the world. So our creativity will fall short, and some of our people will be captured and arrested. They will be paraded on Russian television and photographed for Russian newspapers. The secretary of state and the U.S. ambassador to the Russian Federation will be forced to negotiate for their release. No matter what we do, our operations in Moscow will be gutted for years to come and the United States will be humiliated on a global stage." Cooke finally stopped speaking. Jon was afraid to add anything at all.

Rostow nodded. The president seemed calm and serious. Arrogance was the one emotion Cooke could read well and Rostow had no shortage of it, but she saw none in him at the moment. The man was trying to be sincere, or at least as honest as he could be. "Kathy, I don't doubt anything you said. Not one word," Rostow said. "But the people who sit on this side of this desk don't get to think small, and cutting big deals with hostile nations to save a person here and there is almost always a mistake. I give Maines a pardon and the next Snowden wannabe will see it and think he can jump ship for Russia or China or who-knows-where the next time his agency does something to offend his sensibilities because he'll expect us to forgive everything just to shut him up."

Across the Atlantic, six answers formed in Jon's mind to rebut the president. He considered what Kyra would say, and fought down the urge to speak.

"I'm not a fan of CIA," Rostow continued. "I've never made that a secret, but I'm not stupid enough to think that this country doesn't need it or NSA or any of the other agencies, no matter what sins you people have committed in the past. But you can't run an intelligence community where every officer in it thinks he can toss his secrecy oath out with his classified trash in a burn bag. So Maines gets nothing. And if men die and it goes public, the next Snowdon disciple won't have any doubts about the price he'll have to pay for switching teams. Do your best to save our people and our assets. If you can't, I won't hold you responsible."

Cooke didn't believe he meant the last sentence, but kept her face still. "Yes, sir."

Cooke said nothing on the walk to the Agency car waiting outside on West Executive Avenue. She closed the door and the armored vehicle began to move. She picked up the secure phone mounted between the front seats and dialed a number she had learned by heart in the last two days.

"That was not what I was expecting," Jon said, no pleasantries first. The crypto played games with his voice, stripping it of what little warmth she'd ever heard in it.

"You thought he'd make the deal?" Cooke asked.

"No. Turning us down, that I expected. I didn't expect Rostow to actually listen to us."

"He didn't, until I told him you helped capture that nuke last year," Cooke said. "Presidents don't often talk to the people whom they almost killed with their stupidity. That was probably the first time he's ever shared words with someone his political ambitions directly hurt. I don't know if it will last, but at least he made his decision on the merits for once." Cooke watched a class of schoolchildren cross Constitution Avenue, making their way to the Lincoln Memorial.

"So did he turn us down because he really believes in the decision, or is he just trying to put a shank in your ribs?"

"The former, I think. He's probably right, about not making the deal," she said. "It would be the clean, easy solution now, but it would set us up for more trouble later."

"Doesn't matter now either way," Jon replied. "And there will always be another Edward Snowden or Edward Lee Howard whether we cut a deal with Maines or not."

"I don't doubt that," Cooke agreed, rueful. "But it's not the future traitors we have to worry about now, just the one in Berlin today." She exhaled hard and looked out the car window. The trees along the George Washington Parkway had exploded into their full palette of reds, oranges, and yellows. Along with the temperature, the leaves would start falling soon. "I want you and Kyra to work with Barron and figure out which assets are likely to be first on the Kremlin's list. Prioritize who needs to be saved—"

"And who we hang out in the wind?" Jon interrupted.

"Something like that," Cooke admitted. "It might help if we knew what kind of technology Lavrov is selling now, and who the customer is."

"We're working on that."

CHAPTER FOUR

Vogelsang Military Base (Abandoned)
Vogelsang Village, the city of Zehdenick, Brandenburg, Germany
65 kilometers north of Berlin

The village of Vogelsang barely qualified for the title. The outpost was a tiny borough, not sixty miles west of the Polish border and home to fewer than a thousand people. Kyra suspected that only the solar-energy farm that dominated the southwestern quarter kept the place on the map. The only other site of interest was a deserted facility to the northwest that the Germans here were trying very hard to forget altogether.

Kyra navigated the Zehdenicker Strasse road that ran through the village center until the small town disappeared around a bend in her rearview mirror. A small railway station made of old brick and flanked by large oaks passed on her left as she paralleled the railroad tracks running north and south.

"There should be a turnoff to the left," Jon advised, staring at an iPad.

"Paved road?" Kyra asked.

"We're not so lucky."

There was no marked crossing, so Kyra turned the truck and drove over the median, bushes scraping the undercarriage and doors until she reached the railroad tracks and bounced the vehicle across those too. She navigated down a slope and onto the cleared dirt pathway that ran southwest along the tree line. The trail darkened under the forest canopy as she made a long turn to the northwest. Kyra stopped the truck after a quarter mile.

"What is it?" Jon asked. The road ahead was open.

"I think we should park back here off the road and walk in through the trees. If there's anyone in there, they'll be watching the road."

Jon didn't like the idea, but Kyra could see that he had no good argument against it. She pulled the truck off to the side and killed the engine.

Jon stared at the iPad and manipulated the screen with his fingers. "GPS says we're about a mile off. We could walk it in twenty minutes if we stayed on the road. Stomping through the brush . . . we'll probably need an hour at least."

Kyra shrugged and dismounted from the cab. She hoisted her pack out of the truck bed and fit her arms through the straps. "I've got no place to be right now," she observed. "And it'll take two at least if we're trying to be quiet. I hope there's nobody where we're going, because it's going to be pretty hard to walk quiet through all of this." Jon nodded in agreement and took up his own pack. Kyra took the lead, pushing ahead on foot where their truck couldn't go, Jon following behind.

The Brandenburg woods were so very like Virginia's that Kyra wanted to get lost in them, thinking that she might see her family's home on the James River when she finally emerged. She knew better and chased the childish thought out of her mind. There was a place far less welcoming somewhere down the overgrown path that she and Jon were walking.

After a half hour, they switched and Jon took the lead, trampling down the brush. He hadn't gone a hundred yards before he stopped. "What?" Kyra asked, her voice quiet.

"Concrete wall," he muttered back. Kyra followed his gaze and saw it, a solid obstruction not quite as tall as herself. The gray concrete was stained by weather but still intact. It ran through the woods perpendicular to the open trail to their right before turning northwest and running parallel off into the distance as far as Kyra could see.

"Actually, that's good for us," she offered. "We get behind it and the wall will muffle our sound and hide us from anyone watching the road."

They approached the wall and Jon stopped, locking his hands together to offer the woman a step up. She put her foot in his hands and he lifted her up until she could pull herself over. "How big was this place?" she asked.

"Twenty-five miles on a side, give or take," Jon replied. He gave himself a short running start up the wall and pulled himself over. "It's amazing the spy planes missed it. Vogelsang was the Soviet's first nuclear missile base outside of Russia. Fifteen thousand men and their families were stationed here. They refused to pull out and leave it until '94, a good five years after the Wall fell."

The abandoned base checkpoint was another half mile up the road, a small brick cabin. Bricks were missing from the wall, large sections of paint or siding still hanging from the sides. A pair of large Douglas firs stood watch where the Soviet guards had manned the post decades before them.

"I can't decide whether this would be a good place to meet an asset or not," Kyra remarked, looking around.

"It's remote," Jon offered. "The only people who would stumble onto you would be hikers and hobbyists."

"Or intelligence officers looking for bad men," Kyra responded drily. "But that's the problem . . . it's *too* remote. There's no good cover story for being at a place like this, so far out. You're either here because you're curious, or you're doing something you don't want anyone to see. Nothing in between."

Jon grunted and trudged on.

Reaching the main complex took another forty minutes. The trail broke open into a glade, then into a small city of crumbling buildings that was a horror film waiting to be made. Some of the buildings still looked to be in decent shape at a distance, while others looked like they were one good storm away from coming apart. Every window she could see was broken, whether from vandals or hard weather, Kyra couldn't tell. On one windowsill leading into a men's dormitory, a pair of leather boots sat where their owner had left them or some other visitor had replaced them. Massive hot-water heaters sat rusting outside dormitory buildings, turning green and red from oxidation. Murals still decorated the low concrete walls that ran down roads, showing laborers building fortifications and Soviet flags waving in a nonexistent wind. Cyrillic signs still sat upright, directing nonexistent pedestrians and cars toward the different buildings.

A concrete frieze of Lenin appeared as they turned a corner, the dead Soviet founder dressed in suit and tie, with an overcoat being lifted by an unseen breeze. Chunks of the stone had been torn out, and the bloodred background around the embedded statue had dulled with time and weather. "I'm surprised the Germans haven't knocked that down by now," Kyra said.

"Give them time," Jon answered. "From what I read, the government wants to tear this whole place down."

"Have you ever seen anything like this?" Kyra asked.

"No," Jon admitted. "But I've been places that made me *feel* like this."

"Like where?"

"Auschwitz, for one. The Holocaust Museum, for another," Jon replied. "Don't tell our German hosts I said that."

"I do know how to keep a secret," she assured him. "We could look around here for days and not find anything. Where do we start?"

Jon pulled out his iPad, checked the map, then oriented himself by looking at the buildings around them. "We're here, I think," he said, pointing at a spot in a large cluster of buildings. He moved his finger to a spot a kilometer or more to the southwest, another small village of overgrown buildings. "Strelnikov had a bad knee, so I'd guess he wouldn't park far from wherever the meeting went down. The main road leads here."

Kyra dropped her pack onto the concrete walkway and extracted a folding waterproof map case. She opened it and pulled out an old diagram—a Soviet military map of the Vogelsang facility, offered up by the German government at Barron's request. She held her smartphone over the Cyrillic words, and watched the portable computer translate the foreign-alphabet print into English letters. She held it up next to Jon's iPad. "Commandant's office?" she suggested.

Jon shrugged. "Makes sense that the GRU chairman would take the base commander's old home for himself, I guess."

Kyra saw a sign with Cyrillic letters in neat rows, arrows next to the words pointing in different directions. She aimed her smartphone at the words. The sign appeared on her screen, the handheld computer thought for a few seconds, and the Cyrillic letters disappeared, overwritten by English in the same size. The top line read *Commandant's Office.*

"That way," Kyra said.

The commandant's office was a two-story building with an enclosed red-brick entrance that jutted out from the front. The front steps were half as wide as the entire house, with low brick walls framing the sides. Rusted outlets for lights sat out above the front door, the bulbs long since smashed out. Iron rails topped the entry on three sides, forming a small veranda where the commandant might well have spent his evenings, smoking Cuban cigars and swilling the local beer or something harder shipped in from Moscow. The plaster siding had peeled away from much of the facade, exposing the brown brick underneath. The front door, weathered and split wood, hung open on corroded hinges and Kyra could see through the building all the way to the back. A large dormitory that had housed soldiers of the armored corps stationed at Vogelsang sat off behind some smaller trees a few hundred feet to the right of the house.

"Tire tracks, a few different sets . . . not sure how many," Kyra said, searching the ground. "Pretty recent, I think. The ground is still a little muddy from the rain." She climbed the low steps, stopped, and listened. She heard nothing, not even birds in the nearby evergreens.

"This was probably the nicest home on base, back in the day," Jon observed. "Creeped out yet?"

"It's just an old building," Kyra said with a shrug. Central Virginia, home, had more than its share of abandoned old buildings, some as old as the Revolution itself. She extracted a flashlight from her pack and moved quietly inside.

The walls inside had faired little better than those without. The wallpaper was shredded and large chunks of broken drywall exposed the frames and wiring underneath. Fallen plaster crunched under her boots, and she kicked one of the larger pieces through a hole in the timbers of the floor. It rattled as it fell down a few feet. Kyra looked down.

"Footprints," she said. "Boots by the look of them, but somebody had a pair of dress shoes." The dust had been disturbed, mostly by shoes with fat treads, but also a pair with a flat sole.

They searched the ground floor and found nothing besides the signs of recent movement across the floor. Kyra used her smartphone to document them with digital pictures before the analysts moved up the stairs to the second floor.

The first two rooms were no different from the ones they'd seen on the ground floor, more entropy at work on the wood and wallpaper, but the third was what they'd come to see. A chair sat in the corner, a wooden stool in the center of the room. Both had only the smallest bits of dust on their seats. A length of cord sat on the floor next to a black hood.

"Bet you ten dollars this is where they arrested Strelnikov," Kyra offered.

"Sucker's bet. I'll keep my money. The ante is too low to be interesting."

"You think we should bag that stuff," Kyra asked, nodding at the hood and the rope.

Jon shook his head. "Just photograph the room. If this is where Strelnikov checked out, then it's a crime scene, technically speaking. I don't think the Germans would be very happy with you tampering with evidence."

Kyra shrugged, and photographed the room and its contents. She stared around, looking for any missed details. "There's nothing else here. I don't see anything that could tell us what Lavrov is working on."

Jon's gaze had become unfocused and Kyra recognized the thousand-yard stare that he fell into when he was thinking. "That Syrian officer wouldn't have come all the way out here just to talk with Lavrov," he said, working the puzzle as he spoke. "They could've done that at the embassy, or just over a secure phone. He must've come to Berlin so Lavrov could show him something . . . or give him something."

"Maybe Lavrov wanted to show him that he'd caught Strelnikov?" Kyra suggested. "Show him that his operation was secure?"

Jon shook his head. "A photograph would have done that just as well. No need for him to see that in person, or at least not to see *only* that in person. He must've come here for something that Lavrov couldn't just share remotely," he suggested. "And Lavrov is a technology dealer."

Kyra saw where his line of logic was going. "You think Lavrov brought him here to demonstrate something, or deliver something? A weapon?"

"Or some other piece of technology."

"Why not do that in Russia?" Kyra asked.

"Good question. I don't know," he admitted. "But if the Syrian did come here for a weapons test or a technology demonstration, where would Lavrov set it up?"

Kyra pulled out the base diagram again. "Assuming he wanted to keep the demonstration secure, he wouldn't want to do it around here. The base is enormous. Anyone could stumble in from a dozen different directions. There's no way he could secure the place without bringing in a regiment, and that would be hard to hide from the locals."

Jon stared at the diagram and put his finger down on a spot to the southwest. "The actual missile base? It would be easier to lock down a smaller group of buildings than this main complex . . . and it had its own living quarters, workshops, and hard storage bunkers where everything could be secured. If Lavrov wanted a self-contained space where he could mount up some actual security, that would be the place, because it probably was the most secure place on the base when this place was actually operational. But that's just me doing some mirror imaging. I'm not a Russian intelligence officer."

"It sounds logical. Let's hope that Lavrov is a logical man," Kyra offered in support.

"You think I'm wrong?"

"No, I'm worried that you're right," Kyra replied. "And I'm *really* worried that his people will still be there."

"Then we call the Germans and let them clean the place out," Jon advised. "Maybe everything gets wrapped up nice and neat."

"You don't believe that."

"When have I ever been an optimist?" he asked.

They needed almost another hour to walk down to the missile base. The complex was far smaller than the main base they'd just left, but still large enough to be daunting. They reached the tree line, and Kyra stopped short. "Jon," she said, quiet. "Up there."

He looked up. Two wooden poles six meters tall rose from the ground with a heavy metal cable strung between them over a concrete slab on the ground, then fastened to the earth on either side like the guidelines of a tent. A steel girder, rust apparent on its surface even from a distance, hung suspended from the wire over the slab, five meters square underneath. More dark wires on each side ran down to enormous metal cylinders topped with gold ports, and several other wires ran into a concrete bunker buried in a hillside beyond.

"Are those power lines?" Kyra asked.

Jon nodded. "Good bet. Look where they run." He pointed and Kyra followed the invisible line drawn by his hand to the large silver cylinders topped with gold stubs. "Those look like industrial capacitors."

"No corrosion on them. Those are new," she said. "Big ones too. They look like the ones you'd see in a power substation."

Jon twisted his head, listening. "No buzz," he said.

"Line's dead?"

"Probably, but I'm not going to test it," he replied.

"If this is where Lavrov was set up, he could've just pulled some generator trucks up and jacked in right there."

"I don't think so," Jon countered. "Those wires run over to those buildings. Makes more sense that they'd put up a generator inside. It would be quieter than running it out in the open."

Kyra scanned the close horizon, looking for movement or other signs of life. She saw nothing. "I don't see anyone."

Jon nodded, and they walked toward the odd setup. "It's a test rig of some kind, I think."

"A test rig for what?" Kyra asked. "I don't see any kind of blast or scorch marks on anything. And if they were testing bombs or guns, the locals would've heard it. We're not that far from the village back by the rail station."

Jon pondered the question for a moment. "We should check out the bunkers."

Kyra took the lead, scanning their surroundings as she walked. She stopped as they approached the building that was the power line's terminus. "Any idea what this one is?" she asked, nodding toward the building.

"Missile storage silo is my guess," he muttered.

"Still don't see anyone," Kyra noted. "The place is locked up . . . but the lock looks new from here. Still shines, no rust."

The bunker was a concrete slab dug into the earth behind, with a flat roof that angled down into sloping sides. Moss covered the top side and was growing down the front wall toward the doors. The concrete was discolored where some kind of dark gray paint had started chipping loose near the top. The two doors in front were metal, rusting into shades of red and green. Kyra's observation had been correct. The locks on both were silver, free of corrosion.

"Think you can break in?"

"O ye of little faith," Kyra chided the man. "Wherefore dost thou doubt?"

"As much as I appreciate your talents, you might want to compare your lockpicking skills to someone a little closer to earth."

Kyra extracted her lockpick set from her pack and set to work. Jon kept up the vigil behind her, scanning the buildings and woods for movement. The woman took less than a minute to pop the lock. She pulled it off, set it on the ground, and opened the door.

"No miracles necessary," she offered.

"Very nice," Jon muttered. He stepped inside the bunker and switched on his Maglite.

The bunker's interior was an open cavern, like a miniature aircraft hangar. The floor was concrete, swept clean of debris, with single row of large cement slabs rising up in a line at regular intervals, each with an identical concave arc cut into the center. "They laid the missiles out on those," Kyra realized. She looked up and saw a pair of rails running along the roof near the corners. "Chain and pulley system," she noted. "Would've made it easy to lift and lower them when moving them in and out."

Jon walked toward the far end of the bunker until his flashlight illuminated the back wall. Enormous metal boxes sat on skids, cabled together, with a single power line coming out of the last box on the right and snaking along hooks mounted in the concrete wall toward the entrance. "There are your generators," he said.

Kyra's light caught a dark shape by a pair of worktables and benches that ran along the wall opposite the power line. A backpack sat on the floor, the flap on the front hanging loose. She knelt down by it, lifted the flap, and pointed her light inside. "Camera . . . water bottle . . . notebook," she said, moving the contents around. Other odds and ends were gathered in the bottom.

"Longstreet's, I'll wager," Jon suggested.

"That British hiker?" Kyra realized. "Yeah, I wouldn't bet against that."

"Anything on the camera?"

Kyra picked up the device, a low-end Canon digital SLR. She searched for the power button, pressed it. "Not working. Battery might be dead. We could take it back to the embassy and get a new one . . . unless you want to preserve the crime scene."

Jon looked around with his flashlight. "Something tells me that it won't be here that long. If the Russians are done with these generators and the capacitors outside, I can't imagine they'll leave them here. And if they're not done with them, they'll be back."

"I don't think we want to be here for that." Kyra swept her light over the worktables and benches. They were free of dust and tools, with only bits of wire and electronic parts sitting on top. She picked up a calculator, a cheap Hewlett-Packard. She fiddled with it, but it refused to go on. What appeared to be a digital voltmeter fared no better, as did a radio that sat on the floor under the table. "Busted junk," she said.

Jon frowned. "All of them?"

"Yeah." Kyra took the battery covers off. "Batteries all look fine. No corrosion."

Jon pulled the batteries out of the devices and began dropping them one by one a short distance from each other, just a few inches off the table. Each made a solid thumping sound, and several remained upright.

"What are you doing?" Kyra asked.

"When a battery is used, the alkaline inside undergoes a chemical reaction that produces a gas that gets trapped inside the casing. The more it's used, the more gas it builds up. Drop a charged battery onto a hard surface and it won't bounce. Drop a dead battery, and the gas trapped in it will make it jump. It'll usually fall over. Sounds muffled when it hits too," Jon explained. He held up one of the batteries. "These still have a good charge."

"So why do we care?" Kyra asked.

"The calculator, voltmeter, the radio . . . they all have good power supplies, but none of them work. And I'll bet you that the camera's battery is fine too." Jon looked away from the battery in his hands to his partner, her face only half lit by her flashlight. "It's just a theory, but think about it. Assume Lavrov is doing something up here, something he shows off to the Syrians. We know it's something that he could transport without drawing a lot of attention. It doesn't make a lot of noise, if any, but draws a fair amount of power." He held the battery up again. "And it kills electronics."

Kyra processed the evidence in her mind. "EMP?"

Jon nodded. "Basic physics . . . run enough electricity through metal coil connected to a capacitor and you'll create a pulse that will generate an electrical current inside any computer circuit in range. If there's enough power behind the pulse, it fries everything. Scientists say that one nuclear-generated EMP at four hundred kilometers over Kansas would make the entire continent go preindustrial in a few seconds. The Syrians don't have a missile that could do that, but a Scud could reach Israel in a few minutes. Every time the Syrians face off against the Israelis, they get thrashed because the Israelis have better weapons. We sell Tel Aviv all kinds of high-tech gear that the Syrians can't match, even buying from the Russians. But mount some really powerful electromagnetic pulse bombs on Scud missiles and set them off over the Golan Heights or Tel Aviv, and just maybe the Israeli military gets paralyzed. Same thing could happen to us."

Kyra looked around. "The lights weren't out in the village when we came through. If they were testing one of those, it must've been a small model."

"Lavrov wouldn't have needed to test a big one. EMP bombs aren't complicated to build. The only real variables involved are the altitude when detonation occurs and how much power is behind the pulse. Maybe Lavrov's people figured out how to build a more powerful version in a smaller package."

"What's the altitude ceiling for a Scud?" Kyra asked.

"For a Scud D? A hundred fifty kilometers, more or less . . . but they don't need it to go a hundred fifty kilometers up. If there's enough power behind the pulse, a kilometer or two above the battlefield will do just fine to kill every unhardened piece of gear dead . . . or do the same thing over a major city and kill all of the critical infrastructures in a direct line of sight of the device."

"Strelnikov's grandfather was Jewish," Kyra realized. "It was in the file. Maybe he had a soft spot for Israel. He found out Lavrov was sharing EMP tech with the Syrians and came to us." Kyra pulled out the smartphone and began to photograph everything in sight. Then she picked up the calculator. "Think the Germans would object if I took this?"

"Knock yourself out," Jon said. "Time to be going, I think."

They stepped into the daylight. The sun had reached the tops of the Brandenburg woods and the dark would be settling within the hour.

Jon picked up the padlock from the cement ramp where Kyra had laid it and turned his back to the base. He hooked the shackle over the entry doorway latch—

"Jon!" Kyra yelled.

Jon looked up.

Five men were talking toward them. They were dressed in plainclothes, short haircuts, with pistols drawn. They saw the Americans and shifted from a slow walk to a dead run, guns raised. The man on the far left fired and Jon heard the round strike concrete.

Jon dropped the lock, and the analysts ran for the woods, just to the south. More rounds hit the bunker, closer than the first. The men behind them yelled. *Russian*, he realized. He couldn't understand their commands, but the cadence and guttural sounds of the language were unmistakable.

He heard their pistols fire over the sounds of his own boots tearing through the grass and leaves. The rounds cracked the air open as they passed by the running analysts faster than sound. Kyra sprinted ahead of him, her breath already getting heavy. She looked back, saw she was outpacing her lumbering partner, and slowed up to let him close the distance.

They reached the woods and crashed into the undergrowth at full speed. The brush and weeds slowed them, and the trees forced them to run in anything but a straight line. Three hundred feet into the forest, Kyra ran up to one of the larger trees and stopped for a second, looking back. Jon caught up with her and looked back. He couldn't see their pursuers, but their voices carried well enough as they cursed and yelled at the scrub pines and low bushes tearing at their legs and arms.

"Still coming," Kyra said, her breathing rapid. She pulled her backpack off and tore open a Velcro pocket on the outside. "Which way?"

Jon looked up, and picked out the sun's direction through the green canopy. "We're running south. That means the road is that way." He pointed left. "The truck is a mile down, there." It would be at least a fifteen-minute run through these woods.

"A mile," Kyra muttered. She pulled out a Glock 21, the clip already locked in. She racked the slide to chamber the first round. "Maybe we can slow them down."

A Russian shouted in the distance, not quite so far away now, and the analysts started to run again. "We're on friendly soil," Jon yelled. "You're not supposed to be carrying!"

Kyra leaned around the oak and sent three rounds back at the men behind. "Are you complaining?"

"Nope," Jon told her. "Just don't tell the Germans."

"You keep telling me that."

The woods were pulling on them, trying to slow them down. Surely it was doing the same for the men behind, but every shout seemed closer than the one before. Bullets whined through the trees around them. He could hear them tearing into the trees, dull thuds and hard cracks, but he could not see where they were hitting. Kyra broke stride, turning and firing as often as she dared, but there were far more rounds coming in their direction than she was sending back.

Jon looked left and saw the concrete wall that bordered the open road. They could jump it, get into the open, and put some distance between them and the Russian hunters before the men realized they had left the woods—

He saw movement beyond the wall. The Russians had seen the

road and come to Jon's own conclusion. Two of their pursuers had moved out to the road on the other side of the wall, flanking them. If they were Lavrov's men, then they were Spetsnaz, he thought, and they had a clear path to run all the way to the truck. They would certainly reach it before he or Kyra would.

Five soldiers and five guns at least . . . two analysts and one gun, Jon thought. The odds weren't hard to calculate. Even if he and Kyra turned west and moved deeper into the woods, the men would almost certainly run them to ground. There wasn't enough distance between them and their pursuers, and the men behind were in better shape than he was. Kyra was young and fast, but Jon was past his prime.

He saw Kyra go down hard in the dirt ahead of him, stumbling over some growth in the brush. Jon thought for a moment that one of the Russians had finally drawn close enough to be accurate with his sidearm, but the girl scrambled to her feet and pushed off, trying to recover the speed she had lost. He was hardly fast enough to catch up before she was back at her full speed—

—no, not her full speed, he realized. Kyra was running slow so she wouldn't lose him.

Run faster, old man, he told himself. His body refused to obey. He didn't have more speed in him to give.

He looked at the young woman, the world moving in slow motion around him.

The enemy was too close, there were too many obstacles between them and the truck. Even without him plodding behind, every tree, every root, every dip in the ground would slow Kyra down. She couldn't run at full speed over this damp ground. At every step, the earth was pulling at her feet, forcing her to use her strength to pull her feet back up. The road was in better shape, but it was no escape route. If she jumped the wall, the men on the open road would be in her path and they would have a clear field of fire. If she stayed in the trees, the enemy behind her would get into pistol range long before she reached the truck. She would be forced to stop running and find cover, and then the men on the other side of the wall would climb back over into the woods, get in behind her, and that would be that.

For three years, he'd tried to give her, this broken girl, what little he had to offer. He'd been the best friend he knew how to be, which wasn't much, but she'd taken it and returned more than he'd ever given her.

Kyra needed more time, more space, and she didn't have it. Maybe he could give her that.

He dug deep and decided he might have enough energy for one more sprint.

Kyra turned and fired again. Jon ran up to her and put his hand on the Glock. "Give me the gun," he ordered. His words were labored, his lungs wheezing hard.

"What?"

Jon didn't ask twice. He reached out and put his hand on the weapon. Kyra, confused, released it to him. "Keep running!" Jon yelled. Then he pulled away, running left for the concrete wall.

The Spetsnaz soldiers on the road were twenty yards ahead of them when Jon reached the concrete wall. He ran at the barrier at full speed, sprinted up, and pulled himself over. He hit the dirt on his feet, the mud absorbing some of the impact and the sound. He pushed off and ran after the Russians. The soldiers ahead hadn't heard the sound of his boots in the wet dirt, their ears filled with the sound of their own gasping breath.

Jon raised the Glock, lined up the sights as best he could with one hand on a dead run.

He'd shot men before, once in Iraq. The dreams had haunted him for years, driven him into depression, and left him unsure whether he could ever kill another person again, even in his own defense. He knew the answer to that question now and he was at peace with the answer. The Russians would probably kill him and the act wouldn't have a chance to torture him after.

Jon pulled the trigger.

The pistol kicked hard in his hand, the barrel jerking up. The shot was high, his aim thrown off by his own motion. He'd never shot anyone moving on the run before, but he was close enough. One of the soldiers went down as the .45 round punched into his shoulder, his body twisting and his legs collapsing under him.

The sound of the shot reached his companion's ears just as the man started to tumble to the ground. The second Russian spun around, trying to line up his weapon, but the advantage of surprise had allowed Jon to pull the Glock back down and line up his own. His second shot fired a fraction of a second sooner than his target's and the round struck the Russian's chest on the right side, knocking off the soldier's aim and spinning him as his Makarov pistol fired.

The Russian's bullet tore into Jon's right thigh, ripping his pants and spraying blood from the gory hole in his skin, and sent him into the dirt. His vision went blurry from the pain, fire burning in a straight line through his leg. Still, he tried to focus, scrambling to raise his gun and cover the two fallen Russians with the Glock in case one of them wanted to be persistent, but neither man was moving.

"Jon!" He heard Kyra's voice.

"Keep going," Jon said. The pain in his leg was sharp and burning even hotter now. The femur was broken, he could tell that much. If the bullet had struck the deep femoral artery or the great saphenous vein, he would bleed out right there in the dirt maybe before the other Russians could reach him and their comrades. "Get to the truck."

He looked at the Glock. The pistol's slide had locked open on an empty clip. He didn't know whether Kyra had another clip in her bag or not.

"No! You're—"

He couldn't see Kyra. She was on the other side of the concrete wall. His voice sounded weaker to his own ears now. He was going into shock. He fought it. There were two more pistols on the ground ahead of him. Jon dropped the useless Glock and tried to stand and his leg collapsed under him. He started to crawl through the dirt toward the closer weapon. "Get moving. You have to go."

"No!" Kyra yelled at him. She'd seen his head go down behind the wall, hadn't seen it come back up. The Russians behind her were getting closer. She could hear their shouts. If she ran back a few feet, she could sprint up the wall as Jon had and get to the other side. But he was wounded . . . she could tell that much from his shaky voice. He'd been shot, but where she didn't know. She couldn't help him walk and handle the Glock at the same time . . . and the pain of whatever wound Jon had sustained would wreck his aim. In a few moments, he might not even be conscious.

It didn't matter. She backed up a few feet to get her running start—

—something arced over the fence and landed in the dirt, skidding toward her. Kyra looked down.

It was a pistol . . . not the Glock. A Makarov.

Jon had taken out the soldiers on the other side of the wall.

Kyra picked up the Russian firearm. *I'm coming, Jon—*

She heard another sound, more feet in the dirt on the other side of the wall. The Spetsnaz soldiers had heard the gunshots from the road and jumped over. There was more shooting from Jon's position. A different sound from the Glock. Jon had shot two men, which meant there had been two Makarovs. Jon had thrown her one and gotten to the other. The Russians fifty yards behind her on the other side of the wall returned fire. She couldn't see what was happening.

"Go!" Jon said from the other side of the wall. His voice was hoarse now, weak.

Kyra ran to the wall, jumped, and tried to pull herself over with her one empty hand. A bullet hit the stone, sending small shards into her cheek, and Kyra's reflexes forced her to let go. She fell into the dirt behind the wall, landing hard on her side.

"Jon!" she yelled.

He didn't answer and she heard no more firing from his position. More shouts in Russian came from the road, closer now. She couldn't make it over the wall. The Spetsnaz would reach Jon in seconds and they would kill her if she came over the wall, Makarov in hand.

Her training finally took over, crushing her emotions and forcing her to move, her legs refusing her order to stop, instead determined to carry her to safety.

I'm sorry, Jon.

Kyra ran. It was what he wanted her to do, and she hated him for it.

She heard the Russians' voices grow quieter as she moved farther away. There were no sounds of men crashing through the woods behind her now, no sign they were trying to flank her on the road, no more gunshots. Perhaps the Russian soldiers had contented themselves with capturing one American . . . or had they killed him? Kyra's mind rebelled at the thought, trying to force God or the universe to keep it from being true.

Her legs kept moving of their own accord, her body flying over and around the obstacles in her path without the help of her mind, which was still focused on the place behind her where her friend was lying.

She reached the end of the wood line, where the concrete road turned at a right angle to the east. Kyra ran up the wall, pulled herself over, and landed on her feet in the grass on the other side. The truck was down the road another half mile. Her lungs were wheezing, her legs weak rubber. *Don't stop.* She heard the order in her head but didn't know from where it came . . . certainly not her own conscious mind.

Kyra looked around the corner of the concrete wall back up the road. The sun was behind the trees now, and the shadows had melted into each other. The light would be gone in minutes. She could see no more than an eighth of a mile down the road and there was no one in sight. No yells, no shouts. Kyra pushed herself onto her feet and ran as hard as the adrenaline allowed.

She saw the truck after another three minutes of running, and she didn't stop until she was standing by it. She fumbled for the keys, almost dropped them. Her hands were shaking harder than she could ever remember. She got the door open, threw her pack and the Makarov onto the passenger seat, then managed to push the key into the ignition. She locked her shoulder belt and fired up the engine.

Kyra sat in the seat, hands on the wheel, and looked up the road. Jon was up there, somewhere, dead or alive she didn't know. She thought for a moment that she might go after him, drive the truck at full speed, and run over anyone in her way.

Perhaps she could drive back up the road. She wanted to hunt the Spetsnaz, shoot them or run them over. Then she could help Jon crawl into the truck. The nearby village surely had some kind of medical facility, a first-aid kit if nothing else—

Fool, the thought came. *Idiot*. The Russian men on the road were trained Special Forces soldiers. They outgunned her, and they could simply jump back over the wall if she tried to run them over . . . no, she wouldn't even get that close. She'd have to turn the headlights on, to keep from running Jon over on the off chance he was still alive and lying in the road. The Russians would see her coming long before she would see them. One shot into the truck cab and she would be finished.

Jon had taken out two only because he'd managed to gain the

element of surprise. In the dark, she would have no chance against them . . . and Jon wouldn't have wanted her to try.

Kyra put the truck into gear and U-turned it across the road. She made her way back to the Zehdenicker Strasse road, driving on autopilot, paying no attention to her surroundings. There were no headlights behind her. Her training forced her to notice that much. She turned south onto the highway and continued through the village until she passed the solar farm. Then she found a side road, pulled off, and drove into some farmer's field, where the truck would be hidden from traffic by more thick woods. Then she stopped, killed the engine, and unbuckled her belt.

She stared into space at nothing, then got out of the vehicle. Kyra walked three steps before falling forward into the grass. Her body started to convulse and she lost her lunch, spewing bile onto the ground until there was nothing left but dry heaves.

Then Kyra fell onto her side, curled up, and cried harder than she ever had, great racking sobs that left her shuddering on the ground, until she had no strength left to move at all.

The "Aquarium" — old GRU headquarters
Khoroshevskoye shosse 76
Khodynka, Moscow, Russia

From the outside, the old headquarters of the Glavnoye Razvedyvatel'noye Upravleniye, the Main Intelligence Directorate, was remarkable only for its size. The edifice was a decaying nine-story tower encased in glass that loomed over a family of mismatched industrial buildings and the old Khodynka Airfield. There was no beauty in its design or its cold construction, which fact was demonstrated clearly by the new headquarters building to the east. That structure was as modern as any in Moscow, concrete and glass covered in metal, with all the amenities.

Colonel Anton Semyonovich Sokolov would not have admitted it, but he missed Lubyanka. Not for the finer interior of the upper floors or the larger, cleaner office he'd once used in the KGB's old headquarters when that organization and his own GRU had worked together in a tenuous alliance. Any man would want those amenities again, but the interrogator's desires ran deeper. It was the spirit of the place that he wished he could recapture here. Lubyanka's reputation alone had been enough to break most men and women who'd been brought to his room there. Confessions, whether true or not, had been easy to come by then. Not so much now that he had to work in this unremarkable site. "The Aquarium" just didn't create the same fear in the Russian heart. If his superiors had cared to ask his opinion, he would have admitted that. He would have said that something valuable had been lost, something needed to keep his country orderly and powerful.

Still, there was a job to do, and if the building could not lend him any help, he would have to push on and find other ways when his services were required. There had been little of that in recent years. The unfortunate clientele who had come this way of late had been activists whose crimes mainly had involved discomfiting the political elites, or businessmen who had made the error of thinking that the buyout offers given by those same elites were invitations to bargain, the start of negotiations and not the end. He did not like plying his trade on such people. They were not true threats to the *Rodina*.

The phone on his old metal desk sounded, a shrill electronic ring. An encrypted call, he saw. He lifted the handset. *"Ya slushayu vas."* *I'm listening to you.*

The caller's voice was familiar enough. "Anton Semyonovich. You are in good health?"

"I am, General Lavrov, though I fear the flu is coming soon enough," Sokolov replied. "I catch it every year."

"Then I will tell you *vyzdoravlivay skoreye* now," Lavrov replied. "I trust you are not busy?"

A trick question, always. To say he was unoccupied would have flirted with an admission that he was dispensable. Telling the lie always was safer easier. "Always, but with nothing so pressing today that I cannot shunt it aside if you require my service."

"Very good," Lavrov said. "I am coming home, and I have received some information from a new source that we have some unfaithful colleagues in our ranks. The source is very sensitive and touches on a project of unusual importance. I can trust your discretion?"

"Always."

"I regret that open trials could only threaten the project's security, so they will not be permitted. I will pass you the names one at a time as I confirm the reliability of the information. I will require you to detain the individuals quickly and with no publicity whatsoever. You will be allowed a small unit of men. I will designate who will assist you with the apprehensions. You will not speak of the operations to anyone, even colleagues within the GRU. This will be entirely compartmented. Your duty will be to locate and detain them, then determine quickly what information they have given up to the Main Enemy. After that, you will be free to dispense justice to each criminal as you see fit, but you will report to me the disposition of each case, after which I will give you the next name."

The Main Enemy, Sokolov thought. The United States. The CIA. Almost three decades since the Soviet Union had fallen and his GRU leaders still used the same terms and thought the same ways as before. *"Ya ponimayu." I understand.* There was no question that the general's vision of "justice" would be very narrow despite his promise that the interrogator had the latitude to decide matters for himself.

"*Ochen' khorosho.* You must not delay for any reason. There will be no time for lengthy investigations now. We must repair the project's security as quickly as you can move."

"I can begin today, as soon as you identify the team members. But they must not question my orders, or I will not be able to guarantee you the discretion you desire," the interrogator warned him.

"I will tell them personally that they are at your disposal," Lavrov confirmed. "Stand by. You will have my telex with the first name within the hour."

"Can you tell me how many names are on your list?" Sokolov asked.

"Not yet," Lavrov admitted. "We are unsure as to the scope of the penetrations. The preliminary information our asset has provided suggests at least three penetrations of the GRU itself, but there could be more. So you must not take on any other tasking from any other officers until I tell you that this operation is complete. But I expect the whole matter should not take more than a few weeks."

"Yes, sir. I await your orders."

"*Do svidaniya,*" Lavrov said.

"*Do svidaniya,*" Sokolov repeated. The call disconnected, he replaced the phone on its handset and leaned back, already lost in his thoughts. This was all irregular and surely illegal, not that it mattered. There were procedures for dealing with moles, laws for what came after, and Lavrov had just waived them all aside. *Why?* he wondered. To protect Lavrov's new source? That was possible. Aldrich Ames, the CIA's last great traitor, had given up the names of every CIA mole he knew at once, trying to burn anyone who could identify him. The KGB had taken them all out so quickly that the Americans had known immediately what had happened and Ames's desperate plan had turned on him. His attempt to protect himself had given his CIA colleagues the very evidence they needed to find him. A series of state trials now would surely have the same effect . . . and yet Lavrov had told him to move quickly. No matter how their assets went dark, through public means or private, the CIA surely would realize that its access was being clamped off.

Did the CIA already know about Lavrov's source? Was that the reason the old general was demanding such speed and secrecy? That was an intriguing thought. Perhaps Lavrov wanted to catch the moles before the CIA could exfiltrate them or warn them to run, or before some news service could run a story that would warn them just the same.

A race, then? The CIA and the GRU, both running toward the same set of targets, and he would determine which service reached each mole first.

Sokolov felt a small surge of guilt rise in his chest. It was one thing to extract a confession of guilt from the accused so they could be moved along to a righteous sentence, but that was not his task here. Lavrov clearly considered the word of his source, whoever that was, as good as a confession. Sokolov's only job was damage assessment and control. *Locate, detain, evaluate, neutralize.* Such clinical words.

His orders were set, but orders and duty were not always the same. Sokolov closed his eyes and began to consider whether his heart and his mind were still one and the same.

Lavrov cradled the phone and stared down at the sheet of paper on his desk. It was double-spaced, neatly typed, two columns that reached halfway down the page. He imagined the CIA would gladly have one of its drones put a missile through his window to destroy the list. He was not yet sure that Maines had given him every name the American knew, but there were enough that the traitor's former masters in Virginia must be in a panic.

Where to begin? Every person on the paper would be dealt with, and quickly, but the CIA would be conducting an exercise very much like the one he was performing right now. If they could only save a few before the Russian dragnet fell, who would they choose? Who would they sacrifice that others might live? It was a fascinating puzzle of a kind that Lavrov had never had to tackle before.

The young woman from the roof—Maines had said her name was Stryker—could have been very useful to him right now, were she cooperative. The concept of a Red Cell fascinated the GRU head . . . a group of analysts who, among other things, imagined themselves to be the enemy and tried to think as the enemy did. It was a concept not unknown to his predecessors. The old spy school at Vinnytsia where KGB officers had lived as Americans, shopped at 7-Eleven, and spoken English in homes where they ate roast beef and cherry pie had been a brilliant idea. Even the CIA had thought so. But such techniques had fallen out of use and Lavrov had no training in them.

He touched a finger to the first name. *Are you more important to the CIA than the next name? Or the last?*

Lavrov shook his head and cleared his mind.

Stryker, the woman . . . she had seen the test platform at Vogelsang. His men had caught her and her associate emerging from the missile storage bunker. Had she deduced what he had demonstrated there?

Assume that she has, Lavrov thought. That was easy enough. It was his natural inclination to consider worst cases.

If she knew of the EMP, did she know of the other advanced technologies that the Foundation had shared with America's enemies over the years? It was possible. The Chinese stealth plane had been lost in its first confrontation with the U.S. Navy three years before. The *Abraham Lincoln* carrier battle group had used a very unusual radar network in the Battle of the Taiwan Strait. Had they been forewarned?

The nuclear warhead the Iranians had been constructing in Venezuela had been captured last year, the covert facility utterly destroyed with a Massive Ordinance Penetrator as neatly as a tumor excised by a surgeon's laser. Hosseini Ahmadi, the Iranian program's leader, had been executed on his own plane at the airport, a single bullet to his forehead. It was still unclear who had pulled that trigger and Lavrov hadn't thought the Americans were *that* ruthless, but his own sources in Caracas had confirmed that they had been aboard Ahmadi's aircraft when he'd climbed the stairs, then left just before his corpse had been carried back down.

Assume that she does.

Other operations had come off undisturbed, so the CIA clearly did not know the full scope of the Foundation's work. But if they knew of the program generally and the EMP specifically, would they not try to stop him from sharing that technology, as they had the others?

Lavrov focused on the paper again, reading each name. *Which of you could tell Miss Stryker and her friends of the EMP? Its design? Its location? How we will deliver it?*

Would those be the people the CIA would try to save?

Perhaps not . . . but they would be, he supposed, a very good place for him to start.

CHAPTER FIVE

The Oval Office

Of the innumerable diplomats and foreign leaders that President Daniel Rostow had met, he disliked the Russian ambassador to the U.S. the most. Igor Nikolayevich Galushka smiled so rarely that he frightened most everyone who knew him when he did. The Russian diplomat had come from a background that would have crushed the ambitions of other men in the Kremlin. He was a farmer's son from Fedyakovoan, an unremarkable village seated two hundred miles east of Moscow on the back of the Volga River, and had no advantages of family or business connections to the men who ruled the country. That he had managed to survive the various political and personal purges of the previous three decades and get himself one of the most important postings in the Ministry of Foreign Affairs was more a testament to his lack of ethics than any diplomatic skill. That was fine by him and his superiors. Most important policies between nations were hashed out over the phone between leaders. Ambassadors were used only when the chiefs of state didn't want to answer unpleasant questions, and Galushka excelled at being the bearer of appalling news.

Galushka had demanded, not asked, to see Rostow. The president had granted the request, summoned the secretary of state and his national security adviser to the Oval Office for the meeting, and made Galushka wait fifteen minutes for no good reason before admitting him to the room. The Secret Service officer on duty admitted the Russian diplomat, then took up a position by the closed door.

"Thank you for your time, Mr. President," Galushka began after the pleasantries were finished. "I regret that this will not be a friendly visit."

Rostow doubted that Galushka regretted anything. "I do hope that we can resolve your issue in a fair way."

"To speak in honesty, Mr. President, there is nothing you need do except comply with single demand that I must make," Galushka told him. "As you are aware, I am sure, our security services are the most skilled in the world at counterintelligence. They have been running a major operation for some time, and have confirmed that your country has brought a number of spies into our motherland under the false pretenses of being diplomats and businessmen. This is unacceptable! The presence of a single infiltrator would be unacceptable to us, but the scale of your activity is appalling. Our president has reaffirmed his readiness to expand cooperation with the U.S., including the cooperation of our intelligence agencies in fighting terrorism, but such provocations are in the spirit of the 'Cold War' and undermine the mutual trust we both value."

"I assure you, Igor, your services must be mistaken—" Rostow began.

The Russian reached into his jacket, withdrew a single sheet of folded paper, and laid it on the Resolute desk. "This is a list of the CIA spies that our security services have identified in our country. I am here to inform you that my government has declared them all persona non grata, unwanted persons expelled from our soil for engaging in activities inconsistent with their diplomatic status. Their expulsion is mandatory and they and their families must leave our soil within twenty-four hours."

"Twenty-four hours? That's unreasonable, Igor. You can't expect people to settle their affairs, pack up, and evacuate in a single day."

"Given the scale of American perfidy in this matter, that is all the time we are prepared to offer. The number of spies you have sent into the Russian Federation beggars the imagination."

Rostow frowned, picked up the paper, and unfolded it. The list of names was arranged in two columns and almost filled the page. "Igor, this can't possibly be right. Are you trying to gut our embassy?" Rostow protested. He had abandoned any thoughts of diplomatic phrasing.

"The list is correct," Galushka replied. "Our foreign minister has summoned your ambassador in Moscow to receive our formal demarche and is sharing the same information with him. However, in the spirit of generosity, we will not arrest the ones who lack diplomatic cover. They will be allowed to leave peacefully, but any of them still within our borders after the deadline will be subject to the full penalties of our law."

"Igor, this would not be a wise move—"

"It is done, Mr. President. It was not my decision. I am here only to inform you of it." Galushka stood. "I will take up no more of your time. I am sure that you will need to consult with your cabinet and others to facilitate this new state of affairs."

Rostow nodded at the Russian ambassador, then looked down to reread the list.

Isaac Menard disliked any visit to the White House. FBI directors rarely were the bearers of good tidings and most presidents came to dread any private meetings with them. Six presidents had lived in outright fear of J. Edgar Hoover, the man who'd ruled over the Bureau for almost fifty years. Hoover had menaced so many politicians for so long that Menard was sure that a fear of the FBI had become part of the White House's institutional memory, something that was just part of the air, breathed in and internalized by every president of the United States and his staff, whether they were conscious of it or not. Harrison Stuart, the man who'd appointed him, had been friendly enough; but President Rostow's behavior toward Menard seemed to match the theory, always keeping their visits short and efficient, with no pleasantries exchanged. Menard always had the sense that Rostow wanted the FBI director out of his presence as quickly as possible, like an apostate wanting the priest at his doorstep to leave him to his sins in peace.

Menard had been summoned to the Oval Office this morning, which was a rare event, so he assumed it would be Rostow delivering the unwelcome news today. *It'll be about Maines*, Menard told himself. *Some development in that case*. There were no other active cases that warranted a U.S. president's attention. He had dispatched a small team of special agents to Berlin, but they had nothing new to report since the CIA's woman had met with Maines at the Russian Embassy. Menard had wanted it to be one of his own people who'd gone in, but Clark Barron had persuaded him to let his own person go. The FBI director respected that. Barron wanted first crack at cleaning up the mess one of his own people had made, and Menard would've asked for the same favor had he been in Barron's seat. But the Louisiana-born former special agent was very happy not to be in Barron's chair. He much preferred hunting spies to running them. The moral lines in his mind surrounding the jobs were cleaner, less blurred. Menard liked keeping the black and white very close together, with as little gray between them as possible.

Rostow's secretary admitted him to the Oval Office and closed the northeastern door behind him. "Come on in, Isaac," Rostow ordered. The couches in the room were mostly full, with only one space left. Cyrus Marshall, director of national intelligence, sat to Rostow's immediate right, and Kathryn Cooke, deputy director of national intelligence, next to him. Rostow's dislike of the woman was no secret. For her to be in the room was a sign of unpleasant things.

Menard had known Cooke for years, their respective jobs requiring them to share information about foreign intelligence services working in the U.S. Menard nodded at the woman. *Should've kept you in the top job at Langley*, Menard thought. *Not tried to give it to an amateur who's still waiting for a vote on the Hill.* Maybe Congress would be smart and reject Rostow's pick, opening up another chance for the president to do the smart thing and tap Clark Barron for CIA director. *Not likely,* Menard thought. *Heaven forbid we should ever give the job to people who actually climbed the ranks.* Menard himself had been appointed by Rostow's predecessor, a man who had valued an appointee's potential political capital less than his time in service and the experience that came with it. But Harrison Stuart had been a very rare breed among chief executives.

"Good evening, everyone," Menard said.

"Good evening, Isaac," Kathy replied. Her voice sounded flat, without emotion, as though the woman was trying to hold something inside.

"I know this is unusual," Rostow said, impatient, "but I had a visit with Igor Galushka an hour ago. He said that the Russian security services had just wrapped up a major counterintelligence op and identified a lot of our intel officers over there. They've ordered all of the following and their families out of the country." The president passed out copies of Galushka's list.

Cooke's expression at seeing the paper confirmed the Russian's accusations. "How bad is it, Kathy?" the president asked. There was no current CIA director and Rostow thought it beneath him to consort with acting directors of any agency. Cooke, the last occupant of Langley's top job, was now his best source of information.

The deputy DNI took her time before answering. She scanned the page several times, matching the names on the paper against the ones in her head. "It looks like they've targeted almost everyone the Agency has in the country, including several under nonofficial cover who don't have diplomatic immunity." She folded the paper and set it down. "This wasn't from a counterintelligence operation. This was Maines giving up every name he had, and CIA will be gutted over there for the next five years, maybe longer."

"We won't even have anyone left over there to try to save the assets that Maines's probably named," Marshall added. "This is a death sentence for every last one of them. By the time we can get our case officers replaced, there won't be anyone over there for them to talk to. Recruiting another stable of assets . . . no telling how long that will take."

Menard nodded. "If my people could do this to the Russians and the moles they have in our government, we could give my counterintelligence units a six-month vacation after. It doesn't get worse than this, Mr. President, and there's no upside." The man sounded morose.

"Oh, no, it does get worse. Kathy, tell Isaac what happened yesterday," Rostow ordered.

She turned her head slightly toward the man, but didn't look up. "Clark Barron brought two analysts to Berlin to help him figure out who assassinated General Stepan Strelnikov, who was one of our key recruitments. They developed a theory that General Arkady Lavrov, the GRU chairman, might have met with Strelnikov in the ruins of the old Soviet missile base at Vogelsang before Strelnikov died. They went out there to see if they could confirm that, and they did. They found evidence that Strelnikov was abducted at the old base commandant's office. Acting on a hunch, they also visited one of the abandoned missile storage bunkers." Cooke opened a binder and passed Menard a satellite photograph of the Vogelsang base, with labels identifying the buildings. "They also gathered evidence that Lavrov's people had set up a test rig for an EMP weapon of some kind, probably as a demonstration for the Syrians who were in town earlier this week."

"That's bad news," Menard noted. "They saw the weapon?"

"No," Cooke admitted. She passed the rest of the binder across the table. Menard opened it and found a stack of the photographs Kyra had taken at the site. "But the test rig was still up and they found generators mounted inside one of the bunkers."

She stopped talking for a moment and Menard looked up at the woman, feeling the weight of some piece of news yet to come. "The analysts were ambushed coming out of the bunker. It looks like Lavrov had sent a team back, possibly to break down the test rig and clean up the site. We don't know. We suspect the men were Spetsnaz. The analysts ran for the woods and the Russians pursued them. Only one of the analysts made it back to the embassy."

Menard looked at Cooke, then the men in the room. Marshall was making no effort to hide his anger. Cooke's poker face was impressive, but Menard could see the woman was holding down sadder emotions that were threatening to break through. "And the other one?"

"He got separated from his partner by a concrete barrier," Cooke reported. "She reports that he was shot by the Russians, how seriously we don't know. He could be dead. He told her to keep running. She evaded capture and delivered her evidence to our people in Berlin."

"You're saying that Russian Special Forces may have killed a U.S. citizen on allied soil?" Menard asked.

"That's what she's saying," Marshall confirmed. "Kidnapped him at best, murdered him at worst."

Menard sat back, amazed and trying to process what he'd heard. "That's insane. Have the Germans checked the site?"

"Yes," Marshall answered. The DNI's voice was quiet. "They didn't find anything beyond some blood on the ground. The generators, the test rig, the evidence of Strelnikov's abduction, it was all gone. The Russians cleaned house. If we didn't have those pictures, we wouldn't be able to prove a thing."

"We still can't prove a thing," Cooke corrected him. "If we made these public, the Russians would just claim everything was staged or Photoshopped. Those wouldn't be enough to nail Lavrov on anything."

"We're not going to go public with them," Rostow announced. All

heads turned toward the president. "Russian soldiers have attacked and possibly murdered a U.S. citizen on friendly soil to cover up some covert action. That's not going to stand, especially not when they're about to cut us open like a trout and probably kill a lot of their own people in the process. We're going to talk to them about it in the language they can understand." Rostow opened a folder on the table and passed a sheet of White House letterhead to the FBI director. "Isaac, as of today, I want the FBI to arrest every Russian on U.S. soil who your people ever dreamed might be an intelligence officer. I'm going to talk to the secretary of state and have him start pressing allied countries to do the same. I expect most of the Europeans won't be much use, but the Brits and the Aussies will probably jump at the chance to kick the Russians where it hurts."

"We'll never be able to hold them," Menard advised. "Most of them will be under diplomatic cover."

"I'll declare them persona non grata as fast as you can lock them up, and I don't care if you put most of their embassy staff behind bars. I want tit for tat on this, and I don't care what stories you have to make up about them to get it done," Rostow countered. "Clark, I want your operators to start disrupting every Russian covert operation they know about, and I don't want them to be subtle about it. I want Arkady Lavrov and anyone else over there who's in bed with him to know why we're dropping the mountain on them."

"Sir, if I may," Marshall interjected. "I don't think escalating the situation is the right approach. We don't have our own Alden Maines fingering every Russian intel officer in their embassy up on Wisconsin Avenue. So if we start trying to arrest them en masse, the ones we don't get will know that their cover is intact. They get bolder in their operations than they are now, and we don't know many other potential Maineses they might already be talking to."

"What good is collecting intelligence if we're going to let our enemies murder our people whenever they get the urge? And when our

own people are just going to run over the border and tear us down whenever they get an itch?" Rostow asked. "Cy, I thought snakes stopped walking on two legs when the dinosaurs died out until I met the Russian president. The Syrians drop nail bombs and nerve gas on their own people, and he vetoes any statement of condemnation coming out of the UN just because he can. He sells guns to every butcher with a bank account and murders journalists at home when they dare to talk about it, and no one can touch him. He plays rough and then rubs our nose in it, and the world gets a happy laugh because we look feckless. Well, enough. I'm not going to sit here and look feckless. Am I understood?"

"Yes, sir," the men replied. Silence ruled the room.

Cooke had said nothing. "Kathy, are you with me on this?" Rostow asked.

Cooke looked at the president, murder in her eyes. "We have our orders, don't we?"

"I'd rather hear that you're behind this. The Russians are about to cripple us, and they might have killed one of our own . . . one of *yours*. I would've thought that you'd want to hit them back."

"More people will die if we do this, you know that," Cooke said. She let the silence hang for a minute, then turned loose. "Mr. President, you don't know what you're saying when you call that missing analyst 'one of my own,'" she told him. "And I don't understand how you plan to define victory with this." She held up the White House letterhead that Rostow had placed on the table. "After the Soviet Union fell, the Russian intelligence services practically fused with the mob. Organized crime is running that country, for all practical purposes, so this operation will look like mob warfare in Chicago in the twenties before it's over. You'll get your tit for tat, but it'll be a one-way ratchet of violence and every turn of the handle will be greased with blood. And, with all due respect, Mr. President, I don't think you've considered how we're going to break the cycle once it starts. The Russians assassinate their dissidents abroad by feeding them radioactive poison, and they just shoot the ones at home. So if you're not prepared to fight in the mud, it would be better to walk away now because the Russian security services like it down there."

No one spoke. Rostow stared at the deputy DNI, frowning, but the woman refused to turn away. He saw pain in her eyes that he didn't understand. It was rare that he let a rebuke go, but an instinct, a voice somewhere in his mind, told him to let this one go.

Rostow finally broke the silence that no one else would break. "Thank you for your views, everyone, but I'm not going to back away from this. I consider it one of my primary duties as president to protect our citizens abroad, and I want the Russians to know that they can't just take out our people for free." He turned to the men in the room. "I expect daily updates on this during my PDB briefings, understood?" There were nods and mutters of assent. The president of the United States closed the file on the table, and the meeting was over.

Rostow walked back to his desk as the subordinate stood. "Kathy, my people will need to coordinate with yours," Menard said, his voice low.

"I'll have the Counterintelligence Center contact them," Cooke promised.

"You knew the analyst who got taken down by the Russians?" Menard asked.

"We were close. Leave it there."

"Sure. I am sorry."

Cooke nodded. "Thank you . . . but right now we need to figure out how to manage the damage control on this," she said. Only old Navy discipline was keeping her mind focused on anything other than her grief. "Between Maines feeding the Russians the names of our assets in Moscow and an open ground war between CIA, the

GRU, and the FSB, maybe the SVR too? We'll be lucky if the Russians don't burn our embassy down."

"Yeah," Menard agreed. "But it'll take my people some time to get moving on this, maybe three days. If you can figure out a way to snuff this fuse by then, I'll be a happy man. If not, you said it—we have our orders."

"I'll call you."

U.S. Embassy
Berlin, Germany

"Nothing?" Kyra asked. She was sitting on the conference room table, hunched over, elbows resting on legs that were hanging over the side. Her stare was vacant and she'd hardly made eye contact with him for more than a day now. She was trying to keep it hidden, but Barron heard the anxiety in her voice. He was strangely relieved to hear it. It was the only emotion the woman had displayed since she'd returned alone from the Vogelsang base.

"The Germans swept Vogelsang over," Barron told her. "The test site you reported was clean. They found a fair amount of blood where Jon went down, but nothing else." It had been eighteen hours since the young woman had outrun the Spetsnaz.

"Did he bleed out?" she asked, her voice as empty as her eyes.

"They can't tell," Barron admitted. "The ground was still wet from the rain . . . they couldn't tell how much blood might've soaked into the dirt."

"No leads off that pistol?"

"I gave it to the Germans. The serial number was filed off and the ballistics on it didn't match anything on file. I'm not surprised. Those Makarovs are the Russian version of the Saturday night special. They're so common that just finding one doesn't narrow down the field of suspects," Barron reported. "And Lavrov is gone. The Bundeskriminalamt says he took off for Moscow this morning . . . took an embassy car to the airport and the plane had diplomatic protection too. Without any physical evidence tying him to a crime, the Germans didn't feel they had enough evidence to even ask the Russian government to hold him in the country, much less withdraw his diplomatic immunity. Your testimony alone wasn't enough to convince them."

"Was Maines with him?"

"The Germans aren't sure. Fifteen men traveled with Lavrov. He drove out to the airport in a caravan . . . one town car and two full-size vans. Maines could've been in one of them. The Russians do disguise work as well as we do," Barron said. "But the Germans couldn't even get a good look inside the hangar, much less the people or cargo he took with him. They don't know who or what Lavrov loaded onto his plane before it took off."

Kyra nodded. "What now?"

Barron sat down next to the younger woman, tempted to put his hand on her back. He refrained, not knowing how she would interpret the gesture. He couldn't tell if she was hiding her emotions, or simply had no energy left to feel anything at all. "We go home."

"What?"

Barron offered her a sheet of paper. "We got a cable from Langley. Maines gave up the name of everyone in Moscow Station, every single one. And the Russians figured out that I was Agency a long time ago, so I can't get in there. POTUS has ordered the FBI and the DNI to hit the Russians back," he said. "The Bureau has an open season on every Russian intel officer on U.S. soil, no bag limit. The DNI wants us to disrupt every Russian covert op we know of. Sounds like POTUS wants his own covert spy war."

He expected an explosion from her, some loud expression of satisfaction. Kyra reacted not at all as she read the paper. "My name isn't on here."

"Makes sense," Barron said with a shrug. "You were never assigned to Moscow Station. What's it matter?" He was sure that he would find the answer disturbing, no matter what it was.

"I could go in. I'm not on Maines's list."

"Not a chance," Barron observed. "Maines knows who you are, and I'm sure Lavrov has your picture from the surveillance cameras at the embassy."

"I was in disguise. I can wear a different one going into Moscow."

Barron shook his head. "Even if you could get in, what's the point? In twenty-four hours, there won't be anyone in Moscow who can help you," he protested. "You couldn't possibly save all of our assets over there by yourself. You'd be lucky if you could get to any one of them before the FSB or Lavrov's people did. The Russians have *thousands* of counterintelligence and security officers. And you don't know the exfiltration plans for any of our assets even if you could get to them."

"We can't just walk," Kyra said, her voice quiet and flat. She lifted her head and looked at the clandestine service director.

"Three years in the Red Cell has messed with your head. You'd be lucky to stay out of Lubyanka or whatever other hole the Russians use these days," Barron said after a moment's thought. "I can't begin to count all of the things that could go wrong. You have no plan, you would have no close support. The losses we're going to take are bad enough. I'm not in the habit of giving the Russians freebies."

"That's exactly what we'd be giving them. We stand back and Lavrov just takes out all of those assets for free," Kyra countered. "And then he'll have a clear road for the next decade to keep giving away stealth technology and nuclear weapons designs and EMP bombs. Maybe the Brits or the Israelis will shut some of it down, but they don't have the resources to go after the GRU everywhere on the planet."

"Nice argument. That's not why you want to go."

"No, it's not," Kyra admitted after a long silence, her voice quiet.

"So why?"

The woman turned her head away from the senior officer. "Lavrov and those Spetsnaz soldiers are the only ones who know what happened to Jon." Kyra stared down at the floor, then looked back up at Barron. "I know that the mission always comes first," she admitted. "I know that you would never approve a mission like this just to find out whether Jon's still alive. But he saved my life, last year, in Venezuela. I infiltrated that base where the Iranians were building their bomb. But their security came out, sweeping the buildings, and I was about to get overrun. Jon was up in the hills and he held off a whole regiment of soldiers with a sniper rifle, one of those big .50-caliber monsters that you use to destroy trucks and equipment." Kyra's gaze was distant, like the memory she was describing was playing out on the wall in front of her. She smiled for the first time in days, amused at something only she could see. "He refused to shoot anybody . . . made a good show of killing jeeps, though. Steam and oil spraying everywhere. But he wouldn't kill anyone. He'd done that before, in Iraq during the war, and it still haunted him, so he refused to do it again. Probably saved the president from an international mess, too . . . but he could handle that rifle . . . ended up in a snipers' gunfight a day later with an Iranian Special Forces soldier. Jon was amazing."

The personal movie of her memory ended and Kyra's focus returned to the room. She looked at Barron, focused on his face again. "I have to know what happened to him. If they did kill Jon and we don't try something, they'll never pay for it, and . . ." She stopped to force back a sob. It took her much longer than she'd expected, almost a minute. Barron refused to break the silence. ". . . and how am I supposed to live with that?"

"You'll learn."

"How can you know that?"

Barron smiled, rueful. "I was chief of Moscow Station years ago. You ever hear how my tour ended?" Kyra shook her head. "I was running a night op with one of my officers, Manuela Saconi. I was driving. We were going to use a jack-in-the-box so she could bail out to meet an asset. The FSB had a bug up its butt about something and we drew three cars that night. One of them was aggressive . . . got right up on our rear quarter. The driver had to swerve for I-don't-know-what, turned right into us, and spun me out. Our car rolled, I don't know, five or six times. Ellie died on the scene, massive head trauma, even with her seat belt and airbag. I ended up in a Russian hospital, concussion, major laceration on my scalp. They found the jack-in-the-box in the wreckage. Kathy Cooke's predecessor worked out a deal with the FSB to keep it all quiet. The Agency recalled me and the Kremlin never declared me persona non grata and made sure the local news never covered the story. Ellie got shipped home and was buried before I ever left the hospital in Moscow. But I was furious. I wanted the Russians to apologize, to admit they'd screwed up. Took me a long time, but I realized that wasn't going to happen. I came to see it was for the best . . . that took longer. It's a funny game. The other side screws up and we help them save face, because if we don't, they'll do it anyway by coming after our people and making a big show when they catch one."

"But if Jon's alive—"

"If he's alive, you'll never get near him," Barron told her, his voice soft. "You'll never even get the Russians to admit they've got him. They'd be confessing to the illegal rendition and detention of a U.S. citizen, not that we have the moral high ground on that score anymore. They'd probably kill him and you both before they'd admit it if you did find out he was still alive. So you go in and you might die sooner than you think."

Kyra turned her head away from him. "Even if I can't find him, somebody needs to work the EMP problem. We need to find out where it is, where it's going, how Lavrov is going to deliver it—"

"That's not our problem—"

"Yes, it is. Jon was the one who figured out that Lavrov is selling strategic technologies. We're the only ones who have the whole picture. Sure, the Israelis might catch the EMP coming into Syria, but Lavrov will still be running loose. He'll keep selling the tech and there will always be a buyer out there—"

"And how do you think you're going to stop the head of the GRU from running a global covert op?" Barron pronounced the letters of the acronym slow and precise. "That's like one Russian case officer trying to take on the whole CIA."

"Maybe, but when you think about it, we do that all the time. We're all really on our own when we're on the street anyway. We plan things out, talk through radios, sometimes tell each other to go this way or that, but when the plan comes apart, it's one officer against a whole country, running for a safe house," Kyra observed, not really talking to him. "I've always made it to the safe house. I can do it again."

Barron frowned. "You want to be station chief Moscow that bad?"

"You can keep the title. I just want to get reimbursed for my travel expenses."

Barron smiled. It was a small joke, but he would take whatever emotion he could get from her. "You're insane. You really are."

"No, I'm just motivated. But you can demote me when I get home if it makes you feel better."

"Oh, you're not the one who'll have to worry about getting de-moted," he said. "If you make it out, we'll both be heroes. If you don't, the president will execute me in the Langley courtyard for let-ting you go."

That earned him a small laugh from the woman. "So . . . dead or heroes. Isn't that what we really signed up for when we took this job anyway?"

"Here's the safe house," Barron said, his finger pointing to a street on the Moscow map. "We just set this one up a few months ago, so if there's one that Maines doesn't have on some list, it's that one. Case the place before you go in. Don't assume it's clean. If it is, chances are good you'll have the place as long as you want it, but sanitize the place first so the locals won't find anything sensitive in case they do show up on short notice."

"And if it's not clean?" Kyra asked.

"Then you turn around and you come home. I want you to play this one by the rules all the way. But if it comes apart, whatever you do, don't run for the embassy. The FSB has the place under surveillance at all times. You'll never get to the front gate if they're looking for you."

Kyra stared at the map, repeating the address that Barron had scribbled on it until she'd etched the Russian words in her mind. "Any ideas about which assets I should try to contact when I get in-country?"

Barron held out his hand, a folded note between his fingers. Kyra took it, unfolded it. The list was short, scribbled out by hand in cryptic notes on a sheet of flash paper, nitrocellulose that she could immolate in a fraction of a second with the Zippo lighter that Barron had set on the table. "That's it?"

"That's all the ones that I'm going to give you," Barron replied. "They're the only ones inside the GRU who I think would be in a position to know about any sales of strategic technologies that Lavrov is brokering." There were only three names, but it was, at that moment, possibly the most sensitive document the CIA had in its possession. Even with Maines in their hands, the Russian government still would have murdered anyone in its path to retrieve it without a moment's thought. "If we're lucky, he might have forgotten or withheld some names, and I'm not about to help him fill in any of the blanks. But if he copied everything onto a thumb drive instead of relying on his memory, chances are pretty good that you'll never get near any of them before Lavrov takes them out. So don't try to contact any of them unless you're ready to bet your life that Lavrov's people aren't watching. You take no chances at all, you got me?"

"I should have a few more possibles, in case I can't reach these," Kyra protested. "The Russians can't watch everyone."

"Moscow Rules—you assume that they can. You won't have the time or the resources to focus on anyone else anyway. I don't know how many names Maines might be giving up, but we have to assume he's going to give up all of them. There's no way to even know in what order he might go after them, so we have to assume he'll want to take them all down as fast as he can. The real question is whether the FSB will play ball. If they do, you'll never get to any of them. If they don't, you might have a short window."

"Why wouldn't the FSB cooperate?" Kyra asked. "They handle counterintelligence in Russia."

Barron nodded. "They do, but the FSB director is Anatoly Grigoriyev, and he and Lavrov hate each other. Grigoriyev was KGB back in the eighties, Lavrov was Soviet army intelligence and they were both stationed in Berlin when the Wall fell. They stepped on each other's toes plenty in the aftermath. It's an old professional rivalry turned personal. There's nothing either man would love more than to get the other kicked out of the Kremlin."

Kyra grunted quietly. "That might explain why Lavrov lured Strelnikov to Berlin. He was Lavrov's boy, so it would make sense that Lavrov wouldn't want Grigoriyev to find out about that particular breach until he'd solved the problem."

"Agreed," Barron replied. "That sounds to me like Lavrov doesn't want the FSB to know what he's doing. A major GRU operation to take down Maines's entire list of our assets in short order would be impossible to keep quiet. The FSB would hear about it and someone would start asking questions. That's probably your only prayer of getting to any of these people. Lavrov might be taking his time, working down the list nice and slow so he doesn't aggravate Grigoriyev more than necessary. But if Lavrov is looking to plug his own leaks first, these people could be at the top of the list."

Kyra tried to find some weakness in his logic and failed. "Yeah," she agreed. "And if Lavrov hates Grigoriyev that much, he could get a lot of leverage over Grigoriyev by releasing the rest of Maines's list to the Kremlin once his own holes are plugged. Watching the GRU identify moles in the FSB would probably finish him."

"True," Barron agreed. "And since Lavrov would be the one who cleaned house, he would probably get veto power over the next pick for FSB director after Grigoriyev takes up residence in the gulag. And then there would be no reason not to wrap up everyone on the bottom of the list at once. So all of these people might be dead anyway a lot sooner than we thought." There was bitterness in his voice.

These were his people, Kyra realized. *We're going to lose all of these people on his watch.* She wondered how many of the Russian assets had been recruited when Barron had been the Moscow station chief.

The room fell silent. Kyra picked up the list, read it through three times, then opened the Zippo and spun the flint, igniting the tiny fire. She touched it to the flash paper and it vaporized before she could even open her fingers.

"It's oh-five-hundred. You should get moving," Barron advised.

"Just give me a minute, okay?"

"Don't be long."

Barron marched out of the room. Kyra leaned forward, resting her folded arms on the table, and she laid her head on them, suddenly more tired than she could ever remember being. *You should have stayed with me, Jon, stayed behind the wall*, she thought. *I need your help, old man.* A flood of anxiety rushed into her chest. She fought it down, but the horrifying thought that maybe, just maybe, she was wrong about everything refused to leave her.

Kyra evicted the thoughts, ignored the angry doubts in her chest, and held herself together long enough to fetch her bag from the hotel. Ten minutes after, she was sitting next to Barron in a SUV, pulling out onto the road for the airport. Kyra watched the Berlin embassy recede and wondered again whether she shouldn't give up the fight.

Meeting Room of the Security Council of the Russian Federation
The Kremlin Senate Building
Moscow, Russia

There were seats for more than twenty-five around the long table, but the real governing quorum numbered far fewer and most of them were not present today.

Anatoly Maksimovich Grigoriyev had never pined for the old Soviet Union, but the room had always struck the director of the Federal Security Service (FSB) as too ostentatious, a showpiece that sent the wrong message to the Russian people when the cameras were on. National security was not a subject to be discussed in a place like this. *Too soft*, he thought, *too indulgent.* The people should have seen them meet in a war room, a Spartan place with few comforts that would portray an image of sacrifice and resolve. The floor was dark wood with a geometric parquet pattern running through it. Square columns of dark marble topped with gold capitals stood out against the brown and cream colors that dominated the rest of the room. The front of the room displayed the Russian coat of arms, the two-headed dragon, gold with a red shield mounted high on the wall and flanked on each side by the country's flags. The crowning irony of the place was an ornate chandelier above the table that could have been at home in a czar's palace.

But the cameras were not on, not this time. There were four men in the room and the subject of the meeting was not for anyone's ears but theirs. The president of the Russian Federation, a former FSB director himself, sat at the table's head. The foreign minister and Arkady Lavrov sat to his right. Grigoriyev was quite sure that his position alone on the left side was symbolic.

"Good afternoon, friends," the president said. Polite responses were uttered. "I believe that we are here at your request, Anatoly?"

"Yes, but I don't need to tell any of you why I have asked to meet, I am sure," Grigoriyev replied.

"Then there is nothing to discuss, Anatoly," Lavrov said. "The GRU does not answer—"

"The FSB is responsible for the internal security of the state," Grigoriyev continued, cutting Lavrov off midsentence. "We perform the counterintelligence mission on Russian soil. This is not in dispute. Therefore, I want to know why I was not informed that the GRU had a source inside the CIA that provided a list of all CIA officers currently in Moscow."

"Obviously, for reasons of operational security," Lavrov replied. "Our source is a sensitive one. We could not risk exposing him by sharing the information with the FSB in advance of the announcement."

"There should have been no announcement without consulting me first!" Grigoriyev protested. "And I want to know why our foreign minister cooperated with Arkady in withholding that information while he instructed our ambassador to Washington to tell the U.S. president that we would be expelling all of those officers from our soil." In truth, Grigoriyev already knew the answer. The foreign minister was a Lavrov protégé. Grigoriyev simply wanted to see whether the man would have the good sense to appear embarrassed that he'd allowed the GRU chairman to co-opt his ministry so easily. It seemed he did. The minister avoided Grigoriyev's gaze and remained silent.

The president came to his defense. "Anatoly, I think the greater question here is why the GRU had to do the FSB's duty?"

"Are you accusing me of incompetence?" Grigoriyev countered. "You were the FSB director once, you understand that the CIA is not a club of amateurs. Even in the old days, when we were the KGB and recruited Americans abroad, we never had a source who gave up so much at once. I do not know who this source is, but I doubt very much that Arkady recruited him. No, this is not incompetence on the part of my people. I think it is merely good fortune, a volunteer who came to Arkady's doorstep."

"That does not matter," Lavrov said, dismissive. "How the man became our asset does not change the fact that such a source must be protected. You have seen the list of people we have expelled. You know that everyone you suspected was a CIA officer was on it, and many more who you did not."

"Protected?" Grigoriyev snorted in derision. "Do you truly imagine that the Americans do not know exactly who your source is now? And if you are wrong about him being a genuine defector?" Grigoriyev asked. "How have you verified this source and his information? What if he is lying? Do you realize what you have done if this all proves to be falsehoods?"

"It is not—"

"Open the file to me so that I can verify that for myself," Grigoriyev demanded.

Lavrov exhaled in mock exasperation and shook his head in a display of equally false sympathy. "I think that you are simply concerned that you were made to look the fool, Anatoly," he said. "The GRU has earned the glory that you think should belong to the FSB and now you want a share of something you haven't earned."

"What I want is the opportunity for my people to fulfill their duty to protect the *Rodina* and her interests," Grigoriyev retorted. He turned toward the Russian president. "How can we be sure that this asset was not a dangle or a double agent if we cannot see the file? If that is the case, then expelling all of those Americans will have been a terrible blunder—"

"How so?" the president asked, clearly not interested in the answer.

"The Americans will surely respond in kind. They will expel any number of our people from the United States and disrupt our operations there. If the names that Arkady was given were not, in fact, all CIA officers and merely some easily replaced consular officers, then we could suffer more damage than the Americans—"

"That will not be the case," Lavrov assured the president. "My asset's information is reliable. By tomorrow evening, the CIA will not have a single officer left on Moscow's soil. They know that we know their identities and none of them will risk arrest and imprisonment by staying. Yes, they will certainly expel some of our people from their country, but not so many. With no comparable asset, they could only guess at who our officers are. Unless they are prepared to expel our entire delegation, which would be unthinkable except in war, whatever damage they inflict on us will be less than what we have done to them, so we will be able to reconstitute our operations more quickly. We will have a significant advantage in intelligence operations for at least a decade to come."

"I must agree, Anatoly," the Russian president said. "Do not let your old competition with Arkady blind you to the opportunity that this source presented us. The information that Arkady has given us is truly impressive. We could not wait."

"*We* could not wait?" Grigoriyev said. "Then you knew also?"

"Of course."

"This is foolishness," Grigoriyev groused, the winds sucked neatly from his sails.

"Such sour grapes, Anatoly." Lavrov smiled. "For now, I think it would be helpful to us all if the FSB could ensure that all of the Americans on the list have left the *Rodina*, and I would consider it the greatest of personal favors if you would inform me when their exodus is complete."

I am not a bootlicker, like the foreign minister there, Grigoriyev raged quietly in his mind. *You would throw me crumbs and say I should be grateful for them?*

The FSB director shook his head in disgust. The meeting really had been a formality after all. He should have seen it. Lavrov and his lackey would not have expelled so many Americans without the president's approval. The fact that they had not told him in advance told Grigoriyev where he stood with this group. The path to the president's chair always had gone through the FSB and its predecessor, the KGB. Now Lavrov's good fortune had given the GRU chairman a way to steer that river out of its course.

How to steer it back? Grigoriyev asked himself. He did not have an answer now, he admitted, but a solution would present itself. It always had.

Office of the Director of the Directorate of Operations
Seventh Floor, Old Headquarters Building
CIA headquarters

"You are not serious," Cooke said. Years of practice had taught her to keep her tone calm and measured, especially when the world was burning, but she wanted to scream at her subordinate, tell him in profane terms what she thought about the man's admission. Instead, she gripped the secure phone in her hand and tried to crush it, giving her anger somewhere to go besides her mouth.

"You know better," Barron replied. "She wants to know what happened to Jon. You and I would want to do the same."

"Wanting to do something and actually doing it are very, very different things," Cooke observed. "And the president has ordered everyone out. I'm going to have to tell him that we're actually sending somebody in. He won't take it well." She was being overly polite. She would be fortunate if the man didn't throw the Oval Office Churchill bust at her.

"Not to split hairs, but he ordered everyone on Lavrov's list out," Barron replied. "She's not on the list. And she's got cover for action . . . we really do need someone to sanitize that last safe house. We didn't have enough time to clean them out before everyone had to leave, and that's not a lie."

"What if Maines gave those up to Lavrov?" Cooke asked.

"He might have," Barron admitted. "I've got the Counterintelligence Center checking to see whether he went hunting through those files."

"That's something," Cooke conceded. "Okay, she's in Moscow. The question is what we can do to support her?"

"Not much."

"This isn't a good idea," Cooke observed.

"Probably not," Barron finally conceded. "But it's time we stopped being reactive and started getting ahead of the game. Defense is the art of losing slow, and Maines and Lavrov have been in charge from the start of this. At the very least, we need to start throwing some sand in their gears and slowing them down while we figure out how to get in front of this. If there's one thing Stryker is good at, it's wrecking the best-laid plains."

Cooke didn't know whether to nod or shake her head.

The "Aquarium" — old GRU headquarters

Sokolov's secure phone rang. He answered it, waiting the few seconds for the encryption to go live. *"Ya slushayu vas."*

"Anton Semyonovich." It was Lavrov's voice.

"General," Sokolov answered, "I stand ready at your service."

"I have the first name for you," Lavrov told him. "When can you move on him?"

"At first light, General. The men are here. We will need a few hours to plan the operation. We do not want to give the man any opportunity to slip the net."

"Very good." Lavrov gave him the traitor's name and where he worked. Sokolov's eyes went wide. The man's office was not a thousand yards away. "Report to me when he is in your custody, and then when you have resolved the matter. I will then have another name for you."

"Understood, General." The line died and Sokolov replaced the headset on its cradle. He stared at the name. *And why did* you *turn against the* Rodina? he wondered. He'd studied traitors and their motivations, the better to do his work. There were always so many reasons, but so few noble ones. *I pray that you are a noble one*, he thought. *Perhaps then you will see your death as a fitting end to a life well lived.*

CHAPTER SIX

She'd spent the flight declining the flight attendant's polite questions regarding food and beverages using only hand signals. Kyra couldn't understand what the flight crew was saying and didn't want to make a request for English that would've announced to the entire plane that she was an American. She honestly did not know whether any of the people around her worked for the Russian security services and the case officer decided that now was as good a time as any to start being paranoid.

She looked out the window as the plane began to descend through the clouds. Moscow looked like any other city at night from the air. Kyra indulged her imagination for a few seconds and let herself think she was landing at Dulles. She and Jon would disembark, say good-bye in the baggage claim. A short walk to the parking garage, load her bag into her truck, and she would be home in Leesburg within a half hour—

—but Jon was not here. The pilot's announcement in Russian to prepare for landing fully destroyed the illusion without mercy, not least because Kyra didn't understand a single word.

A sharp wind struck the aircraft sideways and the plane yawed hard just feet off the runway. The pilot held the altitude until he could straighten out the nose. Kyra inhaled deeply when the plane's tires touched the concrete. *Not the best start*, she thought.

She was relieved that she was alone. Half of counterintelligence work was making connections between people and places, and Kyra was free of any here. She was a completely random element as far as the Russians were concerned. If they targeted her simply because she was an American, they would break themselves trying to find any clue that connected her to any of the case officers or assets Maines had revealed. There was nothing for them to connect, and that was the only way to play the game against the FSB, the GRU, and all the rest. The CIA had learned through sad experience that mistakes were small when the Russians were playing at their best, and one could never assume that the Russians were at less than their best. That was the first of the cardinal Moscow Rules.

   1 Assume nothing.
   2 Never go against your gut.
   3 Everyone is potentially under opposition control.
   4 Don't look back; you are never completely alone.
   5 Go with the flow, blend in.
   6 Vary your pattern and stay within your cover.
   7 Lull them into a sense of complacency.
   8 Pick the time and place for action.
   9 Keep your options open.
  10 Don't harass the opposition.

She had no doubt that she would be breaking several of those rules before this was over, and she was sure she needn't have bothered learning the last one. Harass the Russians? She couldn't imagine what case officer would be so stupid even with a full CIA in support to pull them out of trouble. But someone had. Rules were never made until someone had done something that called them into being. Kyra wondered whether the FSB had bashed the offender's face against the asphalt to teach him some humility. She wouldn't have faulted them.

The customs officer was disinterested in the American woman to the point of incivility. The lack of attention, forged documents, and her light disguise—this one changing her into a dark redhead, flat-chested, with wide hips and a round face—granted her admittance into the country without getting called into a private room for a special interview.

Kyra had settled on her method of reaching the safe house before leaving Berlin. Drivers for hire were lined up near the rental car desks. She'd considered one. She didn't read Cyrillic and the Russians' refusal to post English highway signs or obey their own traffic laws was going to make navigation problematic. But the Moscow Rules decreed that *everyone is potentially under opposition control* and she wasn't going to give herself to the FSB or the GRU so quickly. The embassy would have its own fleet of vehicles, but improvisation was going to be the order of the day for this operation and having a car the Russians didn't associate with diplomats would prove useful.

The Russian government allowed foreigners staying less than six months to use their own countries' driver's licenses so long as they had a notarized Russian translation attached. Both were forgeries. The Russian police were known to stop drivers here for no reason at all, but she could risk that. An expert would have been hard-pressed to detect fake documents of this quality. No local traffic cop would manage it standing on the road with his own eyes the only tools at his disposal.

The Volkswagen Tiguan was the last SUV available at the Avis rental desk, and the most expensive transport they had, but Kyra was sure that Langley wasn't going to quibble over prices. Barron's checkbook was open for this trip, which was no small favor. The Tiguan was going to swallow petrol like a parched bull drinking water from the trough on a hot Virginia day, but if Kyra was going to risk surveillance and detention by one of the most efficient intelligence services in the world, she wanted a car with four-wheel drive and as much horsepower as she could buy. She'd been chased before. She knew better than to lose one of those races by choosing an underpowered car that was useless off the paved roads.

She'd memorized the major roads leading into the city on the map in her pack, but she paid for the GPS unit anyway. She didn't know whether the FSB could track it, but if her memory failed her, she wasn't going to spend the next week driving the Moscow streets, hoping to stumble across the safe house. To be fair, that level of incompetence might actually convince them that she was not a spy.

Kyra dropped the handle on her rolling bag, tossed it into the passenger seat, and started the Tiguan. She put her hand on the drive lever and pulled it down, then looked at her dashboard to make sure the truck was in reverse.

The gauges were labeled in Cyrillic.

This is not a good idea.

Kyra exhaled in exasperation as she heard Jon chiding her in her mind. That warning had become his habit and she supposed that he'd never been wrong, technically, despite her successes. Even fools were owed a few victories, she supposed, but she was finally coming to see the truth of his adage that bravery was no substitute for wisdom. If there was any operation that would settle the question, it would be this one. The Russian military may have degraded in the years after the Soviet Union had dissolved, but the security services never had. They had changed names and shapes, allegiances and org charts . . . no, in truth they had *become* the Kremlin, with only the blurred lines between them and organized crime to confuse that fact.

You shouldn't have come here, Jon's voice told her.

God hates a coward, she told him yet again in her mind.

Jon hadn't been a coward. *Gonna make you proud, old man,* she decided.

Kyra put the truck in gear and drove out of the rental lot onto the airport road.

A CIA safe house
Moscow, Russia

The safe house was twenty-five miles from the airport, but Kyra's surveillance detection route had taken four hours to drive. She'd watched the safe house for another two before deciding it was unwatched and undisturbed, but she was still worried the FSB was simply more patient than she was.

She'd cursed in amazement when she saw it. The last safe house she'd seen had been a small apartment in a Caracas slum. This one was a mansion by Moscow standards. A hand-cut stone walkway curved around on a trim green lawn with shade trees and streetlamps for illumination. The exterior of the house was yellow with white brick at the corners and Roman columns that reached up two stories at the front door. A two-car garage connected at a right angle on the side. A black iron fence and high bushes surrounded the property. The estate would not have been out of place in one of the nicer neighborhoods of Loudoun County in northern Virginia, where she lived almost five thousand miles to the west. Kyra was sure that she'd driven off course somewhere, not believing the Agency's largesse extended so far, until the front gate accepted the code Barron had given her in Berlin and moved aside for her truck.

How do they maintain cover on this place? She knew better than to ask such questions aloud back at headquarters.

She parked the Tiguan in the garage and closed that door by hand, hiding the vehicle, then pulled her luggage out of the passenger seat and entered the house by the mudroom door. The building was mostly hidden from the street by darkness, distance, and the bushes, but Barron had counseled her to stay indoors anyway.

The door leading into the house from the mudroom was locked. It looked nondescript, but the locks were heavy and the door and frame both were reinforced with steel.

There was a keypad by the door, twelve black squares with no labels. She pressed a button and the squares lit up, each with a number assigned in random order. No doubt the numbers would be in a different order the next time she came in. The system was designed to prevent anyone from deciphering the entry code by watching the user enter it from a distance and guessing the numbers by following the movement of the hand.

Kyra entered the second code that Barron had given her and the door clicked open.

The mudroom connected with the kitchen, long shadows stretching out on the hardwood floor as the sun moved down behind the bush line. Kyra stopped and listened, not moving for almost a full minute and hearing nothing. She found it strange, but she was grateful that the safe house would be empty. Otherwise, some caretaker would have asked her to *nazovite sebya* with some Russian pass phrase she would have mangled even if Barron had taught it to her hours before.

The Caracas safe house had been a tiny, ugly little space, barely eight hundred square feet with old furnishings, rusting gas heaters, and mold growing in the corners. This house was enormous by comparison, five thousand square feet spread across three levels, the entire space clean, the furnishings modern. A library on the main floor was stocked with both Russian and English books, and the kitchen had better equipment than Kyra's own home in Virginia. The refrigerator was empty, but the pantry and cabinets had enough canned goods to keep her fed for weeks.

Dinner was instant polenta, which she found in the pantry and cooked on the stove. Kyra was no brilliant chef, but her mother had insisted that her daughter could not call herself a proper southern girl if she didn't know how to make a bowl of grits. It was likely the only taste of home she would get here, but it did nothing to soothe her dark spirits. There was an unsettled feeling in the quiet darkness that the comfort food could not dispel and Kyra wondered whether the spirits of dead case officers or assets might not be keeping her company. There seemed to be voices in her head that were not her own.

The light outside had only minutes left before dying and the house seemed to be closing in, getting smaller as the rooms she could see from the table grew darker. She had kept the lights to a minimum, lest the house attract attention, but now she found herself reconsidering the tactic. Kyra had been alone on missions before, never minded it, but none had ever felt like this. Jon had always been at the other end of a phone if she'd needed him. Not tonight.

That's not true, is it? she thought.

Kyra pushed herself away from the table, leaving the dirty bowl and fork to dry, and wandered to the staircase. She walked through the empty hall and found what she was looking for behind the last door on the left, also reinforced. The encrypted phone was stored in a cabinet with a digital lock along with other tools of her trade.

It was a satellite phone, like the one she'd used in Venezuela when that mission had gone sour, but a newer model. She assembled the antenna and worked out which window to point it where it could find a U.S. satellite hung in geostationary orbit. She worked out the interface and began to dial.

The call connected, encrypted, and the phone on the other end rang four times. She knew that no one was going to pick it up. Finally, the Agency voicemail system took over.

"This is Jon. Leave a message and I might get back to you, but probably not. I hate phones and the odds are good that you're not important enough to make me want to use one. So either come see me in person or I'm going to assume whatever you want isn't worth my time. If you were able to track down my number, you can find my vault too."

She'd pestered him into recording a message and that was the one he'd settled on, his own bit of revenge on her coercion.

The answering service sounded the usual tone, and Kyra had to suppress a laugh, lest it be recorded for posterity. She wondered if the Agency or the National Archives kept the voicemails of officers killed in the line of duty.

She called his phone again and listened to the man's voice a second time, smiling as she heard the familiar exasperation in his voice. Kyra disconnected without saying anything, then called a third time, committing his voice to memory as best she could. Jon's dismissive insult to humanity ended once again, the tone sounded, and Kyra cut the call and powered down the unit.

The depression invaded her spirit again as soon as the LED display went black, leaving her sitting in the near darkness. Kyra knew how to fight that, a lesson she'd learned over the last few years.

She opened herself up to anger, letting the hatred for the Russians inside steel her spine. Lavrov was the reason Jon wasn't here, and only he knew whether her mentor was alive or dead and whether an EMP was bound for Syria. Therefore, Kyra needed to connect with someone inside Lavrov's operation.

The flash paper was inside the desk under the computer. Kyra retrieved the notepad, made her way back to the kitchen, and took her seat at the table again. It was two minutes' work to re-create the list of asset names, contact methods, and locations that she'd memorized in Berlin.

She stared down at the asset list. There were three names.

Adolf Viktorovich Topilin
Major Elizaveta Igoryevna Puchkov
Colonel Semyon Petrovich Zhitomirsky

Who do I contact first?
Adolf Viktorovich Topilin, Foundation electrical engineer. Maybe one of the EMP designers? If so, he could confirm its existence . . . maybe

even provide the specs. She was impressed that Barron and his people had been able to recruit a weapons engineer. After the Agency had lost Adolf Tolkachev a few decades before, the Russians had put the screws to every other engineer with access to sensitive designs. The FSB and GRU still knew how to instill fear in the masses when they needed to. Lavrov's engineers inside the Foundation likely wanted to avoid the very appearance of talking to foreigners, lest the security services imagine they were taking a recruitment pitch.

It was full dark outside now, the only light on in the house being the small lamp suspended above the kitchen table. The house creaked somewhere, but Kyra refused to let paranoia creep into her thoughts. If the Russians were going to come in, they would not be subtle about it. She cleared her mind, then stared at the list again, trying to order her thoughts.

Major Elizaveta Igoryevna Puchkov, GRU liaison to the Foundation, logistics specialist. Logistics for what? Kyra wondered. *Acquiring resources for the Foundation? Or helping the Foundation move its cargo around? Both?* Barron had not told her. She considered calling him on the secure sat phone upstairs to ask, but decided against it. If Lavrov had moved an EMP to Berlin for a demonstration, Puchkov would be the best one in a position to know . . . and if Lavrov had flown Jon or Maines back from Berlin, she'd be the best chance to find that out too.

Even if she did know, what could Kyra do about it? What good was information if she couldn't act on it? She cursed herself for going down that path and set that pessimism aside. *Worry about that when the time comes.*

Colonel Semyon Petrovich Zhitomirsky, GRU budget director. Always follow the money, Kyra thought. The money trail could tell an analyst more about what an organization was doing than anything else. Zhitomirsky might not have specifics about any one project, but knowing where the rubles were flowing could at least point Kyra in the right direction. The moneymen always knew where the bodies were buried, even if they didn't know which exact bodies they were. *Save him for last*, she thought. The other two seemed more likely to have specific information she could put to immediate use. She would have to search the computer upstairs, see if the encrypted hard drive contained any information that would help her decide.

Which one to start? Kyra wondered.

Utilisa Lermontov Road
Peredelkino, Moscow Oblast, Russia

Adolf Viktorovich Topilin had stolen his wife's car for this trip. She would be furious when he returned, but her red Ford Mondeo was faster than his own humble Lada Priora. How he would explain to her that they were leaving the country, not to return, he didn't know. She didn't know about his treason and Topilin wasn't sure that Nina would even come with him once he told her. In fact, he believed that she would call the FSB once he told her. He'd considered not telling her at all, just leaving her to the FSB when they came to the house. But he did still love her, even if her affections were far more tenuous than his. He had to give her the chance to come with him, if only to settle his own conscience.

One problem at a time, he told himself. His need for more time outweighed the suffering she would lay on him, and he spurred the car along the forest road much faster than was safe. The trees had combined into a single brown wall that he hardly saw out of the corner of his eye. If a boar or deer crossed into the road, his brakes would not stop the car in time to save the car or the animal. He sped on anyway, but it seemed self-defeating. The faster he went, the more time was stretching out, like Einstein had predicted. The closer he came to the dacha, the farther away it seemed to be and the trip never ended.

He pressed on. Topilin needed to burn the contents of the box and he couldn't do it safely at home. The dacha was the only place for it.

The news of the government's decision to evict so many diplomats from the country by itself had been frightful. Such things were rare and usually reserved for spies caught in the very act of plying their trade. It was not possible the FSB had caught so many CIA officers at once. How, then, had they decided who to expel? Were they all spies? Was the Kremlin merely lashing out at random? It seemed unlikely. There had been no rumors among his GRU coworkers of any kind of confrontation with the Main Enemy, as they still called the U.S., that would lead to mass expulsion. A secret source, then? Some GRU asset who had fingered the CIA's forces in the *Rodina*? And if such a source could access that kind of information, could he not also identify the moles working for the Agency?

That concern had cost Topilin his night's sleep, and his wife had questioned whether he was contracting the flu. He'd denied it, not wanting her to pressure him to stay home from work. Absence might create suspicion, would it not? So he'd risen at the usual hour, trying to hide his anxiety by speaking to his wife as little as possible. He'd shaved, showered, consumed a breakfast of sausage, black bread, and blacker tea. Then his telephone had sounded . . . not his cell phone, but the landline in his home.

"*Ya slushayu vas,*" he'd answered.

"You are Adolf Viktorovich Topilin?" the voice had asked him.

"*Da.*"

"They are coming for you," the voice had said. "The GRU knows that you are a traitor. You will leave now if you value your life." The call had ended there, with Topilin looking at the phone, terror in his soul like he'd never known in all his life. He'd gathered every bit of equipment the CIA had ever given him, thrown it into a box, and loaded it all into the trunk of his wife's car while ignoring her fearful questions and protests.

Topilin pressed the pedal harder and the Mondeo protested, but obeyed.

The irony was that the Mondeo would have been beyond his means to buy had he not been a traitor to his country. His CIA handler had warned him against spending the money and making a show of affluence that he could not explain away, but Adolf Topilin's wife was a relentless woman in her tastes. She had never been happy with the salary the GRU paid him, no matter how high he had climbed. The Russian military was not a generous employer except to its highest leaders and Topilin knew he would never reach those exalted heights. He lacked the personal connections to get such promotions and appointments. In the end, he knew that he would have to leave his job or find some other income to satisfy Nina, or she might leave him for some wealthier man.

But he was an electrical engineer for the Foundation for Advanced Research, had been since its founding, and the Central Intelligence Agency had been happy to give him that outside income in exchange for information. Three years of deliveries to his handler combined with compound interest had given him a sizable escrow account. He'd started tapping into the money in the vain hope that some spending would pacify Nina, but she was insatiable. The more he spent, the more the money fed her tastes. Even buying the dacha here had only quieted her for a year before she had started to demand better furnishings and Western electronics for it. He hadn't wanted to buy it. Topilin knew that he could never explain it away to his superiors. Peredelkino had been a colony for Russia's cultural elites, the writers and poets in the years after the war with the Nazis. Boris Pasternak, one of the Rodina's greatest poets and author of *Doctor Zhivago* had lived here. Now the writers had left for more affordable boroughs and Peredelkino had become a country retreat for the bankers and businessmen. But Nina had her heart, or her avarice, set on this neighborhood and the social status that it would confer.

Another turn and Topilin finally slowed the car. The driveway was to the left and finally he saw the dacha. Two stories, a small, renovated barn with a short deck on the second level. He hated the building, and knew that Nina had no real love for it, only for what it represented. And Topilin had never been able to accept the truth that Nina would leave him when she met some other man better able to pay for the life she really wanted. He had learned in the last hour that loyalty bought was not loyalty at all.

But all that was irrelevant at the moment. What mattered was that the dacha had a wood stove. He would burn everything, then retrieve from the charred metal any devices the fire couldn't consume and throw them into the woods along the drive back at random intervals.

Topilin stopped the Mondeo, killed the engine, and pressed the button to open the trunk. He dismounted and scrambled around to the back to fetch the box. He cursed when he saw the contents spilled out across the carpeting. He grabbed for the small digital camera and the notebook of dead-drop and signal site instructions and tossed them back into the box. It took him a few seconds of searching to find the Short-Range Agent Communications (SRAC) transmitter where it had slid behind the can of kerosene that he'd brought. The onetime pads, the shortwave radio, demodulator unit, the USB thumb drives . . . did he have everything? He swore at himself for not making a list before leaving, and then wondered how he could be so stupid as to think that such a list would have been a good idea. An inventory of equipment used for treason would have been a fine present for the security services—

"I must confess, Adolf Viktorovich, that is a very fine car. However did you afford it?"

Topilin spun around and saw the man standing behind him. He was middle-aged, clean-shaven, his hair still thick and brown, with a few gray hairs around the ears. His overcoat was unbuttoned, hanging open, and Topilin could see there was no paunch around his waist, but he did not seem overly athletic. His face showed no emotion other than weariness, from what exertion, Topilin had no idea. "Who are you?"

"My name is unimportant," Anton Sokolov said. "What matters here is that you are a traitor to the *Rodina*."

"I . . ." Topilin's protest died in his mouth. His brain was churning, considering lies and excuses, and discarding them all. One sentence from this average-looking man had cut through every possible cover story Topilin could dredge up to explain away the CIA equipment in his trunk. "No, I . . . you see—"

The man waved a hand. "There is no point in talking here. We know what you have done. You will come with us."

"'With us'?" Topilin looked around, and finally saw the dozen other men scattered around the dacha. A pair of cars moved out of a side road in the woods and came up the driveway, cutting the Mondeo off from the road. Half of the men, all fit soldiers, entered the dacha without asking his permission. He saw them through the front windows, watched them fan out inside the building. They would search every square inch, Topilin knew. There was nothing inside for them to find, but it hardly mattered. The worst evidence was in his car, hidden by nothing better than a blanket.

The man approached him. "As I said, a very fine car. And a very fine dacha," he said. "I took the liberty of granting myself a tour of the grounds as we waited. It is a pretty little estate. You really must explain to me how you afforded it on your salary. But there will be time for that. If you would come with me to the van?"

"Where will you take me?"

"To the Aquarium."

"GRU headquarters?" Topilin asked. His legs felt suddenly weak, as though the bones had disappeared, and panic surged in his chest.

Sokolov nodded. "I will be your interrogator. I have some questions, and I would be most grateful to hear your answers."

"What . . . what questions?" Topilin stammered, afraid of the answer.

"I simply want to know why you did what you have done," Sokolov explained. "Only that."

Topilin stared at him, uncomprehending. "And you have no questions about—"

"About how you did your business with the CIA?" Sokolov asked. "No. Do you think we would have caught you if we did not already know those details?"

They know everything, Sokolov realized. It would not have mattered if he had managed to burn the equipment and supplies in his car. "And if I cooperate?" Perhaps there was some hope?

"Whether you cooperate or not will have no effect on your sentence, I'm afraid," Sokolov said. "I'm sorry it is so. I think mercy is a trait lacking in so many of the men in our business, but my opinion doesn't matter. In your case, my orders are not discretionary."

No trial? Topilin realized. "And what is my sentence?" he asked, incredulous. He was sure that he knew the answer.

"Surely you remember the history classes that we teach to our officers and staff?" the man answered, a question for a question.

Topilin closed his eyes and his head fell forward. "I do."

The man shrugged. "I thought so. Come—"

Topilin lunged forward, thrusting his hand underneath the blanket in the trunk of his car, where he'd laid his Grach pistol. From the corner of his eye, he saw that Sokolov was not moving. The desperate engineer pulled the pistol out, grabbing the slide and pulling it back to load the first round—

A hand smashed into his face, blinding him, then a hard blow on his wrist, where the radius met the scaphoid, and burning pain exploded through his hand, paralyzing the muscles. Topilin tried to force his eyes open. Too late, he felt the Grach being ripped from his grasp, pulled in the direction opposite the way his fingers could bend.

Then the pistol was gone and he didn't know where, until he felt the metal grip smashed into the vertebrae of his neck. Pain like Topilin had never felt erupted through his body and he went down, all control of his arms and legs lost. His breath gone, he lay on the gravel. He could not speak. He heard himself moaning, like the guttural cries of a wounded cow.

The Spetsnaz team leader offered the Grach to Sokolov. "Sir, we're ready to breach the house."

Sokolov took the pistol, ejected the clip, and made sure the chamber was clear. "Proceed. There could be hidden spaces in the building." He knelt down by the crippled man. "Perhaps our friend Topilin would care to tell us where they are? It would be a shame to tear apart such a lovely home. What say you? Is there anything hidden inside?"

Topilin could not answer. Finally, he shook his head.

"I regret that that is an answer I cannot trust," Sokolov said. "Had you nodded, I would have waited until you had recovered and given you the chance to reveal them. Cooperation would not spare you, but it might have made things to come easier for your wife. But saying there are none? You could be telling the truth, but we will have to see for ourselves. For your wife's sake, I do hope you have not tried to deceive us." Sokolov turned to the Spetsnaz officer. "Proceed, Captain. You need not be gentle with anything. But looting will not be tolerated. Anything that remains intact will be considered potential evidence and any man trying to abscond with such property will answer to me."

"Very good, sir. Also, I suggest that we should leave a detail to watch the property after we're finished. It is possible that Topilin's handler or some other CIA officer could come, trying to connect with him."

Sokolov considered the possibility. "No, I think not," he said after a moment's thought. "They have all been expelled from the country. I think under the circumstances, they would imagine that any kind of operational act would be a serious risk." Sokolov smiled at his subordinate. "Besides, we have already secured our primary objective here. Anything else we find is just sauce for the goose. So take the place apart. Once you are satisfied that there is nothing undiscovered, we will be done here. This all will be the FSB's mess to clean up. Let them watch the house if they want."

"Yes, sir."

Sokolov faced his prisoner. "Come, Adolf Viktorovich, we will talk on the drive home." He waved to two other Spetsnaz officers. They lifted the engineer by his armpits, ignoring his cry of pain as the movement shifted his fractured vertebrae. Helpless, Adolf Topilin hung there in their hands as the soldiers dragged him to the armored van waiting in the road, the last car ride he would ever take on the last day of his life.

Office of the GRU Chairman
New GRU headquarters
Moscow, Russia

Lavrov read the two-page report, then closed the folder in which it was stapled and set it on his desk. "So, I am told that one of the men on your list has been neutralized," he said. "A good start. Several more remain, of course, but a good start." He pulled a beer bottle out of a small refrigerator hidden in a cabinet behind his desk. "I estimate that the immediate threats will be resolved in . . . oh, a week." He pulled a bottle opener from his desk and ripped the bottle cap off the glass neck.

"This is not what I wanted," Maines muttered, afraid to say anything that might offend Lavrov.

The Russian smiled at the pitiful American. "Mr. Maines, you truly do not understand treason, do you? Treason and the nature of information." The Russian sipped at his bottle of chilled beer, a Vasileostrovsky dark. He had offered none to Maines. He was sure the American was thirsty, but Maines's dominant right hand was encased in plaster, his left likely would be shaky from the morphine and other drugs in his system, and it would not do for him to spill any of the alcohol on the expensive rug under their feet. The man's extremity would be crippled for life, barring major surgery involving titanium pins and reconstruction of the muscles. It was a minor miracle he was lucid enough to talk given the painkillers he was taking.

"Some twenty years ago, your country's Bush administration did something so stupid I could hardly believe it," Lavrov explained. "No, it is not what you think, not that business about Iraq. It was the day they declared that papers already released to the public, already filed in your National Archive, some of them decades old . . . they said they were *again* classified documents. Can you believe such a thing? They imagined that information once made free could be pulled back and somehow controlled again. Foolishness. I could not imagine what idiocy, what absurd reasoning could lead any bureaucrat to think it could be done. Oh yes, a government can declare that possessing a document is legal or illegal at a whim. But make people forget the contents? No."

Lavrov took a long swig of the beer this time, draining almost half the contents. "I have heard a saying from some of our computer hackers, which I think originated in your country," he continued. "'Information wants to be free,' they say. Of course, information wants nothing, but what it truly means is that once released into the open, it cannot be taken back. Secrets lost are lost forever. All you can hope is that the world will forget it over time, as the Chinese have tried to manage with their butchery at Tiananmen Square thirty years ago. But only one person needs to remember it or hide a copy of it, written in some journal or copied in some file. Years later they pass it to another, and a new copy is made, repeated over the telephone or posted on some website, and so on." Lavrov took a break to swill more alcohol before continuing. "Information is a virus, always lying dormant until the conditions are right for it to erupt and fill the world again. That is why the state must hold it tight, letting it out most carefully, so that the public is only ever exposed to the most harmless bits . . . the ones that will make no difference, even when the people act on them . . . because people *will* act, and they will do so foolishly. So long as the people can make harmful decisions, they cannot be given the ammunition to hurt themselves or the people around them."

Lavrov finished the bottle and set it on the table in front of the parched American. "Do you understand what I am saying to you?" he asked. "Treason is not a sin for which one can atone. Once you have told the enemy what he should not know, you can never control where that information will go. So there is no restitution you can make. Perhaps you believe that you have done it for some virtuous reason, or perhaps you were just a selfish man. But the fact is that you have hurt your country in a way that will never heal. It will try to compensate for your choice, try to rebuild what you have torn down, but the true effects cannot be undone." The Russian shook his head, frowning.

"You made me tell you more than I wanted," Maines said, his words slightly slurred. The morphine dosage running through him was too high for his body mass, and his mind was foggy. The man would likely end up addicted to the drug.

Lavrov smiled, incredulous. "You surprise me. You, a case officer, and you do not understand the control that an intelligence service has over an asset who has placed himself in its care?"

"I didn't want to be in your care," Maines protested as strongly as the morphine allowed. "I didn't want to defect. You set me up."

"Yes, I did," Lavrov said. "But you made it possible, and, I must admit, quite easy. You are not a clever man, Mr. Maines. You are an educated man, but not a clever one. And that is a terrible failing in an intelligence officer, one I never saw in CIA officers before. The Main Enemy's operatives used to be so cunning. But you . . . a failure of training, maybe?" The Russian stopped short, then smiled, as though some great insight had appeared in his mind. "Perhaps I was wrong. The CIA has forgotten its own past victories? The tactics that let them win the Cold War? Perhaps some bits of knowledge can be forgotten after all."

Lavrov finished the bottle and set it carefully on the desk. "That is the other interesting fact about information . . . it does not care how it is spread. It can be given and it can be taken. How one obtains it is immaterial, the information is the same. And you put yourself in a position where your information could be taken from you, where you could not protect it or call on others to help you do so . . . another terrible sin for an intelligence officer. Perhaps not so serious a form of treason as giving the information away, but a sin nonetheless. To put yourself in the care of others and then think you can decide what to share and what to hide? Naïveté of the worst kind."

"You're a lunatic," Maines dared to say, the words so slurred that Lavrov almost couldn't understand them.

"No, I am not a lunatic, Mr. Maines," Lavrov said. "I am just more clever than you, which is why you are sitting in my office with a crippled hand and a head full of drugs. But I am not an ungrateful man. Quite the opposite, I am very grateful to you for giving me Miss Stryker's name, and telling me about the CIA's Red Cell. I was not aware that such a unit existed. A group of analysts whose job is to consider the improbable possibilities, to go beyond the intelligence on the page and apply history to the present? Brilliant. I must set up such a unit within the GRU . . . that is another reason I should like to talk to Miss Stryker. Do you think she might consider working for me?"

"I think," Maines slurred, "that she'll tell you where you can go and what you can do to yourself while you're waiting to arrive."

"Indeed," Lavrov said, glee in his voice. "But such a unit must be willing to speak truth to the authorities, no? Have the courage to say what no one else wants to say? That is so rare here . . . so rare anywhere really." He stood up, turned to the window, and looked out into the dark at the Kremlin lights. "It should not be so. The authorities always learn eventually that they have been told lies. Do you read history, Mr. Maines?" He waited for a few seconds but the American didn't answer. "There is a story from the Second Great War . . . I do not know if it's true," Lavrov continued. "After the Normandy invasion, Hitler's generals were afraid to tell him day after day of the Reich's many defeats in the final year of the war. So instead, they told him day after day that his armies were winning great victories, killing American, British, and Russian soldiers in large numbers. After many days of this, Hitler finally said, 'If we are winning so many victories, why do the battles keep getting closer to Berlin?'"

Lavrov laughed. "Truth wins the day eventually. Better to hear it early rather than late when there is little that can be done about it."

The Russian sighed. "Yes, better not to delay." Lavrov called out and an aide strode into the room. The general pulled out a notepad and scribbled a name on the paper, then tore it out and gave it to the functionary. "Contact Colonel Sokolov at the Aquarium and pass him this name. He is waiting for it. And please have the orderlies assist Mr. Maines back to his dormitory. He is not feeling well, and the sleep will do him some good."

Utilisa Lermontov Road
Peredelkino, Moscow Oblast, Russia

The signal for a meeting was simple, a piece of tape on an iron fence post. If Topilin wanted the meeting, the tape would be vertical. If the CIA officer wanted the meeting, it would be horizontal. Finding the right street and the right post had taken Kyra half the day thanks to her inability to read Russian, but the GPS had finally led her to the spot. She'd come with a roll of tape in hand, but had been surprised to find two vertical stripes—Topilin's signal for an emergency. Kyra had returned to the safe house after that and pulled up his file on the classified computer, which had taken another hour. His file said that his next steps were to dispose of all incriminating evidence that the Agency had given him, then meet at an exfiltration point in the village of Vyborg, northeast of St. Petersburg near the Russian-Finnish border. His CIA handler would meet him there, where Topilin and his wife would hide in the trunk under a thermal blanket that would mask their body heat from sensors mounted at the border outposts. They would be given a mild sedative to calm their nerves, lest they panic from claustrophobia or some other terror, but that step wasn't in the actual file.

Vyborg was over five hundred miles from Moscow, a full day's drive by car. She prayed that Topilin hadn't left for the village yet. The GPS could lead her to Vyborg, but she doubted she would be able to find a man hiding there. She didn't even know Topilin's face. Even if she could find him, the round trip would take two days that she was sure she couldn't spare. Kyra needed to intercept Topilin before that or he would be beyond her reach as surely as if he'd been captured.

Where to destroy the evidence? Not at home, surely. Kyra knew Topilin's handler would have counseled against that. Burning plastics gave off an unmistakable smell that could raise suspicions. His file said that he had a dacha. That seemed more likely. It was southwest of the city and therefore somewhat out of his way if he was heading for Vyborg, but she didn't know enough about the man to know what other options he might have available to him.

Kyra parked a half mile away down a side road and ran through the woods, navigating her way using the map in her head that she had studied, instead of the GPS. The Russian fall was colder than she'd expected, and she felt a chill until she got up to speed, her own body heat warming her. The dacha appeared through the trees after ten minutes or so, a tidy little renovated barn by the looks of it, with a deck coming off the back. A late-model Ford was sitting in front of the house, her view of it partly blocked by one corner of the house. Kyra felt her spirits surge. *He's here—*

A man appeared from behind the corner, grubby with oil-stained coveralls. *Topilin?* she wondered. That seemed unlikely. She supposed the mole might have dressed in the grubby clothes to keep the smoke and stains from burning evidence off his clothes, but something told her it wasn't so.

She shifted her position carefully to the right, trying to get a better view of the man through the underbrush. After moving a dozen feet, a second car came into view . . . a flatbed tow truck.

No.

The man in the coveralls needed ten minutes to get the Mondeo onto the truck bed and chain it down. He checked the restraints for tension, then mounted the cab, started the engine, and slowly made his way out toward the road, the trees finally taking him out of sight.

Kyra wanted to scream at the receding vehicle, at the driver, at anyone. If this was Topolin's dacha, if that was his car, then Topilin likely had been detained. She felt anger and depression mix inside her, certain that Topilin was a dead man. She prayed she was wrong, but she knew that she was not.

Kyra reset her clock and waited, shivering in the woods for another hour, searching for any other signs of life. The sun was low over the trees by the end of her self-imposed deadline, and she saw no lights in the house. She crept forward, leaned around the corner of the house, and saw no one.

The front door hung ajar. She moved closer and saw that the knob had been torn out. *No no no . . .* she screamed in her mind. She listened, heard no voices or movement inside. She opened the door gently, and stepped in.

The dacha interior was destroyed. There had been abandoned buildings in Vogelsang's decrepit state that had been in better condition. The walls had been torn open, the furniture gutted. The appliances in the kitchen were out of place, moved away from the walls so the intruders could search the spaces behind. A quick sweep of the house confirmed that every room had been dismantled in the same violent fashion.

There was a wood stove on the first floor in the front room. Kyra's family home had had one when she was young, a necessity living in the Virginia backwoods, where a snowstorm could cut off power and escape for days at a time. She'd spent many winter days keeping it fed with split oak logs on her father's orders. She could always get the fire inside raging, far hotter than any oven, a thousand degrees at the center when it was roaring. She loved the feeling of raw heat coming off the old cast-iron sides, which could linger for hours after the fire had burned down to coals.

Heat, she thought. Kyra walked over to the wood stove. If Topilin had come to destroy evidence, he would have used the wood stove to do it.

She reached out slowly. There was no heat from the stove. She touched the cast iron, cold as the rocks outside. Kyra swung open the doors. The inside was covered with a thin layer of gray ash, whatever Topilin had been unable to scoop up after his last fire, which clearly had been some time ago.

Topilin hadn't been able to destroy his equipment.

Kyra could see how it had played out. The man had made it this far, but the Russian security services had been waiting for him. They'd taken him after he'd gotten out of his car but before he'd been able to carry anything inside the house.

She left the dacha, walked outside, and looked at the ground where the car had been. It was dark now, and she pulled out her flashlight, turned it on, and swept the ground. There were footprints in the dust left by the sparse gravel, made by different soles and shoe sizes. Kyra couldn't tell how many men had been here, but it had been several. Then two long lines where the gravel had been knocked aside. She stared at them, confused, then realized they'd been made by a man's shoes as he was dragged along the ground.

Adolf Viktorovich Topilin was a dead man walking somewhere inside Lubyanka Prison, she was sure. Kyra turned off her flashlight and cursed Maines and Lavrov, and any Russian who'd had a hand in Topilin's arrest.

Should've gone for Puchkov first, she thought. The major would've been the better choice. Kyra had been trying to be professional, go for the man who could confirm the existence of the EMP instead of the asset with the broader access to information. Puchkov might have been able to give her a clue to the locations of both Jon and the EMP.

No time for that, a voice in her head chided her. *Topilin is gone. He's a dead man. Two moles left. You have to move.*

Kyra turned back and jogged into the woods, running for her car. Moscow was an hour to the northeast, and she had to get back to the safe house. She needed to be ready to move at sunrise.

CHAPTER SEVEN

The White House

The Russian ambassador to the United States had not expected to be summoned to the White House again so quickly. He had thought President Rostow would have licked his wounds for at least a week as he consulted with his advisers on how best to respond to the Kremlin's expulsion of so many American spies from Moscow's streets. It had been an unprecedented act, but the act of a great power, Galushka thought. Rostow had hidden his reaction to the news reasonably well, but Galushka had read the man's face. The young president had been stunned, even confused. Oh, to have heard the words he had spoken to his staff after the Russian left the Oval Office! Galushka cursed his colleagues in the intelligence services for not being able to tell him that. Instead, he would have to wait a few decades until the American press made their documentaries and wrote their histories to find it out. But he knew what history's judgment of it all would be. The expulsion order would be seen as the starkest evidence yet that the United States was no longer a nation to be feared, and Galushka would be always remembered as the man who had delivered it. Without question, it would stand as the most glorious day of his career thus far, and perhaps the one that opened the door for him to ascend to the Kremlin's highest posts.

Now Galushka could not stop wondering whether the swift summons was not a sign that all of that was being threatened. Like a jury sent out of a courtroom to deliberate a case, a swift verdict was rarely good news for the accused. Now Rostow was being unpredictable. The young president should have accepted his humiliation. Of course, it was expected he would expel a few Russians from Washington in a weak bid to save face. Reagan had expelled fifty-five diplomats in 1986 as retaliation for Gorbachev's eviction of five CIA spies, the kind of disproportionate act the Russian people had come to expect from the cowboy president. Bush the younger had expelled fifty in 2001 after Robert Hannsen's treachery was revealed, but to be fair, that traitor's work had allowed the Kremlin to execute several CIA assets.

But Rostow was no Bush, much less a Reagan, and the man was running for reelection. Politicians like him preferred to rely on the electorate's short memories and bury such embarrassments as deep as they could, and the American president was not following that model. Galushka was concerned. He replayed the secretary of state's call through his mind, asking him to return to the White House. The Russian had asked to know why and the secretary had refused to tell him. The Russian had frowned at that, but no one around him had noticed, the expression being too close to the ambassador's usual appearance.

The chauffeur opened his door and Galushka dismounted onto the asphalt outside the East Wing entrance. The Russian followed the usual security escorts, expecting to be taken to the Oval Office, which route he knew well. His only notice that he would not be following that route came when the man ahead of him slowed to direct him into a room to the north from the center hall. The Russian, focused on his own thoughts, had not been watching his escort and stumbled into him.

Galushka walked through the open door. He'd not been here before, but he came to recognize the White House library, remembering it vaguely from some photograph he'd seen years before. It was a small space, perhaps twenty feet by thirty, decorated in the style of the late Federal period, with soft gray and rose tones coloring the wall panels. It was dimly lit at the moment, the fire in the hearth illuminating the room as much as the gilded wood chandelier above the round table in its center. Galushka was sure that the many books on the shelves were American classics, if any tome written by Western authors ever could be called such. He'd never cared enough to read any of them. Russia's own literary tradition was too rich and deep for him to waste his time on the scribblings produced by so young a country.

The Secret Service escort closed the door behind Galushka and took up a position in the corner to watch the husky diplomat. The Russian waited for his eyes to adjust to the low light. He wasn't a young man anymore and they didn't make the change as quickly as they once had.

"Do you know what this room was used for, originally?" Galushka finally saw President Daniel Rostow standing before the east wall, looking up at a row of books on one of the shelves.

"Mr. President," Galushka acknowledged, "I do not. I have never been in this room."

"It was the White House laundry," Rostow explained. "For almost exactly a hundred years, this is where the staff cleaned up dirty clothes."

Galushka looked around at his surroundings. "It is a more useful space now, I think."

"Oh, yes," Rostow agreed. "Though occasionally it still serves its old purpose."

Galushka frowned, unsure what the young president meant by that. Rostow turned around, made his way to one of two facing chairs before the fireplace, and directed the Russian ambassador to the other. "I'm sure you know why I asked you to come tonight, Igor Nikolayevich."

"You wish to respond to our expulsion of your cadre of spies in

Moscow," Galushka replied. He wanted to smile but it would not have been diplomatic, and he was out of practice anyway.

"That's right, Igor, I do," Rostow concurred. The president of the United States reached over to the table, picked up a large manila envelope, and offered it to the Russian ambassador. "In response to your unprecedented expulsion of so many U.S. diplomats and their families from your soil without provocation, the United States government hereby requires the Russian Federation to withdraw the following individuals and their families from our soil within the next five days. The secretary of state will deliver the formal paperwork to your embassy in the morning, but I wanted to personally give you the advance notice so the people on the list could start packing up tonight."

Galushka opened the envelope and withdrew the contents, surprised to find two pieces of folded paper inside. He straightened them and his eyes widened. Both papers were filled with names, top to bottom, split into two columns on each. He tried to estimate the full total. "There are over two hundred names here," the ambassador protested.

"Two hundred twenty if you'd like to count," Rostow said. "Most work at your embassy here on Wisconsin Avenue, but some are stationed at your consulates in New York, Houston, San Francisco, and Seattle."

Galushka scanned the list. Several names he recognized as GRU and SVR officers under official cover, but he couldn't identify most of them. "This will damage relations between our two countries most severely, Mr. President. It is a shame that you chose this course in an effort to divert the world's attention from the scale of your own intelligence activities and failure. A better course would have been to resolve this matter through private channels and special contacts," he said. "Unfortunately, as you have chosen another way, this step cannot be regarded as anything but a political one."

Rostow smiled. "Well, Ambassador, for the record, you can tell your government that I truly do look forward to finding a way to smooth this matter over and rebuild a productive relationship with the Russian Federation. But unlike some of the previous presidents from my party, I'm a realist. And right now, after your country's unprovoked diplomatic slap, allowing an enormous Russian diplomatic presence on U.S. soil just isn't a good signal to the rest of the world about the kind of relations I want to have with your country. We are equals, after all. It wouldn't do to have your delegation outnumber ours, and asking the Kremlin to approve a lengthy list of replacements for ours would just make me look weak to the rest of the world. Cutting yours down to size is easier and makes me look stronger. So I get to insult you, look stronger for it, get our countries back on equal terms all at once, and boost my poll numbers at home. We Americans call that 'multitasking.'"

The president leaned forward and looked Galushka in the eyes. "Off the record, you can inform your government that the United States of America is not done 'resolving this matter,'" he advised. "And I regret that I must say farewell to you, Igor."

"I am prepared to leave the White House at any time," the Russian replied, offended.

"Not just the White House, Mr. Ambassador," Rostow told him. "Your name is on the list, too. I realize it will cause the Russian Federation some inconvenience to replace its ambassador here, but if the Kremlin wants to make a fresh start with me, they can begin by putting forward a fresh face. But do let your president know that I can expel people just as fast as he can. So you might want to ask him just how far he wants to take this."

Galushka stared down at the papers again, reading the names and finding his own on at the top of the second page. Rostow stood and walked to the door, opened it, and a pair of Secret Service agents stepped inside. "Good-bye, Igor. Do have a safe flight home. I look forward to reading your memoirs." He looked at the senior security officer. "Please see Ambassador Galushka to his car."

"Yes, sir."

The Russian ambassador watched the president of the United States walk out into the central hall and turn left, heading for the West Wing. The Secret Service officer extended his arm, showing Galushka the door, his expression clear that he was not going to be patient with him. The overweight Russian grunted and shuffled out of the library. He knew he wouldn't see the inside of the White House again.

Kurkino District
Moscow, Russia

Major Elizaveta Igoryevna Puchkov pulled around the wrecked cars blocking the leftmost lane of the Leningradskoye Highway and mashed the gas pedal to the floor, determined to recover the speed and time she'd lost to the snarl of traffic she'd just escaped. She seen the now-wrecked car pass her a minute before it had sideswiped a delivery truck. The driver had been drunk, she figured, judging by the lack of control. Not that she minded a bit of inebriation, but the moron should have waited until he got home to chase his stupor. It was early in the evening yet, and the drunk had reaped what his stupidity had sown.

Angry though she was, she could hardly condemn the man. Puchkov had been tempted to pass the evening with a pub crawl of her own, a bad habit she'd picked up during a tour at her country's embassy in London. It had been too long since she'd killed time on a stool at the Bar Strelka by the old Krasny Oktyabr chocolate factory on the man-made island of Bolotny Ostrov. To see the Moskva River at night, lit up by the lights of the Cathedral of Christ the Savior with a bottle of twelve-year-old Green Mark in her hands would be a fine way to forget this ugly day. She was not a Christian, but she could still appreciate the beauty of the buildings the believers erected as an act of worship.

But then the Kremlin itself sat just across the Moskva to the north. Walk the wrong way along the Sofiskaya road while drunk, she would see those spires instead, and Puchkov's loose tongue would be tempted to say something unfortunate. That particular behavior was a luxury she'd indulged in her youth, like most Russian college students. She knew she was a talkative drunk and that was an unfortunate weakness for a CIA mole.

So she'd given it up, but she was at peace with that. Puchkov would do that much for Alexsandr. Her old boyfriend from university had settled on journalism as his calling and he'd been good at it. They'd broken up before the *Novaya Gazeta* newspaper had hired him, but she'd followed his progress, reading his articles and happy that he was making his mark. The *Novaya Gazeta* had been a harsh critic of Putin, enough to draw a charge of violating anti-extremism laws, and Alexsandr had been as daring as any of his peers there. He became a favorite of the Kremlin's opponents, outspoken and never subtle in his writing.

Then he'd turned his talents to writing on corruption in the Kremlin. His new portfolio lasted only four months before his neighbors found his body in the elevator of his apartment building. Two shots to the chest, one to the head, the official report said. The Kremlin had issued a statement decrying his death and promising to find the murderer, but no detectives were ever assigned and no arrests were ever made.

Puchkov had found the Kremlin true-but-unofficial report on Alexsandr's death after a monthlong search in the GRU's files. The folder had included surveillance reports noting Alexsandr's daily schedule. Either they'd killed him or they'd watched while someone did.

Puchkov had volunteered to work for the CIA the next day. Ten years on, her desire to hurt the wicked oligarchs who'd snuffed out her country's brief glimpse of freedom hadn't been satisfied and the GRU major was sure it never would be. Revenge didn't heal the soul, she'd learned. She wished that she could call her actions by some more respectable word, justify them as a covert fight against overt corruption, illegal acts made righteous by evil men who had perverted the law. But, no, it was revenge she wanted, nothing more. Puchkov was at least honest with herself about that.

But now the Americans were in no position to help her. News of the expulsions had raced through the GRU. She had cheered with her colleagues—her finest acting on display—but fear dogged her now. How had General Lavrov identified the American intelligence officers? Would the same source or method let him identify her as a CIA asset? No one had any details that would help her determine this, so all she could do was act as normal as possible and pray that no one came for her at home after dark.

Her cell phone rang in her coat pocket. Puchkov cursed as her lap belt made it a struggle to extract the device. She finally got it out, and took her eyes off the road to look at the screen. The caller ID showed a number she didn't recognize and no name at all. Surely it was someone at work calling. She pressed a button. *"Ya slushayu vas,"* she said.

"You are Elizaveta Igoryevna Puchkov?" the caller asked. The voice sounded odd, digitized. It was not encrypted . . . her phone lacked that capability. Someone was using a voice changer.

"Da."

"They are coming for you," the voice said. "The GRU knows that you are a traitor. If you wish to live, you will go into hiding. Do not go home."

Puchkov's heart began to race, pounding hard enough to hurt her chest. Despite the distortion, she could tell that the caller was Russian. The Muscovite accent was strong enough to survive the digital masking. *Not CIA,* she thought. *Not my handler calling to warn me.*

The Agency had another, more secure way to contact her in case of such an emergency. Was this a GRU trap? Part of a counterintelligence investigation, a gambit to see if she would panic and run, confirming her guilt.

That wasn't one of the GRU's normal methods for hunting moles. Then who was this? This man was a Russian, but no other Russian knew that she was a CIA asset. Puchkov couldn't make sense of it.

"I don't know what you are talking about," Puchkov lied. "I am not a spy."

"You must believe me," the voice said. "They know what you have done."

"I am not a traitor to the *Rodina*," Puchkov retorted. "This is a very poor joke. If you do not leave me alone, I will have this call traced—"

The line went dead. Puchkov set the phone on the passenger seat.

She drove on, her mind paying no attention to the busy road. *What to do?* Was it possible the caller had told the truth? Would the CIA even know if she'd been identified? Perhaps the caller was another CIA asset?

Puchkov knew of only one way to confirm the possibility. She took the next right turn, which led her away from her apartment, less than a mile away.

Magnoliya Supermarket
Kurkinskoye shosse 17k1
Kurkino District
Moscow, Russia

The market was a small, square one-story affair that butted up against the circular red-brick wing of an apartment complex. The file said that the exfiltration signal was to be a chalked diagonal line on a particular brick at the residential building's corner closest to the point where the two buildings met. A line running from the upper left to the lower right was CIA's signal to Puchkov that she needed to run. Puchkov's confirmation was a line from the upper right to the lower left. Puchkov had suggested the site to her handler. The major came here often enough to buy her groceries that a trip would raise no suspicions.

Kyra checked the GPS unit again. She'd been driving for three hours, watching the rearview mirror, and the device finally insisted that she was near the address she had copied from Puchkov's file. She unbuckled her restraint and checked her pocket for the piece of chalk. She would walk a short surveillance detection route, make the mark, retreat to her car, then spend most of the night waiting for Puchkov at the exfiltration site. She couldn't actually get Puchkov out, but she could at least warn the woman and tell her to hide until the CIA could put resources in place to bring her out.

Whether Puchkov knew anything that could help her find Jon or confirm his death was another matter entirely.

There was an unsettled feeling in her chest, and she did not have to guess what it was. *Weird not having you here, Jon*, she thought.

She was sure she heard Jon's voice in her mind. *This is not a good idea*, he told her.

"Yeah, I know," Kyra said aloud, surprising herself. She was gambling that the Russians would be relaxing their security, thinking that all of the CIA officers had left the country.

But only the CIA officers are gone. The Russians know that there are other spies still in the country. They'll still be watching. Jon spoke to her again. *And if Lavrov's boys are here, at the market, you're screwed. Nothing I can do to help you . . . not that I'd get out of the car to save your tail anyway.*

After a three-hour surveillance detection route, I'd think you'd want any excuse to stretch your legs, Kyra chided her absent partner.

If I was going to get out of the car, it would be to run away from the men with the guns, not toward them, Jon's voice in her head replied.

I'm clean, Kyra reassured him and herself. *Three hours looking in the mirror and never saw the same car twice.*

Here's to hoping, her absent partner replied, and then he was silent. Kyra opened the door and put her foot down on the asphalt. She was two hundred yards from the site.

Puchkov pulled her car into the very small parking lot to the south of the market, past the store's own lot, and turned the engine off. She sat inside, working through the rough plan in her mind. She'd parked away from the market so she could walk past the corner where an exfiltration signal would be marked. Whether the signal was there or not, she would go inside, buy some bread and beer, and return to her car. The only question would be where she would go after. If there was no mark, she would go home. If the chalk line was present, she would never see her apartment again. She would drive to the exfiltration point her handler had identified, and fate willing, she would be on United States soil within two days.

Puchkov stepped out of her car, shut the door, and set the locks. She looked for approaching cars. Seeing none, she walked north toward the market.

All she had to do was look at the brick, nothing more.

No one was following. Kyra was a hundred yards from the market when her stomach twisted inward. Her instincts began to scream, and she stopped moving. She swept the scene in front of her, her mind dissecting the picture.

There was very little to see. The only person in sight was a woman, boyish dark hair, short, and a little overweight. She was fifty yards from Kyra's position, but her profile at this distance matched the photograph Kyra had seen in the file. *Puchkov.*

Kyra still wouldn't move, not until she had found the source of her anxiety. She stared at her surroundings.

Finally, she saw it. *This is a supermarket*, she thought. *Where is everyone?*

Kyra's gut twisted.

In that instant, Kyra knew that Major Elizaveta Igoryevna Puchkov was a dead woman.

Puchkov slowed on the sidewalk and turned her head, looking away from the market doors toward the corner where the store met the apartment building. There was no line.

Puchkov was seventy-five yards from her car now, too far to make it back when the trap sprang closed. The Spetsnaz soldiers erupted out of the market, nearby cars, two other buildings. There were at least two dozen of them, maybe more. Every direction in which Puchkov might have run had been identified and blocked off. The Russian woman would have no chance to fight her way out against any one of the men in the circle collapsing around her position.

Kyra wanted to scream at Puchkov, tell her to run anyway, but she knew it was futile. There was no help for the GRU officer now. She would be detained, interrogated, and executed. Kyra could see it, as though it had already happened.

One soldier was moving in a different direction, away from Puchkov—

—toward her. He was yelling in Russian, probably commands to stop, she was sure, but her mind refused to focus on the man's orders. She couldn't tear her eyes away from the Russian woman, watching as the dragnet shrank around her.

The soldier running in her direction was fifty yards away, her car two hundred yards behind her. Kyra's legs refused to move.

Her mind tore the world around her apart, time slowing down for the few seconds she had before the soldier reached her position.

The Spetsnaz had cordoned off the area earlier, before either she or Puchkov had arrived. How was that possible? Even if they had followed her, they couldn't have known where she was going.

There was only one answer. The Russians had known where the CIA would leave a mark to signal Puchkov. Maines had given that to them. The locals had seen the Spetsnaz arrive and known enough to stay away.

Puchkov had been expected, but Kyra's arrival had surprised them, just a stroke of bad timing for her and good for them. Whether she was a random Russian shopper or had some connection to Puchkov, they wouldn't know, but they would detain her for questioning to find out.

It would take them exactly one question to figure out that she couldn't speak Russian and that would settle the issue. They wouldn't accept that it was a coincidence that an American had blundered into their raid site. They would search the airport customs files and security footage to identify her. Eventually, they would know that she was not who her passport claimed she was and whatever had happened to Jon would happen to her.

The first Spetsnaz soldiers reached Puchkov and knocked the woman onto the sidewalk, her face smashing into the concrete, tearing the skin from her cheek. Two men pulled her arms up behind her back, like the spread wings of a chicken, while another forced a rope into her mouth. Two others began stripping her coat and shirt off to remove any means of suicide she might have hidden away. The rest drew their sidearms on the woman, approaching more slowly, ready to put her down in case she had some way of resisting they couldn't see.

The other soldiers circled around her and Kyra lost sight of the GRU major.

Another yell in Russian ripped Kyra's focus away from the arrest and back to the man running at her. He was thirty yards away now.

Kyra's legs finally moved.

She spun around and ran for her car, but she knew that she wouldn't make it. She'd seen how fast the soldier was. By the time she could get up to a full sprint, he could only be a few yards behind her and could run her down on foot, even if he didn't shoot her first. Kyra had no Glock concealed in her waistband under her coat, and it would have been no help anyway. Even had she won a gunfight, which was unlikely, the report of a shot would draw the attention of the soldier's team. With Puchkov down, the rest would be free to lay down fire on her position and she would die. They were a hundred yards from the raid site now. The distance would make for a very long pistol shot, but some of the men would have rifles, and even two hundreds yards wouldn't be a long shot for a Special Forces soldier.

She turned her head to look behind and saw that the soldier had cut the distance in half.

Kyra had trained in Krav Maga, knew how to disarm an attacker, but the man ten yards away had combat training of his own, equal to hers at least, and he was surely at least twice as strong as her if not more. She couldn't take him hand-to-hand. He would put her down like Puchkov and the outcome would be the same.

He was ten yards back and still picking up speed. He was drawing his gun. There was no good cover between her and the car. A few parked cars, some trees, nothing truly defensible.

Kyra had one option left.

She skidded to stop, her hand touching the ground for balance. He was six yards away.

The Spetsnaz officer got his Makarov clear of the holster. Running hard, he had trouble finding the safety. He glanced down at his sidearm. For a second, his eyes were off Kyra and on his weapon.

She rushed toward the soldier, trying to close the distance between them before the Russian raised his gun. Her hand was in her own coat pocket.

The soldier's speed running played against him now and he was unable to stop himself before Kyra got inside his firing arc. The safety was off, the first round in the chamber and the pistol came up, but Kyra was past the end of his outstretched arm. She was going to hit him running full speed.

Kyra pulled the Taser from her coat, flipping off the safety in the same motion.

Foolish woman, the soldier started to think. He was twice her weight, would knock her backward, flipping her over and slamming her down on her spine, probably breaking vertebrae or cracking her pelvis. Either would leave her screaming in agony. He wouldn't even have to waste a bullet—

—the woman veered slightly at the last second before they hit. Her hand came up, something black and thin in her grip, and he heard the loud, machine-gun-clicking of an active electrical current.

Kyra touched the firing trigger on the Taser and raised her right arm the instant before they hit, both moving fast, left shoulders colliding. The soldier was solid muscle, granite in motion. He'd started to turn his shoulder into her. She felt him hit, her lighter body giving way to his solid mass—

—Kyra felt her right shoulder almost dislocate when she slammed into the bulky soldier and the impact sent her spinning, her right arm coming around as she spun left. She saw the dark outline of the soldier through her blurred vision, and she pulled the trigger.

The Taser fired less than a foot from the man's neck, two metal probes exploding from the plastic panel covering the barrel, both trailing thin wires. Kyra's aim was high. She'd meant to shoot him in the back. Instead, the barbs punched through the skin below the base of his skull, digging into the muscle underneath and completing the electrical circuit with the gun.

Five thousand volts arced through the soldier's nervous system, pulsing down his spine, and his body seized up in an instant. The man wanted to howl in pain, but what emerged from his paralyzed vocal cords sounded more like a long, loud grunt as every muscle contracted, his face contorting in agony.

The world blurred and Kyra hit the asphalt hard on the same arm that the man had nearly knocked out of its socket, the same one that a bullet had torn open three years before. She gritted her teeth against the pain, managed not to cry out, but the wind coming out of her forced a grunt from her anyway.

The soldier's inertia carried him forward at full speed but his legs had locked up and he pitched forward, his face slamming against the concrete, shattering his nose. His head bounced up from the hard surface, then gravity pulled him down again, his face connecting with the ground a second time.

His finger was already on his pistol's trigger. The muscles in his right hand contracted and the Makarov fired into the ground. The bullet ricocheted on the asphalt, flying off in some odd direction. It struck a tire, punching a hold in the rubber, and the sound of rushing air sounded in his ears.

The Spetsnaz team had the traitor on the ground. The rope was in her mouth and two men were holding her arms behind her back and stripping off her coat.

The team leader hadn't expected Puchkov to show. He'd thought for certain the primary team would detain her at her home, where

Colonel Sokolov was commanding the detail. The other four teams, including his, were covering sites Sokolov had said were communication points used by the turncoat, but with all of the CIA officers in Moscow expelled, he hadn't expected any of the secondary units to act. But here she was, and the glory of Puchkov's capture belonged to his team.

Colonel Sokolov's information, whatever the source, had been accurate—

Somewhere, a Makarov fired.

The team leader's head jerked around. Puchkov was lying helpless on the cold dirt in front of him, so whichever of his men had fired had not been shooting at her. *Where? Who fired?*

Kyra heard the gunshot. Pain erupted in her right shoulder again as she tried to push herself up. She ignored it and rolled over, trying to get her bearings. Her vision started to focus again.

The soldier was on the ground, still unable to control himself. The Taser was five seconds into a thirty-second cycle, and it was holding the Spetsnaz officer down, his body as hard as the ground it was lying on. His nose was gushing blood.

Kyra pushed herself to her knees and grabbed the Taser off the ground. She didn't know how long the man would need to recover once the weapon stopped disrupting his nervous system, but he was still able to grunt one unbroken, guttural cry of pain.

Kyra let the electrical current flow into him as she searched for the rest of the soldiers. She found them when she heard another shout in Russian. Several of the soldiers surrounding Puchkov were now pointing in her direction.

In a flash of anger, Kyra tried to rip the barbs out of the man's neck. One came out, tearing flesh and drawing more blood for the pavement, but the other probe was stubborn. Kyra ejected the cartridge connecting the probes to the pistol. The circuit broken, the man's body sagged like his bones had melted, muscles still twitching from the residual current firing through his nerves. Then he was still and silent.

Kyra picked up his Makarov. She shoved the Taser back into her pocket, then looked back toward the market where Puchkov had gone down.

More soldiers were now running her way, guns drawn. She heard one fire, then another, bullets hitting cars, the sound of metal punching through metal. They'd seen her.

Kyra pushed off, keeping her head low, running for the Tiguan fifty yards away. The men running toward her position were fast, but they were too far away to catch her now.

She heard more shots, hitting closer to her now. One round missed her by less than a foot, hitting a car as she ran by, a deeper sound than the Makarov rounds, a higher-caliber bullet. Someone had resorted to a rifle now.

Kyra skidded to a stop behind a car, a tiny red Lada Riva that was older than she was. She raised the Makarov and, for the first time on Russian soil, fired a weapon in anger. She sent five rounds downrange, shattering two cars windows and forcing the soldiers to move to cover. Kyra didn't stop. She couldn't spring now. She could only scramble low for the next car, five yards closer to her Tiguan, turn, and send three more rounds back to their original owners.

The Spetsnaz returned fire almost immediately, half shooting while the forward element moved up, then the lead group giving cover fire for the rear unit to catch up. Kyra saw it, and the rounds coming in on her position began to hit the cars around her in a constant rattle. She fired again, keeping low.

Just like Venezuela, Jon. Remember? Kyra thought. *I was trapped against the fence, two hundred soldiers coming in. Then you showed up, on the hill with that big Barrett of yours, like a god with a gun, killing jeeps and lights.*

Kyra was surprised at her own calm. Panic should have set in by now. Jon wasn't here to lay down cover fire for her this time.

The Tiguan was twenty yards away now, the soldiers almost a hundred in the other direction. Kyra fired the Makarov again. She couldn't have more than a few shots left now.

She was almost on her hands and knees, working her way around the last parked cars between her and the SUV. The Spetsnaz had lost track of her for the moment. They knew she was directly ahead, but she hadn't put her head up for almost thirty seconds.

Their target hadn't fired on them for just as long, and their firing grew sporadic as they saved their ammunition for a target they could see. They began to move forward in a low crouch, weapons raised to eye level.

Kyra finally reached her vehicle. She inhaled deep, filling her lungs, then aimed the Makarov and emptied the rest of the clip at the Russians. The soldiers ducked down, scrambling for cover again as their target reappeared.

Kyra pulled the Tiguan's door open, threw herself inside, and closed it up again, putting a layer of metal between her and the enemy. She slammed the keys into the ignition, ordered the truck to life, and it obeyed with a roar. She put it in gear, put the accelerator to the floor, and the wheels began spinning fast, trying to grab the asphalt. White smoke erupted from under the truck.

The soldiers heard the Tiguan come to life, then saw the smoke rising from the ground. They stood and began firing almost in unison.

The wheels finally took hold of the road and the SUV picked up speed, putting distance between Kyra and the soldiers now running in her direction. The sound of bullets perforating the tailgate sounded in the cab, like sharp thumps, rain on a metal roof. She kept her head down until she was at least three hundred yards distant.

• • •

The road bordered the residential complex in a rounded square. Whatever the speed limit was, Kyra went fast enough to break it, hoping the scream of the engine would be warning enough for any-one walking the streets outside the Spetsnaz cordon to stay clear. She pulled to the outside edge of the road, slowed a bit, then accelerated into the turn. The road straightened out for five hundred feet. Three more turns and Kyra was on the Kurkinskoye road again, pushing the SUV as hard as it would go.

Her eyes went to the rearview mirror, and she saw a black sedan pull onto the road a half mile behind her, taking the turn hard enough to convince Kyra that it was a chase car. A second car followed be-hind, an identical model but for its blue color, and both vehicles ac-celerated faster than any normal car could have managed. *Upgraded engines*, Kyra decided. She ran the Tiguan's accelerometer into the red. The chase cars were still closing distance.

Splitting her attention between the rearview and the road ahead, she marked off a passing tree, then began counting seconds. Kyra kept her eyes locked on the mirror, watching until the cars behind reached the mark. *Thirty seconds*, she decided. *They'll catch up in thirty seconds.*

Side road? She considered the option, but she didn't know where any of them would take her. The probability that she would encoun-ter a dead end or get blocked off by the Spetsnaz seemed high.

The main road bent to the right, leading out of the residential area into a more wooded, undeveloped landscape, and the highway began curving gently back and forth. That would slow down her pur-suers and buy her a few seconds.

She couldn't continue on this road. The men behind her would have radios, they would be calling for help, and eventually she would find a roadblock in her path or a helicopter overhead that she would never evade. She needed to break contact and get out of the chase cars' line of sight.

The road straightened out again. She saw empty green fields to both sides, with long tree lines at the far side of each. Kyra searched for a break in the woods, anywhere she could take the SUV that their street cars behind couldn't follow. She saw nothing.

She looked in the mirror. The cars were within a few lengths of the Tiguan. She was out of time. Within a few seconds, they would draw guns and take out her rear tires.

There was one maneuver she could try, the one her trainers in the Agency's "Crash and Bang" course had drawn up on the whiteboard, but refused to let the students practice, citing its lethal potential. She'd never tried it before, didn't know if it would work.

What do you think, Jon? she asked.

This is not a good idea, the absent man replied.

You always say that, she countered. *You got a better idea?*

There was no answer. *That's a no.* "C'mon," she muttered, looking at the Russian cars in the mirror.

Kurkinskoye was a two-lane road. A car passed in the opposite direction, and Kyra saw both lanes ahead were clear for at least a mile. She let the Tiguan drift to the right, almost onto the shoulder, so the lead car could see open path. The driver bit hard on that bait, pulled to the left, and accelerated. Kyra saw the black sedan's front passenger window begin to roll down as it passed into her blind spot. Someone inside would be lining up for a shot.

Kyra tapped her brakes, dumping a little speed and letting the lead car shoot ahead. A pistol shot from inside the other vehicle went wide as the gunner hurried the shot and missed her Tiguan completely. Then she poured on the gas, pulling up and putting her front left tire even with the hostile car's right rear quarter.

Bye bye, she thought.

Kyra turned her steering wheel hard left and the Tiguan's front bumper struck the Russians' rear tire, pushing hard against the black vehicle.

• • •

The sedan's back end skewed and all four tires lost their grip on the asphalt. White smoke began pouring out as the rubber turned molten from the friction. The car's front end spun into Kyra's lane, and she slowed enough to let it rotate until the entire vehicle was sliding sideways down the road at a right angle to her. The SUV shuddered as the passenger-side doors struck her front. She steered her truck left and the car finally spun out. The driver had no control now, his attempts to steer useless as the car slid on pools of liquid made of its own melting tires. The car rotated until it was facing the opposite direction. Kyra stomped on the gas and pulled past it.

The black sedan kept rotating until it was almost crossways in the road again. The blue car's driver had seen Kyra push the other vehicle, watched as it spun until Kyra's SUV blocked it from his view. Thinking that Kyra would swerve right and his teammates' car would come to a spinning halt on the left, he'd swerved to the right side of the road to avoid the coming wreck. But he was following too closely behind to react when the black car appeared in front of him. The lead chase car had pinwheeled across the entire road.

The blue sedan's driver spun his own steering wheel, desperately trying to avoid his black twin, but there was nowhere left to go. The darker car was still spinning, white smoke blinding them both to anything coming ahead. He pushed the brakes to the floor, a mistake that forced the blue sedan's tires to lock up. They too went liquid from the friction as the car's inertia forced it to keep rushing down the road.

The cars slammed into each other, the front of the blue sedan connecting with the driver's door of the black vehicle, crumpling both. The black sedan driver's left arm and leg were shattered on contact, his ribs snapping like kindling from a dead oak tree. Steam and black smoke erupted from the blue car's engine. Fluids gushed out of the undercarriage, leaving a stream of oil on the road and marking the death skid of its owner.

The weight of the black sedan finally dragged the blue car to a stop, its front end still crushed into the lead car's side. The black smoke rising up from engine oil burning on the hot engine block mixed with the white fog of the melting tires and steaming radiators, filling the air with a noxious gray concoction that blocked their view of the Kurkinskoye.

Kyra accelerated until she was out of the Russian soldiers' line of sight, then took the first right turn she found. Five more random turns and she found herself approaching a major highway. She could still see the faint pillar of smoke rising from the Spetsnaz cars now over a mile away.

She maneuvered the Tiguan onto the major artery, and only then asked the GPS unit to show her the way back to the safe house.

The "Aquarium" — old GRU headquarters

Sokolov opened the folder and stared down at the paperwork, still filled out with manual typewriters. Computers were a danger to security and he used them as little as possible. "Elizaveta Igoryevna Puchkov. You had a fine record of service, Major."

The woman in handcuffs across the table kept her mouth closed and didn't look up. She was a pretty thing, not the most attractive woman he'd ever seen, a little short, a bit overweight, black hair cut to a bob. The file said she was divorced, almost forty, childless, though he wondered whether that was by choice or nature's cruelty. The latter, he hoped. The *Rodina* needed strong children and the president of the Russian Federation had all but declared a refusal to bear them an act of disloyalty to the country. Not a crime, technically speaking, but some men would have called it another act of treason to add to the paper stack on the table.

"Have you nothing to say?" he asked.

"Would it matter if I denied the charge?"

"I think not." The interrogator lifted an open box from the floor and set it on the table, then emptied the contents one object at a time. An encryption pad, edible paper, a SRAC transmitter, and other electronics took their places in the space between the two people. "These were recovered from your home. They would seem to establish very clearly that you have been working for the CIA."

"What would you have me say?" Puchkov asked, her voice cracking with anger.

Surprising, Sokolov thought. *No fear, only hostility.* Few people in her place had that reaction. For many, the main obstacle to extracting a confession was the prisoner's anxiety. Terror was nature's most effective paralytic. But the hostile ones, getting a confession from them often was just a matter of touching the nerve that had spawned and fed their outrage. An angry person was usually very willing to explain herself. "The truth. That is all I need."

"What does the truth matter?" she asked. "We both know that I would not be here in shackles"—she held up her hands—"if our superiors had not already decided what the truth is for themselves. What I tell you will make no difference in what happens to me."

Sokolov was confused. *So angry, but unwilling to say why?* That was unusual. He pushed again, trying to find a trigger that would elevate her hostility to a level that would override her self-control. "Perhaps not," he admitted. "But you can still be of service to your country. Surely you still feel some loyalty—"

"Loyalty?" she hissed. "Loyalty to the country that is going to put a bullet in my head? If you were in this chair, you would find that the condemned cannot feel loyalty toward the executioners."

"Or remorse, I suppose."

"No," Puchkov said. She turned her head and looked away, falling silent.

Sokolov frowned. If she wouldn't explain herself in anger, perhaps she might respond to a kinder approach. "Then I ask you, in honesty, why did you commit treason? What was your reason? I truly would like to understand."

"Why? So you can help the GRU become more efficient at spotting a Judas before he can kiss one of the generals on the cheek?"

A Christian? Sokolov wondered. The file said nothing about her being a woman of faith. Were her motivations somehow religious? Sokolov exhaled. "No, not that. I have my own reasons. If you will tell me yours, I promise you, I will not put them in my final report."

"I don't believe you," Puchkov said, her voice flat.

"I understand, but as there has been no trial, I think you will understand when I say that those who have ordered your death have no interest in understanding your motives. I could record them, but no one would read them. Anything I record here will be boxed away in some warehouse where no one will see the papers for a hundred years. Or perhaps they will be burned . . . I don't know. So I am being quite honest with you when I say that I want to know your motives only for myself."

Puchkov stared at him for long seconds, studying his face, trying to decide whether she believed his claims. The interrogator said nothing, giving her all the time she wanted. The woman finally spoke after two minutes had passed. "Because our country is lost," she said. "We could have had a free country. We had our moment . . . and we let the oligarchs and the organized criminals come back, and now we are a tyranny again. Now our leaders kill anyone who leaves and speaks out. Girenko, Novikov, Yushenkov, Kozlov, Litvinenko, Markelov? How many others? How many reporters and writers? They hunt them and shoot them in the street or feed them polonium tea. Even if I left the *Rodina*, if I spoke my conscience, they would come and find me and do the same to me. So tell me, how can I betray a country that feels no loyalty for me? Impossible. You can only betray those who care for you."

A true believer, he thought. Topilin had committed treason for money; he'd seen others do it for ego or excitement, some because they felt slighted by superiors or colleagues. But Puchkov had done it because her morality had driven her to it. But there was a vehemence behind the words. This was no mere ideologue. No, the Kremlin had hurt this woman, hurt her in a very personal way. *Who did we kill, Major?* Sokolov wondered. *A family member? A best friend? A lover?* He doubted she would tell him. Such personal pain was not to be shared with those who had caused it.

"I understand," Sokolov said. "And I do not judge you. You are not alone in thinking as you do. So please believe that you have my respect."

Puchkov glared at him. "And what does that earn me now?"

"Perhaps nothing," Sokolov admitted. "But the most honorable acts aren't those that we perform for ourselves, are they? It is only when we serve others that we become the best of men and women."

"That depends on who we choose to serve," Puchkov said. "And you serve evil men."

Sokolov repressed a smile and closed Puchkov's file. "I am not a religious man, Major Puchkov. And where there is no god to tell us right from wrong, evil becomes simply a matter of perspective."

New GRU headquarters
Khoroshevskoye shosse 76
Moscow, Russia

"I am told that several of your people were injured today, Arkady." Lavrov wanted to slam the phone onto its cradle, but he refused to acknowledge any setback to Grigoriyev. The old FSB director was known for his mind games. He had neutralized more than one opponent by pricking their egos and goading them into mistakes.

"Such things are not unexpected," Lavrov replied.

"They are when your people are engaged in illegal operations," Grigoriyev told him, his voice turning cold in an instant. "It is one thing for you to twist the foreign minister's strings and convince the president to expel Americans. It is quite another for you to perform your own counterintelligence operations on our own soil. That is the duty of the FSB."

"That is true," Lavrov conceded. "But our source has given us the names of CIA moles within our own government. We cannot release those names to you without endangering the source, so it has become necessary for us to take on the responsibility to arrest the traitors. Call the president and discuss the matter with him if you wish."

"Oh, I don't think that's what you are doing, Arkady," Grigoriyev chided. "In fact, I think that there is some other reason you want to keep this all hidden from me. I think you don't want the FSB looking into your operations at all."

"I have nothing to hide from you."

"Quite the opposite, I think," Grigoriyev said. "I am told that your people tried to arrest another person at the scene, a woman. And this woman not only escaped arrest, but she took down one of your Spetsnaz soldiers as she did so, and then left two of your men's cars wrecked in a ditch. Three people were hospitalized."

Lavrov restrained a curse. The old man had his own spies inside the GRU. Lavrov had suspected that, but hadn't been able to confirm it. It wasn't unexpected. The FSB was the spawn of the KGB, and if there was one thing that organization had excelled at, it was spying on its own citizens.

"So I have a theory," Grigoriyev goaded him. "I think that your source did not give you the names of every CIA officer in Russia. I think there is still one out there, probably more, and you don't know who she is."

"If so, it would be your duty to find her," Lavrov countered.

"Oh, no, that is a duty the GRU has accepted, as I recall," Grigoriyev chided his rival. "And I would hate for you to have to admit that your operation has a nasty blemish that you and your people could not manage."

"Competence is best shown by how one manages the unexpected," Lavrov replied.

"Then I look forward to discussing your competence at our next meeting with the president," Grigoriyev said.

"Oh, Anatoly," Lavrov said, "when did I lose your support? Your friendship? We were such comrades once. That night on the embassy roof in Berlin was a great moment for us."

"And a disaster for the *Rodina*. We began to lose our country that night. You lost my support when you began this madness of selling our technologies to third-world runts who do not have the wisdom to use our knowledge in a useful way. You are giving hammers to children who want nothing more than to swing them at each other."

"I am only doing what we all promised to do. We agreed to save the *Rodina*. I regret we could not agree on the way it should be done. Poor Strelnikov became so confused he thought that the Americans were our salvation," Lavrov intoned.

"You are wrong, Arkady," Grigoriyev told him. "Strelnikov did not believe the Americans were our salvation. He simply thought they were the only ones who could turn you out of your destructive course. I am not sure that I disagree."

"Your opinion of me has fallen so low?"

"I think my opinion matters nothing to you," Grigoriyev replied. "And there is the problem. You take counsel from no one. When you will, I think you will find many ready to stand with you again. *Do svidaniya*."

"Do svidaniya," Lavrov said. He set the phone in the cradle far more gently than he would have preferred, but he didn't want to fumble the maneuver and let the FSB director hear a physical sign of his frustration.

The GRU chairman leaned back and stared up at the ceiling. Maddening as Grigoriyev was, it was possible that he was right . . . about the woman. If the woman who had evaded his men during Puchkov's arrest was CIA, then someone had been missed.

Lavrov frowned. No, there was another possibility, wasn't there? Perhaps, in the focus on getting all of the CIA's officers out of the country, another one had come in? And a woman, too, a bold one, capable of facing a Spetsnaz soldier and leaving him a twitching wreck on the pavement.

He had met a woman with such fire recently, hadn't he? *Is that possible?* he wondered. *That she is here?*

Lavrov picked up the phone again and dialed a number he was learning by heart these days. Colonel Sokolov answered after the first ring. *"Ya slushayu vas."*

"Anton Semyonovich, this is General Lavrov."

"Good evening, General. I presume you are calling about today's action?"

"I am. Please congratulate your men on their successful capture of another traitor to the *Rodina*," Lavrov said, his voice warm.

"I will. Thank you, General."

"I regret that is not the end of the matter," Lavrov said. "Your report of a possible foreign operator at the site who interfered is worrisome. We need to find the woman in question. Please contact the security offices at all of our international airports within five hundred kilometers around Moscow. I want the passport photographs of all foreign women traveling from Germany admitted to the country in the last seventy-two hours."

"We will begin immediately," Sokolov replied. "But it will be a very large number. Any information that could help us narrow the search might provide an answer more quickly."

Lavrov paused. "Tell them to focus on women coming from Berlin."

"Yes, sir."

"Very good. And, Anton Semyonovich . . . I think we must accelerate the operation. If the CIA still has officers in Moscow, they will be trying to save their assets. That cannot be allowed, of course. I will assign you additional men, and you will begin moving against the traitors several at a time. I will provide you the names for the first tranche I want neutralized. Understood?"

There was a short delay before Sokolov answered. "*Da*, General."

"Is there a problem, Colonel?"

"*Nyet*, General. I am just concerned about launching a more ambitious set of raids without the opportunity for new men to train with my team. Unit cohesion can be a delicate thing. We do not want to lose any of the targets due to our own mistakes."

"There will be no mistakes, I trust," Lavrov warned. "These men are Spetsnaz, after all . . . and there is no better way to forge a team than a successful operation."

"Of course, General. I will keep you informed of our progress."

"Thank you, Colonel." Lavrov hung up the phone.

Did you follow me here, Miss Stryker? he wondered. *What a happy surprise that would be.*

Kyra's safe house
Moscow, Russia

The door closed behind Kyra's truck and the garage went dark. She had taken a winding route back, running surveillance detection as she went, though she was sure she needn't have bothered. Had the

GRU or any of the other security services picked up her tail, they would have swarmed her vehicle as quickly as they could have called in the help.

Kyra had taken three hours to make her way to the safe house and the sun had set more than an hour before. The garage was shrouded in darkness as she killed the headlights. The woman sat back in the seat, not bothering to unbuckle her restraint. Her eyes adjusted to the dark.

Kyra hit the steering wheel with her fist, then again. She pounded on it, as hard as she could. Then she began to yell in anger, cursing the Russians for their brutality and their skill at it, slamming her hands into the wheel as she did. Her hands began to protest, aching more and more with each strike against the truck. Finally she stopped when the pain was too much. Her chest began to heave. Kyra leaned forward, placed her forehead against the steering wheel. She refused to cry, much as she wanted to.

She'd lost track of the time, how long she was in the truck. Kyra finally emerged and walked into the mudroom, letting her keys fall on the floor. The keypad demanded her full attention before letting her into the house, but Kyra's thoughts disorganized themselves again once she heard the computerized lock open. She entered, the metal door closing itself behind.

The bathroom on the second level was enormous, with a glass-enclosed shower and a tub large enough to disappear in. Kyra thought about cleaning up for the first time since Berlin. She took stock of herself in the mirror. Her right arm ached. She pulled her sleeve up and realized that a massive bruise, black with a green and yellow border, had spread across the muscle. There was ibuprofen in the cabinet and she didn't bother to count how many of the red oval pills she took. The sink water tasted of metal.

Barron had been right. She was never going to get near any of the Agency's assets. The Russian knew exactly who they were, had too much manpower, and knew the terrain far better than she ever could. Kyra had no advantage, no angle to play that would let her seize the high ground even for a few minutes.

I don't think I can do this, Jon, she told her friend, wherever he was.

Maybe not, he agreed. *The Russians aren't amateurs. Fighting them is a team sport on a good day, and this isn't a good day. You don't have any help.*

I got away, she replied. *Again.*

Dumb luck, he chided her. *That soldier draws his gun a little faster and you're dead. You miss with that Taser and you're dead. One of that guy's teammates has a little better aim with a pistol at a hundred yards and you're dead. You didn't plan for any contingencies. You didn't even scout the area before you went in. You shouldn't be sitting here.*

I had to try to reach Puchkov. She was my best chance to find an asset who could help me find you, Kyra protested to the voice in her head. *But I didn't. I couldn't. How am I supposed to figure out where you are, or if you're even still alive, if I can't get to any of our assets inside the GRU before the Russians?*

You're not thinking, Jon's voice replied.

What do you mean? she asked.

Why do you always run straight in? he asked.

Kyra's mind focused in a single moment. Run straight in? It was true. She'd done it every time, in Caracas when she'd gotten shot . . . in Beijing, when she'd been asked to save the Agency's most valuable asset . . . at the CAVIM chemical plant near Morón when the president had wanted to know what the Iranians had smuggled into Venezuela. She'd gone in each time, always finding a way to go through the enemy's security, and always being discovered before she could get back out. Training, Jon, and more dumb luck than she deserved had gotten her home, but she'd had to fight her way out every time. Now she'd finally come up against an enemy that was too skilled to fight. Kyra could go straight at the Russians, but she would never be able to get in.

I'm no coward, she reminded Jon.

Bravery and intelligence are not the same thing, he countered. *And neither one matters without a plan.*

So how do I do this? she asked. *How do I find out what happened to you? How do I stop Lavrov?*

She could almost see her partner smile, that arrogant look he couldn't suppress when he'd figured out the answer before everyone else. *That soldier you took down with the Taser. Did you notice anything about him?*

Kyra sat back and stared at the ceiling, hands behind her head. *Military haircut, hard as steel . . . he carried a Makarov sidearm.*

And who uses Makarov pistols? Jon's voice asked her.

The pistol was the same as the ones the men at Vogelsang had carried. Spetsnaz, Kyra realized. *The GRU control the Spetsnaz. Those were Lavrov's men at the market.*

Don't you think it's interesting that the GRU is arresting traitors on Russian soil? Isn't that the FSB's job? he seemed to say.

Kyra cocked her head. That was interesting. Grigoriyev, the FSB director, hated Lavrov, the GRU chairman. *Why would he let Lavrov run the operations to capture all of the CIA's assets?* she wondered.

What makes you think Grigoriyev even knows what Lavrov is doing? Or that he's cooperating? Jon asked. *What did I teach you about analyzing the enemy?*

Never assume the enemy is monolithic, she replied, answering her absent partner's question. *Never assume that he knows everything that his own people are doing.*

Kyra stared into the mirror, not seeing anything as she tried to focus her mind. She needed to think, but the stress of the past days had cost her all of the energy she had. The fog of sleep deprivation and jet lag was closing in on her. She needed to think. Rest was the only good answer for that, but for now she would have to rely on the false energy of caffeine and adrenaline. She didn't know how long she would sleep if she closed her eyes and she didn't want to give free time away to Lavrov.

Kyra stumbled over to the kitchen and fired up the coffeemaker on the counter. The Russian brands in the cabinet were black and bitter, and Kyra drained three cups to the dregs once the machine started to produce. She poured a fourth mug, set it down on the kitchen table, and looked at her list. There was only one name left on it.

Her hands were shaking hard, her eyes fighting her attempts to focus on the page, and her mind jumping from idea to idea every few seconds. When the caffeine finally passed through her system, Kyra knew that she had reached her limits. The dark living room was close and the couch looked soft, but she refused to surrender so completely. She stumbled up the stairs to the second level, wandered into the first bedroom on the right, fell on the bed, and let the oblivion take her without a fight.

CHAPTER EIGHT

Lavrov had never seen one of his Spetsnaz look so battered outside of a training accident. The man's comrades had brought him to the hospital themselves rather than trusting him to an ambulance crew, and the Botkin was one of the better hospitals in Moscow. It was the facility to which most foreigners in the country came for treatment and was well equipped by Russian standards.

The soldier was lying in a reclining bed, an IV in his arm, dripping saline and morphine both at a slow rate. Both of the man's eyes were badly bruised, deep blue, black-and-green circles surrounding them and stretching into his forehead and cheeks. The surgeon had stanched the bleeding, set his nose, and stitched up the torn flesh on the back of his neck. He'd assured Lavrov that the soldier would suffer no permanent damage from the Taser, something about high voltage but low amperage. But the man's face would take weeks to heal up. He'd tried to refuse the painkiller, but the soldier's team leader had finally told him that there would be no shame in taking it. The morphine had hit his system and the wounded commando had slumped into a deep sleep almost immediately.

Lavrov regretted having to wake him, but the soldier would understand, even if the doctor did not. The surgeon had not wanted to lower the man's morphine drip, but Lavrov gave the order. It was too hard to think and focus one's swollen eyes while riding a morphine high.

"This one?" Lavrov asked, holding up a photograph, the tenth in the stack.

"*Nyet,*" the soldier replied, his voice strained.

Another photo. "This one?" Lavrov asked again.

"*Nyet.*"

Lavrov pursed his lips in frustration. Hundreds of women had entered Moscow from Berlin through the international airport in the last two days. The general decided to skip to the one woman he was interested in most. If the soldier didn't identify her, an aide could handle the rest of the stack.

He rifled through the pictures until he found the only one he wanted. He held it up. "This one?"

The soldier stared, trying to focus on the picture. He forced his head to move forward, bring the image an inch closer. "*Da.*"

"You are sure?"

"I only saw her for a few seconds, and that while running. She had blond hair, not red, and pulled back away from her face, which was thinner. But it could be the same woman." The soldier let his head fall back on the pillow.

"Very good," Lavrov said. "We are most proud of you. You have done your duty." He was surprised the younger man had recognized the American woman through his haze. It had taken the GRU chairman almost six hours going through the photographs to find the one he imagined could have been the same woman he had met on the embassy roof. He would have preferred to let a subordinate take care of sorting through the photographs, but everyone else who had seen the woman was back in Berlin, except Maines. Lavrov didn't trust Maines to pick her out without the threat of pain, and Lavrov had to reserve that tool for another request he might have to give the traitor if his next inquiry turned up empty.

"No, General," the soldier protested, "I failed in my duty. She escaped. I want to return to duty and assist in her arrest."

"Do not worry about that, Captain," Lavrov assured the injured man. "The operation is not done. We do not reinforce failure, but one failure is not the end. You will yet have your chance."

"Thank you, General," the young soldier replied.

Lavrov nodded, patted the young man's hand, then looked at the photograph. *She is here. Miss Stryker is in the* Rodina, he thought. The thought sent a happy thrill up his spine. It was so rare to find an American who was not overly cautious in this business, who was inclined to attack and trust in her skills to finish her mission.

You are a bold one, devushka. *But where are you?*

FSB headquarters
Moscow, Russia

"You humiliate me in front of the president, and now you wish a favor?" Grigoriyev asked, astonished. Lavrov's arrogance was boundless. The FSB director was tempted to cut off the call, but decided that would be unwise. Soothing a wounded ego was a poor excuse for passing up an opportunity to collect some political intelligence that might prove valuable sometime in the future, possibly sooner than he might expect.

"I would not call it a favor," Lavrov objected. "The FSB is charged with internal security. I merely wish to know if a particular woman has been seen entering the American Embassy here in the city. Surely that is a trivial request for you." The FSB kept the Western embassies under a constant watch. The GRU director no doubt was pained that he had to come to Grigoriyev for that information after having ridiculed him twice in the last day.

"And yet you are making the request yourself," Grigoriyev pointed out. "Yes, it would be trivial for me to get you an answer, but not so trivial for you to pose the question. So I presume you have identified the woman who has been putting your men in the hospitals?"

He was sure that Lavrov was frowning on the other side of the phone. "I have," Lavrov replied, surprising the FSB director. "I know where she entered the country, which flight, and when it landed. But making an arrest would be much easier if I knew whether she was operating out of the American Embassy or that of a U.S. ally."

"Ah," Grigoriyev replied. "Of course, we would need all of the information you have on this woman to make any positive identification."

"Of course," Lavrov conceded. "I can have a courier ferry the file to your office immediately if you are willing to assist me."

Assist you? Grigoriyev thought. The man was infuriating. Even when asking for information, the GRU director could not help but twist the conversation to place himself above the person whose help he needed. *Still, if my people could catch this woman before Lavrov . . . yes, that would do nicely*, he thought. Arresting the lone CIA spy in Moscow would shift the balance of influence that had tipped so very dangerously in Lavrov's favor. "Without question, the FSB stands ready to assist you, General," Grigoriyev said. "The security of the *Rodina* is more important than our small differences."

"Without question," Lavrov replied. "Expect my man to arrive within the hour."

"I will admit him without delay," Grigoriyev assured him. "We will have an answer for you as quickly as we can manage."

"Your assistance is appreciated."

"*Do svidaniya*, General."

Lavrov hung up his phone. Losing that small bit of face would be worth the sacrifice if Grigoriyev came back with anything useful. Lavrov's own men were watching the U.S. Embassy, but it was possible that Stryker had entered some other allied embassy, the British or Canadian buildings most likely. His men were not watching those. Grigoriyev's were.

If Stryker was cautious, inclined to self-preservation, the smart move for her would be to leave the country. Her best defense had been secrecy, and the Puchkov operation had stolen that. So it was possible that Grigoriyev's men would catch Miss Stryker trying to escape the *Rodina*. Lavrov doubted she would try to fly out through any of the major airports. With her cover identity blown, she would expect the FSB would be watching all of the major transportation hubs for hundreds of miles around Moscow. No, more likely she would try to cross into one of the border countries in a car, or perhaps even abandon her car and try to hike across. It had been done before and the FSB would be watching.

But he didn't think Stryker would run.

The general retrieved another beer from his small refrigerator, cracked the bottle open, and took a long swig before leaning back in his chair. The young woman knew about his operations. She needed to be neutralized somehow, and Lavrov was prepared to enlist Grigoriyev's help to reach that goal. The FSB director didn't need to know all the details, and he would be happy to have any part in Lavrov's success. So Lavrov would throw him those crumbs. The bigger operation promised glory enough that he could be generous to his old enemy. Besides, being a small part of another's victory could taste more bitter than suffering failure alone, and this game was his and Stryker's to play.

She was a move behind. He had confirmed that she had tried to contact one of the top few names on his list of traitors. Had she tried to contact Topilin? Possibly. Based on the time she had entered the country, he suspected that she wouldn't have been able to get to the now-dead man's dacha before Sokolov had arrested the turncoat. She might have visited the dead man's dacha and found it already sacked.

If so, his men might have been able to grab her there, had Sokolov left a sentry team.

Lavrov frowned. That had been a lapse, but an understandable one, he supposed. Sokolov had had no reason to suspect anyone would have been trying to reach Topilin, and Lavrov had told him that there would be more names to come. The colonel likely had wanted to have all his men available for the next arrest, not leaving them in the woods watching a ransacked cabin. But if Stryker had tried to reach Topilin, then it would be a sure sign that Lavrov had assessed her mission correctly and he knew who her next target must be. The only question now was how to steer her where he wanted her to go.

Grigoriyev didn't call for four hours, time enough for Lavrov to finish half a bottle of Viski Kizlyarskoe–brand whiskey, a single malt produced in Daghestan. It helped the afternoon pass more smoothly. The GRU chairman had long since grown tired of vodka, as had most of the elites who could afford better. He swirled the glass, sniffed at it, and smelled . . . what was that? *Honey*, he thought. Lavrov downed the dregs in the glass. Yes, much better than vodka, easier on the throat, if not the liver. He would never admit it, of course. Vodka was the national drink and had the weight of history on its side. His people loved their liquor and vodka had a special place in the Russian mind and heart. The Kremlin had been cracking down on alcohol consumption for years now, trying to keep the people from drinking themselves to death, but the leadership had never seriously considered prohibition. No, that was out of the question. The Americans had tried that once, with feckless results, and they didn't love their alcohol as the Russian people did. It was said that when Russia had been given a choice between Christianity and Islam, it had chosen the former only because the latter prohibited the drinking of spirits.

The secure-line telephone finally sounded. Lavrov set the glass on the desk and answered the call. *"Ya slushayu vas."*

"Arkady Vladimirovich." It was the FSB director.

"Thank you for responding so swiftly."

"Of course, but you will not like the information I have to report," Grigoriyev advised. "My counterintelligence officer reports that none of our surveillance teams have observed a woman matching the photograph you provided entering the American Embassy during the last week, or any other embassy of any country allied with the Americans. If she is CIA and still on our soil, then she is operating out of some other location. We are reviewing our files now and drawing up a list of possible sites where she could be."

Lavrov narrowed his eyes. He'd expected that answer but he disliked it all the same. It would make finding the woman more tedious. "You have my thanks, Anatoly."

"You will, of course, share any information you obtain concerning her whereabouts with me," Grigoriyev told him. He didn't mean it as a request, though he knew Lavrov would tell him nothing.

"Of course. *Do svidaniya.*"

"*Do svidaniya.*" The line went dead. Lavrov cradled the phone, then sat in his chair and tried to think through the whiskey-fueled haze that had settled over his mind. He'd drunk too much waiting for that call and now found it difficult to assemble his thoughts.

Stryker is here, but she is not operating out of her country's embassy or any other. A safe house, then. It had to be, but where?

Grigoriyev's FSB had the information on that, and Lavrov groaned at the thought of calling his adversary back and having to plead with him for access to those particular files. It would pile shame on humiliation.

Lavrov had considered letting her go and making contact with her in the United States, but that seemed too great a risk. Trying to turn a hostile target on her own home soil could backfire in such spectacular fashion. She had to be brought in.

But does she have to die? Lavrov asked himself. Possibly not. She was an intriguing young lady, and she could be a great help in establishing his own Red Cell in the GRU. He doubted that she would betray her country. She did not seem the type, but he saw no reason not to make her the offer. There was no risk in it for him, and the reward could be a tidy one, however improbable.

But he could not make the pitch until they could talk. *So how to find her?* he wondered. He stared at the phone, thought about dialing Grigoriyev's number. There had to be some other way—

Yes, there was another way, and he would have come to it sooner but for the whiskey twisting his thoughts out of shape. The GRU director wondered if Alden Maines might not be willing to give up the information in exchange for some of that fine drink. *Probably*, Lavrov mused, *but why waste it on him?* He didn't need to bribe the American to talk anymore. Fear of the hammer was enough now. He should have asked the traitor about safe houses before but it had not seemed like a priority. With all of the CIA officers forced out, their covert facilities should have been neutralized, left waiting to be identified and sacked at his leisure.

The only questions now were whether Maines had familiarized himself with his former services' safe-house locations in Moscow, and if the traitor could focus long enough to remember. It was one thing to try to remember information while drinking alcohol. It was another to do so with morphine running through the veins. That brave Spetsnaz officer had done it, but Lavrov suspected that Maines was neither so driven nor so resilient.

He picked up his telephone. "Please tell Mr. Maines that we need to have another conversation in my office. When is he due for his next dose of medication? Very good. Withhold it from him, and let him know that it will be waiting for him when our discussion is done." Lavrov hung up the phone and retrieved a box of pushpins and a map of greater Moscow from his desk. He wondered how many locations Maines was going to mark down for him.

She had driven for more than an hour into the countryside with the GPS turned off. If she didn't know where she was, she figured the Russians wouldn't be able to predict her path either. They were going to try to triangulate on the signal she was about to send and she didn't want them to have any kind of head start if they had any clue what neighborhood the safe house was in. Kyra's sense of direction was good and always had been. It was one of the blessings granted by a childhood growing up in the foothills of the Blue Ridge Mountains, where back roads were plentiful and the sun and landmarks were hidden more often than not by the forests that swallowed the gravel roads where she'd learned to drive. Moscow was behind her to the east, and Kyra was reminded how similar the world always looked when there were no signs in foreign languages to remind her that she wasn't home.

She stopped the truck on some side road, barely a dirt trail that probably belonged to some farmer, and sat in the cab until the sun slipped down below the horizon and the world around her went dark. The Russian stars looked no different from those she'd watched in Virginia as a girl. She was in the right hemisphere to see the familiar constellations. In a few hours, the same sky would hover over her home in the United States, but the thought did nothing to calm her anxiety. The darkness felt oppressive, like it was Lavrov's personal ally.

She spent the afternoon in the cab of the truck, sleeping on and off, her mind unwilling to let her go for more than an hour at a time. She stepped outside, stretched, ate what little food was in her pack, and then sat in the grass, trying to reason her way through the situation. In truth, there was only one course of action. She only had the name of one final asset and only one means of communicating with him. Kyra crawled back into the cab and lay on the seat. The hours passed by slowly, and she faded out in the truck again, a deep sleep this time. She awoke to see the Milky Way above her head, a sight that was always washed out back home by the light pollution of Leesburg. Stars were everywhere, the sky alive with a picture of the entire galaxy that stretched out above her in all directions. The sight was peaceful and she stared at it for an hour before deciding to move.

Kyra loaded the shortwave transmitter into the backpack, extending the rubber antenna through the port on the top of the pack. She pulled out an LED light and turned it on, pushing the night away from her path and wincing at how bright the beam was. The woman looked around, but saw no lights anywhere in the distance that could suggest another person was anywhere within her line of sight.

There was a hill a quarter mile beyond and she hiked through the grass until she reached it. It was steep but not especially high, less than two hundred feet to the summit, with rocks and roots bursting out of the dirt. Kyra reached the top in less than thirty minutes, checking her watch at a constant rate as she climbed. She was almost out of time and she wanted to get as much altitude as possible before she had to reach out to the asset.

The man's name was Colonel Semyon Petrovich Zhitomirsky. The file said that he was a GRU chief of staff in some office whose name meant nothing to her, but which had some dealings with the Foundation for Advanced Research. Kyra honestly did not know what kind of access the man might have, but he was her last hope as far as she could see. The other assets on the now-vaporized list were all positioned further and further from the Foundation that seemed to be the center of Lavrov's operation. If Zhitomirsky could not help her, she was out of options.

Kyra set herself and the backpack on the grass. Crossing her legs, she opened up the pack and turned on the shortwave transmitter. The screen lit up the darkness. The communications plan Zhitomirsky's handler had set up for him five years earlier called for him to monitor a shortwave frequency once a month using a small radio the Agency had provided. Once a month, on the day corresponding to the number of the month—1 January, 2 February, 3 March, until year's end—the Russian would turn on his radio for one hour beginning at nine o'clock. The handler would speak only one word, a woman's name, either "Olga," "Anna," or "Nina," each of which would tell the man which meeting site they would use.

The fourth name, "Valery," would trigger an emergency meeting two hours after the transmission at a prearranged site. Kyra hadn't bothered to memorize any of the sites tied to the other names.

She twisted the knob, tuning the transmitter to the frequency that she'd memorized from the encrypted file on the classified computer on the receiver. Her earpiece barraged her with a cacophony of broadcasts . . . an American broadcaster discussing the coming End of Days . . . a political broadcast in Spanish denouncing U.S. interference in Venezuela . . . a Frenchman singing off-key some folk song . . . some Chinese broadcast that sounded like a news report from the speaker's tone of voice, but Kyra really couldn't tell. She finally pulled the earpiece out to save her ears until the screen reported she had arrived at 26770 kilohertz.

Kyra replaced the earpiece and checked her watch. She had to wait three minutes, and then held off two more for good measure in case Zhitomirsky was late. Then she picked up the microphone and depressed the button on the microphone.

"Valery," she said. Kyra released the button, waiting to hear for Zhitomirsky's response. There was none.

Kyra stared at her watch, waiting until one minute had passed, then pressed the button and repeated the name.

"So you are here, *devushka*."

It was Lavrov's voice.

Despair tore through Kyra like the claws on a bear might rip through her skin. She grimaced hard, squeezing the microphone in her hand until her knuckles wanted to crack and she had to hold back a sob.

Lavrov had Zhitomirsky. She didn't even know when or how the general had arrested the asset. He must've had multiple teams, running multiple operations at once. She was one officer, operating in the black. She couldn't even begin to keep up.

She'd been a fool to come, to think she could make any difference at all.

I failed, Jon, she told her missing partner. *I can't beat him. He's everywhere.*

Are you going to quit? the voice inside her head asked.

Kyra opened her eyes, and anger rushed into her, taking over. She pushed the button on the mic again. "Yes, I'm here."

"I had so hoped we could talk again," Lavrov said. "I would have preferred to see you when we did, but I can accept this for now."

"And why would you want to talk to me?" Kyra asked, not trying to keep the disgust out of her voice. She wondered who else might be hearing their conversation.

"Because I admire you, young lady," Lavrov said, not bothering to hide the pleasure in his own. "You are a bold one. I have worked in our business for a long time, longer, I think, than you have been alive, and never have I met one such as you. To walk into our embassy and demand to see a turncoat? How could I not reward such initiative? And then you came here, rushing in when all of your comrades were scurrying out because I told them to. A woman who will not be cowed? Oh, that is its own kind of beauty, and so rare. It must be appreciated . . . but I must ask . . . why did you come here? When all of those who could help you went home, what reason did you have for running toward the sound of the guns?"

"You killed my partner," Kyra accused, the words escaping through clenched teeth. She wondered how many people around the world heard the accusation. The transmission was unencrypted and shortwave signals broadcast at night could reflect off the ionosphere, traveling over the horizon for thousands of miles. In her fury, she didn't really care now.

There was a pause before Lavrov spoke. "The man taken at Vogelsang? Oh, he was a brave one too, that one. To throw himself at two of my best men? He must have cared about you very much to do that. I should like to have known him better, but I have little spare time and he is not a talker."

Kyra's breath caught in her throat.

Is?

Lavrov was a Russian. Had he misspoken, chosen the wrong word as he translated his speech from his native language into hers? No, the man's English was too good . . . no broken sentences, no dropped words, too many rhetorical flourishes.

Jon was alive. Or was Lavrov playing on her emotions, trying to unsettle her thinking, get her to make a mistake?

The despair in her mind vanished and Kyra felt the adrenaline begin to take over. She gathered her thoughts, then lifted the microphone to her mouth again. "He's a talker, if he likes you," Kyra corrected him. "But he doesn't like many people."

"A sensible man, then," Lavrov said. "Perhaps I shall try again with him. In any case, I do wish you to understand that my admiration for you is quite real."

"I don't care what you think about me," Kyra told the man.

"Oh, I do know that," Lavrov replied. "Courage and disdain for the opinions of others grow together. You could not be what I admire so much if my thoughts and desires matter to you at all." There was a pause in his speech, and then Lavrov spoke again. "But now you must care what I think, *devushka*. I have a choice to present and you will make it. I want you to work for me. The other gentleman you met on the embassy roof that day is no longer in a position to feed me useful information, but you could return home and fill that role. Agree, and

I will release your partner to you. You will go home, a hero who pulled her partner out of the ashes. Refuse, and I cannot let you go free. I will catch you. The *Rodina* is my home, my battlefield, and you will lose. So I offer you the only way out that exists. Go home with your friend but in my debt, or not at all, *Miss Stryker*."

Kyra stared down at the microphone in her hand in horror. Lavrov had called her by name, her true name, not the one listed on her passport and other identification papers. *Maines gave me up*, she fumed, anger burning hot in her chest. She should have expected it. The man had given up every other bit of information in his head, why not her name too?

She shook her head. *No time for that*, she ordered. *He wants you confused, angry, off balance, so you'll say or do something stupid.* She had to focus on Lavrov's choice.

No, not Lavrov's choice . . . a Hobson's choice, she thought.

No, he wants you to think it's a Hobson's choice. He still doesn't know where you are. He has Jon, so he thinks he has leverage over you. He thinks he knows what choice you will make. Kyra thought for a moment that it was Jon's voice, but realized that it was her own.

He hadn't really spoken to her since Vogelsang, she knew. It had always been her own thoughts. *So what are you going to do? Become another Maines? An Aldrich Ames? A Robert Hannsen?*

Kyra searched her own feelings. It took her only a few seconds to settle on the answer she had really known all along.

"*Molōn labé*, General," Kyra told Lavrov.

"Ah, an educated woman," Lavrov said. "We are at the pass at Thermopylae, you are Leonidas and I am Xerxes, am I? 'Having come, take?' But you came here, to me."

"We say things a little different back home. 'Come and get me.'"

"You do not like to let others set the rules of the game, do you, *devushka*?" Lavrov replied. "You will reconsider . . . but my patience is not infinite. You can contact me on this frequency any night at this time."

"Don't bother. I'll meet you soon," she told him.

"Indeed," Lavrov said. "I do look forward to it, Miss Stryker."

Kyra turned off the transmitter and the screen faded. *Assume Lavrov isn't lying. He has Jon, but Jon's alive,* she told herself again. *Where are they holding him? How do I find him? Even if I can find him, how do I get in and get him out? How—*

Why do you always run straight in? Jon's voice repeated in her head. *Find a better way for once.*

Kyra lay on her back in the grass, staring up at the stars. She did not move until the answer came.

When it did, she pulled out her smartphone, launched the secure recording app, and began to talk. "This is GRANITE. I have reason to believe that all assets in this AOR have been compromised . . ."

The "Aquarium"—old GRU headquarters

Sokolov pulled the keys from his pocket and unlocked the door to the incinerator room. He pulled it wide open and held it as the guards led the accused in. The man shuffled along as best he could with the shackles keeping him from taking a full stride. The interrogator was patient and let the prisoner move at his own pace. There was no hurry now.

Sokolov dismissed the guards. "Stand outside until I call you, please," he said. They nodded, took up their places in the hall, and closed the door. He pulled out a chair for the prisoner. "Please, sit," he said to the man in chains. "I'm sure that it was a difficult walk."

The prisoner looked at him, suspicious, but reclined in the chair.

Sokolov reached into his coat pocket and pulled out the folded papers he'd carried there. "You are Semyon Petrovich Zhitomirsky," he said.

"I am," the prisoner replied.

"And you were a colonel?"

"I am," Zhitomirsky said.

"You were," Sokolov said. "Your commission in the Glavnoye Razvedyvatel'noye Upravleniye has been revoked, I'm afraid. That is the first and least punishment given to traitors to the *Rodina*."

"I have been convicted of nothing. I have confessed to nothing," Zhitomirsky countered.

"It does not matter," the interrogator told his prisoner. "You have been identified as a spy for the United States of America. The source who revealed you is unimpeachable, or so I'm told, and the evidence found in your dacha leaves you guilty beyond question."

"Lies. I am innocent."

"You did not even try to run."

"As I told you, I am innocent."

"And you have proof of your innocence?" Sokolov asked.

"I cannot prove a negative. Neither can I prove that our fellow officers planted their evidence in my home—"

"Please, sir, you insult me," Sokolov scolded him. "The evidence was neither planted nor fabricated and we both know it. You are not here to defend yourself. Your guilt has been confirmed to the satisfaction of the highest authorities and there will be neither a trial nor appeal. You are here because I am offering you a chance to heal your conscience, if you still have one. If you are a religious man, you may think of me as a priest to whom you can confess your sins. If you are not, you may share with me any words you might care to have recorded. Beyond that, there truly is nothing to say."

Even in the harsh fluorescent light, Sokolov could see Zhitomirsky's face turn white, almost the color of his dress shirt. "No!" the shackled Russian protested. "This is not the Soviet Union! Not anymore! The old ways . . . we don't—"

Sokolov sighed as the prisoner ranted, then waved his hand in the air, signaling for silence. "Sir, protesting to me is pointless. Even if I had the authority to release you or alter your sentence, I would not because then our superiors would execute me in your place. But you are here because you chose to be here—"

"I did not!" Zhitomirsky objected.

"Yes, you did," Sokolov told him. "I am always amazed at the shortsightedness of traitors. Did you honestly believe that you would never be found? And of course you knew what would follow if and when you *were* found. You were an officer of the GRU for twenty years. You took the counterintelligence training. You knew how past traitors were treated. And you still chose this course."

Zhitomirsky stared at him, the inevitable finally settling in his mind. His head fell, his chin almost to his chest, and great racking sobs exploded out of him. The interrogator had seen it many times. He didn't judge the man or think him a coward, but neither did he feel pity for him. The prisoner was simply going through the cycle that every condemned man suffered in his closing moments.

"Semyon Petrovich, if you have nothing to say that you want me to carry back out of this room, then I hope you will do me the kind favor of answering a single question," Sokolov said.

Zhitomirsky raised his head, tears on his cheeks. "What is it?"

"Why did you do it? Surely you had a reason."

The silence lasted for almost ten seconds before the heaving sobs returned, and it took the prisoner two minutes to compose himself enough to speak again. "I hated my superiors," he said, finally. "They told me that I would never be promoted to general."

"And wisely so, it seems," Sokolov said. "Petty revenge. You had no better reason than petty revenge. To salve your ego, you sold your country. Utter selfishness at its worst. I could have respected you had you shared some noble reason for your actions. If a man is going to betray his country, he should do so for his principles." He folded the papers, returned them to his pocket, and stood.

"I have done you the favor you asked," Zhitomirsky said. "Will you do one for me?"

"I will consider it."

"Let me stand up when you shoot me," the prisoner asked.

"I regret that I can't grant that favor," Sokolov said. It was the truth.

"You would deny me that? Such a small request?"

"I must, because you are not going to be shot."

Zhitomirsky blinked, and hope passed across his face. "I . . . I am to go to prison?"

"No," Sokolov said. "I am under orders that you are not to leave this room. But your hated superiors have such contempt for you that they do not wish to waste a bullet on you." He closed the file, stood, and opened the door.

Two men walked in, both dressed in coveralls. The lead man, a muscular, balding man, reached into a pocket, pulled a Taser, and moved toward the prisoner. His partner, a skinnier, younger man with a military haircut, kept walking toward the incinerator.

Confusion took hold of Zhitomirsky and he stared at the men until he figured out the simple riddle, and his face went pale again. "No!" he shouted, drawing back. The larger man pressed the Taser against Zhitomirsky's neck, silencing his yell as every muscle in Zhitomirsky's body seized up. The prisoner convulsed, then fell off the chair onto the floor.

The muscular guard replaced the Taser in his pocket and pulled out two pairs of handcuffs as his comrade opened the incinerator door, which squealed on ungreased iron hinges.

"The stretcher is in the corner behind the furnace," Sokolov told them as they pulled the table and chair toward the corner to free up space for maneuvering. "Advise me when it is done." He took up the file and left the room. He'd seen many a man die during his years of service, but one of Zhitomirsky's superiors must truly have hated the man to have ordered this punishment. *I truly wish you had escaped*, Sokolov thought. *No man deserves this, no matter what he has done or why.*

Office of the Director of the Directorate of Operations

The secure phone called for Barron's attention. He'd come to hate the machine over the years. The mere fact that he needed a phone that could encrypt a conversation was evidence that there were enemies who would listen if they could and use what they learned to hurt his country. Barron had come to that realization early in his career and he'd started to see more such proof everywhere he looked. The guards at the gates, the badge readers at the entrances, metal doors to every vault, locks on every door. But soon he'd seen that it wasn't just the physical barriers. The training courses, incessant reminders of "need to know" and "honor the oath," the very artwork on the walls that paid tribute to great operations of the past where Agency officers had done unto others what the Agency desperately was trying to ensure would never happen to its own. Even the classification markings on every sheet of paper that he handled every day, dictating who did and didn't qualify to read the information . . . all reminders that hatred for the United States was a constant in the world outside.

The head of the Directorate of Operations wished that he'd never had that particular epiphany. Langley was a jail of steel, glass, fiber-optic lines, and paper, and like any true prison, someone who served time became institutionalized . . . accustomed, even dependent on the culture it imposed, unable to adjust to the world outside, where people were free to speak what they knew. So many retired, only to come back as contractors or consultants. Others went downtown to other jobs where they could earn more but stay in CIA's orbit. Just different prisons in the same system.

Barron had better plans. He'd long since exceeded whatever

youthful ambitions he'd harbored and the loftier heights within his reach held no appeal. There was a Montana farm with his name on the deed and the day he gave his blue badge to the security office would be the last time he saw Langley. Whatever neighbors he met north of Billings were never going to know that the man who'd moved in had spent his life fighting Russians and Chinese and terrorists in the dark corners of the world.

The phone sounded for the fourth time, shaking him out of his thoughts. "Barron."

"This is the Ops Center, sir," announced the caller. "A secure transmission has come in and you're going to want to hear it."

"Bring it in."

"Yes, sir."

The voice on the computer file was Kyra Stryker's. The young woman, wherever she was, had set up a sat phone, recorded the message on her smartphone, then compressed and encrypted it, and transmitted it in a single upload that likely took less than a minute. The Russians would never have been able to track it. They would have been doing well just to detect it.

"I have reason to believe that all assets in this AOR have been compromised. Whether they have been captured is unknown, but I can confirm that my three priority assets have been neutralized," she said. Barron listened, pen in hand, but he knew that he would be writing nothing down until he'd listened to the transmission at least twice. *"Also, I have no safe way to communicate with any who might have evaded capture. My hosts demonstrated during my last attempt that they knew the details of the assets' communications plan, so we must assume that all communications methods are compromised. I also must assume that all meeting and dead-drop sites are known. To my knowledge, my safe house is still secure but that may not last indefinitely. I would appreciate any information HQ could provide on that."*

Barron closed his eyes. He'd expected this when the first news of Maines's treason had reached him, but hearing that the Agency's Moscow networks had been decimated was one of those pieces of news that no mental preparation could soften. After Lavrov had finished rounding up their assets, he would almost certainly turn his attention to the Agency's safe houses and other facilities. His people would have to start from zero to rebuild everything, and they would need decades to do it.

"*. . . Also, the host country knows my identity. Our former friend appears to have burned me to his new friends. However, I have reason to suspect that our officer believed KIA last week is alive and in host country's custody,*" Kyra reported. Barron's eyes opened wide at that announcement. "*I have no information on his condition or location, but host-country security services has offered to return him in exchange for my agreement to become their asset. I refused.*"

"Good girl," Barron muttered, nodding. Kyra could have agreed, trying to lure the Russians into a double-agent operation, but that was an exceptionally dangerous game and Lavrov would have prepared for it. Barron suspected that Lavrov's offer never had been genuine at all, but a baited hook to get Kyra to come in from the field. For what reason, Barron wasn't sure. He was sure that any answer would have come at a high and ugly cost that Kyra would have been made to pay.

No assets to save, no way to communicate with anyone who might be free, no safe houses, Barron reasoned. No resources. Maines had burned the Agency's operations to the ground in Moscow. *It's time to come home, Stryker,* Barron decided. There was nothing else for her to do. The question now was how to get her out—

"*I have an operational plan that I want to propose,*" Kyra announced. Barron's head jerked toward the laptop playing the file. "*I am uncertain about chances for success, but at this point, I see no other options. We will need time to reestablish operations in this AOR and creating confusion might be the best we can hope for. Accordingly, I propose that the following . . ."*

Barron put pen to paper and began to scribble notes as the woman spoke to him from the Russian countryside. Kyra finished talking and the recording went silent. He played it again and reviewed his notes as she talked, making sure he had missed nothing. When she finished for the second time, he read everything over and sat back in his chair.

You devious woman, Barron thought. Kyra's admission that she was "uncertain" whether it would work was an understatement . . . he wasn't even sure what would constitute success or whether he could properly call it covert action. Stryker had been brave even to propose it, but he knew from his own experience that an officer trapped in a hostile country viewed risk and reward very differently from those sitting behind desks in northern Virginia.

And I really am one of those now, aren't I? he thought. He'd spent most of his own career in the field, and had so often despised those above him, the former case officers who'd gotten so comfortable in the chairs they'd really been chasing all along . . . the ones who liked to claim "I'm one of you, I know what it's like out there," but who so clearly had forgotten, who'd never really wanted to be out there at all and whose eyes really had always been focused on a desk on the Agency's seventh floor.

Barron capped his pen. *Not going to be one of those*, he decided.

He walked out to the foyer that separated his office from that of the director of analysis twenty feet away. Barron looked down to his secretary. "Julie, I need you to get Kathy Cooke on the line. Whatever she's doing, tell her office that she'll want to cut it off and call me." He paused. His assistant knew better than to ask why he needed to call the deputy director of national intelligence. But Cooke would want to know. "Tell her it's about Jon."

The secretary had no idea who Jon was, but answered "yes, sir" anyway and reached for her own phone. Barron returned to his office, closed the door, and waited the hour it took for the deputy DNI to free herself and return his call.

"You think this has a prayer of working?" Kathy Cooke asked. The deputy DNI stared down at Barron's notepad, rereading the man's scrawl as best she could. He made it to her office at Liberty Crossing less than fifteen minutes after she'd returned his call. Barron's explanation of Kyra's operational plan had taken another five.

"If it was just her with the resources she has right now, not a prayer," Barron replied. "With our help and a little bit from the embassy staff in Moscow, maybe. Lots of variables we can't predict or control. Everyone's timing will have to be on the money and it's going to cost us a very nice safe house no matter what happens, but it's ambitious and we're desperate enough that I'd love to try it just to find out. If it doesn't work, every asset we've got in Moscow is dead."

Cooke's mouth twisted into a wry grin, but Barron knew the woman wasn't feeling much happiness at the moment. "She's trying to use mental aikido on the Kremlin. The question is whether she could sell it."

"It would be an easier sell if she had some serious evidence to prove her own *bona fides* to the Russians," Barron suggested. "And someone to vouch for her."

"Yes, it would," Cooke agreed. "And she's sure Jon's alive." That was not a question.

"She is. Me, not so much," Barron admitted. "But if he is, this might be the only way to get him back. I don't have a better plan and I don't know anyone else who does. But the beauty of it is that this doesn't even qualify as covert action . . . no need for the president to sign off. This is just the kind of thing we do every day, with a twist."

"True, but we'll have to warn him," Cooke said. "If it hits the papers, he won't appreciate the surprise."

"If it works, it won't hit the papers. That's the real beauty of it," Barron observed. "There's no way the Kremlin will advertise it."

Cooke nodded. She stared at the paper, reviewing it all in her mind, and then she looked at her subordinate. "I'll brief Cyrus."

"You think he'll approve?"

"He's been giving me a very long leash," Cooke replied. "Sign me up and I'll sign the check."

"Will do," Barron said. "Wheels up at midnight, Dulles Airport. You know the hangar."

CHAPTER NINE

Kyra had spent the night in the truck. Without blankets or enough clothes, the cab had gotten cold, the temperature easily in the mid-forties. She had slept a bit, running the engine every hour so the heater could keep her warm, as much for her own morale as for comfort. The cold could sap the spirit along with physical strength, and she was going to need both for what she hoped was coming next.

The sunrise caught her by surprise. Kyra hadn't realized that she'd slipped back into oblivion, as her dreams had been nothing more than an extension of her worried thoughts. She checked her watch and realized that almost twelve hours had passed since she'd transmitted her opplan to Langley. They would either approve it or order her home. How she could even get home now, she wasn't sure. Maybe headquarters would give her a route out of the country. In any case, it was time to go. The question was how.

She dismounted the cab and felt the cool morning air rush over her face. Kyra slung the sat-phone strap over her shoulder, shoved her hands down in her pockets, and began to make her way back to the hill. The temperature was climbing a bit now that the sun was up, still cold enough to be unpleasant but just barely so.

She scrambled up the grassy hillside, slipping often on the dew. It took a bit longer to reach the peak this time because of the damp, wet slide under her feet, but she held on as best she could. Her legs and triceps were burning by the end, and she took a few minutes to rest, sitting on a flat rock, before she assembled the phone, positioned the antenna, and made the call.

An encrypted digital file was waiting for her, and she downloaded the message and transferred it to her smartphone. She took a deep breath, then touched the screen.

"*GRANITE, good to hear your voice.*" Kyra recognized Barron's own voice dictating the message. "*Message received on all counts. Also, several seniors were very happy to receive the good news that your friend may still be kicking around. Roger your report that all assets and facilities in AOR are compromised. We hoped for better but weren't surprised. We retasked some birds to watch our safe sites and observed one house being raided by your hosts. Your present location shouldn't be considered safe and you should evacuate as soon as you possibly can.*"

There was a short pause in his message, then he switched gears. "*Roger receipt of your proposed opplan. Plan approved. We're contacting friends in your AOR and arranging for transfer of resources. Will advise soonest once they are in place as to how you can access them . . . check back every hour after you receive this message. Also, we're ordering a change to your plan. We have some friends who will join you in-country who will be en route by the time you receive this. Details to follow. Stay safe, good hunting.*"

Several seniors were happy to receive the good news? Kyra smiled at that. Barron had told Kathy Cooke that Jon might still be alive. She wondered how the woman had taken the news. The case officer supposed that the deputy DNI had been happy enough to approve the proposed operation.

Friends who will join you in-country? That was a surprise. She couldn't imagine how Barron could get anyone into Russia under the present circumstances. Maybe the Brits were coming to help? Aussies? She doubted either country would want to risk its own people and assets given what the United States had just suffered.

Kyra shook her head and cleared her mind. Speculating would

just be a waste of energy that she needed to conserve. She sat on the rock, staring out at the green valley below her position, and passed the time trying to think about nothing at all.

There was no message waiting for her the first time she called back. The second call an hour later yielded another encrypted recording. Kyra didn't recognize the voice and the message was far longer than Barron's first message. She listened to it three times, memorizing the key details. Her task done, she broke down the satellite phone, packed up, and walked down the hill to the Tiguan.

Kyra's safe house

It had taken less than an hour to find all of the supplies she needed in the house except the twine. That had required a trip to a Russian hardware store. She'd managed to fake her way through the purchase without talking and judge more or less correctly the amount of petty cash needed to cover the expenses. Kyra had pulled into the safe-house garage long after dark, the long, winding routes she'd had to take coming and going having added to the time and subtracted from her energy. She drank two cups of the strong Russian coffee, enough to make sure she would stay awake for hours but not enough to make her hands shake. She was going to need some steady hands.

It had taken her an hour to carve up the twenty bars of soap she'd found upstairs in the bathroom closet using the box grater that had been in one of the kitchen cabinets, and she had a large bowlful of green shavings to show for her work. A storage can from the garage and a siphon pump had allowed her to extract three gallons of gasoline from the Tiguan. Had it been warmer, she would have used motor oil instead, as gasoline would have started to evaporate after a few hours and reduced the volatility of the end product; but the Russian cold was her friend in that respect.

Napalm had been one of the simpler incendiaries the Agency had taught her to make. It would be harder to make the fuse than the jellied gasoline, but not overly so. The several gallons of household bleach she'd found in the basement would provide her with all of the potassium chlorate she would need for that and there was no short-age of granulated sugar in the pantry.

She'd worried about building an ignitor until she realized that Lavrov's men would provide that for her when they came.

Barron wouldn't be happy with what she was about to do, she was sure, but if Lavrov's men were coming, then the safe house was lost to the Agency anyway. Its only useful purpose now would be to send a message to the general that neither Kyra nor the Agency intended to go out so quietly.

Kyra fetched a large metal pot from its home under the counter and turned on the stove. She uncapped the first bottle of bleach and began to pour it into the pot.

New GRU headquarters

"Your report, Colonel?" Lavrov leaned back in his chair, using his shoulder to hold the phone to his ear. Russian breweries had not mastered the art of the twist cap and opening a bottle took both of his hands.

"We have completed raids on four of the homes that your source identified," Sokolov said. "All were abandoned, all sanitized. If they truly were CIA safe houses, the evidence of it was thoroughly re-moved before the custodians left. Impressive, given how little time they must have had."

"Indeed," Lavrov said. "It does not matter, Colonel. I expect they will all be abandoned and stripped except one, and it is that one you must find." The bottle top finally came loose and the general took his first taste. The brew inside was bitter and not quite as cold as he liked it.

"There are six more on the list you gave me, General," Sokolov advised. "It takes several hours to plan and conduct a proper raid on each one to make sure no one evades capture. It will take at least another day, possibly two to target them all."

"Understood. No delays, Colonel."

"Yes, sir," Sokolov said.

Kyra's safe house

Kyra set the plastic bucket down and peeled the latex gloves off her hands. The napalm was plastered in every major room of the house. Running the improvised string fuse to each incendiary site was going to take another half hour. Setting up the front, mudroom, and back doors to ignite the entire system would take less than a minute.

An hour later and the job done, Kyra looked to the clock. She still had twelve hours before she had to go out on the street.

The coffee had long since stopped doing its job and Kyra wanted to stumble back up the stairs to the bedroom. She would need some sleep and then some food in her stomach for what came next. But it was not safe to stay, as tempting as the soft bed was. Kyra might easily wake up to find the Spetsnaz standing over her, or, more likely, the house burning around her if the ignition system worked as she'd planned.

She could sleep in the Tiguan after she'd found some hidden field miles from here. Her last chore here was to turn on the short-wave transmitter, tuned to the frequency she'd used to talk to Lavrov last night, and leave it on. Then she would drive out. The Spetsnaz would come—

A telephone rang.

Her mind hazy from lack of sleep, she needed several seconds to realize that it wasn't any ringtone on her cell. No, it was the house phone. *Headquarters?* she thought. Langley surely had the number, but Barron wouldn't be so stupid as to call her on an open, unencrypted line.

She stumbled off in search of a handset, finally finding one on the sixth or seventh ring, having lost count. The caller ID showed nothing.

Answer it? she wondered.

Why not? Jon's voice in her mind said. You're heading out the door anyway and not coming back.

She picked it up, then froze in place, realizing too late that she didn't know how to answer a call in Russian or whether there was any kind of security phrase assigned to this location.

The caller saved her the embarrassment. "You are American?" the man asked. His voice was disguised, digitized somehow.

Kyra said nothing. "You must leave house if you are American," the voice said, the man's English accented and broken. "They are coming to your safe site. You have maybe one hour, maybe more, but they come and they arrest you. You must leave now."

She heard a click on the other end, then a dial tone, and she stared at the phone in her hand. Kyra set it back in the cradle.

It had not been some mistaken caller dialing the wrong number. The man had expected that an American would answer, which meant he'd known that he was calling a safe house. That, together with the fact that he had been able to get the telephone number, which was unlisted, yelled that the caller was someone who had access to official information.

But he'd spoken quickly, not waiting for a response from her, but simply had spilled what he knew and cut the call. *Worried that someone might hear him?* she wondered. Then she understood. The caller hadn't merely been someone with access to official information. *No,* counterintelligence *information.*

There was a mole in Lavrov's operation. Someone knew about Lavrov's operations against the Agency.

Someone Maines didn't give up? Someone he didn't know about? she wondered. Or maybe just someone Lavrov hadn't arrested yet, but that seemed unlikely. If there was anyone in a position to know about his counterintelligence operation, Lavrov would have been a fool not to neutralize that traitor first. No, there was someone in the Kremlin, maybe the GRU, who was moving against Lavrov and who wasn't on whatever list Maines had given up.

Kyra checked the caller ID again and cursed the empty display. The caller might have been someone who could help her find out what had happened to Jon. The ID might have given her somewhere to start, some bit of information she could have used to reconnect with the Russian caller, whoever he was.

The quiet of the house seemed hostile to her now, the shadows of the hallway oppressive. *Maybe one hour*, she repeated in her mind.

The adrenaline surge cleared her mind and her vision. She ran across the hallway to the equipment room, threw the door open, grabbed for the satellite phone, and began stabbing at the keypad. The call connected, encrypted, and she heard an American accent for the first time in days.

"Operator."

"This is site GRANITE," Kyra announced. "I have reason to believe this location will be raided within the hour. All remaining equipment and papers will be sanitized and I am evacuating."

"Roger, copy that," the male voice on the other end said. "To which other site will you evac?"

Kyra sucked in a deep breath. "None of them. All sites in this area have been compromised."

The man on the other end was professional enough to keep his thoughts to himself about that. "Copy that, all sites in your immediate area compromised. Are you requesting evac from the country?"

"Negative. I'm heading for the embassy."

"Copy that, good luck and stay safe." The operator disconnected the call.

Kyra pulled the crypto card from the phone and stuffed it in her pocket. Breaking down the sat phone and its antenna took her less than a minute. That job done, she sat down in front of the classified computer and launched the program that would wipe the hard drive. The machine made her confirm twice that she really wanted the program to execute. She told it yes both times and the machine obediently began to overwrite every file on the system.

The file-deletion utility reported that it needed ten minutes to chew up all of the encrypted data on the hard drive.

Ten minutes. It had been almost forty-five minutes since the anonymous Russian had called. She looked out the windows toward the main road, saw nothing. Kyra pulled the chair to the window, sat down, and stared out, waiting for the enemy to come. The watch on her wrist showed the seconds passing by more slowly than she had ever thought possible.

The hard-drive utility reported that it had finished its work on time, which Kyra thought was no small miracle. She powered the machine down, pulled the removable hard drive from its chassis, and fed it and the sat phone's crypto card into the industrial shredder in the storage closet connected to the room. The sounds of grinding metal were, at once, the most hideous and beautiful noise Kyra had ever heard as the shredder turned the drive platters into shavings. The shredder finished dining on the storage device and the card, and Kyra powered it down.

She ran for the garage.

It truly was an enormous house by Russian standards, and if it was a CIA safe house, Anton Semyonovich Sokolov could not fathom why the Americans had chosen it. The gates and fence provided no true security from the security forces, as the Spetsnaz had just proven by climbing the iron spikes, and the relative wealth on display could only draw attention. Perhaps the Agency had expected that to deflect suspicion, a daring move in a mind game that had stretched on for decades. Or, perhaps, some mindless bureaucrat had simply had money to burn. Whatever the logic, Lavrov's source had rendered it moot and cut through the illusions that had kept the building secure.

The sun was behind the trees and the house itself cast a long shadow that reached to the gate, giving the Spetsnaz a dark trail to follow as they ran across the lawn, carbines raised. There was no obvious movement inside the house itself, which was mostly dark. There was a light visible on the upper floor and one in the kitchen, but the rest of the windows were black. The size of the building itself had required every man at his disposal for the raid and two dozen, four teams, were moving into position to enter the house, the rest positioned on the ground to catch anyone who tried to run.

"All teams in position," the team leader called out over the radio.

Sokolov frowned. "No response from inside?"

"*Nyet*, Colonel."

The GRU officer scanned the compound, then looked through his field glasses at the house itself. The light inside let him see into a room on the upper story, and some secondary illumination cast a glow into one of the front rooms on the main level, but there was no movement anywhere. He pursed his lips. Something was amiss, he was sure, but he could not see it.

"Proceed," he said, finally giving the order.

At the front, the team leader nodded to the officer heading the stack of four positioned by the door. The lead man nodded, drew back with the heavy sledge in his hands, and slammed the breaching tool forward into the knob. The door shuddered, but held fast. The man pulled back and swung the sledge again, this time battering it against the middle hinge. The door shook again but stayed fixed in place.

"Front door is reinforced," the team leader reported, speaking into the microphone clipped to his uniform.

"Rear entry is reinforced," his radio announced. The team behind the house was having no better luck.

"Side entry is reinforced." A different voice this time, same report.

"Garage door breached, garage entry to the house is reinforced and door is secured with a keypad."

So it is *a safe house*, Sokolov told himself. *Or the owner is very paranoid. Probably a criminal who should be arrested anyway.* He raised his field glasses. Still, there was no movement inside the house.

"All teams, proceed with ballistic breach—"

"This is team four," Sokolov's radio announced. "The doorframe of the garage entry is reinforced with heavy metal. Hinges are nonstandard. Ballistic breaching round likely will not penetrate. Permission to perform explosive breach."

Sokolov's eyebrows went up. The teams all had specialized breaching rounds that vaporized on impact to protect the shooters and teams from ricochet. "Team four, is solid slug an option?"

"*Nyet.* The first slug almost certainly would not penetrate, and likely would ricochet. I would prefer not to risk that, given that we are standing in an enclosed space."

Sokolov's eyebrows went up at that news. They had not run into this particular problem at any of the other reported safe houses. Those had all had wooden doors, solid oak to be sure, but nothing the men hadn't been able to breach with sledges or shotguns. The specialized shotgun rounds were preferable, as a solid slug fired point-blank from a twelve-gauge shotgun could overpenetrate a door, blowing through the wood and killing a suspect on the other side. That assumed the door was even composed of wood. Someone willing to install a hardened metal doorframe likely would not use a wooden door. The entry likely was a metal plate covered with wood veneer. His teams were trained to fire two rounds at a knob, three at a hinge, just to be sure the chosen weak point of the door was destroyed. Fired into a metal door, those rounds might go in every direction but into the house itself.

Armored against a ballistic breach? Someone is paranoid indeed, he thought. A metal door suggested that they had found one of the Main Enemy's primary facilities outside his embassy. "All teams, prepare for explosive breach at your discretion," he ordered through his own mic.

The team leader in the mudroom pulled a flexible linear charge from his pack. Doing the math in his head, he began to run lines of detonation cord the length of the door, top to bottom by the hinges. One line would have taken apart a hollow door, two would tear apart anything made from particleboard, and three could cut through solid wood. Not knowing how thick the metal core at the door's center might be, he opted to tape six lines onto the barrier. If that failed, getting through the door would require a specialist to cut through the door with a plasma torch. His team would have to resign itself to guarding the room and preventing any escape while the other teams swept the house.

He ordered his men out of the mudroom, attached the blasting cap, and connected the firing line.

The team leader at the front door nodded to the stack lead and the line of men while he pulled a two-inch-square block of Semtex from his pack. He fastened the putty brick to the doorknob with a loop of detonation cord connected to the explosive with uli knots. Loose ends of detcord hung down and he tied them into a square knot. He tied in the blasting cap and connected his own firing line, then fell back to his own safe position. Then he tied the detcord line into the fuse initiator.

"First team, breaching charge in place. Standing by to breach." The other teams reported back within seconds, their own charges fixed and ready to fire.

"Go," Sokolov ordered.

The team leader ripped the cotter pin from the initiator, a hard, sharp pull.

The detcord ignited, followed by the Semtex, and flames and smoke exploded from the door, with simultaneous eruptions coming from the rear and side of the house. The explosion inside the garage was deafening and the team leader out front hoped that his counterpart hadn't miscalculated the explosive required. Overloaded breaching charges had deafened more than one soldier performing such duties.

The front door slammed open and the stack of soldiers rushed forward, carbines raised. They entered the house, pushing through the gray haze—

The stack leader felt the pressure wave of the igniting gasoline before he smelled it. The room went up in an instant, flames spreading across the floors and walls in every direction. He saw lines of flame travel out of the room into the kitchen, the hallway, the library, faster than he could move.

A large glass jar, sealed with a lid and filled with a colored gelatin, sat in the middle of the room, the flames not quite touching it.

"Fall back!" he ordered. "All teams! Evacuate the building *now!*"

His stack turned and filed out as fast as they could move. The team leader still on the porch jumped the railing and ran with them across the lawn toward Sokolov's position.

• • •

Inside the front room, the glass jar heated enough to ignite the napalm inside. The makeshift bomb exploded, glass and burning jellied gasoline spreading out to fill the room in a fraction of a second. Identical explosives went off in the kitchen and by the rear and side doors.

The gas trails Kyra had laid down led the open flames to every other room in the house, where the napalm she'd spread across the walls and floors lit off, each starting a small inferno. On the second floor, the gas fumes that had collected since her departure ignited, sending a mild fireball through the upper floor, igniting the napalm puddles and everything else flammable they touched.

With less than a minute, the funeral pyre for Moscow Station was burning against the dusk, smoke rising high enough to be seen from the Kremlin.

A mile away, Kyra lay prone in a copse on a small knoll, looking at the abandoned estate through her own field glasses. The building was nothing more than a house-shaped flame with men in tactical gear standing at a safe distance, helpless to do anything but watch the immolation.

One man was dressed in civilian clothes, a business suit and overcoat, no hat, and speaking into a phone. She could not make out his features from this distance, but his profile was different enough that she could tell that it wasn't Lavrov. She'd hoped he would be here to see the safe house burn in person, but she was sure that he'd get the message all the same.

She pushed herself up to standing and walked back to the Tiguan. She tossed the field glasses inside, crawled in, started the engine, and drove across the green field between her and the road, not caring if the soldiers in the distance could hear the engine.

CIA Operations Center

The exact moment of the excited phone call had been a surprise, but the call itself was not. Barron entered the bullpen, his eyes immediately drawn to the array of monitors that covered the front wall. At the moment, they were mated together to display a single image, in this case a live video feed from an orbiting satellite controlled by the National Reconnaissance Office.

Barron stopped and smiled when he saw the image. Everyone in the room stared at the head of the Directorate of Operations, unable to fathom why anyone should be happy to watch an Agency facility burn so early in the morning.

The senior duty officer sidled over to his superior. "You seem very chipper for a man who's watching a very expensive safe house go up in flames."

"Better torched than in the hands of the GRU," he said.

Kyra's safe house

Sokolov stepped inside the charred remains of the safe house. Spetsnaz officers in tactical vests and balaclavas were still sweeping the gutted structure, Bison SMG carbines and Makarov pistols raised to eye level. They would be thorough, but Sokolov had no doubt that there was nothing to find. There had been no cars in the garage, no lights, no signs of life, but Lavrov's information had again proven correct. This had been a CIA safe house. The incendiary traps had erased any doubts he'd had about that.

The sweep took less than ten minutes to complete. "Nothing to recover?" Sokolov asked.

"*Nyet*" was the answer. The Spetsnaz team leader pulled his black hood back over his head and away from his face. "Any specialized equipment or papers have been destroyed. We found the remains of an industrial shredder on the second level and its wastebin in the cellar next to a furnace. There was one computer in the same area with the shredder, but its hard drive is missing, probably fed into the shredder. Any papers were probably shredded and burned before the house went up. We will recover nothing."

"They knew we were coming."

The Spetsnaz leader looked around, thought, and nodded. "They used gasoline as an accelerant, possibly other chemicals as well," he said. "Our own breaching charges ignited the fires."

"They tried to kill our teams," Sokolov noted.

"I don't think so," the soldier replied. "The napalm jars were left in plain view where the teams would see them immediately. Whoever arranged this could have set up a very efficient ignition system, but just left them sitting in the middle of the room for the heat to ignite. They were not even covered in accelerant, if our men's observations are accurate. I think that our arsonist wanted to give our men a chance to get out." He scanned the ruins. "I have never heard of the CIA rigging a house to burn this way, but I suppose they might have done so in desperation. The general gave them little time to leave the country. They may have hoped to return one day, but left the incendiaries in case that proved impossible."

Sokolov nodded. "I suspect that you are right. Still, it would be a callous thing. Had we not come, some civilian would have in time and might been killed, delayed napalm bombs notwithstanding." *But if they knew we were coming? That we would be the ones to encounter those homemade explosives? It would not be callous then, would it?* He looked around at the remains of the living room, what had been a vaulted ceiling, plush carpet, and leather couches. "It surely was a lovely home. The Americans do like their comforts, do they not?"

"They do, I think," the soldier agreed.

"Indeed," Sokolov replied. "Sweep the rubble again. Look for any secret compartments. Tear out any floorboards you find intact. I doubt very much that you will find anything, but we must be thorough. Report to me by nineteen hundred hours tonight. General Lavrov will be expecting an update." Sokolov frowned, then sighed. "And I must disappoint him." The soldier nodded, saluted his commanding officer, then moved off to organize the sifting of the ash and char.

He pulled out his own encrypted smartphone and dialed a stored number. "General Lavrov, this is Colonel Sokolov."

"Your report, Colonel?" Lavrov demanded.

"My teams have all reported in. We have taken control of all of the sites on the list you provided, but found them all abandoned. All but one had sensitive equipment either removed or rendered unusable. There is evidence enough to confirm that they likely were CIA safe houses, but there will be little of use to be recovered from any of them."

"All but one?"

"The last one. The doors were all reinforced with strong metal and we were forced to breach the doors with explosive charges. There were incendiary traps set at the entrances, which our charges ignited. The house burned."

"That is where she was hiding," Lavrov noted.

"Almost certainly," Sokolov agreed. "But she was not here when we arrived and she has no safe haven now, if your source's list is complete."

"I do not think that worries her," Lavrov replied. "She did not have to burn the house, but chose to do so. That was a message and a dramatic one. She is confident that she can escape our country. Your team's surveillance of the Western embassies has suffered no lapses?"

"None, General. She has not been observed entering or exiting the U.S. Embassy or that of any close American ally," Sokolov confirmed. "It is always possible that she could have entered hidden in some vehicle, as we cannot search those. But we have kept a very tight watch on all pedestrians entering on foot."

"Good. Make sure that they remain under watch. I want her found."

"We may yet hope there will be some bit of evidence here missed in the initial sweep."

"Hope is a poor substitute for competence, Colonel, if you understand my meaning," Lavrov advised.

"I do, General," Sokolov replied. "I will report to you with our findings by nightfall."

"I will be waiting." The call went dead. Sokolov replaced his phone in his pocket. *So, young lady, you got out,* he thought. *Run, little rabbit. I do not think you would like to be Lavrov's guest.*

Moscow, Russia

Joshua Ettleman shifted his laptop bag in his hand, nervous about the contents for several reasons, some of which he would have been hard-pressed to put into words.

Espionage was not something he'd ever aspired to practice, and the newest foreign service officer at the U.S. Embassy was quite disturbed that he'd managed to get roped into an operation four months into his tour, however minor his role. But the order, polite though it was, had come from the ambassador. Why she had chosen him, Ettleman was sure he didn't know. He'd been quite surprised that his country's chief diplomat to the Russian Federation had agreed to participate in any operation the CIA had organized and he assumed it had something to do with the mass exodus of U.S. citizens from the country a few days before. He'd heard the scuttlebutt that the Russians had declared a huge swath of his countrymen persona non grata, but the ambassador had locked down the information on orders from Foggy Bottom. Ettleman and the minions who worked at his level were left only with the rumors, but that was plenty. Bureaucratic leaks often turned out to be more accurate than the exalted leadership would have liked and what Ettleman had heard was so strange that it fell squarely into that category of events that no one could have made it up from whole cloth.

As for the request that he perform an operational act, few moments of thought had given him the time to grasp just how few people in the U.S. government could even make such a request of honest diplomats. Someone with serious pull at a very high level was desperate enough to ask the State Department to take on a job that the spooks from Langley usually performed. Ettleman thought the order had to have come from the secretary of state at least, which suggested the National Security Council was involved or possibly the president himself. In fact, he was sure that CIA's leadership must have been galled at the thought of asking a diplomat to help; that they had was surely a sign of how desperate they'd become.

They were CIA, all of them. It had to be true, and if it was, the CIA station in Moscow had been gutted, maybe down to the last officer. How that could have happened, the State officer had no idea, and his clique at work had posited one theory after another, each more insane than the last. If even the least improbable of them was true, the Russian government had done tremendous damage to his country's national security.

Ettleman was no spy, had no particular love for the CIA, but he considered himself ambitious, and if the Agency's fat was that deep in the fire, he didn't need long to figure that agreeing to perform this single duty would earn him the favor of someone very, very senior. Still, there was the small issue of completing the operational act without getting caught, and he couldn't imagine why he'd been chosen. The young man had met the U.S. ambassador to the Russian Federation exactly once and that had been the perfunctory greeting that all new embassy staff received during their orientation on their first day at the diplomatic outpost. Now he'd been called in and asked to take this assignment that was far out of his lane. It seemed simple enough. He was to take a bag home, acting entirely normal on the walk, and deliver it to a CIA officer who would meet him there. He wasn't to open the bag under any circumstances, but he wasn't to resist if he was detained by the host country's security services. Ettleman had agreed on the single condition that the ambassador never, ever make any such request of him again. The young diplomat was willing to take his chances once in the pursuit of a commendation that would guarantee his next promotion and choice of assignments, but had no desire to see the interior of Lubyanka or risk eviction more than once from the country for actions "inconsistent with his diplomatic status," as the Russians would call it.

Taking the assignment had seemed like a smart move until he'd stepped outside the embassy gates with the nylon bag slung over his shoulder. He was just another diplomat going home, but all of his senses were heightened and he was sure that everyone around him knew that he was on a special mission, that even the most casual Russian pedestrian knew he was carrying something valuable. Serious anxiety set in once the embassy was out of sight and he was sufficiently agitated that a fellow commuter on the Moscow subway had asked him whether he was taken ill. The winter was coming on and Americans were not as hardy as the average Muscovite after all. Drink more vodka and buy a good hat, he was told. Even an American could get through a Russian winter with one of the latter and enough of the former.

Once he was aboveground again, Ettleman wondered whether he was being followed, but the young diplomat had no training for detecting surveillance. He simply walked home, fighting the urge to hurry his pace, but it was like his body was fighting him, trying to break out into a dead run. The fight-or-flight urge was strong and it took all of his self-control to keep it checked.

Reaching the top floor of his apartment building, Ettleman scanned the concrete landing to his small apartment three times to make sure he was alone. The amount of adrenaline flooding his system was truly impressive and he hated what it was doing to his senses. *Langley morons*, he muttered inside his head. *Get themselves all evicted and now they need us to do their job and just maybe I get evicted too.*

He set the nylon bag on the floor by his feet, leaning it against his leg so he could be sure it wouldn't move while he fished the key out of his pocket. There was no one anywhere nearby that he could tell, but Ettleman found his mind was running through every worst case it could conjure. At the moment, he was sure that the Russian FSB had some world-class sprinter racing up the stairs to grab the nylon bag. But there were no sounds other than his own heavy breathing and the clinking of his key against the door as his shaking hand failed to get it into the lock until his fourth attempt.

The door opened, Ettleman retrieved the bag and stepped inside, trying and failing to look casual. He was a poor actor and he knew it, but the door was closed within a few moments, locked and bolted. The need for pretense gone, the young man felt a small bit of his anxiety subside—

"Joshua Ettleman?" the voice asked. The diplomat yelped and spun around, scrambling for anything he could use as a weapon and scanning the room in a wild panic, his heart now pounding hard enough that he could feel the blood running behind his eyes. Nothing was within reach.

There was a young woman sitting on the couch. She was dressed in khakis, tactical pants, and low brown hiking boots, her dirty-blond hair pulled back away from her face. The woman was about his own age as best he could figure and quite pretty, he realized, after he was able to start thinking rationally again, which took several more seconds. She waited patiently until he could calm himself, as though she understood the irrational fear she'd inspired just by asking his name . . . but her accent was American, he realized. She was not a Russian, and therefore he had not been caught by the FSB.

"Who are you?" he demanded, the questions coming out far ruder than he'd intended.

The woman stood, blue jacket and khaki pants not hiding her curves very much. "You can call me Kyra," she said, smiling. "They told me that you would be expecting me. I promise, I'm harmless."

He noticed that she didn't explain who "they" were, and as for her being harmless, Ettleman doubted that very much. He tried to take some deep breaths, and it took a few seconds for the shock the adrenaline had given to his system to subside. "*They* told me that someone was going to meet me at my place," he said. "They didn't say you were going to let yourself in. I thought my locks were better than that." He regretted the stupid observation as soon as he said it. *She's CIA, moron. She knows how to pick a lock.*

The woman shrugged. "Sorry, not so much. You know the Russians probably have already been in your apartment at least once, right?"

"I . . . State is supposed to install a security system, but they haven't gotten to it yet . . . you know, paperwork . . . our security office moves at the speed of government—"

Kyra smiled. "A security system won't help. The FSB isn't going to let a commercial system stop them if they want to come in here. I can show you some other ways you can figure out whether you've had an intruder, but you're not going to be able to keep them out. Don't worry, I swept the place, didn't find anything. Doesn't mean it's clean, but you probably haven't really come up on their radar yet."

"I've only been here since July," Ettleman stammered. His initial panic was gone, finally, and now he was finding himself anxious for another reason entirely. The young woman was the first visitor to his apartment and he was sure that he hadn't made much of an impression on her.

"I know," Kyra said. She smiled.

"You do?"

"Your clothes are all American brands, suggesting that you haven't been in-country long enough to need to shop at any of the local stores for replacements," she replied. "And I don't see any obviously Russian souvenirs. You have some very nice ones from Turkey and Argentina, nice enough to show you have decent taste. So the lack of anything local means this isn't your first overseas assignment, but you haven't been here long enough to pick up anything you think is worth showing off to visitors. And there was that lack of a security system."

"Oh," Ettleman said.

"Sorry, but that's probably why they picked you," she told him. "They needed someone who the locals probably figured was an unlikely candidate to act as a courier."

Ettleman was silent for a moment while he absorbed her admission. "And someone dispensable if they got caught." He cursed himself. *The ambassador picked me because I'm nobody.*

The woman looked at him, as though she could divine his thoughts from the look on his face. "Have you read Churchill?"

"Winston Churchill?"

The woman nodded. "'To each there comes in their lifetime a special moment when they are figuratively tapped on the shoulder and offered the chance to do a very special thing, unique to them and fitted to their talents. What a tragedy if that moment finds them unprepared or unqualified for that which could have been their finest hour.'" Kyra smiled at him. "Right now they needed someone to do a 'very special thing' that was fitted to you. They needed someone who could fly right under the Russians' radar, and you did. I know that carrying a bag around doesn't seem like much, but if everything works out, what you just did is going to help a lot of people. Your moment came and you stepped up . . . your finest moment, until you have a bigger one. You should be proud of that."

Ettleman tried not to gape at the woman who had just turned his anxiety into elation with a few words. She nodded toward the nylon bag. "I assume that's for me?" she asked.

She was looking at his laptop bag. "Oh, yeah," Ettleman said. He offered it and Kyra took it from him. She unzipped it and looked inside.

"I don't know even know what's in it—"

"A quarter million euros," Kyra said. She pulled out one of the bundles and rifled through the bills to prove the point. "And a disguise kit and a false passport, all sent through the diplomatic pouch from Langley."

"A quarter . . . *million*?" Ettleman repeated in quiet surprise, his voice quavering, much to his embarrassment. He looked inside. The bag held euros, all €500 banknotes. The foreign service officer didn't know the day's exchange rate, but he was sure that he'd been carrying more than his annual salary, enough that any Russian thug would have gutted him for the pile without a thought. "They told me not to open it. I didn't, swear to—"

"I believe you," the woman assured him.

Idiot, he thought. *Now she thinks you didn't have the stones to even check out what you were carrying around.* "I mean, I wanted to, but I thought, maybe, you know, operational security—"

"You followed your orders. That means you're not stupid." She exhaled, then smiled, sheepish, which sent Ettleman's heart rate up again. "I'm sorry, that was rude of me. It's been a tough week and I've . . . the guy who trained me was kind of blunt and I've picked up the habit."

"That's okay," Ettleman said. He would've forgiven this woman of murder if she would smile at him again. "They said you'd need a few other things?"

The woman nodded. "Nothing exotic," she advised. "I'll raid your closet later. Do you have a laptop and a printer?" Ettleman nodded.

"Unplug everything from the Internet and shut down any wireless connections you have running. You're fluent in Russian? I need to type a letter and I'll need you to translate it after I'm done. And a hot shower would be very kind."

"Oh, uh, sure," Ettleman said. "The shower is at the end of the hall. I'll get you a towel."

"That would be lovely, thank you." Kyra smiled at him again. "And you don't have to be nervous. You're doing fine." Then she turned away and headed for his shower.

The man's heart soared and sank at the same time. Maybe he'd applied for the wrong career after all, Ettleman thought. Delivering huge piles of money to strange and attractive women who showed up in his apartment, reading his mind through his body language and asking for his services and amenities? He could get used to that.

Chapter Ten

A craft, her father had once explained, *is a marriage between science and art. You have to master the science before you can aspire to the art.*

Kyra was an analyst now, but she'd been a case officer once and had worked the street before. She understood both the science and the art of it. She'd been in war zones before, had been involved in some serious fights, violence and gunfire coming from plain enemies out to do her harm. Street work was different; it was subtlety and advance planning. There was a learning curve to it, but just knowing the science of a spy's tradecraft would not be enough here. It was not a place for beginners and Kyra was wondering now whether she truly was ready to face the Kremlin machine. The Russians were efficient and unforgiving. They had practiced on these streets for a century now and Kyra was neither stupid nor arrogant enough to imagine that her experience and intelligence alone put her on equal ground with them anywhere on earth, much less here.

This was their home. They knew it intimately and would defend it. She was the criminal, the invader, the thief come to rob and steal. She was the villain here.

She did have one advantage. The Russian experience gained practicing counterintelligence on their own territory was predicated on the idea that both sides shared the same ideas about success and failure, the same definitions. Kyra hated that anyone ever called it a game, but the contest did have its own rules about how to win and lose. The Russians always assumed that the Americans would send their best people and use their best tradecraft, that they would never make an unforced error. The Americans usually assumed that the Russians had enough manpower and practice that they could be everywhere and see everything, omniscient enough that they could make an unforced error and still recover. They didn't have to be perfect to win here.

Kyra couldn't win the old game, but she might be able to win her *own* game, where a different set of rules decreed that a lack of skill on the street was a tactic, not a weakness.

Kyra's advantage was that she was both a case officer and an analyst. Jon believed that she would be a better analyst than he one day, or so Marisa Mills had told her before she'd been killed the year before . . . someone with a foot in both worlds who could fuse the two. She brought practical experience into Jon's theoretical world. Now, she thought, they might turn the world on its head by doing the reverse.

Why do you always run straight in? Jon's voice had asked her. She'd found the answer. She had always been thinking like a case officer, always moving, always trying to take the initiative by moving. Now it was time to think like an analyst.

Jon had spent years teaching her where analysts' mind-sets and biases had led them wrong, where their long experience with one subject had carried them to exactly the wrong analytical conclusion. The Russian mind was no different, she was certain. She could win if she could bring them to a place where their experience dictated exactly the wrong move.

Kyra had left Ettleman's apartment and abandoned the Tiguan two hours and three miles ago. Most of the equipment it had carried was at the bottom of the Moskva River, including the satellite phone. She'd thought about leaving it all with the State officer, but she had decided against giving the man anything incriminating. The Russians would be in his apartment eventually and she didn't want to cause him trouble. She didn't need any of the equipment now. Either the operation would work or it would not. None of the gear she'd carried would make the difference, so she'd laid it to rest at the river's bottom.

She marched north up the Smolenskaya highway. The Moskva was to her left. Three years ago, she'd been walking by a river like this one in downtown Caracas, the Guaire, a concrete channel that became an artificial river that split the Venezuelan city in half during the rainy season. She'd been shot during that operation. Maines had brought her home. Now the world seemed to be working in reverse. She was out to bring him home, even if he didn't want to come.

The Moskva turned away from her to the northwest. She'd passed the British Embassy on her right a few minutes before and her own country's diplomatic outpost was not far ahead. Kyra didn't know how far out the FSB or the GRU surveillance cordon would reach from that point, but Lavrov would surely have had both embassies under watch. She'd started looking for surveillance a mile before approaching the British compound and had seen nothing, but that was meaningless. The Russians could throw a hundred men and women at her and she would never see the same face twice.

Kyra had come wearing a light disguise, baggy clothes, glasses, a wig, and a hoodie. Some of it she'd scrounged from Ettleman, the rest from stores around his apartment. It wasn't a very good disguise and therefore it was good enough.

Lavrov would have found a picture of her, from the cameras in customs at the Domodedovo Airport or the embassy in Berlin. His people would have scanned it in, then created a hundred variations on her face, different hair colors and styles, with glasses and without, cheeks fatter or sunken in. He would have distributed them to whichever teams were watching these streets.

They would see a young woman approach. They would sort through the pictures and find one that wasn't far off her current appearance. *Is it her?* they would wonder. A small team would start to follow behind. She was walking toward the U.S. Embassy. Was that her destination? Would she turn off?

Are you behind me? she asked the Russians. *Did you pick me when I walked past the British Embassy?* She was going to be very disappointed if they hadn't, but they would start to follow her eventually.

She stopped under the overpass where the Kutuzovsky Avenue crossed the Moskva and the Smolenskaya highway. She didn't bother looking behind. If the Russians weren't there, she would give them more opportunities to find her. If they were there, so much the better.

Kyra made a show of fumbling with the satchel she was carrying over her right shoulder, then took her time pulling out the fur *ushanka* hat that she'd kept inside and put it on her head. It was an innocent act, one that thousands of people might do on a cool fall night like this one . . . or it might be an attempt to change appearance. Security officers were a paranoid lot and Kyra was giving them just enough to keep their attention.

She turned east and walked alongside Kutuzovsky Avenue. Cars roared past on the roadway above. The U.S. Embassy was only a block north but she was going to take the long way around. She looked up at the sky. It was night and she wished she could see the stars. They were all washed out of the sky by the city lights and smog. She kept walking, one block east, the cool air brushing over her face.

She slid the satchel off, then removed her coat and felt the cold air invade her shirt. The coat was reversible, gray on the inside, brown on the outside. She turned it inside out, then put it back on. She practiced the maneuver a thousand times and she had to work now to mess it up.

Kyra reached the intersection and crossed north along the Novinsky road. She walked another block, not bothering to look behind for anyone following.

One block and she turned west, doubling back the way she'd originally come. *Come on*, she thought. *You have to have figured it out by now. You can't be that dense.*

She was still free and approaching the corner. The embassy was a half block to the north. *One more to be sure.*

There was a Dumpster jutting slightly out of an alley ahead to her right. Kyra gently idled toward it. Within arms' reach, she reached up and pulled the *ushanka* hat and the dark wig off her head and dropped them in, a movement that took less than a second. She pulled the jacket's hood over her hair, and turned right onto the Smolenskaya again.

Kyra heard the van pull up behind her, the side doors opening before it came to a stop.

There we go, she thought. Not looking back, she pushed off and ran.

Four men dismounted on the move. A series of parked cars kept the van away from the sidewalk, giving her six feet to spare from the men spilling out of the vehicle. The first one tried to hurdle one of the cars, caught his foot on the bumper, and went down. Kyra angled away from the street as she picked up speed. The second man made it between the cars, but he overreached trying to lay hands on her and lost his balance stumbling forward and went down on the asphalt. The third man behind hurdled his teammate, but Kyra was accelerating now. She was pulling away. She heard the van speed up and the woman pushed herself, now sprinting as fast as she could go.

The embassy gate was fifty yards ahead. A series of white concrete planter boxes, really barricades, formed a low wall to her left, the parked cars still blocking off the road to her right. She heard the footsteps behind her getting close. Even at her best speed, the men were going to run her down.

A brick wall rose up on her left, the boundary of the embassy compound. She passed a security camera suspended over the sidewalk. *Please tell me you saw this*, she thought.

The gate would be closed. Embassy security would open it only when approved vehicles approached. Beyond the gate was the small security building.

The wall flew by on Kyra's left, the bricks melting into a single red blur, and she moved her legs faster than she ever had before. *Almost there.*

The brick wall fell away and she saw the gated entrance, then the embassy beyond, the American flag flying unfurled in the courtyard, brilliant colors in the high-powered spotlights. She heard the screeching tires of the van chasing behind her.

A man leaned out of the security building door . . . embassy security. He reached for her, to pull her inside, where she would be safe. They'd seen her running on the camera and opened the door. Barron had told them that she would be coming—

Kyra felt the hit between her shoulder blades, sending her sprawling forward. She got her hands up before hitting the ground, stopping the concrete from stripping the skin from her face, but she went down in a rolling heap. She struggled to pull herself to her feet, then lunged toward the American guard at the door—

The Spetsnaz officer coming out of the van put his shoulder square into her diaphragm, a football tackle that caught Kyra under her center of gravity. She had no leverage against the man, and he was at least half again her weight. He slammed her onto the grass strip in front of the brick wall that extended out from the other side of the security annex.

"American!" she yelled just before the man's body put her into the ground, driving the wind from her, and she could yell no more.

Hands grabbed both of her arms, lifting them up behind her back until she felt her shoulders begin to scream in pain. Russian shouts that she didn't understand came from all sides and a camera flash began to blind her every few seconds. A knife came out and cut the shoulder strap from the satchel, and it was pulled from her body.

Kyra closed her eyes and didn't bother to fight as her wrists were zip-tied together behind her back.

Her attackers kept her prone on the ground for almost a minute, long enough for the cold to seep up from the cement through her clothes. She heard the guard yelling in poor Russian at the men pinning her to the ground, but they held her head down. She couldn't turn to see it. Finally, they lifted her by her armpits and dragged her stumbling to the van. The U.S. guard was a Marine, she thought, given the quality of the English profanities he was dishing out to the Russians. If the Russians understood any English at all, they would know that much.

Other hands reached out of the darkness in the vehicle and took her, pulling her inside onto a seat. The last Russian turned away from the American guard, who continued to harangue him in vile terms, and crawled inside with his teammates. The side door slammed shut and the van moved away. Kyra stared out the window as she was shackled at the feet to the floor. Through the side window, she saw the United States flag waving in the light of the flood lamps and receding as the van picked up speed. Then a black hood came down over her head and the entire world disappeared.

Domodedovo International Airport
28 kilometers south of Moscow

The Russian liaison was waiting at the customs exit for Cooke and Barron. He knew the woman on sight, doubtless from the photograph of her that the FSB kept in a dossier somewhere. "Director Cooke, m*en-ya za-voot Vitaly Leontyevich Churkin. Zdras-tvooy-tyeh.*

Dobro pozhalovat' v Rossiyu," the man said. *My name is Vitaliy Chur-kin. Greetings and welcome to Russia.*

Cooke spoke no Russian, and so let the former chief of station Moscow handle the pleasantries. "It is our honor to meet you," Barron said in the other man's native language. "We are most grateful to Director Grigoriyev for his willingness to meet us on short notice."

"In light of recent events, he felt that a discussion with a counterpart of Miss Cooke's stature would be most illuminating," Churkin replied.

"I assure you, it will be," Barron advised. "However, we need to visit our embassy here before meeting with the director. Last-minute instructions from the president, that sort of thing."

"Of course," Churkin agreed. "I believe your embassy has sent you a driver who is waiting for you. Of course, we will be happy to give you an escort to the embassy, and from there to Lubyanka."

"Many thanks," Barron told him.

"Everything okay?" Cooke asked, her voice quiet.

"Just the usual pleasantries," Barron replied, switching back to English. "Welcome, we're going to follow you everywhere, don't be stupid and try any operational acts, that sort of thing."

Cooke smiled. "Of course not."

Somewhere in Moscow, Russia

The van drove for a half hour by Kyra's estimation, one violent turn after another, and she assumed that the driver wasn't obligated to obey traffic laws. The hands holding her arms never let her go and the men inside never said a word.

The van finally stopped, Kyra heard the door open, and she felt movement around her. Someone unlocked the shackles binding her legs to the van and the hands on her arms pulled hard, dragging her out. She stumbled getting out, unable to judge the distance to the ground and falling to one knee. The unseen hands pulled her up and led her roughly along.

She felt the warm air of a building on her face and the sound of men's shoes changed from a rough scrape on concrete to the softer sounds of rubber rustling across carpet to an echo inside the closed walls of an elevator. The doors closed and the car took several seconds to think about whether to move or not before finally ascending. The ride was smooth, the passengers silent, and Kyra couldn't tell how many floors they'd passed before the car stopped.

Kyra was led out and guided down another hallway, then finally into a room where her captors seated her in a chair. The zip ties binding her wrists were cut, freeing her arms at last. She wasn't foolish enough to try removing the black hood cutting off her sight. She sat still, hands in her lap, listening to the conversation around her and trying to pick out any words she recognized. That proved to be a feckless exercise.

Another five minutes passed before the hood finally came off of Kyra's head. The world appeared, blinding and bright, and Kyra squinted until her eyes could adjust. The room around her was non-descript, painted concrete walls, no other furniture than the chair on which she was sitting, nothing to give her any clue as to where she was.

The contents of Kyra's satchel were laid out on a table in front of her. Some functionary was using a Nikon camera to document the captured gear . . . a Moscow tour map, an envelope, a passport, a ziplock bag with a disguise kit sealed inside, a pair of English paperback novels, some power bars, and several stacks of euros, the paper bands removed.

Kyra's escorts took their places by the gray metal door. A photographer aimed the camera in her direction and began taking pictures.

A Russian colonel stood behind the table separating them. "Good evening," Sokolov said. "Your name, please?" The command being in

English, Kyra had no doubts that it was intended for her. She said nothing. The Russian officer looked at her for several seconds, studying her, then leaned forward, putting his face only inches from hers. "Your name?"

"I am a diplomat," Kyra said, lying. "I'm not required to answer your question. There are rules governing the interrogation of diplomats and you know them. You will advise my embassy of my whereabouts immediately."

"A *diplomat*," Sokolov said. Kyra furrowed her brow. There was no venom in the Russian's voice, no sarcasm. "We know the kind of diplomacy that Americans practice with tools such as these. But I think you do not understand that diplomatic immunity does not apply right now."

U.S. Embassy
Moscow, Russia

The Russian escort cars peeled away, blocking off the street. The security gate slid open, the embassy car pulled through into the compound, and Cooke felt some of the tension in her shoulders ease. She was still a stranger in a hostile land, but there was a feeling here, a tangible spirit that hovered over this little spit of American-held territory that made it feel very much like home.

Her traveling companion had a fool's grin on his face. "Your old playground?" she teased him.

Barron nodded. "Three years, until the FSB almost killed me," he replied. "They did kill one of mine. That stupid car accident I told you about a few years ago. The locals here always did play the surveillance game a little too rough."

"You don't have to come with me to Lubyanka. You could stay here, preserve your cover."

"Nope," Barron said. "I'm almost ready to retire anyway and I want to see how this all turns out."

They stared down at the monitor as the embassy security chief restarted the video from the beginning and watched the replay for a second time. The time index on the screen showed the video was two hours old now. On the screen, Kyra came sprinting into the picture, reaching for the security guard's outstretched hand as a Russian chased her down, pushed her from behind, and the young woman tumbled to the white concrete. She pushed herself up, tried to get to the gate, only to be tackled. "American!" she yelled, clearly audible on the footage. Then three men were on her, the American guard helpless to step off U.S. territory onto Russian land and do anything. The Russians pinned her arms up, zip-tied her hands, and wrestled her into a waiting van as the U.S. Marine screamed profanities at the smug Russian standing between him and their captive. Then the Russians piled into the vehicle, closed the door, and pulled away. The entire incident had taken less than one minute.

"The question is which one got her," Barron said. "FSB or GRU? Any clues?"

"I gave a copy to some of the FBI special agents here," the security chief replied. "It's not much to go on . . . we're trying to match the license plate or the van, but good luck with that. The FSB would have to cooperate and they won't tell us jack just on general principles. But my gut tells me they weren't FSB. Military haircuts, and there are a few frames here where it looks like one of them is carrying a Makarov pistol in his holster, but I could be wrong. And the FSB doesn't usually play it like this, but I couldn't prove anything right now if I had to."

Cooke nodded. "That's okay. If the FSB grabbed her, they'll tell us. If they don't, we know who has her."

"You ready to head out?" Barron asked his superior.

"Yeah. Let's get this done."

The "Aquarium" — old GRU headquarters

"Explain, please, why you were in possession of this?" Sokolov asked, his voice loud for the recorders, waving his hand toward the table.

"I am a diplomat," Kyra repeated. "I'm not required to answer your questions. You will advise my embassy of my whereabouts immediately."

"That answer is tiring." Sokolov picked up the envelope. The seal was broken, leaving no question that he already knew what was inside. Still he made the dramatic show of pulling out the letter, printed in neat Cyrillic.

Dear friend,

We were most grateful to receive your last communication. We have always valued your information and were distressed not to hear from you according to the schedule. Your help in the past has been invaluable and we do not want to lose your friendship.

We regret the actions you had to take with regard to your friend, but we concur with your decision. While he was valuable to us, you have proven yourself more so and your protection is paramount. Your security means a lot to us.

As you know, we have sent one of our friends to support the story you had to report to your superiors. This is a difficult assignment for him, as he will be a guest in your country for some months, perhaps longer than a year before his claim that he is disillusioned with life there will be credible. We ask that you assist him in every way possible without endangering your own security.

Because of the recent troubles, we have found it necessary to alter the emergency travel plans we worked out with you some time ago. In this package, you will find new travel documents and the personal kit you will need to use it. Please keep them somewhere safe.

We are very concerned with your recent demand to change the terms of our financial arrangement with you. In particular, sending home so many consular officers to demonstrate your influence was unnecessary. As your friends, we are happy to discuss additional compensation for your help and information in the future. To show our sincerity, we have deposited $250,000 in the escrow account in addition to the payment here.

We look forward to working with you again in the nearest future. Your friends

"For who was this letter?" Sokolov asked. Kyra winced slightly at the man's stiff accent, but said nothing in response. *"We were most grateful to receive your last communication,"* he read from the page. "You are trying to reach a spy in our government, and an important one, I'm sure." He hefted one of the stacks of euros and made a show of flipping through the bills. "A quarter million. Fine wages for a mole, but I suppose a rich country like the United States can afford to pay such amounts for traitors." It was not a question.

Kyra held her peace. Sokolov picked up the passport and opened the cover, then shoved the front page at her face. The Russian pointed to the photograph. "Who is this? The Foreign Ministry assures me that they have issued no passport with this number, nor does the photograph match any on file."

Kyra just looked at him. Sokolov pushed the disguise kit across the table at her. "There is no reason not to tell me. It is a very good forgery, done by a skilled artist. But the false attachments in this bag—" He held up the ziplock pouch. "They are the same as the beard and glasses and other additions to the man's face in this picture. Do you think we have no computer experts? One of our best technicians is erasing them from the picture so we can see what the man looks like without them. We will find this man. You cannot save him by refusing to answer."

"As I told you, I'm a diplomat and not required to answer your questions," Kyra said.

The Russian sighed in mock resignation. "You are very calm," he observed. "I have seen many people in that chair, where you are now. Few have shown such reserve. You've had training, I think. Yes. You've been taught how to handle an interrogation. But we understand the way to drive a woman past her limits. You know that as well, I am sure, but I respect your discipline. You have done your duty and this does not need to be unfriendly. We understand the business of intelligence services. You spy on us, we spy on you. We are professionals about this, are we not? In the end, you will answer the questions, so I will not think less of you for choosing to avoid the agony."

Nice show, Kyra thought. "I want to speak to a representative from my embassy," she said.

"I can make that happen," Sokolov assured her. "But your refusal to cooperate with me can only delay that process. How can I tell them who has requested their assistance if you will not give me your name? You had no identification with you when you were detained. You must give me some information about yourself or I cannot help you. I do not even know which embassy to contact," he said.

Okay, time for a little reward, Kyra decided. "The U.S. Embassy."

"So you are American."

Kyra fought down the urge to roll her eyes and insult the man's deductive powers. "Yes," she said, her voice oozing condescension. The Russian's English accent was heavy enough that Kyra suspected the man wouldn't understand the emotion when he heard it.

"That is a start," Sokolov said. "And your name?"

"You don't need that. Just advise the embassy that you have a U.S. diplomat in your custody."

Sokolov turned to his Russian subordinates. "Leave," he ordered in their native language.

The photographer moved immediately to the exit, but the escorts stayed rooted, their faces perplexed. "You will leave," the Russian ordered a second time. "She is uncooperative. I must apply other measures. You will stand the post outside."

More hesitation, but the escorts finally obeyed, leaving the Russian alone with Kyra.

**Headquarters of the Federal Security Service
of the Russian Federation (FSB)
1 Bolshaya Lubyanka Street
Moscow, Russia**

The FSB's current home, strictly speaking, was across the street from old Lubyanka, the home of the KGB before it. If asked, Kathy Cooke would have admitted that the older building was an impressive piece of architecture, a four-story neo-Baroque edifice made of yellow-brick-turned-gray. CIA headquarters was an ugly complex to her eyes, but Lubyanka, originally built to be the home of an insurance company before the 1917 Revolution, had some real old European beauty in its design. It radiated a sense of history to her.

Not the good kind of history, she thought. The artistry of Lubyanka's design belied the fact that its ground floor had been a prison where thousands had entered and somewhat fewer had emerged. So much of Stalin's reign of terror had its epicenter in Lubyanka.

"Never thought I'd get this close to it," Barron admitted.

"Never wanted to," Cooke replied. "Too many people walked in and never came out. You can feel the ghosts."

"I never took you for the type to believe in the supernatural," Barron said.

"I'm not," she told him. "But I'm just religious enough to think that if the dead are walking the earth anywhere, it's here. You ever heard of Vasily Blokhin?"

"Can't say as I have."

"He was the chief executioner of the Soviet Union, handpicked by Stalin himself. It was an actual government position, if you can believe it. Nobody even knows how many people he personally killed, but I've seen claims as high as fifty thousand. He oversaw the executions of seven thousand Polish soldiers in one *month* in 1940," Cooke recounted. "He set a goal of killing three hundred people every night . . . brought his own briefcase full of Walther pistols because he didn't think the Soviet sidearms were reliable enough. The man even had an official executioner's uniform . . . leather butcher's apron, hat, long leather gloves that ran up to his elbows. A guard would march the prisoner into a little antechamber called the 'Leninist room,' which Blokhin had designed himself . . . soundproof walls and a sloping floor with a drain, to make it easier to wash the blood off after each kill. They'd put the prisoner down on his knees and Blokhin would shoot him in the base of the skull. They'd drag out the body and bring in another one. His unit helped him kill them at the rate of one man every three minutes, ten hours every night for a month. Stalin gave Blokhin the Order of the Red Banner for it." Cooke raised an arm and pointed at Lubyanka. "And he did it all in there. So, yeah, I can believe in ghosts."

"You know, the Russians probably believe our predecessors were doing the same thing at Langley."

"We've had our share of bad men, but we never had a prison in the basement, and we sure never kidnapped our own citizens," Cooke replied.

"Yeah, good luck convincing the Russians of that," Barron said. He felt like the building in front of him had drained the humor from his bones. "How'd Blokhin check out in the end?"

"Lost his job in '53 after Stalin died," Cooke recalled. "Became an alcoholic and went insane. The official record says he committed suicide in '55."

"Couldn't have happened to a nicer guy," Barron mused.

"I've never understood how someone can become so indifferent to life."

"'That which we persist in doing becomes easier, not that the task itself has become easier, but that our ability to perform it has improved,'" Barron said. "Ralph Waldo Emerson. Unfortunately, that applies to evil talents as well as good ones. Do something often enough and it becomes banal . . . ordinary."

"Maybe," Cooke said. "But he committed suicide. Maybe it never really became ordinary to him after all."

"You really believe he killed himself?"

Cooke pondered the question, then nodded. "Actually, yes. Maybe the ghosts of all the people he murdered tortured him until he went mad. That would be justice. A man who kills that many people by his own hand . . . I can't imagine what that does to your soul."

"What soul?" Barron asked. "A man would have nothing left by the end of that." He shook his head in disbelief. "And we're going to talk to the successor of guys like that. Makes me think this operation can't possibly work."

"Maybe," Cooke replied. "The question is who Grigoriyev hates worse, us or Lavrov."

"My money's on Lavrov. Grigoriyev was the FSB director when I was the station chief here, so I got a pretty good feel for him. He's a professional. He doesn't like us, but it's not personal. We're not trying to put the old man out to pasture. Lavrov is, and the anger between those two runs deep. If there's one thing the Russians do well, it's hold a grudge."

"You're right on that score," Cooke agreed. "You ready to do this?"

Barron shrugged. "Why not?" he asked. "You know, the Russians never filed the paperwork to PNG me after that car wreck. We've always assumed they know I'm Agency, but they never confirmed it. I guess they're going to find out now."

"If you're going to blow your cover, might as well go big and nuke it hard," Cooke advised.

"Like Slim Pickens riding the bomb." He dismounted the car and held the door for Cooke. Churkin and a Russian security detail got out of their own vehicles and formed a cordon around the Americans, leading them toward the visitors' entrance.

They approached the guard post. The Russian officer held up a hand. *"Ostanovites' i identifitsirovat' sebya!" Stop and identify yourself!*

Barron nodded, reached into his coat pocket, and pulled out his CIA credentials. "This is Kathryn Cooke, deputy director of national intelligence for the United States government. My name is Clark Barron and I'm the director of the CIA Directorate of Operations." Churkin's head whipped around in surprise at that revelation, proving conclusively that he spoke very good English. "We're here to speak to Director Anatoly Maksimovich Grigoriyev," Barron said in Russian. "He's expecting us."

The FSB officer manning the door gawked at the American, took Barron's credentials, and stared, then picked up the phone.

The conference room to which the escorts delivered them was more ornate than anything Barron had ever seen at Langley. The walls were hardwood, lacquered and polished to a perfect shine, with gold trim around the ceiling. The table in the center had a similar wooden border, the center covered in green leather. The chairs matched the table, with blue-and-white-checked cloth coverings, and Barron thought that the office chair under him was possibly the most comfortable in which he'd ever sat. There was no telephone in the room, no computer, no way to communicate outside. Barron wondered where the cameras were.

Grigoriyev stared hard at Barron, murder in his eyes. "You have lived in Russia before, Mr. Barron," he said. "My men retrieved our old file on you. It said nothing about you being a CIA officer."

"I lived here for three years," Barron confirmed. "I'd like to think I was good at the business."

"It appears you were. But you were in a terrible car accident," the Russian noted.

"Some of your counterintelligence boys were tailing me and one of my officers," Barron told him. "They got a little aggressive and ran into us . . . flipped our car and killed the young woman who was with me."

"They thought they were trailing diplomats and thought they could intimidate you. It was a new team and they were reckless. My condolences, though such accidents do happen from time to time. For their stupidity, the team responsible was reassigned to some very unpleasant duty in our far northeast, if that gives you any satisfaction at all." Grigoriyev's tone announced that he could not have cared less about a dead American spy. He turned to the senior U.S. officer in the room. "I was quite surprised to receive your request for a meeting, Miss Cooke. It is rare for American intelligence officers to meet with us at all, and when it does happen, months of planning occur in advance. Rushed meetings are rare things, so you must forgive my suspicions and concerns about your honesty right now."

"Not at all, Director," Cooke said. "I would feel the same if I was sitting on your side of the table."

"So we understand each other," Grigoriyev agreed. "Then why did you wish to meet with me?"

"There is a situation with one of our assets here in Moscow that has gone out of our control and we need your assistance to resolve it," Cooke replied.

Sokolov leaned in to Kyra, close enough to whisper. "I turned cameras off, so they cannot hear us, before they came in with you. Will look like equipment failure. You know where you are, yes? This building is old GRU headquarters, but GRU does not handle counterintelligence in the *Rodina*. That is FSB. They don't know you are here and Lavrov will not tell them or your embassy. FSB would turn you over to your embassy and expel you from country after making you a . . . what is the word . . . spectacle? But FSB does not know about what Lavrov is doing here and he does not want them to know. So if you want me to tell your embassy that you are here so they can tell FSB to come, you must give me your name."

Kyra looked at the man in disbelief. "I have wanted to work for your people, long time now," Sokolov said.

Kyra stared at him, watching him twitch. The arrogance had disappeared so quickly and completely that she wasn't sure it hadn't been an act all along. "I don't believe you," she finally said, cautious. He was showing none of the physical signs of deceit, but he was a Russian intelligence officer after all. The GRU trained its men to hide them, she was sure.

Sokolov saw her expression. "For thirty years, I am interrogator for GRU," he said. "I am good at it, but I am sick of it. Seeing people brought to me who have done nothing but make angry or insult some senior man. Then our Soviet Union falls and I had hope we would be a better country. We *are* a better country, for a few years. They do not bring people to me in here for long time. Then Putin takes over and I see him and his friends taking us back, making us again what we were. And then they start bringing people to me again—" He stopped talking, almost in midsentence, choking on whatever he was going to say next.

Kyra didn't try to fill the silence. Finally, Sokolov looked up. "And I am a coward," he said, self-loathing in his voice. "They bring these men to me . . . sometimes women, sometimes journalists who try to solve murders done by government . . . officers and spies who tell superiors that they are evil men . . . sometimes just businessmen who do not want to sell things to the Kremlin at prices the Kremlin wants to pay. And I ask them questions, and if they do not give me answers that my bosses want to hear, then I step outside and let guards come in and beat them until they give me answers that my bosses want to hear. And I am afraid to say no because I know the names of so many people that my bosses kill. I am afraid that if I stop, they kill me too."

The Russian colonel slumped, resting his backside on the heavy metal table. "So I think maybe I can be a spy, but I never volunteer because I am afraid. And then Lavrov tells me that he has source who is going to give him names of Russians who I need to kill. And I think, if names come from his source, then Russians brought to me must be working for CIA, yes? And I think, maybe I can warn the men who the source names, so they can maybe escape. So Lavrov gives me the name, I find the person, and I make private phone call and tell them to run. But my unit, they are too good and catch them anyway, and I have to act like I am pleased and do my duty so they do not kill me."

He had hardly looked at Kyra during his explanation, but he raised his head and looked at the analyst's face. "But now Lavrov brings me Americans, you and the other man. He will not talk and I have to try to make him. Lavrov does not want me to kill him, but I think maybe it would be better. If you do not talk, maybe Lavrov will tell me to do to you the things I had to do to him. I do not want to hurt you. I hope you can tell your bosses about me and help me escape my country. Will you help me? Will you help my family? If you say yes, I try to save you. I cannot get you out of the building. The escorts have orders from Lavrov. The only way to get you outside is to tell FSB. Grigoriyev hates Lavrov and to hear that Lavrov is holding and torturing diplomats will give him a chance to hurt Lavrov. But FSB, they will contact your embassy first to confirm you are diplomat. They will need your name to do that. If your embassy agrees, FSB will come—"

The door opened behind them. Sokolov's face switched from one of depression and despair to a mask of nonemotion in an instant. He turned around.

General Arkady Lavrov stood at the door. "I am told that we have an American guest," he said, in English.

"Yes, General," Sokolov replied in the same language. "I am asking her questions, but she says only that she is diplomat and will not answer questions. She wants us to tell U.S. embassy—"

"Yes, yes," Lavrov said, waving the explanation away. "You are dismissed."

"I—" Sokolov started. Then he decided that silence was the better course, looked at Kyra, and retreated from the room. The door closed behind him.

FSB headquarters

"And this 'situation' . . . who does it concern?" Grigoriyev asked.

Play it up, Cooke thought. *People believe what they want to believe . . . even Russians.*

"Three of our officers and GRU Chairman Arkady Lavrov," Barron said.

Grigoriyev held up a hand. "You have never admitted to having intelligence officers on Russian soil."

"And we're not admitting it now. You understand how this is all played, Director," Barron told him.

"I do. But to the best of my knowledge, Arkady Lavrov and the foreign minister have expelled all of your people. Are you telling me now that they missed some?"

"We're not at liberty to confirm or deny whether any of the people

Lavrov had expelled were intelligence officers," Cooke countered. "They're not the issue. The officers that Lavrov is holding is the issue."

Grigoriyev frowned. "The GRU has no authority to detain foreign citizens for espionage. Such arrests are strictly the purview of the FSB."

"Director Grigoriyev, there's a very good reason that Chairman Lavrov hasn't told you about the arrests," Barron told him.

"And that would be . . . ?"

"Because he was working for us," Barron replied.

Grigoriyev furrowed his brow. "An extraordinary claim requires extraordinary proof."

"The proof is sitting in a cell at GRU headquarters," Cooke said.

The "Aquarium" — old GRU headquarters

"When my subordinates told me that they had caught an American spy trying to take sanctuary in her country's embassy, I had so hoped it would be the young woman I met in Berlin at the embassy," Lavrov said, exultant.

"I think I'm a little young for you," Kyra replied, deadpan.

"There is no such thing," Lavrov said. "But you are a woman of deeper morals, then?"

"More than you, apparently."

Lavrov laughed at her response. "Yes, I think that is true. But we are both spies, and it is also true that the longer one is a spy, the fewer morals are left to her."

"Only if she's weak," Kyra replied. "If she's strong, the longer she's a spy, the more devoted she becomes to the morals she believes in."

"You are a thinker, then? Very good." Lavrov chuckled. "But you do not know me—"

"You're Arkady Lavrov, chairman of the GRU," Kyra said. "And for the last twenty years, you've been selling strategic military technologies to foreign buyers. You sold stealth materials to the Chinese recovered from the wreckage of an F-117 Nighthawk shot down in Serbia in 1999. You sold nuclear weapons designs to the Iranians and have been helping them with uranium enrichment and nuclear waste reprocessing to manufacture plutonium. And now you're trying to sell an electromagnetic pulse weapon to the Syrians, probably for use against Israel." Kyra grinned. "I could be wrong about that last one."

Lavrov smiled in surprise, nicotine-stained teeth showing between his lips. "And why do you think I do these things? Do you think I do it to destroy your country?"

"Actually, I think that would just be a bonus for you," Kyra replied.

"Again, very good." Lavrov looked down at her. "Destroying countries is the grandiose ambition of lunatics, movies, and fiction books," he said. The man's English was refined, very smooth compared to Sokolov's diction. "But if that were my goal, I would need do nothing. Your own politicians are doing it efficiently enough. The irony is that you're doing to yourselves what you once did to us. Your leaders are wasting your wealth, spending more on your military than the next ten countries combined, trying to keep the world in a bottle. But I promise you, I am very interested in building up your country."

Kyra frowned. "You'll forgive me if I think you're a liar."

"Of course," Lavrov replied. "But I am quite telling the truth when I say that I have a proposal for you."

"Such as?"

"I would like you to work for me."

FSB headquarters

"If Lavrov is one of your assets, why would he be holding your officers?" Grigoriyev said, disbelieving.

"That's complicated—" Barron started. He was playing the idiot, giving Cooke's more generous answers greater credibility.

"I am not a stupid man," Grigoriyev cut him off.

"No, you're not," Cooke replied. "Lavrov was a volunteer, but not for ideological reasons. Simply put, he was feeding us information about you, sir, and the FSB. I don't think you'll be surprised to hear that he's wanted to remove you from your post for a long time. To that end, he gave us information about FSB operations that let us protect our operations and undercut your efforts. In short, Lavrov wanted to neutralize *you*."

Grigoriyev gave no reaction to the accusation. "Continue," he said, his voice showing no emotion.

"We were happy to cooperate with that effort until we learned about some of Lavrov's own operations. I presume you know about the Chinese stealth plane that the U.S. Navy shot down over the Taiwan Strait two years ago?" Cooke asked.

"Yes."

"Lavrov sold the engine and stealth technologies to the Chinese to make that plane. Its engine designs matched those of Russia's fifth-generation fighter, the Sukhoi T-50," Barron said.

Grigoriyev frowned. "Those engines are not for export and the plans are classified."

"And you also know about the Iranian nuclear warhead that we recovered in Venezuela last year?" Cooke asked.

"Yes," Grigoriyev said.

Cooke extended a USB thumb drive to the Russian. "It was a Russian design, last generation."

Grigoriyev took the thumb drive. "That cannot be true. That would be treason of the highest order, unless the order came from the president himself."

"Yes, it would," Cooke said.

"Work for you?" Kyra asked. It was the least subtle pitch for treason she'd ever heard. "Like Maines?"

"I thought Mr. Maines could understand my views. But when he arrived in Berlin, he proved to me that his interest was money above anything else. I knew then that he was not the person I needed inside the CIA. So I refused to give him anything," Lavrov countered. "But I have greater hopes for you, young lady. Our conversation on the embassy roof . . . you showed me then that you see things in a different way. Shall I explain?"

"Oh, please, by all means," Kyra told him. "I want to hear this."

Lavrov dragged a chair over toward his captive and set his bulk on the seat. "Some years ago, Vladimir Putin said that the collapse of the Soviet Union was the disaster of the century, and he was correct. He was thinking of the plight that faced the Russian people in the years after, but he failed to see the plight that our collapse left for yours."

"I think being the world's only superpower worked out pretty well for us," Kyra observed.

"Then you have been blind," Lavrov told her, his voice suddenly cold. "There must be opposition in all things, don't you think? For almost fifty years, your country faced nuclear annihilation at our hand, but that did not break your spirit, your sense of who you were . . . quite the opposite, in fact. But you spent so long fighting us that when we could no longer fight, you found yourselves without direction. Then September eleventh. Terrorists are vicious people, to be sure, but hardly a threat to your national existence. But how did your leaders respond? They dropped expensive bombs on people who lived in caves and huts. They kidnapped and tortured. They tried to control chaos with tools designed to fight an organized enemy."

Kyra said nothing. She wanted to tell the man that he was wrong, but she wasn't sure that he was.

"During the Cold War, two great powers offered a single choice to every country in the world . . . whose side will you join? And the world was more stable for it." Lavrov stopped talking, ran his hand through his thinning gray hair. "Do you see it?" he asked. "Two fallen countries that could be great again . . . but neither without the other. We need our enemies, *devushka*. That is why I don't want to destroy your country. I only want to build mine up, but it cannot rise to its full stature without yours to oppose it. We will draw other countries back into our arms—"

"So you can take them over again?" Kyra asked. She didn't try to hide her contempt.

"Not so much. That did not work so well for us before . . . but weaker countries do turn to stronger ones for guidance. That is to be expected. And it is the nature of almost every person, as soon as they gain a little power, that they begin to exercise it to control those around them. No, it is better, I think, to offer them something they want and attach conditions to receiving it. Better to bribe than to bully or butcher. People will fight to the death for their freedoms, but they will sell them quick and cheap for something they want."

"Like weapons?" Kyra accused him.

Lavrov shrugged. "There is no moral law of the universe that says the Chinese may not have stealth planes or the Iranians can have no nuclear weapons, or the Syrians no EMP bombs. You only want to stop these because they scare you."

"We're afraid? You're the one hiding from us," Kyra replied. "You don't sell your technology out in the open."

"Privacy is good business. Surely the United States doesn't make public all of its weapons sales? And there is nothing I have sold to other countries that your country has not. Stealth, nuclear weapons, EMPs . . . have you held any of these back from *your* allies? No."

"We demanded that General Lavrov stop his proliferation activities immediately," Cooke continued. "He refused, saying that he was making more from that business than he was from us. The fact is, we can't get approval to pay him the kind of money that he's making from proliferating strategic technologies to foreign buyers. President Rostow is afraid it would set a precedent and he doesn't want to reward men who traffic in illegal arms. So we told General Lavrov that we would burn him ourselves by reporting him to you. Whether your president had approved or not, he would have to stop Lavrov to protect his own interests."

"Then Lavrov killed Strelnikov to protect himself," Barron added. "He could blame all of his activities on Strelnikov and say that he'd already found and executed the mole himself. It was a stalemate. So we decided to negotiate a truce. We sent a CIA officer named Alden Maines to Berlin to meet with Lavrov. Maines's cover story was that he was defecting and had burned Strelnikov to prove his *bona fides*. The general detained him. We sent two more officers to find out what happened to Maines and Lavrov grabbed one of them. The other escaped, but we believe the general is holding our two officers at GRU headquarters. The U.S Embassy also informed us a short while ago that he arrested a third officer just this evening, a young woman who was investigating Maines's detention."

Girgoriyev frowned. "As I told you, the GRU has no authority to detain foreign citizens engaged in unlawful actions on our soil. That is the duty of the FSB."

"We have the security footage," Barron replied. "It's on that thumb drive. Feel free to confirm it. I won't be surprised if the men in the video don't work for you."

Grigoriyev stared at the thumb drive in his hand. Cooke couldn't tell whether he could separate the truth from the lies. "So you believe he is trying to neutralize everyone who could confirm his treason, whether Russian or American," he said.

"We're not sure, but that's our working theory," Barron agreed. "And we think he's tried to push the point by evicting mass numbers of U.S. citizens from the country, probably hoping that we'd back off. At this point, Lavrov is beyond our control, has undermined our operations, and could kill three of our officers. Since he's broken Russian laws by detaining foreign citizens on Russian soil without valid legal authority, we're going to the only person with the authority and resources to stop him."

"But we know that some of the people who Lavrov evicted from the *Rodina* were CIA officers, not diplomats. We are very good at counterintelligence," Gregoriyev replied.

"Some were," Barron conceded. "Mostly senior officers who were already nearing the end of their rotations in Moscow. The rest were just State Department employees."

"So the bulk of your officers, they are still in Moscow?" Grigori-yev asked, suspicious.

"That I cannot confirm nor deny," Barron replied.

Grigoriyev leaned back, clasped his hands together, and stared at the Americans.

GRU headquarters

Lavrov leaned back in the chair, looking suddenly tired. "So I ask you, the final time . . . work for me. I will not insult your loyalty by offering you money, though I can and will arrange that if you agree. You spoke the truth when you said you were a moral woman, and I need such a person. In return, I can give you the intelligence you need to win some battles and rise through the ranks. I will give you what you need to become one of the CIA's leaders. You will be in a position to influence presidents. Help me to rebuild my country so that yours can be strong again."

Kyra stared at him, trying to read his face, his movements, to get some look into his mind. "Will you answer one question?"

"Perhaps."

"How much money have you made selling technology to other countries?" she asked.

Lavrov's smile froze and melted in seconds. He turned to the table where the contents of Kyra's pack were still organized. He picked up the letter and showed it to her. "They showed me a photocopy of this letter. Who was it meant for?" he asked.

Kyra refused to answer and Lavrov read the letter aloud. *"We regret the actions you had to take with regard to your friend, but we concur with your decision. While he was valuable to us, you have proven yourself more so and your protection is paramount."* He looked back at the analyst. "I think this letter is not meant for anyone," Lavrov offered. "I think this letter is a forgery, a prop for a play on a stage, and we are the actors. I believe you wanted to get caught, hoping that this letter would reach the highest levels of the FSB. Grigoriyev would read it and think that I am a CIA asset. Grigoriyev hates me, as I am sure you know, and he would use this as an excuse to denounce and jail me . . . possibly execute me."

Kyra gave him no reaction. "But you did not think that the GRU might detain you instead of the FSB. A shame, it was clever." He pulled a lighter out of his pocket, ignited it, and touched it to the paper. He held it until the fire reached his fingers, and he dropped it. Then he picked up the stacks of euros. "But I will keep the money, for which I thank you."

"So it *is* all about money," Kyra said.

"No, *devushka*," Lavrov said. "It truly is as I said. I want my country to be great and I need your country to stand against it for that to happen. But great men deserve great rewards. Your country thinks so. Why else do so many of your politicians become wealthy in the service of your nation?"

He sighed. "I regret that we could not come to an accommodation." Lavrov walked to the door and opened it. "You have your orders?" he asked the guards.

"Da," they said, not quite in unison.

"Very well. I will be at the Khodynka Airfield. Let me know when you are finished." Lavrov turned into the hallway and walked out of Kyra's sight.

Moscow, Russia

Director Grigoriyev's car was one of the most comfortable armored vehicles in which Kathy Cooke had ever traveled. The U.S. president's limousine was a finer ride, but not by much.

The FSB director himself sat in the facing double seat across from Cooke and Barron, holding a conversation in Russian with the station chief. Two guards sat in the front of the car, and chase cars bracketed them ahead and behind. The motorcade was ignoring traffic lights and laws with abandon. *Grigoriyev has better job perks than I do*, Cooke thought.

Grigoriyev and Barron reached some break in their conversation and the Russian senior officer pulled a cell phone out of his pocket and placed a call. Cooke leaned over to the station chief. "Where are we going?" she asked, her voice low.

"GRU headquarters," Barron said.

"Oh, joy," Cooke said, deadpan. "Did Grigoriyev believe us? Or is he just using us to shiv Lavrov?"

"I don't know," Barron admitted. "Could be either one. I wouldn't put it past him to be playing both sides. You should read his leadership profile sometime. He's not one to pass up an opportunity."

"Fine by me either way," Cooke replied, approving. "I don't care if he uses us, as long as he's letting us use him."

"Let's hope he's looking at it the same way," Barron advised. "It's one thing to be strange bedfellows. But Russians love their chess and I'm not sure who the pawns are here."

Khodynka Military Airfield
One quarter mile northeast of GRU headquarters

Lavrov took the long way to the hangar, driving his jeep slowly past the small boneyard of retired MiGs and Sukhois and Ilyushins that sat in a line on the eastern half of the field. He could see them all from his office window, decaying reminders of what Russia had once been. It was an infuriating sight to him. Each of those planes had had its day, the finest aircraft in the world of its time, a terrifying reminder that his country could exert its will where and how it chose. Now they were rusting in place, never to grace the sky again. Oh, the president was making a show of pouring money into new weapons, trying to show the world that the Kremlin was not to be ignored. He was a fool. It was simply more of what Stalin and Khrushchev and Brezhnev had all done, and look where that had taken the *Rodina*. The president had learned nothing from history, grasped no lessons.

Such as this field . . . there was such history here in this field. Fourteen hundred people had been trampled to death here during a celebration of the coronation of Czar Nicholas II in 1896, soaking the field in the blood of peasants. The czar had cared so little for the massacre that he hadn't bothered to cancel his coronation ball that evening. It was a day remembered less than two decades later when the Bolsheviks rose up. The man who had shown so little regard for his people found that his people had none for him when the day of execution came. Did the Kremlin even remember what had happened here, and what had sprung from it? Lavrov was sure they did not, else this field would not have been left strewn with weeds and rusting metal and broken asphalt. It would have been a monument, not a boneyard.

Lavrov shook his head. It was a cruel thing, to have a vision that no one shared. To have to manipulate others and fool them into joining a cause was maddening. Why did no one else see what he saw? Grigoriyev did not see it. Maines certainly did not see it. He had hoped that the *devushka*, Kyra Stryker, would see it. He was not sure why, but that one pained him the most of all. Their conversation on the embassy roof in Berlin had given him such hope. She had read his operation against Maines like a voodoo witch reading the tarot cards. She had divined his entire campaign to strengthen America's enemies by selling them technologies . . . but she had disappointed him at the critical moment. She should have seen him for the man that he was, not a greedy arms dealer.

He would go on. All of the great Russian leaders had been lonely men. He supposed that he had been a fool to expect better for himself.

Lavrov's jeep slowed as it rolled into the hangar, the cargo truck trailing behind carrying men and crates. He killed the engine and stared up at the Mil Mi-26 cargo helicopter being serviced. The truck continued around him to the unloading station and men began leaping from the bed before the vehicle had stopped. The general dismounted and walked across the bright concrete floor to the rear cargo ramp to find the crew chief. The soldier was inside the cavernous metal stomach of the helo, checking the chains and straps binding the cargo boxes to the floor. "How long?" Lavrov asked the man.

The crew chief saluted the general, then rubbed a hand across his face, stretching out the leathery skin wrinkled before its time from abuse of cigarettes and cheap alcohol. "Another hour, I think, General. The cargo is ready, but we have to finish the maintenance checks and then top off the tank. But we will be ready on schedule."

Lavrov nodded. "Very good. A Syrian friend of mine is waiting for this delivery and he is the impatient kind. I will be in the maintenance office."

"Yes, sir." Lavrov trudged down the ramp and exhaled, depressed in his spirit. He looked at his watch and wondered how much longer it would take Sokolov and his men to kill the woman and the other Americans.

GRU headquarters

The drive from Lubyanka took eighteen minutes. There had been traffic, but Grigoriyev's motorcade had used lights and sirens to force its way past the civilian traffic and ignored whatever inconvenient laws would have slowed the trip. Cooke saw an airfield to her right, the sun glinting off a series of decrepit fighter planes lined up in a sloppy row. There was no movement on the tarmac, no trucks, no planes fueling. There were no lights in any of the buildings save one hangar near the center, and she wondered why the Russians had let a military airfield in the heart of Moscow sit unused and decaying.

The car turned left and slowed as it approached a security gate. The driver rolled down the window and showed his identification. Cooke heard them exchange words in Russian, then heated arguments mixed with several phrases she was sure were insults. The guard began waving wildly at the line of SUVs and cars behind Grigoriyev's own.

The FSB director rolled down his own window and motioned the guard to come over. Barron leaned over and began whispering to Cooke, translating the conversation.

"You know who I am?" Grigoriyev asked.

"Yes," the guard asked.

"Good. Open the gate."

"Director, I must call my superiors for orders—"

"No, you do not. I am not a military officer, but I am in charge of the security of the *Rodina* and there are men inside your building who are traitors to your homeland and mine. So you will open this gate and allow this entire motorcade into this facility, and you will not warn anyone about it. If you fail to follow those orders, you will be arrested as a co-conspirator along with anyone else I decide to detain in the next hour, and no military officer in your chain of command will save you. Do you understand?"

The guard nodded, mute.

"Good. Now, again, open the gate."

The guard returned to his post and spoke to his comrades. Cooke saw the young men look at their car, fear on their young faces. The guard pressed an unseen button and the gate opened, the barricade lowering beyond. Grigoriyev's driver eased the car forward and the other vehicles behind rolled forward to follow.

"I never thought that fear of Lubyanka Prison would work in our favor," Cooke whispered.

"Enjoy it," Barron advised. "I suspect it's a once-in-a-lifetime event."

"I am sorry," Sokolov said. "I cannot help you now. Lavrov knows you are a prisoner and expects me to execute you and your friends. If I do not, he will execute me, I am sure."

Kyra stared up at the man, trying to judge whether his sorrow was genuine. She thought it was, but she wasn't sure that Russians expressed their emotions in quite the same way as her own countrymen. "Can you tell me what time it is?" she asked.

Sokolov looked at her, surprised, then at his watch. "It is nineteen forty hours."

Kyra tipped her head back a bit and stared at the ceiling as she did the math. "I don't suppose I could ask you to wait an hour."

"Wait? You ask this as last request?"

"Do Russian prisoners get a last request?"

Sokolov shrugged. "No."

"Then I suppose it's a good thing that I'm not Russian. But if you'll wait an hour, I don't think you'll have to follow General Lavrov's orders," Kyra advised. "That would be worth your time, if you really are sick of killing good people."

Sokolov furrowed his brow in confusion. "What are you saying?"

"I'm saying that sometime in the next hour, I think there will be some visitors coming and they'll want to see me."

"Visitors? From where?" Sokolov demanded.

"The FSB," Kyra replied. *I hope*, she thought.

Grigoriyev stomped ahead of his security detail, much to his protective officers' frustration. Cooke and Barron kept pace twenty feet behind. The deputy DNI looked over at her subordinate. Barron was smiling, happier than she'd ever seen him. "You're enjoying this?"

"Do you have any idea how many times I wanted to see the inside of this place when I was the station chief here? Getting here would've been like walking into the holy of holies. Besides, I think we're about to see one wild show from the expensive seats."

Grigoriyev pushed the main doors open to GRU headquarters and stormed the building, his detail behind. Cooke and Barron stepped inside. The front lobby was brightly lit, with white marble walls and a marble parquet floor. The center of the floor was decorated with the GRU seal, which looked for all the world like Batman's symbol.

The guards at the entry post rose in confusion. "You men will sit down," Grigoriyev ordered, pointing a leathery finger at the junior officers. "I am Anatoly Maksimovich Grigoriyev, director of the Federal'naya Sluzhba Bezopasnosti. Where is General-Major Arkady Lavrov?"

They had recognized Grigoriyev before he'd identified himself.

The head of the FSB, like his KGB predecessors, was always an infamous figure among his countrymen. "Sir," one of the guards replied, "I . . . we do not know. We are not privy to the general's schedule. But if you could wait here, we can try to—"

Grigoriyev marched over to the security desk and stared down at the young guard, a boy of twenty perhaps. "You will call upstairs to the general's staff and determine his location in the next five minutes. You will not report who has made the request." The FSB director pulled a set of photographs out of the inside pocket of his overcoat and laid them on the desk. "Also, these Americans are being detained somewhere in this facility. You will find out where they are being held, also in the next five minutes. If you do not meet my deadline, I will have you arrested and dragged in chains to Lubyanka, and then I will give the same order to your replacement and we will try again. Am I understood?"

"Yes, Director!" the guard said, trying desperately not to stammer out the words.

"Very good. When you have fulfilled my request, you will then escort me to the general, and you will provide an escort for a detachment to wherever the Americans are being held. Do all of this and you will go home free men tonight."

"Yes, Director!"

"I'll say this for the Russians," Barron whispered. "Intimidation is an art form over here."

"First lesson, don't bluff," Cooke said. "I don't know what he just told that boy, but I'm sure he meant every word."

"He did," Barron confirmed. "If this was the warm-up, it was worth blowing my cover to see what's coming when he finds Lavrov."

"I do not think that General Lavrov will wait so long for me to call," Sokolov said. "He will call others to come and see why—"

An insistent pounding on the door interrupted the interrogator's apology. Sokolov frowned, moved to the door, and opened it. A conscript stood in the hallway outside, looking nervous. He saluted the senior officer. "Colonel Sokolov! The director of the FSB is at the main entrance. He is demanding to see the American."

Sokolov's eyes grew larger and he looked over his shoulder at Kyra. "*Neveroyatno!*" he muttered. "I am under orders from General Lavrov himself to expedite the . . . the interrogation."

"I . . . I don't know what to tell you, sir," the conscript stammered. "General Lavrov is our ranking officer . . . but the FSB!"

"I know," Sokolov replied. "Very well. Bring Director Grigoriyev here."

"Yes, sir!" The conscript saluted again, then fled down the hallway as fast as he could run.

Sokolov turned back to Kyra. "I think you have gotten your wish," he told her. "I think I will not have to kill you after all. This makes me very happy."

You and me both, Kyra thought.

Grigoriyev and his entourage made the walk to the interrogation room in five minutes almost to the second. The FSB director stormed into the room without announcing his arrival, paying no attention to Sokolov. Kyra's clothing and restraints made it clear what role she was playing. She saw Kathy Cooke and Clark Barron stride into the room, surrounded by Russian officers, and she exhaled long and slow with relief.

"I am Anatoly Grigoriyev, director of the FSB," the man said to her in English. "You are the American, Kyra Stryker?"

"I am, Director," she replied.

Grigoriyev muttered a curse and turned his gaze on Sokolov. "Under what authority is this woman being detained by the GRU?" he demanded in Russian.

"I cannot answer that question," Sokolov admitted. "She was detained and brought to me under direct orders from General Lavrov. I have been following his orders. One does not question orders."

"I want to see any effects that were on her person when she was detained."

Sokolov pointed at the nearby table. "Her equipment is there."

Grigoriyev leaned over and examined the contents of Kyra's pack. "This is everything?"

"No, Director. There were two other items, a letter and a considerable quantity of euros."

"And why are they not here?" Grigoriyev demanded.

"General Lavrov took the euros and burned the letter," Sokolov said. "But our photographer documented everything. He can show you a digital picture of the original letter."

"I want to see it. Bring it to me now."

"Yes, Director." Sokolov stepped out of the room.

Barron and Cooke stepped over to Kyra's side. "Good to see you," Barron said. "You're in one piece?"

"More or less," Kyra confirmed.

"Have you seen Jon?" Cooke asked.

"No," Kyra replied. "They brought me straight here and I haven't been out of this room. The colonel there was under orders from Lavrov to execute me. He wasn't anxious to do it, but I don't think he was going to wait much longer."

"Lavrov was here?" Barron asked.

"Yeah," Kyra confirmed. "He pitched me to work for him again. I turned him down."

"Good choice," Barron said. "After Grigoriyev is finished tonight, I don't think Lavrov's people are going to have much job security."

Sokolov reentered the room, a tablet computer in his hand. "This was the letter," he announced in Russian.

Grigoriyev took the tablet, pulled reading glasses from his overcoat, and put them on using one hand, then stared at the screen. He said nothing for almost a minute. "And Lavrov burned this letter?"

"He did."

"You handled it?"

"*Da,*" Sokolov confirmed.

"In your opinion, was it genuine?" Grigoriyev asked.

Sokolov looked at Kyra, a look of concentration on his face. *If you want to switch sides, now's the time,* Kyra thought. *Back me up if you want to get out from under Lavrov.*

The colonel turned back to the FSB director, still thinking. Then he straightened his spine and looked Grigoriyev in the eyes. "*Da,* Director Grigoriyev. I believe it was."

Kyra tightened her fists, channeling all of her adrenaline and excited energy into her hands.

"And he talked to your prisoner?"

"*Da,*" Sokolov confirmed.

"You heard the conversation?"

"I did not. The general ordered me out of the room."

"I want to see the security tapes," Grigoriyev ordered.

"There are none," Sokolov said.

"Why not?"

"Because General Lavrov ordered me to have them switched off," Sokolov lied. "He said that an operation that required detaining the Americans was too sensitive to record any related interrogation on the tapes."

"So, the general came in, ordered you out of the room and the cameras turned off, then had a private conversation with an American spy, burned a letter that appears to incriminate him as a CIA asset, and walked out with a large amount of euros that this woman had on her person and which the letter said were for his services. Is that accurate?"

"It is," Sokolov said, trying to look embarrassed. He was finding his footing now.

"Colonel, you are a fool. You will release this woman into my custody immediately," Grigoriyev ordered. "And you will do the same with any other Americans you are holding in this facility."

"I think General Lavrov will dispute your request—" Sokolov protested, not very hard.

"General Lavrov will be very fortunate if he does not end his night in Lubyanka!" Grigoriyev snapped. "The question of this moment is whether you will share a seat next to him. The answer to that question will depend on the amount of cooperation you offer me in the next few seconds."

Sokolov pulled back, apparently intimidated. "There are two others," he said. "Two men. They are in the infirmary under guard."

Grigoriyev pointed at Cooke and Barron. "You will release her and take us to them. You will also tell me where General Lavrov is."

"He is at the Khodynka Airfield," Sokolov said. "He left here a half hour ago. If he is not there now, I do not know where he might be."

Grigoriyev made a curt nod toward Kyra, and Sokolov unfastened her restraints. "I am pleased that you will leave this place," he told her, almost a whisper. "I did not want you to die tonight." He stood up and helped Kyra to her feet. "If you follow, I take you to the infirmary."

Kyra followed Sokolov down the stairwell, afraid to say anything to the man. She saw security cameras at every turn, but wasn't sure whether the Aquarium hallways and stairwells weren't filled with audio taps and bugs in every corner. She didn't want to say anything that would incriminate the man. The colonel had just set up his commanding officer as a traitor to his country and she didn't want Lavrov to find some way to lay the same crime at Sokolov's feet.

The infirmary was in the new GRU headquarters and the crossover between the old and new buildings was unmistakable. The

Aquarium had smelled of old must, its architecture a testament to Soviet design. The new building was clean and modern, brightly lit with new carpet and light-colored walls. Kyra could have mistaken it for a U.S. government facility had the lettering on the signs not been in Cyrillic.

Sokolov turned a corner and slowed. He pointed at the door ahead. "They are inside," he said. "The man who came with Lavrov from Berlin, the traitor, he was injured before he came here. They break his hand with hammers. The other, they shoot him in his leg. I know the men they left with him. They are efficient and lose any pity for others long time ago."

"Thank you," Kyra said.

Barron pushed open the door to the infirmary.

It looked like any doctor's office, with a nurses' station, a waiting room, and a hallway leading back into private offices and other rooms. A faint antiseptic smell pervaded the air and Kyra's stomach churned a bit.

Grigoriyev filed in behind her, approached the nurse on duty, and had a short conversation with her. She hesitated, saw the armed men behind the FSB director, and decided that compliance was the wiser course. She pointed down the hall.

Grigoriyev marched ahead, Kyra and the other Americans behind. The Russian made a few turns, then stopped. A pair of guards, hard young men, flanked the last door on the left. Kyra's instincts told her they were Spetsnaz.

"You know me?" Grigoriyev asked in Russian, approaching the soldiers.

"Yes, sir," one of the guards confirmed.

"Good. Open the door."

"*Nyet*, Director. We have orders from general—"

"General Lavrov's orders do not apply to me. I am in charge of counterintelligence and internal security in the *Rodina*. The men in that room are American civilians, and therefore the GRU has no jurisdiction here. Open the door."

"*Nyet*, Director. We cannot without orders from the general."

Grigoriyev's patience snapped. He barked an order in Russian that Kyra didn't catch. Grigoriyev's men drew their sidearms and leveled them at the Spetsnaz guards, who drew their own weapons on instinct and pointed them at the FSB director, both sides yelling at each other, frenzied orders demanding each side surrender their pistols.

The guns hadn't cleared the holsters before Kyra felt Barron's hands grab her from behind, and the man almost threw her and Cooke into a doorway, then positioned himself between them and the guards.

Grigoriyev raised his hand and his men fell quiet. His eyes tore into the GRU officers. "You are outnumbered and there is nowhere in this hallway to take cover. If you shoot me, it will be a race to see whether my body or yours reaches the carpet first." The guards stared at the half-dozen guns pointed at their heads. "The Americans are coming with me. Lower your guns and I will report to your superiors that you did your duty. No charges will be brought against you."

The Spetsnaz took another five seconds to consider the offer and work out the math. They lowered their Makarovs, replacing them in their holsters.

"A good decision. Now step aside."

The room was small, barely larger than an average patient's room in any American hospital, the equipment similar except for the strange lettering on every console. The lighting was dim and it took several seconds for Kyra's eyes to adjust, her night vision coming to bear.

Alden Maines lay in the first bed, unconscious, a large clear bag of morphine running into his forearm through an IV drip. He was handcuffed to the bed rail, which saved Kyra the trouble of asking Grigoriyev to take care of that piece of business.

A curtain hanging from a sliding rail separated the American criminal from the patient in the far bed. Kyra stepped forward, her heart trying to beat its way out of her chest. She took the white cloth in her hand and pulled it aside.

Jonathan Burke was lying in the bed, dressed in hospital scrubs, an IV drip of his own attached to his arm. Kyra rushed forward, kneeling down by his bed. He turned his head to the side, saw Kyra, and he smiled a bit. "Heard the yelling. Figured it was you. Didn't think anyone else could make Russians want to shoot each other," he said, his words slurring together. Whatever drug they were feeding into him was industrial grade and she thought it was amazing that he was awake. A few minutes more and she might see him fade back into sleep.

She grabbed his hand and squeezed. "You idiot."

"Good to see you too—" His eyes shifted and looked behind her. Kyra heard a gasp, then felt Kathy Cooke push in next to her. Kyra stood and moved to the side. "Hi, Kathy—" Jon started.

"Shut up, Jon," Cooke said. She leaned over, her eyes playing over his face, and then she kissed him.

Grigoriyev pushed his way over to the end of Jon's bed and lifted the clipboard hanging off the end. He scanned the page, then handed it to Barron. "What's it say?" Kyra asked.

"Gunshot wound to the leg," Barron said. "Looks like whoever shot him treated him on site with some coagulant, the Russian equivalent of QuikClot. Surgeons here sewed that up. But . . ." He paused. "They tortured him."

"Hurt too," Jon muttered.

"What did they do to him?" Cooke asked. Her voice was cold, venom in her tone like Barron had never heard.

"He's been treated for dehydration and pinpoint burns, probably from electric shocks," he said, reading off the paper. "Kathy . . . they crushed his knee."

Kyra looked down at the sheet. Jon's right leg formed a strange angle under the white cloth. "Didn't work," he muttered. "Asperger's gives me a low pain threshold. I kept passing out. So they gave me painkillers to keep me awake, but I couldn't feel anything so I didn't care what they did. Drove 'em crazy." He laughed quietly.

"I don't know what they're giving him, but whatever it is, I want some," Barron said. "That must be some quality stuff, and judging by the drip rate, he's getting plenty."

Cooke did not smile at the joke. "Director Grigoriyev," she said, "I expect you to help us evacuate this man to the United States immediately, where he can receive proper medical attention under the supervision of our own doctors." Her voice left no doubt that she was not asking a question.

Grigoriyev nodded. "We will move him to our best hospital. Our surgeons there will examine and treat him until an arrangement for a medical flight can be made," he said. "If you are satisfied, I need to find General Lavrov." He stared at Kyra. "And you are coming."

"No, she's not," Barron objected.

"I need her there," Grigoriyev said. "Lavrov ordered her execution because she is a witness to his illegal arrests of Russian citizens. When he sees that she is with me, he will know that I have the evidence to remove him from command of the GRU. If she is not there, he might not believe that she lives and will resist arrest."

"He might resist anyway," Barron told him.

"He might," Grigoriyev conceded. "But if she comes, he might surrender."

"I'll go with her," Barron replied. "That's not a request."

"That will be acceptable."

"Clark, I'll stay here with Jon," Cooke said. "Director Grigoriyev,

I do not speak Russian. I will need an officer who speaks English to help me coordinate the medical flight and other arrangements."

"I believe Colonel Sokolov speaks English. He will help you." The FSB director put his hand in his coat and felt the sidearm he was carrying. "Now, we go to Khodynka."

Khodynka Military Airfield
One quarter mile northeast of GRU headquarters

The hour had passed and Sokolov still had not called. Had the man forgotten? Lavrov doubted that. Even if a soldier could forget a direct order so easily, the colonel had always been an efficient officer, a man who paid attention to the details. He would have remembered. Something was amiss at the Aquarium, but there were no sirens, no alerts. The general stepped outside the hangar and looked past the line of barracks to the old headquarters. The skyline of buildings looked like they always had in the dark.

Lavrov pulled out his own cell phone and dialed the number to Sokolov's office. There was no answer. He tried the GRU operator and had him connect the call to the interrogation room. That phone stubbornly continued ringing until Lavrov disconnected. *What is going on over there?*

"General Lavrov." The crew chief approached, saluted, then nodded toward the Mi-26 helicopter. "Maintenance is finished, the tank is full, and the cargo loaded. We will tow it out and it will be ready to travel once your pilot arrives and performs his preflight check"

"Very good." Lavrov said. "The pilot . . . he should have been here by now, correct?"

'The crew chief wiped his greasy hands on a rag. "He was due five minutes ago. No one has called to explain the delay—" He stopped, looked out into the darkness, and pointed. "Maybe that is him."

Lavrov twisted his head, following the imaginary line from the crew chief's finger out onto the tarmac. A line of cars was crossing the runway in front of the boneyard. "No," Lavrov said. "There are too many cars." He stared at the approaching convoy, then turned back to the hangar. Whoever was coming was no friend.

I have friends of my own here, he thought.

"There." Grigoriyev's driver pointed to the open hangar. "There is a transport still inside."

Grigoriyev answered nothing. The driver accelerated a bit, closed the distance to the metal building, and finally stopped, parking the car to block the Mi-26 from being towed outside. The other four cars fanned out, parking in a staggered formation behind the director's vehicle.

Lavrov looked out through the helicopter's windshield and counted a dozen men stepping out of the cars, none wearing a military uniform. *Grigoriyev.* He saw the old FSB director dismount and stand, hands in his overcoat, his breath visible in the cooling air.

There was a woman with them. Lavrov cursed. *Stryker.* Grigoriyev had stopped the colonel from carrying out his orders. This would be a problem.

The general turned to the Spetsnaz squad standing behind him, carbines suspended from their vests. "You understand the orders?" he asked. The Special Forces soldiers nodded in silent agreement. "Very good." Lavrov turned and walked down the cargo ramp.

"Arkady!" Grigoriyev called out. "We must talk."

There was no answer before the GRU chairman came around from behind the transport. He approached the FSB chief and stopped, making a show of counting the men behind him. His eyes lingered on Kyra. "Why are you here, Anatoly?"

"I am here to arrest you."

"I think not."

"You are a traitor to the *Rodina*, Arkady. You have sold yourself to the CIA for money and you killed Stepan to cover your perfidy. I do not care that you tried to extort the Americans for more money, but you made illegal arrests and executions of Russian citizens to prove your leverage. Your CIA 'source' was actually a dangle that you swallowed. The people you expelled were just common diplomats. The CIA cadre here in Moscow remains intact, while you have given the U.S. government an excuse to expel our officers from Washington, including our ambassador, and move against every intelligence operation we are running on their soil. You have left us at a severe disadvantage that will cripple us for years and the price you paid for this failure was the blood of loyal Russian citizens. Therefore, you are charged with treason and murder," Grigoriyev said.

"The president will not agree—" Lavrov began. He shook his head slightly, a laugh of derision escaping him.

"I saw the letter, Arkady . . . the letter which you burned. And he will see it."

Lavrov's eyes narrowed. "It was a falsehood, created to implicate me. I burned it so that would not happen."

"Or so there would be less evidence of your treason."

"*Less* evidence?"

"Your Colonel Sokolov tells me that you took the quarter-million euros that were recovered with the note, which Miss Stryker admitted under questioning was meant for you. Why would you do that, Arkady, unless you considered it payment due for services rendered?"

"Money recovered from spies is put to other purposes. You know that," Lavrov protested.

"Indeed. So I presume you took it directly to your chief of staff and ordered him to account for it and have it deposited?"

Lavrov pursed his lips and said nothing for several seconds. "No," he finally admitted.

"I know," Grigoriyev told him. "We asked the man. If my men search your jeep and this helicopter, will they find it?"

"I presume she told you those lies?" He nodded at Kyra.

Lavrov's eyes turned on Kyra, hatred visible on his face now. "What are they saying?" she asked Barron.

"Grigoriyev is twisting the shiv," the NCS director replied. "Nice work on the setup. Everything he did has two explanations and our friend here is running with the one that makes him look like a sellout."

"They hate each other," Kyra said, her voice a whisper. "It's easy to think the worst about someone when you've already primed."

"You are under arrest, Arkady. You will surrender—"

"I will not," Lavrov told him. He raised his hand.

A thunderous avalanche of boots on metal echoed inside the hangar, sounding like a battalion of soldiers storming in from all sides. A squad of Spetsnaz officers exploded out from behind the helicopter, moving to covered positions behind the Mi-26, carbines raised. Grigoriyev's men began yelling, fanning out, and pulling their own sidearms. Barron grabbed Kyra's arm and pointed toward Lavrov's jeep, still parked a few dozen feet from the help. "Go!" he ordered. She sprinted for the vehicle, the senior officer and a pair of FSB officers behind. The Russians knelt at the corners of the vehicle, handguns raised.

Grigoriyev and Lavrov stood unmoved in the middle of it, staring at each other.

"What now, Arkady?" Grigoriyev asked.

"You are outnumbered and outgunned," Lavrov told him, explaining the obvious. "I would think the wiser choice would be apparent."

"And what would you have me do? Let you leave here with a fortune in euros and technology for sale to anyone ready to pay your prices?"

"I would have you believe that I am not a traitor."

"Threatening to have me shot is no argument in your favor," Grigoriyev noted. "You will surrender yourself and order the GRU to cooperate with my investigation. If you are innocent, you will be freed—"

"You will ensure I am proven guilty, Anatoly. What I have actually done will not matter—" Lavrov said.

The Spetsnaz officer crouching on the extreme left of the his team's firing line was the youngest man on the squad, new to the Special Forces and the least experienced. He had not intended to position himself on the flank, preferring to leave that to one of the more senior officers, but there had been little time to coordinate their movements before Lavrov had raised his hand to call them out. There was little space behind the helicopter and several men were bunched together, almost pushing him out from behind cover. It would not take much to find himself exposed here.

He scanned the hangar. Most of the FSB officers had managed to find good cover behind equipment and other cargo stacks, but the helicopter denied them any good line of fire. The two who had moved behind Lavrov's jeep were a problem. They were far enough over so that they would be able to flank his team's position. That needed fixing.

A pallet of cargo boxes was stacked a few meters to his left, a forklift waiting next to it, the tines lowered to the ground. From there, he could hold them down if things turned unpleasant. It would be a short run. He might even be able to move farther over and gain a line of fire on some of the other hostiles. He could trade his current position for better cover and expose the enemy in the process.

He took a breath, released it, and pushed off, running for the forklift.

Kyra saw movement in her peripheral vision. The FSB officer to Kyra's right jerked his head, swung his pistol out of reflex, yelled, and fired.

The 9x19mm Parabellum round punched through the soldier's upper thigh, just missing the pelvic bone and breaking the femur near the upper joint. Blood spurted from his leg and the man went down with a scream. His teammates heard the shot's report, saw their colleague drop, and returned fire.

Kyra yelled as bullets tore into Lavrov's jeep, shattering the windows and spewing glass in every direction. The Spetsnaz were carrying AEK-919s, automatic submachine guns for which the FSB's pistols were a poor match. The volume of fire that erupted from behind the helicopter was deafening, streams of lead pouring out in every direction at once. Lavrov and Grigoriyev both fled for cover, the general around the side of the aircraft, the FSB director back toward a low wall of metal boxes.

The FSB unit fired their Grachs as fast as they could. The sound of metal punching through metal added an ugly melody to the fight, low thumps mixing with the higher-pitched whine of ricochets and the angry snapping of the guns.

The tires on Lavrov's jeep blew out, tilting the vehicle to one side. Barron pushed Kyra behind the front wheel well, then moved back and took up the same position to the rear, putting solid metal in front of her feet and his. The Russian to her right fired three more rounds, then screamed and pitched over, clutching at his shattered hand where a bullet had smashed into the fingers closed around his pistol's grip, nearly amputating one of his digits. Kyra lunged to the side, grabbed his coat, and pulled the man back to cover. He curled up in the fetal position, trying to suppress his own screams.

His Grach sat in the open where it had landed, ten feet beyond her reach.

Lavrov pushed himself up to a kneeling position behind a metal crate, drew his Makarov, and looked for a target. Grigoriyev gave him nothing, hiding as he was behind his own makeshift parapet of cargo boxes. Lavrov unloaded three rounds at an FSB officer who raised up to fire, the second bullet catching the man in the sternum and rendering him unable to scream as the air in his lungs flooded out through the hole in his windpipe.

Kyra picked up a piece of shattered mirror and used it to look around the jeep's hood. The Spetsnaz officer covering his team's flank fired his 919, and the weapon ran dry. She saw him raise it to eject the clip.

Kyra dropped the mirror, pushed off, and sprinted low to the fallen Grach, keeping her eyes focused on the gun.

"No!" Barron yelled, but the woman was already in motion. He started to move toward the front of the car she had just abandoned, but a shattering window above made him think better of it. The Russian beside him raised up in a half crouch, fired, then toppled back as a 9mm round tore through his head. The man's own Grach clattered onto the ground, still behind the vehicle. Barron scrambled over to retrieve it.

Kyra slowed just long enough to grab for the Grach, and felt the grooved handle of the pistol in her palm as her hand wrapped around it. She picked up speed again, closed the distance to the next pallet of cargo in less than a second, and threw herself behind the metal boxes.

She lowered herself onto one knee and looked around the crates. The Spetsnaz were behind cover, several in a line almost at a right angle to her position.

The soldier at the end of the line finished loading the clip into his weapon, looked up, and saw Kyra's head before she could pull back. He racked the slide on his carbine, loading the first round, and raised it—

—Kyra's rounds caught him high in the shoulder, smashing his collarbone and knocking him to the floor, his gun clattering on the concrete as he landed.

Kyra's pistol locked open. She stared at the Grach in disbelief? *Two rounds? I ran for a gun that had two rounds?* She was a sitting target if the Russian soldiers moved on her position.

She looked over, saw Barron firing a pistol over the trunk of Lavrov's jeep. He looked back over at her. "I'm out!" she yelled.

Barron cursed the woman for having left her position. He drew himself down behind the vehicle, set his Grach on the ground, and threw open the jacket of the dead Russian at his feet. The man had been carrying two spare clips in pouches on his belt. Barron pulled them both out, held one up for Kyra to see, and threw it across the floor to her.

The clip skittered over and Kyra stopped it with her foot. She ejected the empty, loaded the replacement, and jacked the slide. She raised herself up to fire again, then dropped back when bullets began tearing into the crates. The Spetsnaz team had seen their comrade go down and was not going to give her the chance to fire again.

Barron looked over the trunk and saw one of the soldiers firing on Kyra's position. The woman was crouching low behind the crates, but she was pinned down. The soldier couldn't tell how many people had moved around the flank and he was chewing into the metal barricade as hot and fast as his gun allowed.

The soldier was focused on the threat to his flank and had lost track of his own position. His head leaned forward, exposed from behind the crate hiding him.

Barron swung his pistol onto the trunk, took half a second to line up the shot, and pulled the trigger.

The 9mm round punched through the soldier's head, spraying

blood as it left an open hole behind. The soldier fell sideways, his rifle clattering on the ground as he crumpled over.

Kyra peeked over, saw the man pitch sideways, blood flying out from his shattered skull in a red mist. The enemy's flank exposed, she raised herself up, bringing her own fully loaded weapon to bear, and began pulling the trigger.

Lavrov heard Spetsnaz officers scream, one after another as bullets tore into arms and legs, a torso. Two of his men tried to move around the other side of the helicopter for cover and the lead soldier went down as FSB officers watching that side opened up. The second man grabbed his comrade by his drag collar and tried to pull him out of the field of fire, but he went down, a bullet in his leg.

"Inside! Inside!" Lavrov ordered, pointing at the helicopter's open cargo door. The Spetsnaz called out their acknowledgments, then began laying down covering fire as men dragged and carried their wounded up the ramp to the safety. Lavrov saw Kyra look around from behind her barricade and sent three rounds in her direction. The woman jerked her head back.

The last of the Russian soldiers scrambled up the metal incline and Lavrov followed, stepping through the line of four men covering the entrance.

The hangar fell quiet, a disturbing stillness after the wild chaos of the single minute the firefight had lasted. Grigoriyev and his men looked up, weapons still raised. The FSB director pointed his men forward, and they began to move toward the aircraft in a low crouch. He pulled his cell phone from his pocket and dialed a number.

Barron, head down, ran to Kyra's position. "They would've eaten us alive if you hadn't threatened their flank," he said. "I thought it was stupid to make the run, but I won't argue with the result."

"Good, 'cause I'm out again." She held up the Grach, which was locked open on an empty chamber again. "Never thought I'd help the FSB shoot other Russians."

"I hope you enjoyed it, because we're done. This is not what we signed up for when we agreed to come here to help arrest Lavrov. This is Grigoriyev's problem now." Barron waved over to the FSB director and motioned for the man to send reinforcements. Three officers crouching near their director saw the signal and moved without orders. "Come on, we're moving," Barron ordered.

He led Kyra back behind Lavrov's vehicle, then around to Grigoriyev. The Russian ended his call and replaced his cell phone in his coat. "An exciting evening, I think," he said.

"A little too much for our taste," Barron advised. "This is your problem, not ours."

"Mr. Barron, I think you will want to stay. The more exciting part is still coming." Grigoriyev turned back to the helicopter and switched to his native language. "Arkady!" he yelled. "It is time to surrender. You cannot stay inside."

Lavrov heard Grigoriyev's voice and cursed him under his breath. The man's arrogance was maddening. He could not have forgotten that GRU headquarters was a stone's throw from the hangar. "You should leave now, Anatoly," he called back. "We are in my backyard. One radio call and a battalion of men will arrive here in five minutes."

Grigoriyev shook his head. "Send your battalion, Arkady. Send a division! It will not matter. I have already made my call. We will have a visitor soon. You might kill us before he arrives, but you will not be able to hide what you have done."

"And who is coming?" Lavrov yelled back, contempt thick in his voice.

"The one who will settle this." Grigoriyev turned back to the

Americans. "You must forgive my lack of hospitality, but I must con-fiscate those guns and place you under arrest. A temporary measure only, but you are American spies in the *Rodina* and his security detail might shoot you on sight. Foreigners with guns on our soil make them unhappy . . . and it would look very bad to him if he saw that you were not only free but helping to suppress an armed insurrection."

"Look bad to who?" Barron asked.

"Who do you think, *devushka*?" Grigoriyev asked.

Kyra smiled. "The only one who can settle this," she said.

"And that is . . . ?" Barron asked her.

"The president of the Russian Federation." She handed Grigori-yev the Grach pistol she was holding, then offered both arms for the handcuffs.

The motorcade arrived on Grigoriynv's schedule, a half-dozen Volks-wagen Caravelles surrounding a heavy stretch limousine, an armored black Mercedes Benz S-class with solid rubber tires, dark windows, and a motor that growled low under the weight it carried. The small fleet pulled to a stop fifty meters from the hangar and men spilled out of the vans, every one carrying a carbine.

Kyra watched the team leader confer with Grigoriyev in Russian, then walk toward the cargo helicopter, his hands raised high in the air. Lavrov yelled something back and the man made his way around and disappeared up the cargo ramp. He was inside the aircraft for two minutes, then reappeared, Lavrov walking beside him.

"Are you ready to talk, Arkady?" Grigoriyev asked.

"Your men fired first," Lavrov noted. "But as a demonstration of my innocence, I have ordered them to surrender their weapons." He looked at Kyra, murder in his eyes. "If anyone is to visit Lubyanka tonight—"

"He will decide who visits Lubyanka tonight," Grigoriyev said.

He pulled out his cell phone, dialed the same number as before, and shared a few words with the caller on the other end before disconnecting. The FSB director looked back at the parked motorcade.

The driver dismounted, opened the rear passenger door, and the president of the Russian Federation stepped onto the tarmac.

His dark suit was bespoke, impeccable, and expensive. The man was shorter than Kyra had expected, but built solid across the chest and arms. Kyra couldn't determine the color of his eyes in the hangar light, but she saw they were cold. He approached the small group, slowing only slightly when he saw the two Americans standing by Grigoriyev, in restraints and under guard. He reached the FSB director, stopped, and scanned the hangar, taking note of the bullet holes that seemed to cover every flat surface in sight. He sniffed the air, smelled the odor of burned gunpowder that still wafted through the open space.

"Anatoly Maksimovich," he said. "I see that you were not wasting my time when you asked me to come."

"I would not, sir," Grigoriyev said.

"Very good. You have arrested some American spies, I'm told."

"I have, but the matter is more complicated than that. There is evidence that these spies were working with one of our own," Grigoriyev told him.

"And you have detained this traitor?"

"That is why I came here, to detain the man." Grigoriyev turned and looked at the Russian general. "But Arkady Vladimirovich would not surrender. He ordered his men to abet his attempt to resist arrest. I have several wounded men, some seriously."

"An extraordinary accusation," the Russian president noted. "I presume you have extraordinary evidence. Arkady has done much for the *Rodina* over the years."

"More for himself, I think," Grigoriyev replied.

The Oval Office

President Daniel Rostow looked up from the file in his hands, the FBI's summary of the Russian ambassador's departure from the country. "It's a start," he said. "Not a good one, but I'll take something over nothing." He closed the file and passed it back to the FBI director. "I'd be a happier man if I was sure that more of these Russian diplomats lined up at the ticket counter at Dulles were really intelligence officers."

"Yes, sir." Isaac Menard's tone was an unhappy mix of embarrassment and resolution, heavy on the former. "We listed everyone who we ever imagined was a spy and plenty more who were just abusing their diplomatic immunity to get out of driving violations. We have a second tranche who are members of the Russian delegation to the UN in New York City under review, so we'll be able to hit them up there if this goes on."

"Good," Rostow encouraged him. "And I want you back here tomorrow for lunch. I'm calling down the House and Senate Intel Committee chairs. I want to discuss hiking your counterintelligence budget—"

The telephone on the Resolute desk sounded, calling for Rostow's attention. He touched the button. "What is it, Vickie?"

"Mr. President, the Watch Office has the deputy director of national intelligence on the line. She's asking to speak with you."

"Kathy Cooke?" Rostow rolled his eyes and looked to Menard. "What's it about?"

"They didn't say, but she is calling from Moscow," the secretary replied.

"*Moscow*? Put her on." The line went mute as the secretary began to connect the call. "How did Kathy Cooke get into Russia?"

"No idea," Menard said, shaking his head. "They stopped approving visas for any of our people the minute this started. Maybe she called someone senior over there."

"I don't like this—"

"Mr. President, now connecting you with Deputy DNI Cooke," the secretary announced.

"Kathy?" Rostow asked. "What are you doing in Moscow?"

"Sir." The distance delayed Cooke's answer a second, and the president found even that short wait intolerable. "I came over yesterday with Clark Barron from CIA to meet with FSB Director Anatoly Grigoriyev. We've recovered our analyst who was abducted in Germany, and Alden Maines is presently in my custody—"

"Kathy," Menard interrupted, "it's Isaac. You have Maines?"

"Technically, he's in FSB custody, but they're going to release him to us," Cooke told him. "I'll need as many of the Bureau's special agents at the embassy as you can muster to report to GRU headquarters as fast as they can get over here."

"How did you manage that?" Rostow asked, incredulous.

"This is an unsecured line, Mr. President, so I can't explain the details here. I'll call you from the embassy as soon as I can. But we need someone to arrange a medical evac flight for two seriously wounded officers. Maines and Jonathan Burke were both tortured by the GRU. I want to evac them to Rammstein for treatment."

"I'll have the Pentagon set it up," Rostow confirmed. "I want to hear back from you in a half hour."

"I can do that, if Isaac's people can get over here and take over for me," Cooke replied.

"I'm on it." Menard's hand was on the Oval Office door and he was setting his course for the White House Watch Office before Rostow disconnected the call.

Khodynka Military Airfield

"Can you explain this, Arkady?" The Russian president stared down at the quarter-million euros filling the satchel retrieved from Lavrov's car. Bullets had struck the bag and perforated several stacks of the bills.

"My officers retrieved the funds from this woman—" Lavrov pointed at Kyra. "She is a CIA officer detained by my men when she attempted to enter her embassy."

"A partial truth," Grigoriyev added. He held out his smartphone, Sokolov's picture of Kyra's letter on the screen. The president took the phone and stared at the photograph, zooming and scrolling as he read. "Arkady, this could refer to you."

"I am not named—"

"Of course not!" the president snapped. "The CIA is not stupid enough to name an asset in a communiqué like this one! I was the FSB director once! You think I do not know how assets are run?"

"No, sir—" Lavrov started.

"Enough!" The president turned to Grigoriyev. "Is this all?"

"No. I have a GRU interrogator in custody who has confirmed that the general personally interviewed this woman alone, outside the presence of witnesses and with the cameras turned off on his order. General Lavrov personally destroyed that letter, not realizing that a photographic copy had been taken. Then he left with the money in hand and did not deliver it to his staff for accounting."

The Russian president frowned and returned the smartphone to its owner. "And then you resisted when Anatoly asked you to come with him to explain yourself. This looks very bad, Arkady."

"He wants to remove me from my post," Lavrov protested. "You know this."

"Politics is no defense for this," the president replied, anger flashing in his eyes.

"This is a deception operation!" Lavrov yelled, thrusting his finger at Kyra and Barron again. "I have gutted their operations and now they are trying to undo me!"

"And yet you killed General Strelnikov without discussing the matter with Anatoly or myself. You have executed three other Russian citizens without trial or any evidence of their guilt other than the word of a source who you have allowed no one to interview." The president shook his head. "I believe I have given you too much latitude, Arkady. Your successes in straining the Main Enemy by providing technology to our allies blinded me to your excesses."

"Mr. President—"

"No, I will hear no more from you here. You will surrender yourself to Anatoly. He will investigate your actions and then we will decide what to do. You are relieved of your command of the GRU and your Foundation for Advanced Research will cease all its dealings with foreign buyers until I decide otherwise." The president nodded to Grigoriyev, who waved his hand. An FSB officer approached the Russian general and pulled his arms behind his back.

"Sir, we have his alleged source and the wounded CIA officer he kidnapped in Germany in our custody. That matter needs our attention," Grigoriyev said.

"What would you suggest?"

"We have no grounds to hold the kidnapped officer. His forced extradition to Russia was entirely illegal and would complicate our relations with Europe. I believe he should be sent home," Grigoriyev offered. "As for the general's source, his information cannot be trusted. At this moment, we do not know whether he truly is a traitor to his country or a loyal officer who Lavorv tortured for information. But in either case, he committed no crime on our soil, none that we would want to bring to public trial anyway. I suggest he be sent home as well."

The president nodded. "See to it. And these two? Do they have diplomatic immunity?" he asked, nodding at Kyra and Barron.

"Technically, no," Grigoriyev admitted. "But I think that consigning them to prison would be to waste an advantage."

The president looked at his FSB director, considering the implication. He turned to the head of his security detail. "Fetch me the secure phone from my car."

The Oval Office

"Mr. President?" It was the second time in ten minutes that his secretary had asked for his attention and Rostow was already getting tired of the woman's voice.

"Yes, Vickie?"

"Sir, it's the Watch Office again. The president of the Russian Federation is standing by to speak to you."

Rostow's eye's widened at the news. "Put him on."

The connection took almost ten seconds. "Daniel, how are you this morning?" The Russian president's English was quite good, his accent strong but his diction still understandable.

"I'm doing well. And yourself?"

"My health is good. What more can I ask?" the Russian replied. "There have been several unpleasant exchanges between our two countries of late. That is unfortunate. This business of expelling so many of each other's diplomats? The great powers should not be so hostile to each other."

"I agree," Rostow said. "How can we mend our fences?" *What are you selling?* he wondered.

"There has been an incident here in Moscow this evening . . . very unpleasant business. Two of your intelligence officers have been detained by the FSB, neither with diplomatic immunity, and the GRU has two others in its infirmary. I believe that one is wanted by your FBI. As an act of my good faith, I would like to return the injured men to you after we treat them in our finest hospital."

"That would be a very gracious act. On behalf of the American people, I would like to thank you for your concern and generosity."

"It is my pleasure. As for the other two, they are more problematic. Without immunity, it would be our standard practice to try them and consign them to prison. But I believe that a better solution might be possible," the Russian offered.

"I would be pleased to hear any proposal you would care to offer," Rostow said. He wanted to gag on the words. The American president was skilled at the language of diplomats and had no issue with the hypocrisy behind it, but he hated to ever look like he was at the mercy of others.

"We have both expelled a number of the other's diplomats from our respective countries these past days. You have sent our ambassador home and we were preparing to do the same to yours. This has all been very disruptive. I would suggest a trade. If you will agree to withdraw the expulsion of a select number of our diplomats, I would be pleased to do the same for an equal number of yours. I will send these two home as an incentive. They would be persona non grata to us forever, of course."

"Of course," Rostow replied. He let the silence hang for a few moments. The Russian would know that he wasn't really thinking things over, but appearances had to be maintained for the benefit of the security officers on both sides who were listening in. *You want to send some intel officers back to the U.S., we get to send back some of ours.* Whoever went back in on either side would spend at least a year under intense surveillance, but the CIA wouldn't lose its entire brain trust in Moscow. *It'll still take 'em a couple of years to get back on their feet, but that's less than the alternative. We'll have to get some new people over there to work the street, but at least they'll have experienced people running things from the office.*

"I think that's a very generous offer. On behalf of the United States, I accept," Rostow said. "Please let Ambassador Galushka know that he can return to Washington at his convenience. I will have our ambassador in Moscow provide you with a list of our people we would like restored as soon as I can discuss the matter with him and the secretary of state." *And the director of national intelligence,* he didn't add.

"Excellent!" the Russian exclaimed. "I am gratified that this matter will conclude in an agreeable way. I do hope that we can avoid any such unpleasant quarrels in the future."

"As do I," Rostow replied. "Good night, Mr. President."

"*Do svedaniya,* Daniel." The line died, and Rostow set his own handset on the cradle. *Kathy is going to have to explain what in heaven's name just happened,* he thought.

Khodynka Military Airfield

The Russian president turned off the phone and looked at Barron and Kyra. "You will be returned home," he announced. "You will have to spend the evening in Lubyanka, of course. There are protocols we must follow. You are also persona non grata to the Russian people and will never set foot in our country again."

"We understand," Barron said.

"Then this matter is concluded, for you anyway." The Russian president turned to Grigoriyev. "I leave this in your hands, Anatoly Maksimovich. I regret that I did not listen to your advice sooner. I will take it as a lesson that the wisdom of FSB men is not to be discounted so lightly."

"Thank you, Mr. President," Grigoriyev said. The Russian president turned away and began the walk across the tarmac back to his car. The FSB director stared at the group. "The FSB will not charge the Spetsnaz officers who participated in this affair with any crime. You may return to your duties and deliver your wounded to your infirmary. You were only following your orders and did not realize that the man giving them had betrayed you." He turned to his own men. "Take the general and the Americans to Lubyanka, separate cars. Also, advise their embassy of the need for the medical flight. These two are being expelled from the country and will leave on that aircraft. They may have escaped prison, but we do not have to allow them the luxury of a soft seat on a commercial flight for their trip home."

"Always wanted to see Lubyanka," Barron muttered.

"Just so long as we get to walk back out again," Kyra replied.

CHAPTER ELEVEN

Somewhere over Poland

The C-130E Hercules was a cavern, loud, though brighter and smaller than Kyra had imagined. The four Rolls-Royce turboprops filled the flying tube with a steady buzz, but the air outside was calm enough to keep the ride smooth. Kyra was grateful for it, more for Jon than herself. The flight nurses had hung a new bag of Dilaudid and increased his drip in the last hour to keep Jon asleep, but Kyra still wondered if he could feel the pain. She'd been shot once herself. The morphine injection she'd given herself had wiped the pain away like an eraser across a chalkboard and knocked her cold. Despite the doctors' later assurances that it was a dream, she was sure that the agony had broken through the oblivion in fits and spurts. She imagined that whatever Jon would feel now if he awoke would eclipse the agony she'd suffered after that bullet had torn through her arm. She prayed Jon wasn't hurting that way, but the lack of turbulence would be a blessing if she was wrong.

They were an hour out of Rammstein. A bus was waiting on the tarmac to move Jon and Maines to Landstuhl Regional Medical Center, where they would spend three days at least. The Russian doctors at Botkin Hospital had been as professional as any Kyra had known in the States, and appalled to the last man at the state of Jon's gunshot wound to his leg. The chief physician had declared Jon was lucky that infection had not set in and had muttered some Russian profanity Kyra didn't understand when the X-rays of Jon's knee were delivered and posted on the light board.

The stay at Landstuhl would end with a return to Rammstein, where a C-141 Starlifter would ferry them to Joint Base Andrews east of Washington. Jon would spend weeks at the Inova Fairfax Hospital in Falls Church, where they would rebuild his destroyed joint. Months of therapy would teach him to walk again and he would probably use a cane ever after. Kyra wasn't sure whether he would grouse about that or embrace it, claiming it made him look dignified.

She felt a presence behind her and looked up. Kathy Cooke was standing over Jon, looking down at his pale face. She reached out and moved a stray bit of hair off his forehead.

"What did they say?" Kyra asked.

"They didn't tell you?" Cooke asked. Kyra just shook her head. "Those Russian doctors wouldn't tell me anything. Persona non grata, if you'll recall."

Cooke grunted, a quiet laugh. "He's stable. They don't think there was any permanent trauma to his brain or other organs. It looks like the only real permanent damage is to his leg. The surgeons will have to replace the knee." Kyra looked down toward Jon's lower limbs but couldn't see the damaged joint under the sheet. The image of his leg hanging at a strange angle when the GRU soldiers had transferred him to a gurney for his trip to Botkin broke into her thoughts.

She tried to push the image away. "I thought he was dead for a second when I saw him. Just for a second . . . then he was laughing," Kyra said, her voice flat, and the memory surged up in her mind of Jon in the metal chair. She had to fight down the urge to vomit. The image had been stalking the edge of her thoughts since that moment Sokolov had opened the door, and it had come through more than a few times. "I wish he hadn't jumped that wall. I would've burned every asset we have in Moscow myself before I would've let Lavrov's men do this to him."

Cooke knelt down beside her, staring at the man she loved. "Kyra, do you know why Jon joined the Red Cell?" she asked.

Kyra stared at the man, watched his chest rise and fall as the tubes fed oxygen into his nose. "He told me about that ambush in Iraq . . . the one in the Triangle where he saved Marisa Mills. He never gave me the dirty details, though. I didn't tell him but I looked up the after-action report on it. He killed two men. I assumed that the post-traumatic stress disorder was why he quit the field."

"Actually, it wasn't," Cooke replied. "He was determined to tough it out, but Marisa didn't think he should be in the field. So she asked headquarters to reassign them to someplace where they could still work counterterrorism without being on the front line. I don't think she expected the Seventh Floor would be stupid enough to send them to one of the black sites. Jon ended up working with the interrogators. Some of the detainees had been held in custody by foreign intel services who . . . well, they had no moral objections to torture."

The deputy director of national intelligence reached out and brushed Jon's dark hair back from his forehead again, but it just fell back into place. "He saw what torture does, both to the subject and the men who carry it out. Jon was handling his PTSD okay until he saw that. That's what finally broke him. He told me that he saw men lose their souls and he walked out before he got comfortable with it. He joined the Red Cell and that's when he started closing his office door to everyone else. Between shooting those men and seeing others hurt in custody, Jon suffered more emotional pain in a shorter time than anyone else I've ever met. He closed his office so no one could do that to him again . . . and so he wouldn't hurt anyone else, any more than he could help it, anyway."

Cooke laid her hand on Jon's and squeezed it. "One of the best men I've ever known. He didn't close himself off because he despised people. He just didn't want to hurt any more."

"He never told me that," Kyra replied.

"I'm not sure he would have," Cooke said. She smiled, a memory playing on her face. "Do you remember that first day I took you down to meet him?"

"Yes."

"I thought for sure he was going to kick you out," Cooke told her. "Or find some reason that you couldn't stay there. But he surprised me. He figured out what had happened to you down in Venezuela a few months before and I guess he decided that you'd been hurt like him. I think it touched a soft streak in him."

"I didn't think he had a soft streak in him, not until he came out and saved my tail with that rifle last year when we got caught out in the bush . . . when the revolution broke out in Caracas," Kyra replied.

"He did," Cooke told her. "Kyra, I think Jon jumped that wall because he'd seen torture. He knew that there are ways to torture a man, and there are entirely different ways to torture a woman, and you're a beautiful girl. I suspect Jon was worried that Lavrov's men would break you in ways that can't ever be fixed."

"He was probably right," Kyra said, her voice flat. "He's always right."

"Yes, he usually is," Cooke agreed.

One of the flight nurses came over to check Jon's vitals and the intelligence officers fell silent until the woman had left. Kyra watched her go, then looked at Maines strapped down on his own litter between two special agents and handcuffed to the fuselage. "What happens to him?"

"Maines?" Cooke asked, seeing the direction of Kyra's stare. "I talked to the attorney general this morning. There'll be a trial, of course, but he'll end up in supermax. Life with no parole."

"He's the one who pulled me out of that safe house three years ago. I owe my life to a traitor," she said. "I don't suppose those Bureau boys would let us drop the ramp and just push him out."

"I won't stop you if you want to ask," Cooke told her. She stood.

"Ma'am . . . do you think he'll come back to the Agency?" Kyra asked, nodding at Jon.

Cooke studied Jon's swollen face, as though trying to reach into his thoughts and discern how he might answer the question. "I don't know," she admitted finally. "He really never belonged at the Agency. He has a sense of justice that's hard as rock, and in this business, most of the time, all we have are bad options . . . all we get to do is pick who's going to get hurt. So we save the ones we need, not the ones who deserve it. Sometimes we get lucky and they're the same people. But Jon could never make that call. He would save the deserving ones. That makes him a good man but a terrible intelligence officer."

"Maybe we should be more like him, instead of thinking he should be more like us," Kyra said.

"Probably," Kathy admitted. "And in the end, the CIA would become the most moral and least useful intelligence service in the world. We deal with the devils, Kyra. But I don't want him to have to do that anymore . . . or to do it myself. Whether Jon comes back or not . . . I'm going to resign. And I'm going to ask him to marry me."

Kyra looked up at the woman, surprised. Cooke smiled, rueful. "Jon's been more patient than I ever asked him to be . . . and I've given up as much for my country as I can stand. I almost had to give up too much and I'm not going to let that happen again." She put her hand on Kyra's shoulder. "I have to call the White House. President Rostow wants another update. Thank you for staying with him."

Cooke trudged toward the front of the plane, and Kyra turned back to her patient.

EIGHTEEN MONTHS LATER

"The Alcatraz of the Rockies"
United States Penitentiary,
Administrative Maximum Facility (ADX) aka supermax
Florence, Colorado

There were fewer than five hundred men who lived in the prison proper. The al-Qaida terrorists and other extremists had their own wing, the H Unit with its own security ready to deal with their hunger strikes and refusals to cooperate with the female guards. Two men were in Range 13, the "ultramax" block where their isolation from all human contact was total and they could not even see their own guards. Thomas Silverstein of the Aryan Brotherhood had earned that home for murdering three inmates and a prison guard. He had been in isolation since 1982 and some of the guards wondered whether the old man, deprived of almost all human contact for almost four decades, hadn't simply gone insane. That he was still alive was all they really cared to know.

Maines stared at the Rocky Mountains on the drive, knowing they would be the last view of the horizon he would ever see. Three consecutive life sentences with no possibility of parole defined his future. His lawyer had argued at the sentencing that such crimes didn't merit supermax confinement, that Aldrich Ames's treason had killed more men and the courts hadn't seen fit to send that old man here. The judge had been unimpressed.

The former CIA officer arrived through the underground garage, chauffeured in the rear seat of a white SUV. The armored vehicle came to a stop, ending the last car ride Maines would ever take. The garage door closed behind them and only then was he allowed to climb out of the vehicle.

"A clean version of hell," one of the prison's former wardens had called it, and Maines saw that the man's observation had been accurate. The cavernous space was white, concrete walls and floor, and empty but for a fish-eye surveillance camera mounted on the wall. Maines was quite sure that he would see a camera in every room, every hallway. He would die in this place and he would never know a moment of true privacy until that day came. It was ironic that, most days here, he would be isolated, having almost no contact with another human being, but he would never be alone. Some guard controlling some camera would always be staring at him. He would finally know privacy again when they closed and locked his coffin lid.

Four prisoners had found ways to take their own lives over the years. Maines wondered whether he would want to follow their example, and whether he could find a way around the guards and the cameras and the controls to kill himself if his mind ever broke down so completely.

Three officers and an administrator were standing in the garage when the car pulled in. Maines was shackled, hands, waist, and legs, which made dismounting from the SUV a challenging task. The prison guards searched him for contraband despite the restraints. When he was pronounced clean, they led him through the halls, his chains forcing him to shuffle. They came off only when he was inside the last room that would ever be his.

The cell was twelve feet long and barely wider at seven feet than he was tall. The bed was a concrete slab extending from the wall covered by a thin mattress. The low desk and seat were also concrete slabs, unmovable, unbreakable. There was no wood in the room at all, nothing for a prisoner to shatter into splinters that could serve as weapons. The shower had no separate enclosure and a timer that turned the water off every minute, so he would have to push a button to keep it flowing. There was television on a low shelf, a twelve-inch black-and-white. He'd been forced to watch the Administration and Orientation Program on Institutional Channel 4 before they'd brought him to the room. Channel 14 was dedicated to religious and psychiatric broadcasts. A quick turn of the dial revealed that a few other channels offered him educational shows and some entertainment programs. He considered that he could smash the television and try to electrocute himself or use the glass to slash his wrists, but he dismissed the thought. Surely some other inmates had tried and the staff would be ready for that. If he failed, they would take his television and he might never get another.

The functionary who had processed him had explained his routine. Twenty-three hours a day, he would stay in the room. He would eat all three meals every day in this space. Refusal to eat would result in an involuntary feeding using restraints and a nasogastric tube they would insert through his nasal cavity. If he found a way to remove that, they would use an anal tube. He could have one hour of solitary exercise in the recreation pen each day if he behaved and submitted first to a strip search. He could read books, even order them from the outside, but only paperbacks, lest he find some malicious use for the book boards inside the covers. He would be allowed letters but only from recipients approved by the prison. He wondered who might write to him. One fifteen-minute phone call per month was permitted, monitored of course. Who to call? He would have to think about that.

Think . . . that was what they truly wanted him to do. *Think*. A man found himself here because his conscience had lost its ability to torture him, so his country had ensured that his mind would accomplish the task instead. Time, loneliness, and his thoughts would create all the pain they could ever want. It would mount slowly over the years, would never be a sharp agony, just a growing madness that would build inside him until it crushed his capacity to feel joy. One day, he would try desperately to remember what pleasure and happiness were and would find that he could not.

Maines looked out through the four-inch-wide window. He could see sky, but a wall of red concrete bricks blocked his view of the earth. Some days he might see clouds, maybe rain, or a bird, others there would be snow or lightning. The stars would be there, rarely the moon. Earth itself would always be denied him, but he would always see the heavens. But they would be denied him in the end too, wouldn't they? Maines didn't believe in God, and hoped that he was right on that score now more than he ever had. If there was some Deity out there, surely He despised a traitor. Then Maines's eventual death wouldn't be an end to his punishment but the start of a new kind that would go for an eternity that would make his stay here feel like a small moment.

He turned back to the cell door, now closed and locked behind him. His imagination had been telling him for months now that Stryker or Barron would be there, to mock him or curse him when they finally locked him up. But there was no one.

Maines sat down on the cement bed and closed his eyes. The room already felt smaller than it had five minutes ago.

Kyra hadn't asked the Federal Bureau of Prisons to let her accompany Maines into supermax and she suspected they would have refused the request outright had she made it. Such dramatic gestures were the fantasies of fiction and the U.S. Department of Justice cared more about efficiency than drama. ADX Florence was a hole in the ground where men were sent to be forgotten by the society they had done so much to harm, and the actual forgetting would begin before they arrived.

But Kyra had wanted to see where the man would end his life. She was searching for something here, though she didn't know what . . . closure or understanding, maybe even sympathy. Alden Maines had decided that his country deserved to be hurt. She wasn't sure she wanted to understand his line of reasoning, but something inside whispered that it was necessary. Kyra Stryker was in a position to do what he had done. Every CIA officer was. Kyra had read about other such traitors, sat through the lectures and heard the dire warnings. Every CIA officer had. And still, some turned anyway. Someday the temptation might reach her and she wanted to be sure she would make the right choice.

Kyra had never seen the Rockies before this morning and she could hardly digest their raw size. Virginia had its mountains, but most were covered by trees that hid their true size from view. Even so, she could see that the Blue Ridge Mountains were just a line of hills compared to these.

Such beauty was the last thing Maines or any other resident of supermax would have seen before they were locked inside for life, and she wondered if the Department of Justice hadn't chosen this site for that reason, just to add a final bit of punishment onto their sentences.

Kyra pulled the smartphone from her pocket, called up the number she needed from the contacts list, and dialed. "It's me," she said. "He's inside."

"Ah, supermax . . . our landfill for human garbage. You didn't go in with him?" Clark Barron asked. The CIA director did not sound surprised.

"I'm done with him."

"I wish we could forget about our traitors. They'll be teaching classes about him for the next fifty years. Speaking of which, the Kent School wants you to give a lecture on Maines in the Bubble."

"Any chance we can get Jon and Kathy to come back in? Guest speakers?" Kyra asked.

"We have to unveil Kathy's portrait in the Directors Gallery soon. I'm sure the Burkes wouldn't mind spending a few minutes onstage talking. Well, Kathy will be happy to do it. Jon, not so much," Barron offered. "Do you want an extra day out there? You've got the leave hours."

"Depends," she replied without thought. "You don't need me for anything?"

"We do have a report that some advanced body armor showed up in Libya," Barron admitted. "Nothing that's going to change the big picture over there, but not something we like to see. But I think we can handle it without you."

"I was thinking about driving back. I've never seen the battlefields at Shiloh or Chickamauga. I thought I might take the opportunity."

"Avoid Kansas," Barron advised. "Swing south through Texas and Louisiana. Barbecue and gumbo country."

"Noted. I'll call you from the road."

"Take your time." Barron hung up and Kyra replaced her smartphone in her pocket.

She stared at the Rockies again. The winter snows hadn't melted off the peaks yet. They were tall enough that she wondered if the powder ever melted, even in the summertime. It was a sight fit for a painting, grays and blues everywhere she looked. But it wasn't home. The greens hills of Virginia were more beautiful still, to her eyes anyway.

The chief of the Red Cell turned away from the prison and walked back toward her rental car. She could be home in three days if she wanted to drive hard. Virginia was two thousand miles east, but she was in no hurry. The world was quiet, for once.

ACKNOWLEDGMENTS

My first acknowledgement, as always, must go to my dear wife, Janna, without whom it would be impossible to write the first page, much less an entire book. I love you.

Jason Yarn and Ken Freimann, my agents who keep things moving in a productive direction. Not all of my ideas are good ones, and these are the gentlemen who must occasionally prune the tree of my imagination so the good fruit can flourish.

Lauren Spiegel, Miya Kumangai, and Shida Carr, my editors and publicist at Simon & Schuster who are forever professional and encouraging. My work is always better for their having read, edited, and promoted it.

Steve S. for help with Russian language and culture and years of friendship and mentoring. The world is both a safer and more interesting place thanks to him.

My friends and family and those readers who are forever encouraging. I write for you as much as for myself.

The Agency managers and Publication Review Board members who have to read my manuscripts and call out the bits that need to be changed or redacted. Their unfailing politeness makes the review process far easier than it otherwise could be. Their persistent professionalism strongly suggests to me that ex-Agency authors who complain about "censorship" are trying to publish details they know darned well that they shouldn't and are either just mad that they're getting blocked, trying to gin up publicity and therefore sales, or both.